Dear Readers:

Please, come and join us at the beautiful, Victorian-style Seascape Inn, a magical bed-and-breakfast nestled on the Maine coast. A short walk from the graceful and alluring inn lies Sea Haven Village, where Fred and Lucy will welcome you to the Blue Moon Cafe, a picturesque eatery where you can dine in summer by the gentle ocean breeze and, in winter, be intrigued by the shroud of mystical fog and crisp, cool sea mist.

After your meal, stop across the street at The Store, a fairly modern grocery and gas station owned by Mayor Horace and Lydia Johnson. There you can pick up most any incidental you might have forgotten in your haste to pack. Should you arrive by car, rest assured it'll be in good hands with Jimmy Goodson at Jimmy's Quick Service Garage.

Other residents ready to welcome you to the peaceful village include Pastor Brown, a handsome, young minister; Miss Millicent Thomas, the elderly owner of Miss Millie's Antique Shoppe; Sheriff Leroy Cobb, who stops in at the cafe every afternoon for a slab of Lucy's homemade blueberry pie; Hatch, who maintains the lighthouse; and, of course, the ever-nurturing Miss Hattie, caretaker of Seascape Inn. Oh, and do try to ignore the rantings of Miss Hattie's neighbor, Beaulah Favish, insisting that strange things are going on at Seascape Inn, mmm? She's reportedly a touch eccentric—even when it comes to relaying the Seascape Legend.

Please, come join us by reading the sixth *Seascape* series novel, *Tomorrow's Treasures* by Rosalyn Alsobrook, and let the magic of Seascape Inn work for you as it is rumored to have worked for those special few who've dared to . . .

Live the Legend

From the *Seascape* Creators,
Victoria Barrett and Rosalyn Alsobrook

The Seascape Romance Series from
St. Martin's Paperbacks

Tomorrow's Treasures

A SEASCAPE ROMANCE

ROSALYN ALSOBROOK

St. Martin's Paperbacks

NOTE: If you purchased this book without a cover you should be aware that this book is stolen property. It was reported as "unsold and destroyed" to the publisher, and neither the author nor the publisher has received any payment for this "stripped book."

TOMORROW'S TREASURES

Copyright © 1997 by Rosalyn Alsobrook.

Excerpt from *The Endless Sky* copyright © 1997 by Shirl Henke.

Cover photograph by Steve Terrill, courtesy The Stockbroker.

All rights reserved. No part of this book may be used or reproduced in any manner whatsoever without written permission except in the case of brief quotations embodied in critical articles or reviews. For information address St. Martin's Press, 175 Fifth Avenue, New York, N.Y. 10010.

ISBN: 0-312-96394-7

Printed in the United States of America

St. Martin's Paperbacks edition/December 1997

10 9 8 7 6 5 4 3 2 1

This book is dedicated to Lowell and Christine Rutledge, who somehow managed to turn their own rowdy little tomboy into someone society could tolerate. Miracle workers, both of them.

Miss Hattie's Cranberry Bread

Preheat oven: 350 degrees

      2 cups white flour
 1½ teaspoons baking powder
      1 cup sugar
      3 tablespoons oleo, melted
      ¾ cup nuts, chopped (pecans or walnuts)
      ⅓ teaspoon salt
      ½ teaspoon soda
      1 medium or large egg, beaten
      ¾ cup orange juice
      1 cup cranberries, halved

Mix the dry ingredients first, then stir in the rest. Spray a loaf pan with cooking oil; fill with mixture, and bake in a 350 degree oven for 50 minutes to one hour. Best served warm.

Tomorrow's Treasures

❧ *Chapter 1* ❧

For lack of a weapon, Damon Adams shot his friend an angry look, then reached for the telephone. "Aren't you worried that this could all backfire on us?"

Blair tapped a red fingernail on his desk. "It won't backfire. Do it."

Out of arguments, Damon let out an annoyed huff. *Why did life have to be so complicated?*

Wishing Blair anywhere else, Damon divided his attention between the old, worn maroon and white travel brochure open on his desk and the stormy gray telephone receiver gripped in his hand. Reluctantly, he punched the lighted buttons in correct sequence with a pencil eraser. With elbows planted on his note-stuffed, ink-scribbled desk pad, he listened for that first ring. Four rings later, Miss Hattie finally answered.

"The Seascape Inn, Sea Haven, Maine. Hattie Stillman speaking. May I help you?"

Despite the purpose of his call, Damon relaxed at hearing the natural warmth in Miss Hattie's familiar voice. How he loved that jaunty clip so characteristic of her fellow 'Mainiacs of the mid-coast'. Only someone as pleasant as Miss Hattie could make him want to smile at the same time he contemplated pulling out large needed hunks of his dark hair. Or better yet, he could pull out large hunks of Blair Brockway's short, transient-brown locks. How he hated being manipulated. Or was blackmailed a better word?

His glower returned. *Some friend she turned out to be.*

"I certainly hope so," he replied in a friendlier voice than he'd expected. "This is Damon Adams. I know this is late notice, but I need to see if I can reserve a third room for eleven days of those two weeks Jeri and I will be there. You wouldn't happen to still have a vacancy during that time, would you?" *Please say no.*

"I just might. Which eleven days are you talking about?"

"Starting that Friday."

"Let me check." She clattered the phone, then leafed through papers, probably the pages of that oversized reservation book of hers. After a minute or so of her humming the first stanza of *Amazing Grace*, she came back on the line. "Aye, that's what I thought. You are in luck, Damon. The couple who had booked the Cove Room for the last two weeks in July called just yesterday to tell me they would be staying only through the first Thursday. How nice for you because having that room will give you the entire second floor right here in the house. That will afford you a little more privacy than most guests have since you won't have to share the bathroom with any strangers."

"Then add it to my reservation." Damon sighed inwardly. *Of all the rotten luck.*

He wrinkled his nose beneath the bridge of the designer, gold-rimmed glasses he had slipped on to read the unreasonably tiny print on the brochure. Had there been no vacancy, he would have had a good reason to tell Blair to forget the whole thing. After all, there was no way Jeri would allow anyone of the adult female persuasion to share her room. The kid was going to be furious enough just having one join them there. Even though destined to become one, his daughter did not yet trust anyone female who had the audacity to be over the age of eighteen. But then, her own mother had had plenty to do with that. "Do you need my credit card number again?"

"No, no, I still have that right here. Besides, I trust you to pay your bill. You haven't failed me yet." She paused a moment. "What name shall I put down as the occupant for this third room?"

"Paige Brockway." Aggravated, he tapped the metal pencil band against the side of the telephone base. It looked like he would have to go through with it after all. *Drat.*

"A close friend of yours?"

"No, she's more like a friend of a close friend." He cut his gaze to Blair seated primly on the only chair in his office that was not cluttered with paperwork. "Or rather the sister of one. She should arrive sometime Friday to help keep Jeri entertained and out of trouble while I put together a bid for a very important contract. It's one of those unexpected last minute deals that can't be helped."

"How old is this Paige?"

If anyone but dear, sweet Miss Hattie had asked, Damon would have simply told her it was none of her business and been done with it. But Miss Hattie had a true interest in people, and liked knowing a little about her guests beforehand so she could make them feel more at home.

"How old is Paige?" he repeated, and thought a moment. "She's about twenty-five."

"No, Damon, twenty-*seven*," Blair corrected. She leaned forward to be sure he heard her. "Paige is now twenty-*seven*."

Damon frowned, distracted from the conversation with Hattie. "Already?" He pulled the receiver away from his mouth, but didn't bother to cover it with his hand. "She can't be that old already. Why, it was just yesterday the little twerp was out riding that goofy looking white bicycle with the plastic pink and purple tassels and—"

"That wasn't *yesterday*, Damon." Blair wagged a perfectly manicured nail in his direction. "Paige gave away that old bike when she was thirteen and we had to move. Paige really is twenty-seven now."

He groaned at the reminder. If Paige was twenty-seven,

that meant he was thirty-three. He didn't like being thirty-three. Scowling deeply, he jerked his reading glasses off and shoved them aside before talking again into the telephone receiver. "Ah, my mistake. Seems the years are getting by me without enough notice. It looks like little Sticks is now twenty-seven. And to save you from your next questions, she's a women's fashion designer who I understand is very good at what she does. She lives in New York City for now but is about to move back here to Mt. Pine."

"No, Paige is *not* moving back here to Texas!" Blair came out of her chair with a regal vengeance. "She's not going to throw away her career like that. She's going to stay right there in New York with me. You are about to make sure of that, remember?"

Damon didn't care to explain away another blunder so he simply went on with his description. "She's single, educated, and nauseatingly successful for someone so young—and most importantly—she is not coming because I have any sort of romantic interest in her. Got that? You are to do none of that matchmaking thing you're so noted for. This is strictly business."

"Mmmmm, strictly business?"

"And I don't mean monkey business," Damon cautioned. There was something in Miss Hattie's tone that made him nervous enough to want to lie. He had seen Miss Hattie in action. "I guess you should know, I'm dating someone else right now who would have a royal conniption if she thought I was up there fraternizing with the help. Please, keep that in mind while we are there."

"Oh? You have found enough time to date again? How nice. Why don't you bring your new lady friend with you, too? I'll have another room empty in the carriage house at that time and I'd truly love to meet the woman who finally made you realize what your life was lacking. What's she like?"

Not in a creative mood, Damon cut the conversation short. "I have to get back to work, Miss Hattie. I'll tell you all about her when I see you in a couple of weeks. Goodbye until then.''

After he jabbed the off button, he laid the handset down beside those hated eyeglasses and rubbed the pad-dented bridge of his nose with a gentle finger and thumb.

''Okay,'' he muttered. Dropping his hand, he returned his attention to Blair, now seated again. ''I did it. Your sister now has a room at the Seascape Inn.'' He slid the pencil into the empty pocket of his dark red cotton shirt. ''But what makes you so all-fired certain she'll agree to go to Maine with us?''

''Oh, she'll go all right,'' Blair replied with a slightly impish smile—the same deep, dimpled smile that had made her famous world wide. It was the same smile Damon had learned to be wary of years ago.

''Don't you worry, sweetie. My sister will be there. I'll see to it.'' Her smile deepened as she braided her slender hands together and rested them gracefully on a silk draped knee. ''And she will loathe every minute she's there. *You* will see to that. After which, my friend will give your bid very special consideration. *I'll* see to that.''

''If that's what it takes to cinch that contract and save my father's business.'' Damon let out a tired breath, rolled his head back, and rested it against the top of his worn, leather chair. ''Then that's what I'll do.''

Checking to make sure she left the door locked, Paige Brockway shook off the odd feeling of being watched. There was no one around to notice her as she slid the oversized room key into her hip pocket and took the front stairs back down to the foyer at a fast clip.

Having had to be so fashion conscious all the time, it had been years since she had worn a pair of simple, double-stitched blue jeans and a white T-shirt, much less white cotton socks and a pair of plain lace-up tennis shoes. Doing so again made Paige want to run, skip, and jump like a child just let out for recess.

It was all a reflection of her new found freedom. She

had finally made up her mind to follow her heart and leave New York, and had already put the hardest part of that decision behind her. Not only had she given notice to her boss and worked the final two weeks following, she had already found the courage and told Blair. All Paige had to do now was get through these next eleven days, return to pack the rest of her belongings, then she would soon be on her way back to Mt. Pine—*foot loose and guilt free.*

"How was the room?" Miss Hattie asked with an inflection typical to Mainers when she glanced up from an assortment of mail scattered across an otherwise tidy registration desk. Miss Hattie was the lovely woman who managed the Seascape Inn all alone despite her many years—which Paige guessed totaled over seventy.

"The room is wonderful," she answered honestly. "My view of the village, the cove, and the forests beyond are incredibly breathtaking. I can't believe how beautiful this area is."

When Blair first told Paige about the little-known seaside bed and breakfast hidden away in some obscure part of the country, she'd had her doubts. But now that she had seen it, *had felt it*, she understood why Blair's good friend, Damon, brought his daughter there every year for vacation.

There was something remarkably invigorating about the modest little inn—yet at the same time emotionally soothing. The brochure Blair had given her in no way did the place justice. The inn was more than simply picturesque and restful, as stated in the blurb. It was magic. So amazingly magic that Paige was now glad she had agreed to come there to try and force a little good influence off on Damon Adams' twelve year old hellion, as she'd once heard Blair refer to her.

Having seen Jerina Adams only once, though quite by accident, Paige wasn't sure what she was faced with trying to convince that child to become more poised and proper. Jeri, as Blair most often called her, was a beautiful girl with plenty of feminine potential, who had yet to realize her softer side. Helping make a lady out of that would not be easy.

But whatever trials lay ahead these next several days, they would be well worth braving if, in the end, they allayed even part of Paige's ever-nagging guilt. Guilt that had shot to life the day she decided to leave Manhattan and move back to Mt. Pine, where she could live her life the way she'd always wanted. Getting rid of some of that guilty feeling was the main reason Paige had traveled there.

Blair was right—*of course*. Performing this one small favor was the least Paige could do for her *considering*.

"Surely all those years I spent helping care for you account for something," her older sister had been very quick to point out. And that was true. Her sister's many sacrifices did account for plenty. Paige would be forever grateful for her sister's loyalty and help, especially during those emotional years right after their father's death. It had been hard enough for Paige to cope with their mother's early death, but being only thirteen when their father died, too, Paige would have had no one to care for her had it not been for Blair.

That was why Paige loved her sister so dearly. Blair had taken Paige in during a time in Blair's modeling career when it would have been very easy not to. She also had been the first to notice Paige's natural talent for fashion design and had encouraged her in that direction, seeing her through all the frustrations and joys that followed.

Truth was, Blair had supported Paige through every emotional crises of her life, including her failed engagement, and she had celebrated even the smallest of achievements with her. Blair was more than just an older sister. She was Paige's most trusted friend, and Paige would do anything for her—except stay in New York. The time had come to break away and live life the way she'd always wanted.

Having made it this far already, Paige could taste the independence—as clearly as she could taste the salt in the seaswept air. Twenty-seven years old and she was about to be on her own for the first time ever. How much more thrilling could life get?

"And the gardens in the yard below my window are *heavenly*," she continued her assessment in earnest. "I love all those flowers."

"I'm glad you're pleased." Miss Hattie nodded, her smile etched in age lines as soft as the charming lilt in her voice. "Were there enough towels?"

"Yes, that young man who led me here from the village then showed me to my room pointed out where they are. There are enough in the closet to last me several days, thank you. He also showed me the bathroom across the hall, and explained about hanging out the occupied sign whenever I think I might have to be in there for long so others will know to come downstairs instead. I peeked inside and can hardly wait to try out that monstrosity of a bathtub. Of course, I'll be sharing the bathroom with other guests, so I'll try not to hoard it."

"Oh, but you'll only be sharing with Damon and Jeri. You three together have that whole floor to do whatever strikes your fancy. When my other guests arrive, they all go into the carriage house—that largest building outside. The one just beyond the biggest garden." She waved a partly opened envelope in the general direction. Her green eyes sparkled with untold mischief when she glanced first to where she had gestured, then back again at Paige.

The look of mischief fell in direct odds with Miss Hattie's sweet, grandmotherly appearance. She was not only ample and round, she also wore her silvery white hair in a neat bun at the back of her head. She was the sort of person one longed to hug close—and one who shouldn't look as if she planned a serious bit of chicanery.

"Are Damon and Jeri Adams around?" Paige asked, finished with the assessment of her host. No reason to delay her duties. "I should let them know I arrived a couple of hours earlier than I'd thought I would." She glanced into the quaint sunlit parlor across the hall. It was filled with comfortable looking antiques and colorful throw rugs, but was otherwise empty. No guests at all.

"Aye, those two have been here a couple of days now. Last I heard tell, they were heading over to that lot beside the church to see if they could put together a baseball game with some of the locals. With the Bakers' nephews here for the week, that shouldn't be too hard to do. They've always enjoyed playing with Jeri and her father."

Paige frowned. How odd that a father who so desperately wanted his tomboy daughter to start behaving more like a young lady would be so willing to pull together a baseball game for them.

Did the man expect *her* to do all the work without any help at all? Maybe she *should* have called him beforehand to find out a little something about his expectations. But Blair had cautioned her against that. The problem with his daughter was not something he liked to talk about. The less said, the better. "Where is this lot?"

Miss Hattie set the envelope down and picked up a small handkerchief edged in lace. She fluttered the scrap of crisp white in the direction of the nearby village. "It's on the church side of the post office. You passed it driving in." She dabbed lightly at her temple then slid all but one lacy corner into the front pocket of her mid-sleeve, sea-green dress. "The post office is that small red-brick building with the flag out front. It also doubles as our City Hall."

"It's walking distance then?"

"For most folks."

"Thanks." Eager to breathe that fresh sea air again, Paige hurried through the front door, again invigorated by the distant purr of the ocean and a soft, warm breeze spiced with the scents of salt, cedar, and roses. She had already clamored out into the yard when Hattie called out one final directive. "Just look for the church steeple. That will guide you right to them."

Spotting the white steeple through the top branches of the lofty cedars nearby, she cut across a grassy field rather than follow the driveway to the patchy strip of asphalt that curved along the rugged shore. A stone path beyond the old highway would have offered a far more majestic view of the ocean while she walked, but she wasn't there as a tourist. She was there to work—and, in doing so, rid herself of at least part of the sisterly guilt that plagued her, freeing her to leave.

Even though Blair still loved life in the city and always would, Paige had long since grown tired of it. Fed up with the pressure and the politics that lay at the very core of the fashion world, all Paige wanted to do now was to move back to Mt. Pine, Texas, and find something a little less stressful to do with her life—like open her own dress boutique.

Oh, but Blair couldn't understand that. She couldn't perceive how anyone would choose such an ordinary existence over being surrounded by the thrill and energy of the city. To Blair, a move to Mt. Pine would be a major step backward, something Paige would regret for the rest of her life.

In truth, when Paige first started designing clothing for MissTeek Fashions, life in New York City had seemed as exciting as it was challenging. But after reality eventually set in, the challenge of being one of MissTeek's top designers was no longer worth the aggravation or ruthlessness that came with it. The lure of glitz and glamour had worn off long ago for Paige, but she had yet to convince Blair of that.

Granted, Blair's dreams for Paige to be wondrously successful and eventually develop her own line of designer fashions were nothing short of admirable; still, they were just that—Blair's dreams and not her own.

Even so, Paige couldn't help feeling guilty about the decision to move back to the town where she grew up, and finally take charge of her own life. It's what prompted her to do this one last special favor for Blair. Helping Damon Adams to turn his daughter around so he didn't have to continue dealing with the girl's tomboyish behavior should also help make up for what Blair considered a direct betrayal.

Damon Adams. The name alone caused Paige shivers of concern. Why, of all Blair's friends, did it have to be Damon Adams who needed help right now?

Damon was without a doubt the most handsome, most athletic boy ever to graduate Mt. Pine high school. He was also the most elusive and most arrogant. Every girl who ever knew him had developed a crush on him, though he had had eyes only for the elite few.

Even Paige, only twelve-years-old when he graduated, had thought him impossibly handsome. Yet like most of the girls in Mt. Pine, Damon had never really noticed her. He'd never thought of her as anything more than the skinny little sister of his close friend, Blair. *Sticks* he'd called her. How humiliating that had been. And how amusing it must have been for him. But then Damon had always enjoyed a real talent for making awkward girls like her feel awful, which undoubtedly pumped up that over-inflated ego even more.

But then Damon had every right to an over-inflated ego. "Why are you letting all that bother you now?" she asked herself aloud. "That was over fifteen years ago—nearly half your lifetime ago." Back when Damon was still in his prime, and back during one of the most impressionable and most emotional ages a young woman faced. Twelve. The same age Jeri was now. *Poor kid.*

Holding on to that perspective, Paige counted the years again. Fifteen. Damon graduated the same year as Blair. That made him thirty-three years old by now. Or maybe thirty-two. Hardly of an age to still have that sleek, hard body or a head covered with that thick, dark brown hair he'd always worn rakishly long. No, by now, time would have taken its gracious toll on that athletic body. She could well imagine the paunch he'd developed while sitting behind his father's desk most of the day. Running the two family businesses he'd inherited had to take up most of his time. Wickedly, she hoped he had gone bald as well. She could hardly wait to see the ravages time had made on Damon's appearance.

Stepping around a large black and yellow dog sleeping in the middle of the sidewalk in town, Paige sighed with the memory of that lovelorn little girl who might as well have been invisible. How it had broken her heart that next year to have to move away from Mt. Pine. If only she had known then that when Damon returned from college, it would be with a wife and child.

Just my luck, she thought, then laughed: as if she would have ever had a chance of catching his eye even later, after she had finally filled out in all the right places. No, not when women far more desirable than she ever hoped to be had beckoned his attention and failed.

Oddly disappointed by that thought, she wondered what the woman who finally landed him was like. Probably nothing short of gorgeous. But then a lot of good being gorgeous had done the poor soul. Eventually, Damon dumped her just like he'd dumped every other woman in his life.

Still headed toward the narrow wooden steeple that stood high above everything else in the quaint little seaside village, Paige glanced off to the right. There was the red-brick building with the post office emblem on the front. On the far side of that was a small grassy field with a dilapidated backstop and well-worn baselines where three men and children of all ages indulged in a noisy game of sandlot baseball.

Paige's stomach knotted with anticipation. From that distance, she could not make out faces, but she guessed all three men to be somewhere in their thirties. Two were slender, of medium height, and dressed in worn jeans and cotton shirts, while the third was a little shorter and a bit paunchy—although not quite as paunchy as Paige had hoped.

She squinted to see what the shorter man wore. Coming from northeast Texas where the men tried to stand as tall as the native pines, he had on western style boots instead of athletic shoes and a pair of blue-striped overalls—the trademark of most construction people. The overalls looked loose enough in the legs but appeared a little snug around his middle.

So Damon hadn't fared as well as he might have liked.

Malevolently pleased, Paige headed toward right field where he stood shading his eyes though the afternoon sun was behind him. He was one of the few without either a baseball cap or sunglasses.

Next trying to pick out Jeri from the children, Paige crossed a sandy area to the baseball field. Having caught a glimpse of the girl a couple of weeks ago while in Mt. Pine visiting her childhood friend, Susan Carmichael, Paige already knew what Jeri looked like. Susan had remembered the crush Paige had on Damon during junior high and pointed Jeri out to her while coming out of the maternity shop where Paige had longingly bought her pregnant friend several adorable outfits. Though she had seen Jeri just once, Paige now spotted the girl easily.

The long shimmering-blond ponytail dangling through the adjustment gap in the back of her red baseball cap was a dead giveaway. So was her half-tucked-in bright red baseball shirt with bold white letters that read *Adams Lumber and Construction*. Evidently the girl played on a sponsored team back home.

"Come on, Dad," she whined loud enough for Paige to hear. "He's got the idea already. Move out of the way so I can finish striking him out."

Dad? Paige skidded to an abrupt halt, still a dozen yards behind the lopsided backstop. The man she had thought to be Damon Adams still stood out in right field, now impatiently twisting what appeared to be an oversized gold ring around his pinky. But the man Jeri had just referred to as Dad stood directly behind the batter, helping a boy who looked to be about nine years old straighten out his batting swing.

She couldn't see the second man's face from where she stood, but when he bent forward to place his arms around the small batter, his worn jeans pulled taut, allowing her a nice view of what could only be described as one lean, hard, muscular behind. The light blue short-sleeve shirt stretched around a pair of wicked shoulders, and gave stark contrast to his dark tan. His arms flexed with smooth, agile strength while he gently moved the boy's arms, using his hands.

He was one of those men who made simple mass-manufactured clothing look top designer.

So much for the softening with age theory.

A hard knot the size of the baseball in Jeri's hand formed in the pit of Paige's stomach. Suddenly, she wasn't so sure she had done the right thing coming to Maine. There had to have been other favors she could have done for her sister.

"No, Barney, hold it more like this, and swing level when she pitches it to you."

Paige sucked in an unsteady breath at the sound of his voice. Even that was every bit as sexy as it had been back in high school. Maybe more so, what with the deepening of age. *How unfair.*

"Come off it, Dad," Jeri complained. She shoved her hat back a half inch, all her placement of ponytail allowed. Not yet noticing Paige, she jutted her hip out and tucked her gloved hand under her pitching arm. Dirt stained the side of her pleated shorts. "He isn't even on our team."

"I'm just helping him a little with his batting problem," Damon pointed out needlessly. He continued to manipulate the boy's arms.

Jeri blew out an exasperated breath and shifted her weight to the other leg.

"It's the Godly thing to do," came an immediate retort from the bearded man standing near third base. Judging by the way he stood to the inside of the diamond and kept his foot on the base, he was a runner on little Barney's team. It made sense that he would support any help the boy got.

"Yeah, Reverend Brown, I know that," Jeri granted, then shifted her weight to the other leg. "But he's holding up the game. I've got two strikes on Barn. All I need is one more and you guys take the field.''

"Patience," he cautioned, then flashed a wide, even grin through his dark, well-kept beard. "It is not the good Lord's fault that your team is behind by one point."

"No, it isn't," Jeri agreed, then cut an annoyed look out toward right field. "And it sure isn't *my* fault either."

The man in overalls slumped his shoulders in an exaggerated show of remorse and Jeri laughed in spite of herself. "Just stay awake out there, okay?"

He nodded vigorously, then clicked his boot heels and saluted.

Paige smiled despite her growing trepidation.

What fun these people had playing to their audience of one: a pretty blonde girl, who looked to be about sixteen or seventeen. She sat cross-legged in the grass not very far from third base, dressed in a pair of tight stone-washed jeans and a pink blouse. Having seen the melodramatic salute of the older man, the audience merely shook her head and moaned.

Finally Damon stepped away from the batter and took his position as the catcher. His form fitted Levi's stretched to their limit around taut thighs when he squatted and slid his hand back into his glove, then held it upright. He had yet to turn around and notice Paige. His attention remained on the batter. "Ready."

Paige waited for the next pitch and was pleased when the boy hit a slow line drive to third. She held her breath. By the time that ball finally reached the young man playing third base and was thrown home, the preacher just might make it in safe, and the little boy will have hit a runner in.

It would have been an excitingly close play had the third baseman caught the ball.

"Andy, no!" The girl in the grass covered her eyes so she couldn't watch while the teenager named Andy scrambled after the ball.

"Pitch it home. Pitch it home," Jeri shrieked, headed in to back up her father at the plate.

Andy stumbled and fell, but not before scooping up the ball and tossing it wildly toward home. Jeri intercepted it and spun around to toss it to her dad. But too late. The Reverend Brown had cleared the plate and now danced around happily.

Barney had made it to first, and stood staring at the dancing man with a proud grin. The shorter boy beside him stood with his arms crossed, clearly annoyed. Judging by their appearances, those two were brothers.

"Uncle Fred, I don't want to be on your team no more," the younger one said, his lower lip stuck out about as far as it could go and still stay attached. "It ain't fair when your own catcher helps the other side."

"Hailstones, Bobby, it's not my fault you and David ended up on my team. It was the luck of the draw, remember? Besides, we still have another turn at bat. We can pull this out yet."

"If we ever get them out again," he muttered, then took a deep breath and resumed his stance at first base.

Paige waited until the preacher finished his victory dance and had joined his teammates under the only tree before approaching the man she now knew to be Damon.

Prepared to feel insignificant again, like when she was twelve years old and he was eighteen, she called out his name.

Everyone turned to look at her. Including Damon.

Paige's reaction was immediate. A combination of awe and disappointment struck her at the same time.

She had so hoped that in concession for having kept such a strong, healthy body, he had forfeited immensely in the face. But he hadn't. From this distance, he looked even better than he had fifteen years ago. But close up surely she would discover a whole network of age lines and such, especially when it was obvious by his tan skin, he spent a lot of time out in the aging sun.

She headed toward him, again hopeful.

"Yes?" Having squinted against the sun despite the shade the billed cap provided, his nose was still wrinkled when he first turned to face her. But, instantly, that expression gave way to one of obvious surprise. "Can I help you?"

Jeri had not yet returned to the pitching mound and stood just a few feet in front of her father. She cocked her head and gave Paige a quick once over, apparently not pleased with what she saw. Her disdainful expression reminded Paige of that younger Damon she remembered so well.

With Jeri blocking her path, Paige stopped several paces away and desperately sought something intelligent to say. But words failed her. She was still too stunned by how very little Damon had changed in fifteen years.

"Dad, is *this* the woman you told me about?" Jeri scowled and gave Paige another cynical sweep. "Is she the one who is supposed to help keep *me* entertained while we're here?" She rolled her eyes and gave Paige a *get real* kind of look. Clearly, the girl thought Paige unqualified for the job.

Perceptive child.

"I don't know," Damon admitted. He'd tugged off his glove and stepped around his daughter. Eyes that were every bit as blue as those Paige remembered met hers questioningly when he came to a halt only a couple of feet away.

Paige drew in another disappointed breath. Dear heavens. Hardly any age lines at all. Her heart did a little jazz dance while she considered how disgustingly handsome he still looked.

"Are you Paige Brockway?" He blinked hard as if not quite expecting the answer to be yes. The shadow from his cap slanted across a still handsome face while he studied her more closely. "Are *you* that skinny little kid who used to follow Blair around all the time? The one who was so bony, I called her Sticks?"

"Yes," Paige snapped. Obviously, the attitude part of

this man hadn't changed either. He was still incredibly insulting. "But I happen to have grown up since then."

Great, she thought. Not even a minute in Damon's company and already she was on the defensive. It was like being twelve years old all over again.

Chapter 2

Paige shifted under Damon's studious gaze. Suddenly, she felt awkward and ugly—and deeply offended. "Not only have I grown up since then, I happen to have filled out, too." She lifted her chin proudly. "You can't go around calling me Sticks anymore."

"I'll say," he nodded, his wide-eyed expression not revealing if he approved of the change, or was simply shocked by it.

He blinked twice more, then slowly smiled, his teeth a brilliant white against all that dark tanned skin. Dimples formed deep, familiar curves in both his cheeks. Oh, how Damon had used those same dimples to his advantage back in high school. There wasn't a female student or female teacher who hadn't been at least somewhat affected by Damon's long, curved dimples.

But Paige refused to be swayed by them today. Jaw hardened, she reached up to shove a wind-tossed curl away from her face. She wanted him to have a clear view of the determination flaring in her brown eyes. She was not that same trod-upon little girl. Not now.

"Well, then, I guess I won't be calling you Sticks anymore, huh?"

"Not if you want to live to be any older," she warned, presenting a smile of her own, though not a sincere one.

Having developed what she thought a genuine self-confidence during her past several years as the head designer for the internationally renowned MissTeek Fashions—a position landed after a skyrocketing start to her career—she was not used to feeling this vulnerable and insecure. She hated it. But, judging by his widening smile, he enjoyed watching her squirm.

Did the man find some sort of perverse pleasure in making others feel about as meaningful as pond scum? *Sticks, indeed.*

"Come on, Dad. We have a game to finish," Jeri said. She glared at Paige a second more before soundly thwapping her father across one solid shoulder with the tip of her glove. "Let's get back to it. We are now two points behind. We've gotta do something about that."

Finally, Damon pulled his attention off Paige and shifted it to his daughter. "Okay, you're right. Let's get back to it. Whose turn is it to bat?"

"Barney just went," Jeri answered, already headed for the pitcher's mound. "So it has to be Frankie's turn again." Back into position, she stood with her weight shifted to her left leg and resumed glowering at Paige.

Paige could not believe the animosity coming from that child. Did the girl already know the real reason she was there? Blair had assured her she wouldn't, since that might work against what they hoped to accomplish. Surely Damon hadn't warned the girl.

Paige chewed nervously on her lower lip. She should have called. Even though Blair had cautioned her not to, she should have called. If she had, she would know more about what she faced there.

Finally, Jeri tore her gaze away. "Come on, guys. This should be an easy out." Having dismissed Paige for now, Jeri glanced back toward right field and shouted in a louder voice. "Or it will be if everyone on our side stays awake."

Rather than be insulted, the man laughed and saluted again. Judging by the friendly rapport, these two had known each other a long time.

Paige's attention shifted back to Damon, who hadn't

moved yet. Again, he stared at her, making her swallow around the lump in her throat.

"I guess introductions will have to wait," Damon commented with a helpless shrug. His blue eyes still on her as if still having a hard time believing how much she'd changed, he gestured toward the teenage girl sitting in the grass just the other side of the backstop. "Why don't you go over there and sit with Nolene Baker? We should be through here shortly."

Paige would have preferred waiting for these two back at the inn. That would give her a chance to get over the unpleasant shock of discovering that Damon looked even better now than he had back when he was the sexiest senior ever to grace the halls of Mt. Pine High. The years had certainly been kind to him—if not revoltingly benevolent.

After a quick exchange of hellos with Nolene, Paige sank down into the soft grass beside her. She quickly learned that Nolene was a local girl whose father was the outfielder taking the brunt of everyone's complaints. He and her mother owned the local cafe down the street. Nolene next told her a little about the people playing. Although there was no shade to the side of the backstop where they sat, a constant breeze kept the mid-afternoon heat at a comfortable level while they watched the game.

With Damon more to the side of her than directly in front of her, Paige was better able to concentrate on the eclectic mixture of ball players while Nolene revealed tidbits about them. There were seven people on each team, ranging in age from the current first baseman, who appeared about eight, to Nolene's father in right field, who looked nearly forty.

All but two of the sandlot players were male, some more so than others. Paige glanced again at Damon, busy adjusting his glove, then quickly away, her heart pumping harder than ever.

Trying to get over that, she next studied the only two girls in the game. They were on opposite teams and looked to be about the same age. Both were blond. Both wore ponytails, though Jeri had the longer ponytail of the two. Jeri was also a year or two older, and prettier.

At the moment, all eyes were on the two girls as they faced each other, pitcher to batter. All eyes except Paige's. She could not seem to keep her gaze from straying to the still strong lines of Damon's face. Nor could she keep her pulses from pounding a little harder each time it did. She truly had not expected him to look quite so perfect.

"Are you ready to strike out there, Frankie?" Jeri asked, tugging her ballcap bill back down as she bent forward to assess her batter with a narrowed gaze.

"Send me your best shot," Frankie responded, a death grip on the wooden bat as she gave it a good, hard practice swing then stepped back up to the plate. "I'll knock it clean into the forest where Mr. Baker will have to spend the rest of the afternoon lookin' for it among the ferns."

Damon chuckled as he squatted down and lifted his glove. He balanced his weight evenly on the balls of both feet. Although he'd been a lead pitcher in high school, he had obviously had a lot of practice playing behind the plate.

"Strike one," he called out a second after the ball thumped into his glove. He stood and threw it back in one smooth, involved motion. "Frankie, you should have taken a piece out of that one. It was right over."

Scowling, Frankie stepped back and hit the ground a couple of times with the large end of her bat, like Paige had seen professional ball players do.

"Good pitch," Paige shouted, hoping to make the still frowning pitcher feel a little better about her being there— if indeed she was the child's problem. Until they talked, there was no way to know what had her so upset.

"She is good isn't she?" Damon turned and gave Paige a wink so playful and sexy it took Paige's next breath away. What she would have given for him to wink at her like that fifteen years ago. It would have sent her young heart spiralling into the heavens. As it was, her now much older pulses lurched forward with a noticeable force. From just a wink?

His attention back on the game, Damon knelt again, glove ready. Again, Jeri zinged one in dead center. When he stood to toss it back, little Bobby on first base shouted for a time-out then pointed to home plate. "Frankie needs to tie her shoe again."

Frankie glanced down, sighed, then stepped back and bent to take care of the stray laces with fumbly fingers. Waiting on her to finish, Damon strolled over to where Paige and Nolene sat with such male grace, he put most of the professional models in Paige's fashion world to shame. His attraction went far beyond any pretty boy looks.

"You know, I just can't get over how much you've changed." He pulled his ballcap off and ran three curved fingers through his still thick brown hair.

Even damp, Damon's hair fell evenly back into place. Had time not done one single thing to ugly this man?

"And just what did you expect?"

"I'm not sure. But I don't think I would have known you if you hadn't told me who you are. It's truly amazing."

Paige couldn't help but smile at that. He sounded sincerely bewildered. Perhaps his comments about what she used to look like hadn't been said to make her feel awkward and ugly again. Could it be that had just been his way of pointing out how different she looked now? Perhaps she had misjudged him. "It has been fifteen years, you know."

His dimples disappeared the second his mouth flatlined. "Don't remind me." He knelt, allowing her a better view of the crystal clarity in his blue eyes—so pale and glittering beneath that thick fringe of dark lashes.

The sexiest eyes Paige had ever seen on a man.

"Please, I do what I can to forget that I'm starting to get on up there in years. I don't like the idea of starting to fall apart."

If he was digging for a compliment, he did not get one. While Paige considered a safe yet still honest response, Nolene nodded with understanding. "But everyone gets old, Mr. Adams." She plucked a long blade of grass and tipped her head to one side while she tickled her cheek with the frayed end. "Just take a look at my pop." She pointed the green tip toward the outfield. "That poor man is nearly ancient."

"Nolene, your father is thirty-six," Damon pointed out with a questioning lift of his brow, but he didn't follow her request to look outfield.

"See?" she replied brightly, as if that had been her point all along. "I told you. *Everyone* gets old."

Damon moaned, then laughed, recovering quickly from the unintended insult. "It's all in one's perspective, bright eyes. I live by the popular saying, you are only as old as you feel and, fortunately, I don't feel quite ancient yet." He flicked a hopeful gaze to Paige. "Do I look quite ancient to you?"

Paige drew a quick breath. She had been so busy studying how incredibly radiant his eyes were, she hadn't paid that much attention to the conversation. Something about getting old?

He leaned closer, boosting her pulses to yet a faster rate. Was the man flirting with her? Or had she misjudged the situation yet again? What was it about him that jammed all her circuits?

"Well? Do I?"

"Da-ad!" Jeri called out, interrupting the cozy threesome. She stood impatiently, with her left hip jutted out again. "Frankie's shoes are tied already. Get back behind the plate."

Damon tossed a look over his shoulder, then let out a short breath as he stood again, putting his denim clad legs in Paige's direct line of vision. "Sorry, but duty calls."

He gave Paige one more quick glance, plopped his hat in place, and headed back to cover home plate. Paige's attention remained with the graceful movement of his muscular legs until he knelt again, then it shifted to the pitcher's mound. Her next breath snagged inside her throat when she saw the malice in Jeri's expression. Every muscle in the girl's face and neck was rigid. More so now than earlier.

What was that girl's problem?

Finally, Jeri returned her attention to the batter and Paige released the breath she hadn't even realized she'd held until she heard it escape. Damon's daughter was most intimidating for a twelve year old. It was hard to think of her as the *poor, motherless waif* Blair had so ineptly described.

"You ready, Frankie?" Jeri pressed her lips together in preparation.

Frankie twitched her nose and tightened her hold on the bat as Jeri brought the ball forward to the tip of her glove, stretched it back to gather as much speed as possible, then flung it forward with all her might.

Paige, having taken that next second to glance at Damon again, barely looked back in time to duck out of the way. As she slammed her shoulder into the grass, the ball missed her by mere inches. Had she not fallen back, it would have caught her square in the chest.

"Paige!" Damon slung his glove aside in his rush to see if she was hurt all the while his daughter stayed put and continued to deliver that accomplished glower of hers. "Paige, are you okay?"

Kneeling beside her, he held out a hand to help her back into a seated position. Paige accepted that help hesitantly. She had never touched Damon Adams before, although once when she was twelve, she remembered touching his school books.

As expected, when his fingers closed around hers, his hand felt warm and his grip firm, causing something so startling inside her, it cut off her next breath. A profound bolt of electricity had shot up her arm then scattered in all directions like a starburst, affecting her from her fingers to her toes.

Paige swallowed hard while praying her lungs would kick in again. She had not responded that strongly to a man since Edward Simmons. And look how awful *that* turned out. *Major red flag there.*

She didn't dare let Damon get to her the same way her just as handsome ex-fiance had. She didn't do humiliation well at all. That was the primary reason she'd sworn off handsome men forever. Good looks were more a detriment than an advantage as far as she was concerned.

"Did the ball hit you?" Worry etched his face when he leaned forward. Balancing his weight on one knee, he peered over her shoulder to check for injuries there.

Having already felt around for possible knots or scrapes and finding none, Paige returned her attention to Damon. While he quickly brushed the grass off the back of her shirt with quick, agile swipes, she breathed deeply the warm scent of his cologne. Or maybe it was his shampoo that smelled so good. Whatever the fragrance, she indulged herself, and at the same time wondered why he didn't smell like sweat and old leather. "It came close, but it popped the ground not me."

While Damon continued brushing the tiny pieces of grass from her back and shoulders, she turned a questioning glance to Jeri. The girl pursed her mouth into a tight, malevolent smile while she rocked her weight to her left leg and planted her pitching hand on her hip. Clearly, she had wanted to bean her. *The brat.*

"Jeri, I can't believe you slung such a wild throw." Damon spoke loud enough to be heard by his daughter, yet without looking back at her. He next brushed broken grass off Paige's sleeves, but paused with his hand in midstroke when he started to brush at the few blades that clung to her breasts.

"Yeah, I know," Jeri responded. She sounded far more innocent than she looked. "I was all set to strike out Frankie; but the ball just sorta slipped from my fingers before it was supposed to." She shook her head as if concerned.

"And that was my fast ball. It could have bruised her bad. Good thing she's quick and ducked back."

"Isn't it though?" Paige muttered, then noting what Damon's problem was, finished the job of brushing the grass off her new white t-shirt. When plucking at the last of it, she spotted the bright green grass stains that streaked her right sleeve. Dear heavens. She hadn't had grass stains since she was a kid.

"Yeah," Jeri continued her act. "At first I didn't think you were going to see it coming in time to get out of the way, and I was too blown away by it happening at all to cry out a warning."

Paige glanced at her again. She didn't look too blown away by anything. All she looked was annoyed that she'd missed. "Well, no real harm done."

Jeri snorted loud enough to be heard across the field. "I guess you should have been watching this direction instead of staring so hard at something else."

Afraid of what might be said next, Paige tensed. Was the girl about to point out to everyone that she'd been all but drooling over Damon? Surely not.

"If you hadn't been so busy staring at my dad like that, you would have had more time to get out of the way."

Paige groaned. Something definitely had to be done about that child; and, fortunately, she was just the one to do it. No wonder Damon wanted a woman's gentler influence for the girl. The child definitely needed it. "I'll keep that in mind."

Damon said nothing. Either he didn't want to inflame the child more, or he simply hadn't heard the comment. Paige couldn't decide which.

Andy, who had hurdled the low picket fence and darted across the cemetery to retrieve the ball, was on his way back when he shouted a heads up to Jeri so he could throw it back to her. "Miss Hattie is not going to be happy with you. You just clipped most of those yellow flowers she always puts on Tony Freeport's grave right in half. Those flowers were supposed to last till Tuesday when she comes around again and brings another batch.''

"It's not like I did it on purpose," she protested, catching the ball with a quick flick of her glove. "It was a wild throw. The ball slipped out of my hand."

Still kneeling beside Paige, Damon continued to watch her, mesmerized, while she finished plucking at the last few pieces of grass clinging to her breasts, then at the blades in her lap. It wasn't until Paige lifted a questioning eyebrow that he coughed twice, and quickly stood. His gaze lingered on her t-shirt a second more before he headed off to where Frankie stood waiting.

"Is the lady okay?" Bobby on first base asked, watching while Damon bent to pick up his glove. "Was that crack we heard her head or the ball smacking the ground behind her when it bounced?"

"Must have been the ground," he answered, slipping the glove back on his hand. He glanced at Paige again, though briefly. "She's fine."

Bobby nodded, but frowned when he looked again at Paige. His freckled nose wrinkled speculatively. "Is anybody ever going to tell the rest of us who she is? Because, you know, if she does end up catching one of Jeri's fast balls in the head, and we all have to go to her funeral, I'd at least like to know who it was we killed."

Damon chuckled at the boy's reasoning, and looked like he was just about to answer when Jeri piped in. "Her name is Paige Brockway. And we're all supposed to believe she's come all the way up here to be my baby sitter because Dad has suddenly decided I need a private keeper."

"I can certainly understand that," Fred Baker piped in from right field. He gave Damon a thumbs up for such a sound decision and chuckled. "If ever there was a young lady who needed her own keeper, it would have to be you."

She shot him a warning glance. "Don't you find it a little weird that the keeper he found for *me* happens to be such a young, hot babe? Especially when my sitters in the past have always been such old, dumpy women.''

Having bent forward to smooth out the legs of her jeans, Paige jerked her head up to look at Jeri again, startled the girl had just called her a young, hot babe. She had expected only derogatory comments from her. But then, the way Jeri spoke the words, being a young, hot babe *had* sounded derogatory.

''Why would I find such a thing weird?'' Fred asked, coming in ready defense of a fellow father. ''An old woman would have a blessed hard time keeping up with the likes of you these days.'' He laughed again as he jerked the tip of his thumb in Paige's direction. ''Hailstones, even a young woman like her will have a hard time of it. I don't envy her any at all.''

''Very funny,'' she returned, jamming her free fist on her hip. ''If you can't see the real reason she's here, then I feel sorry for you.'' She cut a quick look toward Nolene, now seated directly behind the backstop, with Paige only a few feet away. ''No. I take that back. I feel sorry for Nolene.''

Damon cleared his throat loudly, as if to give a warning.

''Well, I do,'' she responded to the noise, her tone defensive. ''Nolene is the one who has to put up with him everyday of her life.''

Damon cleared his throat again.

''I can't help how I think.'' She took a swipe at a fat yellow butterfly that fluttered around her head, then dropped her shoulders in defeat. ''We going to finish this game or not?''

After that, Jeri had a hard time putting the ball where she wanted it, and the other team eventually won by four points. Clearly, she was not happy with the score, her father, and most especially with Paige when the three headed back toward the inn afterward. Opting for the more scenic route, they followed a winding path that curved along the rocky shore.

Damon and Jeri walked side by side, with their gloves tucked under their arms, while Paige came along a half-pace behind. From that vantage point, she noticed how, even with a tired swagger, Damon moved with superb grace. The man had no physical flaws. At least none that Paige found.

How depressing.

Yet how intriguing.

She continued to watch the pair from behind. If Damon was surprised or duly upset by his daughter's continued obstinate behavior, he didn't show it. At least not that Paige could tell. There was not one smidgen of annoyance or anger in his voice when finally he spoke just loud enough to be heard over the ocean's constant roar.

"You know, Jeri, you were probably the only person there today who didn't welcome Paige to Sea Haven with a friendly smile and a handshake," he commented, while gazing off across the dark blue water. Damon had already established that he wanted Jeri and Paige on a first name basis to encourage an eventual friendship between the two. "It's not as if our having lost that game is her fault."

"But, it is her fault," she answered, surprising Paige. Jeri slapped her glove repeatedly against her thigh while she walked. "Our team would be the one at the cafe having Cokes and ice cream sundaes right now if it wasn't for her."

"How do you figure that?" He looked at Jeri questioningly, clearly as baffled by that claim as Paige. "We were already one point behind before she even arrived."

"Because I was still pitching good before she got there. I didn't mess up hardly at all until then. But after she sat down to watch, no matter how hard I tried to put that ball over the plate, it just wasn't in there." She sliced a quick, accusing glance over her shoulder, then stared again at the path ahead. "She jinxed us."

"Don't blame Paige because you couldn't last the entire game. She had nothing to do with your arm giving out on you like it did. As I recall, you managed to put two in dead center *after* she sat down."

"Yes, I even commented on that first one," Paige put

in as a reminder, trying to second guess where all this would lead.

Without missing a step, Jeri bent over and scooped up a small flat, gray rock, and Paige allowed another few feet of distance between them.

"All I know is that before you got there, I pitched fine. After you got there, it was like something invisible stood in front of that plate blocking the ball, knocking my pitches off to one side or the other. I couldn't put them even close to where I wanted them after that. That's not like me. Even with a tired arm, I still do pretty good. Why else would I be the starting pitcher for our team?"

Could it partly be because your father is the team sponsor? Paige thought, and glanced again at the advertising on the back of the girl's bulky red shirt. But rather than make that comment aloud, she let Damon reply. So far, he had defended the situation eloquently.

"It could be you pulled something in your arm when you accidentally threw that hard, fast ball that almost nailed Paige but bounced off into the cemetery instead. As I recall, it was right after that, your pitching went haywire. Or, you may have hurt something just before that pitch, which is why that throw went so wild in the first place."

"But my arm doesn't hurt." She rotated her shoulder and elbow in different directions to prove her point. "There's no pain at all and it doesn't feel too tired. It wasn't *my* fault we lost that game." Angrily, she faced the ocean and chunked the rock as far as she could. She watched while it sailed straight out, then slowly lost its speed and plunked into the water below. "See? The arm still works fine."

Damon was quiet several minutes, but continued to walk at the same steady pace. Finally, he let out an audible breath. "We'll discuss this later. In private."

Blair was right. Damon hated other people knowing how little control he had over his intractable daughter. No wonder he was having such a hard time turning her into the little lady he wanted her to be. He was nowhere near forceful enough with the child. He obviously didn't like the idea of being considered the bad guy. But sometimes parents had to be the bad guys.

After a sharp bend in the path that had cut through a patch of mixed trees, he pointed ahead to the inviting, three-story gray and white Victorian house that lay just ahead. "Right now, I want you to hurry on upstairs, take a quick bath to cool off, then change into clean clothes for supper. I'll be up in a minute. Paige and I have to talk first."

Jeri snorted then took off running at an amazing speed for someone so young. By the time Damon and Paige reached the wide, sloping front lawn, Jeri had already bounded up the stairs and across the shaded veranda. She paused just outside the front door to give Paige one last hateful glower before jerking the door open and darting inside.

Paige swallowed around the tight knot of dread obstructing her throat. Blair was right again. If ever there was a little girl who needed a woman's gentle influence, it was Jeri. Turning that little hellion into a manageable young lady was not a task for the weak at heart. It would be easier to make a bridal gown out of a tow sack.

No wonder Damon wanted someone else's help. He had hold of one bad situation here.

❧ *Chapter 3* ❧

Damon gritted his teeth when Jeri slammed the screen door behind her. If he hadn't needed his daughter to act just the way she was acting, he would have stormed in after her and grounded her to her guest room. A few hours of time-out would likely tone down that snippy attitude a level or two. But as it was, Jeri was behaving just the way he and Blair had hoped she would—only worse. Or, in this case, *better*.

From the beginning, he and Blair had both known that Jeri would not like having a stranger join the two of them during their annual vacation at the Seascape Inn. Who could blame her? The three-story clapboard house with its simple white shutters and spindled wooden banisters had been their private haven for seven summers now—since a few months after the divorce when Dr. Westworth first suggested Damon and his daughter go there for a little bit of emotional healing. It was the one place he and Jeri could go and rejuvenate at the same time they enjoyed each other's company. Their two weeks at the cozy inn had become a heavenly tradition for both of them. Something they'd looked forward to each summer.

And he had ruined it.

Or rather Blair had.

Remembering her last visit to his construction office, Damon let out another pent up breath while he and Paige continued across the lawn. Blair had certainly been at her most formidable that day. He never stood a chance. Anymore than Paige did now.

"I'm glad Blair was able to talk you into coming up here and helping out," he commented as a way to restart a conversation. She'd fallen notably quiet. "I imagine helping a near stranger take care of a pre-teen you've never met is not something you'd normally agree to do." But then Blair could be incredibly manipulative whenever she wanted something important—choosing all the right but-' tons to push to get exactly what she wanted. His friend since early childhood, Blair knew his buttons only too well.

If it meant salvaging his father's businesses, he would indeed help Blair turn her foolhardy little sister, Paige, against the fruitless idea of returning to Mt. Pine.

"Trust me. It isn't something I'd normally do," she told him. "But Blair told me how important this is to you—as it is to her. My sister obviously treasures your friendship a great deal." She paused a moment to think about that. "Having been good friends for as long as you two have, I guess there's nothing you wouldn't do for each other."

Damon didn't argue with that, having discovered no limit thus far. But then, to prevent the inherited family businesses from failing, he would gladly do Blair's bidding. He would do what he could to make Paige see that staying in New York with Blair and continuing her successful career as a fashion designer was a much wiser choice. She would one day regret having acted on impulse, giving up everything she had fought so hard to gain.

And if a man ever understood regrets, it was him.

He shook that last thought. Dwelling on what might have been did no good. It only distracted him from what needed his attention the most. *Paige.* From what Blair had told him, Paige wasn't working with all tools in place. Not only did she intend to blow most of her savings on a small house a few blocks from his, and on a small boutique downtown, she also planned to go out and find herself a

Mr. Right so she could eventually lay claim to a family of her own. Blair maintained that if she didn't step in, Paige would ruin her life trying to find happiness based on someone else's gauge.

"We do need to talk," he repeated, stressing what he had just told Jeri.

"About what?"

"Oh, about a lot of things." But for now, he'd stick with the topic of his recalcitrant daughter. One accomplishment at a time. "Your duties for example. I thought you might like to know more about them."

He glanced at Paige, watching while she moved a little ahead of him. For some reason, she had gotten it into that pretty head of hers that true happiness and small town family life were synonymous. That was probably because her old high school friend, Susan Carmichael, whom Paige probably still remembered as Susan Sellers, had proved fortunate enough to find such happiness. But then, who was he to say where happiness lay for other people? Paige could be right. She might indeed find hers in Mt. Pine. Stranger things have happened.

Trouble was, Blair did not want Paige leaving New York in search of the impossible. She didn't want the same thing happening to her little sister that had happened to their mother, and Damon certainly wasn't the person to try to argue her out of that particular fear. Personal experience had proved marriage to be highly overrated. He and Trana had demonstrated just how wretched married life could turn out—in spades. It wasn't the sort of lifestyle he could personally recommend to anyone.

Parenthood, though, was another matter. Trying as Jeri might be at times, she was the one true joy in his life. He would not change her, or change having her for the world. Jeri was one of the few things about his life he never regretted—even when she behaved like a brat.

"So would you rather we sit over there in the garden, or go inside into the front parlor?" He glanced again at Paige, but only briefly this time. There was something unsettling in how very much she had changed during the past fifteen years. He couldn't look at her long without gaping in awe.

Who would have thought skinny little Paige Brockway with her oversized brown eyes and her unkempt brown hair would turn out to be such an attractive, alluring woman? Unlike Blair, destined to be gorgeous from day one, Paige had been such a gangly, awkward kid. So much so, he had hardly noticed her while growing up.

But he definitely noticed her now.

While Paige moved ahead of him, he couldn't help but observe the natural, fluid movements of her shapely legs and arms. No, there wasn't one awkward bone left in her sweet, supple body.

"I think I'd rather sit in the garden," she finally replied, already veering in that direction.

Lulled by her easy grace, Damon bit his knuckle to keep from groaning with appreciation. The woman exuded sensuality from the very top of her sun-glistening brown hair to the tip of her white lace-up tennis shoes.

"It's such a beautiful day," she pointed out needlessly for it was a day that had grown more glorious by the minute. She turned her face to the cloud-dotted blue sky, the curved ends of her silky hair bunching softly against her cotton clad shoulders. "It would be a shame to waste any of it cooped up inside the house."

Even Paige's voice had gone through an amazing change during the past dozen years. Back in her youth, Paige had had a very high-pitched, whiny voice, the kind that grated on one's nerves. But now it was deep, soft, and as smooth as a plank of freshly sanded pine. *Downright seductive.*

Startled, Damon ignored that last thought. The last thing he needed was to end up physically attracted to the very woman he'd vowed to turn against marriage, children, and small town life. He would do well to remember that the future of Adams Lumber and Construction was at stake.

If he didn't swing that big contract, it was sunk. And so was he.

"I considered calling you right after Blair first told me you had agreed to come up and help out with Jeri." He hurried to catch up with her even though he would have enjoyed trailing along behind awhile longer. She moved in a way that left him hungry to watch. It wasn't a slinky walk, like Blair's, but a smooth, steady movement with a more than enticing sway to her hips. "I thought maybe we should talk a little about what you could expect while you were here; but Blair told me if I did that, you might not come at all."

Odd, at the time, he had thought that was exactly what he wanted—for Paige to change her mind and back out of the deal so he and Jeri would be free to vacation in peace. If Paige had backed out like he had hoped at first, then it wouldn't have been his fault when everything fell through.

None of this was his idea anyway.

But after seeing Paige again, and seeing how very much she'd changed, he was glad he never bothered with that telephone call. It intrigued him to no end that such a goofy looking kid had turned out so stunning.

He gave her another quick appraisal. Even with her drawn expression, her face was absolutely gorgeous. Practically flawless. So, why hadn't Paige become a model, too? She might not be quite as tall as Blair, nor was she quite as rail thin, but she was every bit as graceful and every bit as striking. Maybe more so.

He studied her profile a moment longer, noting the upward tilt of her nose and the smooth, rounded lines of her forehead and chin. Why was this woman without a man? Were the men in New York City all blind? Or had Blair made sure no man had a chance with Paige for fear he might take Paige away from her? Paige was the only stable thing within Blair's ever changing life.

That stability made Blair need Paige every bit as much as she claimed Paige needed her. It could be Blair's careful interference through the years was what had kept Paige's love life to a minimum. Why else would this gorgeous creature be unattached?

Even with Paige's dark brown eyes diverted for the moment, Damon well remembered how large and expressive they were. Perfect for her dark, silky complexion. The sort of eyes a man could get lost in. Bedroom eyes, some called them, making him wonder what they might look like languid with passion, those long lashes weighing heavily over them.

He cleared his throat, hoping she would look at him again so he could observe those eyes first hand. But her attention remained on the path ahead. Clearly, Paige was not as interested in him as he was in her. Fortunately, it was his duty to change that. How else could he establish a close enough relationship to have the proper effect on her reasoning?

"Blair was worried about me calling you, too," she admitted. She glanced at him briefly, giving him another delightful glimpse of her glittering dark eyes. "She said she didn't want me to cause you any bad feelings. She knows how extremely sensitive you can be about your daughter."

So *that* was how Blair had kept her from calling him and talking her way out of all this like he had first hoped. "I can't help but be sensitive where Jeri is concerned. She's my kid and I love her. Fact is, she's the most important person in my life. I want the world for her."

"Which I suppose is why I am here."

Damon thought about it, then nodded. Wanting to save the family business from ruin was as much to secure Jeri's future as it was to preserve his father's life long dream. Upon entering the largest of Miss Hattie's many flower gardens, he gestured to the most comfortable looking group of chairs. Paige headed immediately toward them.

"As you may have already guessed, your job is not going to be easy. But then taking care of Jeri is never easy. Like most children, she can be a handful at times."

When Paige rolled her eyes, indicating that had to be an understatement, he wanted to laugh. Jeri had indeed been on her very worst behavior these past couple of hours. It should be easy enough now to convince Paige that parenthood was not all it was cracked up to be. Nor was any other part of domestic life. Just because Susan Carmichael had made it all sound so wonderfully gratifying, didn't mean it was like that for everyone.

Damon watched Paige pivot on one narrow tennis shoe then sink gracefully into the soft cushions, tucking one leg up into the chair with her. Something about the way she folded herself drew his attention. Perhaps it was the way those blue jeans hugged her curves in all the right places. "I guess it is only fair I warn you that Jeri is jealous of you."

"Jealous of me?" Clearly baffled, she turned those immeasurable brown eyes on him and all he wanted to do was stare into them. How compelling they were.

"Why on earth would your daughter be jealous of me?" She glanced down as if thinking her clothes might provide a clue, and brushed at the grass stains on her sleeve as she looked up at him again, clearly baffled. "She doesn't even know me."

"She doesn't have to know you to be jealous of you. Not when she has obviously decided that the real reason you came was to be with me. Not to entertain her while I work."

"Jeri thinks I came here to be with you? Why would she think that?"

Disappointed by how ludicrous she made that sound, he shifted his weight to one leg. Most women liked the idea of being with him—at least until they had had more time to assess the total Adams package. Maybe that was the problem here. Paige had already met and assessed the rest of the Adams package. In this instance, being an attractive man wasn't going to benefit him as much as it normally would. Paige obviously didn't care what he looked like. Too bad. It was his looks that usually lured people into wanting to get to know him. That was why he dreaded the thought of growing old so much. Without good looks, no one would bother getting to know him at all. Sad, but true.

"Yes, I think she has decided that you and I are an item. Or at least that we're trying to be. To Jeri, that means I'll be looking to give up part of what little vacation time I have to spend with her so I can spend it with you instead."

He hesitated, almost losing his train of thought when the tip of Paige's tongue darted out of her mouth, leaving an enticing sheen behind on lips that were so full and so sexy that, well . . .

Shaking yet another wayward thought, he continued, "Jeri has never liked sharing me. She doesn't like for me to be around attractive women at all—especially if she has it in her head that those attractive women just might have eyes for me. I think she's afraid, if I were to ever really start dating again, we would lose some of our father-daughter closeness."

"You don't date?" That apparently surprised Paige. Odd reaction, considering Blair had told him that Paige rarely dated.

She studied him with a disbelieving crook in an otherwise perfectly shaped forehead.

"Not often." When did he have time? Between his father duties, and running the lumber and construction businesses, he stayed far too busy. Besides, until now, no one had really interested him. Not in the way Paige did. She did strange and wonderful things to his libido. Each breath grew harder to draw while his thoughts turned to what it would be like to pull this beautiful woman into his arms and devour her.

With someone like her to tempt him, dating had definite possibilities again. Too bad his goal was to persuade her *not* to live in Mt. Pine. Keeping her around for awhile had definite possibilities.

He shifted his weight back to both legs, hoping that might shift his thoughts as well.

"Why don't you date?" She was clearly having a hard time with that whole concept.

Rather than list all the reasons, he shrugged. "I do

sometimes have a date with me when I attend an occasional banquet or some other social event. And every now and then I take a woman out for a quiet dinner and a movie, but no relationship I start ever lasts very long.'' He sighed at how very true that was as he, too, finally sat. Women just didn't find him worth the trouble.

"Why doesn't it?"

"Because Jeri won't let it. In the past six years, she has managed to run off every woman who has shown even a glimmer of interest in me. She's gotten to be a regular little pro at it."

Paige studied him, her expression doubtful. "Isn't it just a little too convenient and a little too unfair to blame Jeri for having run off all the women in your life? Don't you think that maybe you could take at least some of that blame?"

Damon fisted his hands against the insecurities she had struck, then relaxed them again. He could not let her know how painful that question had been. "Maybe. But I don't like thinking that I am the one running them all off. Besides, you have watched Jeri in action. You've seen how offending she can be when she wants. She can be downright militant when it suits her needs."

"Yes, but I'm not so sure that combative behavior is because she mistakenly thinks I'm interested in you. Could it be that she's found out the truth about why I'm here?"

Damon frowned, puzzled. Why would that make his daughter so hostile? True, Jeri didn't like the thought of having a *keeper* as she had so melodramatically labeled it; but she would not be against any attempt to save her grandfather's company. But then, Paige didn't know anything about that. Or did she? Surely Blair hadn't admitted the bribery she'd offered him to her sister. No, not when telling Paige would have prompted her to ask Blair what it was she expected to receive in return for swinging such a lucrative contract for him.

Paige would be furious with Blair for interfering like that. Rightfully so. Trading business favors in exchange for help manipulating her life wasn't exactly praiseworthy.

"No, the only thing Jeri has been told is that you are Blair's sister, and that you have agreed to come here to help keep her entertained and out of trouble while I work on an important bid I need to have ready no later than the end of next week." A formality that would make it a little easier for Blair to see to her end of the bargain. Although the deal was supposedly already set, Blair's friend needed an official bid to work with. One that fell pretty much in line with the others.

"Are you sure that's all she knows?" Paige's attention fell to several geraniums clumped near the border of the flower bed, not too far from her foot. She bent down to trace the lacy edges of the vivid red clusters with the tips of her fingers. An act Damon found strangely seductive.

"That's all. But that doesn't keep a girl her age from speculating. Pre-teens have quite a wild imagination." Which was why she had decided Paige had come there to be with him. Too bad it wasn't true. It would be nice to have Paige Brockway interested in him. Even if only for awhile. All the while she felt of the flower's many petals, he imagined what it would be like to have that same delicate touch run over his heated skin.

"I suppose we need to discuss my duties next." Stretching further, she broke off a bloom and sat up again. She stroked the flower's velvety petals against her cheek, making him wonder which would prove softer. He ignored the desire to find out.

"Yes, that's probably a good idea. That way we both know what's expected of you."

"What Blair told me was that I'll be expected to spend as much time as possible with the girl, whether you are around or not."

"That's right. The more time you spend with her, the better. It'll be trying at times, but that's just the way it is with a youngster her age. Nothing on this earth tries your patience more." If little else came of these next eleven days, he had to make sure Paige understood that being around kids was not always enjoyable. No matter *what* Susan Carmichael said.

"I can handle anything that girl throws at me," she assured him, then chuckled while twirling the flower stem between her delicate fingers. "Including baseballs."

Damon grimaced. Jeri had thrown that ball on purpose. He hadn't expected her to do anything quite so drastic, but she had. "Just be forewarned. Jeri is quite the individual. You will have your hands full these next several days. I hope you have a lot of patience. You will need it."

"When do I start?"

"Tonight. I'll be returning to my room right after supper. That should give you two at least a couple of hours to get to know each other. Then I'll wait until after she's gone to bed before I come to your room to find out how your first time alone together went. Be sure to leave your door unlocked so I don't have to knock. I'd hate for Jeri to look out and discover me at your door so late at night."

Paige didn't look very pleased over the thought of him slipping into her room. "Why my room? Why not talk downstairs?"

"Because I don't want Jeri to see us together anywhere that late at night, not even downstairs," he answered, not ready to send Jeri off the deep end just yet. "She'd think only the worst."

Paige chewed on the inner wall of her lower lip a minute, then finally nodded. "What time does she normally go to bed?"

"In the summer, around 10:30. I'll wait until about 11:00 to come see you." Damon drummed his fingers against the sides of his chair with nervous energy. The thought of being alone with this woman inside her bedroom at such a late hour intrigued him. He considered what it would be like to be invited to sit with her on the bed while they talked—close enough to slip his arms around her slender shoulders. He swallowed hard at the mere thought of where that could lead.

Again, Paige looked hesitant.

"Don't worry," he vowed. "I can be very discreet."

Headed for bed, Miss Hattie started for the front stairs just as the elegant old grandfather's clock in the gallery struck nine o'clock.

Watching her go, Paige tried not to think about what was set to occur in just a couple of hours. Even in her wildest youthful imaginings she never thought that she and heartthrob, Damon Adams, would ever have a reason to be alone together in a bedroom—no one else aware. Would he try to hit on her while alone with her, hoping to add her to his long record of conquests? Or worse, would he make fun of her again, reminding her what an ugly, awkward youth she'd been?

Uncertain of what might happen during their private bedroom visit, and not wanting to worry about it, she kept her thought on the task at hand. It was important. Until she had accomplished what she'd come there to accomplish, she would be burdened with a full load of sisterly guilt. She had to take care of this one last big favor for Blair before she could feel right about thinking of herself again—even if it meant having to deal with all her old insecurities for a few days.

Her attention again on the task at hand, Paige tried to decide the best way to handle the situation with Jeri. The girl had managed to be civil throughout supper, yielding a few minutes of false hope, but the moment Damon disappeared upstairs and Miss Hattie had left to go wash dishes, Jeri turned hostile again.

She indignantly refused to play cards or chess, and most certainly did not want to take a walk out by the ocean where they might chat and try to get to know each other. Instead, all she wanted to do was slump sideways in a small, damask covered settee in the parlor and watch television—an activity that made it easy for Paige's charge to ignore her completely.

Bored with the girl's selection of comedies, Paige moved to the turret area where she turned a winged chair around to face out. Little lamplight reached the turret, allowing her a magnificent night view of the Atlantic Ocean through the dark window screens. Twinkling lights danced across the inky water like scattering diamonds while boats of different sizes crept into a brightly lit marina nearby. Why they would be coming in so late, Paige couldn't imagine.

"Do you see Miss Beaulah out there?"

Paige started. Those were the first words Jeri had spoken since Damon left. Was she bored with tonight's program selection, too? Or had she simply decided the heavy silence wasn't worth the effort?

Not sure which, Paige glanced at Jeri still slouched across the settee closest to the television, her blond ponytail flung haphazardly over one shoulder. She sat at an angle to her, allowing Paige a partial view of her expressionless face.

"I don't know. Who is Miss Beaulah?" After learning that the neighborhood dog was named Walter, Jr., Paige thought perhaps Miss Beaulah might turn out to be a friendly raccoon or, at this hour, perhaps a cranky old night owl.

"Miss Beaulah is the nosy neighbor who likes to creep around in the dark and watch this house with a big old pair of hunting binoculars." She swung her feet to the floor, straightened a strap on her right sandal, and stood. The bottom of her oversized red striped t-shirt fell halfway to her dark, suntanned knees, hiding all but a trace of her carnation pink shorts.

Not exactly a fashion statement, mused Paige, wondering why Jeri chose to look so rumpled. The sloppy-grunge look was well outdated, even for teenagers.

"You expect to find a neighbor out there?"

"Yeah, the old woman is right fond of nights like this when there's just enough moonlight for her to see where she's going but not enough to give her away."

Looking outside again, Paige studied the distant shadows, but saw nothing that looked remotely human. "Why would she do that?"

"Because she's old and batty." Jeri turned off the television then sauntered in Paige's direction. The shadows cast by the antique lamps scattered about the room moved softly across an expressionless face. For the moment, there was no sign of all that earlier anger.

Dr. Jekyll and Mr. Hyde.

"My friend, Frankie, says Miss Beaulah sneaks around out there hoping to get some sort of proof that the Seascape Inn has ghosts, so everyone will finally believe her wild stories."

"Ghosts?" Paige glanced out into the hall, and an odd chill washed over her. Just the suggestion of ghosts made her feel eerie—like someone or something was carefully watching her. Amazing, the power a simple suggestion had. Was the girl serious? Or just trying to frighten her? "The woman thinks this place has ghosts?"

"Yeah." Jeri paused beside Paige's chair. Wisps of her blond hair stirred while she faced the open windows. With the lamplight behind her now, it was harder to make out her expression, yet there was enough glow to tell there was still no scowl. "For some reason, Miss Beaulah's got it in her head that this place is haunted."

Jeri chuckled as she turned the other chair to face the windows and plopped down in it. For the moment, her earlier animosity was completely gone. Paige noted how pretty Jeri looked with a smile instead of that incessant scowl. The girl lay destined to be a real heartbreaker one day. Just like her father.

Paige's stomach did a funny little flip just thinking about Damon's wide, deep-dimpled smile. Dear heavens. The man wasn't even in the room with her and she felt flushed. What was it about him that caused such severe reactions in her?

Jeri's grin crooked to one side, she slid further down in the chair, still facing the windows, her well-muscled, sun-tanned legs sprawled in front of her. "Last summer, Frankie and I almost had the old busybody convinced she'd finally found her ghosts. We spotted her moving around out by the pond one night so we took flashlights and the sheets off my bed, and snuck out on the roof to make it look like big old spooky ghosts were climbing in and out of the windows.''

Jeri chuckled again, her gaze lost in the breeze tossed shadows she saw fluttering across the sloping lawn. ''We heard that woman screeching happy-as-could-be all the way back to her house. It wasn't ten minutes later that Sheriff Cobb came by wanting to know if there had been anything strange going on out on the roof that night. If Frankie and I hadn't gotten a bad case of the giggles, I think we could have convinced him, too, that there were ghosts here.''

''You climbed out on the roof at night?'' Paige worried, not sure she had understood right. Having such a deep fear of heights, she couldn't understand why anyone would purposely do something like that. ''Don't you realize how dangerous that was?''

''Not for me. I'm used to climbing all over some of my dad's construction sites. There wasn't much danger to it at all. Dad tells everyone I'm as sure-footed as a mountain goat.'' She smiled proudly. ''Like him.''

''Maybe it wasn't all that dangerous. But it was extremely unladylike, don't you think?'' Might as well get started with what she had come there to do. The sooner she did, the sooner she could rid herself of some of those guilty feelings from wanting to leave New York City and move back to Mt. Pine.

Jeri stiffened, as if suddenly aware she had let down her guard. ''So?''

''So, even if you aren't afraid of heights like I am, don't you think a young lady like you should try to act a little more dignified than that?'' Feeling quite clever to have found a way to ease into the topic of concern so early into her visit, Paige prepared for a long, thoughtful discussion like those she and her sister often shared back in her own youth.

''Let's get something straight right off.'' Jeri's expression turned bitter-hard. ''I don't like it when people—especially stupid strangers like you—go around trying to make me into something I'm not. I don't like it when people tell me to do things like sit up with my shoulders level, or walk around with my chin high and my back rigid, like I have a metal spring up my butt.'' She snorted at the thought. "I can assure you right now, the one sure thing I'm *not* and never *will* be is a dignified young lady.'' Eyes narrowed, she wrinkled her nose with disgust over such a foul thought. "So don't even start that with me.''

Paige had never seen such hostility in a child's expression, not even earlier when accused of having had something to do with their team losing the baseball game. She noted how the muscles shaping the outer fringe of Jeri's jaw had tightened and turned rock hard. "But don't you—?''

"Save your breath.'' Jeri's eyes turned into two determined slits of ice blue. "I told you. I'm not a young lady, and what's more I don't want to be a young lady. As it just so happens, lady, I'm happy with being who I already am, and the sooner you get that fact straight in your head, the better it will be for both of us.''

"But you are—''

"I said not to waste your breath.'' She slammed a fist against the winged arm of the chair and sat forward. "Look, you may think you are doing me some sort of big favor by griping at me about how I don't go around acting like a lot of the other girls my age do, but the effort is wasted. It just so happens, I like being a tomboy. I like getting dirty, and playing sports like baseball and soccer. I even like climbing out on rooftops at night when the mood hits me. And, most of all, I like hanging out at construction sites and being best buds with my dad.''

She wagged her head with such sharp resolve, her ponytail whipped forward like a golden curtain across her shoulder. "What I *don't* like is having to sit up in chairs with my feet together and my hands in my lap, or having to put on silly looking dresses with shiny shoes, or going around acting prissy and batting my eyes a lot. I know some girls do all that, but not me. I can't see any good reason to go around behaving like a twerp the way some of the other girls do.''

"Not even to attract a cute boy?''

"No boy is that cute.'' She stood, body trembling, her hands balled into tight fists at her side. "Look, just because some of my friends have started to primp and wear stupid looking clothes in stupid looking ways doesn't mean I have to. You know, you are just like your snooty sister. You won't be happy until everyone else walks around acting just like you do. It's sick really. You both think just because my dad happens to like you, that gives you the right to go around telling me what to do and how to do it. Well, you don't have the right. Nobody does. *Nobody.*''

Tears brimming, Jeri stormed across the room toward the hall but stopped just short of the darkened door. "And don't you think even for a minute that I care one bit that the boys who were once my best friends now all seem to want to spend most of their time being around those other girls.'' Her voice rose with each word spoken until it strained at the top. "Because I don't care. Not one bit. And you want to know why?''

Paige wasn't given time to respond.

"Because I know for a fact it won't take them long to figure out that those other girls don't share the same likes that they do anymore. Those girls don't want to play baseball, or ride bikes, or even climb trees anymore. Once the boys finally get that figured out, they'll forget all about those stupid girls and find time for me again. Just you wait and see.''

Paige had not moved once throughout Jeri's sudden tirade. She was too stunned by the unexpected outburst to do anything more than sit there, mouth open, while the angry girl spun on her heel and bolted out of the room.

Barely a minute later, a door slammed upstairs and the house fell quiet again.

Paige looked toward the ceiling and blinked twice. *That certainly went well.*

❧ *Chapter 4* ❧

Paige drummed her fingers against the stark white window frame while she stared through her own reflection to the moving black shadows that stirred beyond the lighted flower gardens below. With so little moonlight, she could barely make out the shape of the little white gazebo shaded each afternoon by a single giant poplar, or the low, native stone wall that divided Seascape land from the neighbor's.

She could also barely make out the spring-fed pond from the grassy field and the lumbering shape of the burly oak that grew at the water's edge. The only vivid detail was the dozen or so lights scattered across the small, seaside village, peeking playfully through several banks of fir and poplar.

So few lights for such a thriving little village. But then, most locals were probably in bed by this hour. Curious about the time, she glanced over her shoulder at the only clock—a small frame alarm clock with a bright red digital display, hard to miss in a room with only one overhead light burning.

Ten o'clock.

She cut her gaze toward the hall door, set away from the rest of the room. She had barely an hour before Damon was due for that private talk. Her heart skipped its next beat.

"Oh, great," she thought as she drew in a long, deep,

miserable breath. "Barely an hour to figure out the best way to explain that disaster downstairs. But how, when I don't even understand it myself?" Paige rolled her eyes, noting she had now started talking to herself.

"Well, that may be, but at least I am not answering myself," she defended quickly, then frowned. Was she now arguing with herself? *Good grief.* Time to get a grip.

Releasing the green-print curtain made from the same washable fabric as the hand-stitched pillows atop the dark green bed, she pushed away from the window, too restless to stand still.

What had she gotten herself into? Helping Jeri realize her femininity and become the proper little lady her father wanted her to be was not going to be anywhere nearly as easy as Blair had led her to believe.

"That child needs far more encouragement than I can offer." The truth was, Jeri needed professional help. Judging by that irrational outburst downstairs, the girl had some deep emotional problems lying beneath that aggressive behavior. Those were real tears.

"Yep, Blair, you grossly overestimated this one," she muttered, already pacing. Jeri needed more than someone helping to pattern her behavior. *Far more.* "That kid desperately needs someone skilled to talk to, someone who knows kids a lot better than I do."

Paige sighed. She was talking to herself again.

But then, she'd never been around a kid Jeri's age, much less a kid with so many problems. If she hadn't made that foolish promise to Blair, she would give up on all this right now and go back to packing up for her new life. She wasn't cut out for this sort of problem.

"But, noooo, you had to go and promise, didn't you?" Paige massaged her temple with the cool pads of her fingers. "And before you'd even met the child." Had she met her first, Paige definitely would have found some other way to lose the guilt. How did someone deal with a high-strung kid like that? Even Jeri's own father hadn't a clue— or he would never let her get away with so much.

And what was with all that misdirected anger? Apparently, Jeri felt alienated from the other girls her age who already viewed boys in a whole new light. But Paige suspected that Jeri's anger went far beyond that—and was well rooted in her past. So why had the girl transferred all that anger over to her? Paige gave a frustrated shake of her head. She'd done nothing to try to provoke the girl.

Could Damon be right? Did Jeri view her as a personal threat? But, no, that was just too ludicrous. Damon could never be romantically interested in someone like her. They were far too opposite. Always had been. Always would be. But Jeri, being only twelve years old, might not understand just how different they really were, or how problematic those differences could be.

Paige paced the room, trying to figure it all out. It could be Jeri really was worried that Paige hoped to move in on her father, thus taking him away from her. Undoubtedly, that sort of thing happened often to Jeri, what with having a father as attractive as Damon. Often enough that Jeri feared one day some beautiful woman would succeed at winning her father's heart, and then his hand.

"Poor kid." Judging by her comments, Jeri considered her father her only real friend right now. All her other friends, including the boys, had already started down that painful trek toward adulthood, leaving her behind hanging desperately onto childhood—and to her father, who she feared might also soon desert her.

How was Paige supposed to help the child deal with frustration like that? If the transition to adulthood, or lack of it, was causing Jeri that much turmoil, she needed someone professional helping her work through it. Couldn't Damon see that?

Shaking her head, Paige continued to pace. She had enough of her own problems to deal with right now. That's why she had come there with a firm resolve not to become emotionally involved with either Jeri or Damon. It wasn't time to let anyone else in her screwed up life just yet.

Still, she couldn't help but sympathize with the girl.

What an awkward age twelve years old could be. She well remembered her own emotional upheaval at that age. Only in her case, her libido had gone to the opposite extreme and had shoved her toward adulthood long before her body was ready to accept the notion.

Talk about *frustration*.

It was at that same age she'd started pining away for Damon, cherishing him from afar while daydreaming of a day when he would finally notice her. How many times had she dreamed of being all alone with him in some dark, romantic setting, his arms around her holding her close while he worked up the courage to kiss her?

She laughed at how silly that fantasy had been. Damon had never been the type to have to work up any courage to kiss a girl. He had been quite the lover in high school, dating a different popular girl every few weeks—*a real love-them-and-leave-them kind of guy*. With so many girls falling all over him, he had been the subject of many a female fantasy, each longing to be caught alone with him in the most compromising of situations while dreaming she had what it took to make him stay.

How ironic that fifteen years later Paige should be pacing her bedroom like a caged animal, waiting for Damon to visit. She laughed again as she slid onto the bed, still in the pink shorts and the sleeveless pink and white plaid blouse she had worn to supper.

The forest green comforter felt cool and silky-soft against her skin, making her senses all the more acute. While studying first the dark cherrywood furniture then the crisp pleating in the green print curtains, she breathed deeply the fresh sea air that drifted in through the open windows. Noticing next the antique wash stand in the far corner with its cream colored porcelain bowl, she glimpsed her reflection in the large-frame mirror. As she rolled onto her side to study that reflection, she heard a door close somewhere on that same floor, but paid little attention to the sound.

"Not bad for someone my age," she mused. She might

not be the raving beauty Blair was; but she was by no means dog-ugly either. Even sporting minimum make up and a simple, easy-care hairstyle, she had definite possibilities.

Wondering what a few sexy improvements might do for her, she carefully unbuttoned the top pink button on her notch-collared blouse. Pretending again, just like when she was twelve, Paige propped on one elbow and slipped the pink plaid off her shoulder siren-style. Glancing down to see how that looked from a closer angle, she quickly tucked her bra strap out of the way then checked the mirror again.

"Oh, you wicked woman," she chortled, dropping one sultry eyebrow.

With one shoulder now bare, she arched her back, smoothed back her hair with several long strokes of her fingers, then undid yet another button—all the while pretending to seduce Damon Adams with her best come-hither look. Glancing down again, she decided not enough cleavage showed to attract the likes of a man as experienced as Damon. Time to undo yet a third button, making sure the material draped in such a way her breasts looked their fullest and most inviting.

"No, not bad at all." If only she could have had this body back when she was still such a hormonal twelve year old. She might not have attracted Damon Adams even then, but she sure as heck would have attracted a few of the less popular boys in school.

She laughed again at just how many adolescent boys she would have had following her around had her body been this mature way back then, and was about to rebutton her blouse and stop her silliness when suddenly her door creaked open.

"Huh?" She questioned the unexpected sound and looked again at the clock beside her bed. Only five minutes after ten. Puzzled, she looked toward the tiny foyer and gasped at the sight of Damon standing there, the door already closed again. He wasn't supposed to arrive for nearly an hour.

"Damon!" Strangling, she sat up and swung her legs around to the side of the bed.

Not until she noticed where his gaze rested did she accept that not only was the man she had just shamelessly fantasized about really there, but she had yet to rebutton her blouse. Horrified that he had caught her in the middle of behaving like an over-sexed twelve year old, she looked down to see just how much skin lay open to his view, her bra covering the barest of her essentials.

Oh, great move, Brockway. Jerking the fabric closed with one quick yank, she shot her attention back to Damon, who stood frozen just inside the door. Her heart pounded with amazing force while she quickly moved her hands to the buttons. "I thought you weren't coming until after eleven."

At first he didn't comment while she fumbled with the contrary disks, then finally responded. "I heard Jeri come upstairs a lot earlier than I expected. When I went in to find out why, I saw she had already gone to bed. Since she was in her pajamas and was tucked away under the sheets reading a comic book when I left her, I figured it should be safe enough to go ahead and come see you."

He swallowed hard, then lifted his glittering gaze to hers. He hadn't blinked those thick dark eyelashes once since entering. "It didn't dawn on me that you would be—" He hesitated as if not quite sure what it was he had caught her doing. "I guess I should have waited until eleven o'clock like I said I would. Should I leave and come back later?"

"No." Her lips suddenly dry, she dampened them with several swipes of her tongue while fumbling with her last button. "That's not necessary. Since you are already here, we might as well go ahead and have that talk." After she finally shoved that final button through, she glanced at the only chair in her room, surprised to see her jeans from earlier still draped across the back. She could have sworn she'd moved those jeans earlier to clear that chair for Damon when he came. But evidently she'd imagined it. The pants were still right where she had tossed them earlier when changing into something cooler.

Eager to clear that spot for Damon, she slid forward on the bed; but before she quite made it to her feet, the mattress gave way to his weight. Paige's next breath caught. Damon had already sat down. Right beside her.

Her pulses flew at an impossible rate when she spotted a long, lean denim clad leg only an inch from her bare skin. This was just all too bizarre. Who would have thought she and Damon Adams would ever have a reason to sit this incredibly close to one another—and on a bed of all places?

This just wasn't happening. It couldn't be. She must have fallen asleep in the middle of her musings, and her dreams now carried her farther into her adolescent fantasies.

"So how'd it go?"

His deep, vibrant voice certainly sounded real enough. Too real. Her heart rate jumped another level when he then shifted his weight and the bed jiggled in response. Figments of the imagination didn't make beds move. Nor did they smell anywhere near as wonderfully sexy as this one did.

She breathed deeply, trying to figure out the brand of cologne, but couldn't. It surpassed any she'd ever known.

Compelled to do more than smell him, she lifted her gaze to the solid lines of his face and, for a moment, the room lost all its air. She had never been quite this close to perfection before. They sat practically nose to nose— close enough to detect the silvery flecks in his blue eyes after they caught the light from the brass fixture overhead.

"Did you and Jeri manage to get to know each other a little better?" Again, he focused his attention on the front of her now buttoned blouse, to the area that moments earlier had been open to his view.

Only too aware of what occupied his thoughts, Paige

drew in a long, unsteady breath to try to calm her racing heart, and at the same time slow the hard flow of adrenaline. Finding a problem with releasing that same breath, she tried audibly clearing a small obstruction blocking her throat; but the mass only grew larger. As did Damon's eyes.

In an attempt to bring his attention back to her face, she finally spoke, "I-I'm afraid it didn't go as well as I'd hoped between us."

"Why? What happened?"

He continued to stare boldly at the rapid rise and fall of her breasts. *Good grief.* Did he plan to seduce her? Right there? Right now? But why on earth would he do something like that? She wasn't even his type. *Oh, but if only she were . . .*

That unfinished thought brought a hormonal rush similar to what she had experienced back as an enamored twelve year old. The sudden longing, coupled with the fact he still stared brazenly at her breasts, made it difficult to concentrate on the conversation. "Your daughter told me about the prank she and a friend of hers played on some nosy neighbor last summer."

The heat from his body somehow jumped the four-inch gap between them while he continued giving his view a lot of attention. She swallowed hard, still fighting whatever growing thing had filled her throat. "I-I made the mistake of pointing out to Jeri that climbing around on the roof of this house while trying to make some nosy neighbor think she saw ghosts was not exactly a ladylike thing to do."

"Oh, I can well imagine the reaction that got." His gaze lifted to hers briefly, then lowered again with easy distraction. "I'm surprised she let you live." He dampened those full, sexy lips with a short flick of his tongue, making them invitingly moist. Then, without a word, he lifted both hands toward the front of her blouse.

Paige's heart quickly joined whatever blocked her throat. *He was going for it.* Without a word of warning—

with no seductive groundwork of any kind—he was going for her clothes.

Floored by his boldness, she didn't know whether to slap his hands, or simply move out of his reach. *Or* move further *into* his reach. The idea of sharing a night of wild passionate love with someone as sexy as Damon Adams still had definite appeal, maybe more so now than ever.

With as much carnal experience as Damon had surely collected through the years, he was bound to be one fabulous lover. But did she really want to be just another of this man's many conquests? Would one night of pleasure be worth the shame she might feel later on?

Dear heavens. What should she do? At age twelve, she had often wondered what it would be like to be thoroughly kissed by Damon Adams in some darkened corner of the world. Her young fantasies were ladened with such wanton thoughts. But now, fifteen years later, she took those wayward thoughts a step further and wondered what it would be like to be bedded by him. As fit as he still was, and so well proportioned, he would look phenomenal naked. A tingling warmth invaded her at the mere thought of seeing him unclothed.

"My daughter doesn't yet care much for the idea of one day being a woman," he continued his explanation, though by now Paige had lost all interest in their conversation. Her attention was riveted on those ever-so slow moving hands. "Jeri doesn't even want to think about anything like that."

"So I discovered." Feeling as bold as him, she dropped her gaze to where the V of his collar revealed a tempting patch of dark, curling hair. Surely more such springy hair grew beneath that light blue shirt, trailing down his taut skin into those soft, snug jeans. Mmmmmm?

Oh, dear heavens. Was she really undressing the man in her mind? But then, she might as well. He was clearly undressing her in his. And if those unbearably slow hands of his ever reached their destination, he'd soon attempt to undress her for real.

Still uncertain of what to do, quite aware she could be on the brink of fulfilling a fantasy that had plagued her for more than half her life, she drew in a quick, sharp breath and held it deep in her burning lungs. With pulses still racing wildly, she tried to think through the situation before it progressed to the point where she couldn't think anymore. Should she stop him now? Or should she allow him to undress her as he obviously planned, then see what happened after that? After all, it was four long years since she'd been with a man. Four long years since her failed engagement to Edward. Did she dare—?

Her hands trembled while she considered what to do with them. Even though she'd had so little experience with such matters—having been intimate with only two men in her life—it seemed appropriate that if Damon unbuttoned her blouse for her, then she should unbutton his shirt for him. But could her heart take it if she actually touched his clothing? The way the thing already pounded nearly out of her chest, she wasn't too sure.

Another breath lodged in her throat as his fingers gradually closed around her top button. Could she possibly go through something this sexually explosive and survive? She continued to stare at the body hair peeking out from the opening in his shirt, her fingers itching to touch the crisp softness.

Well, she had wanted to become an independent, take charge kind of woman. That was part of why she wanted to leave New York and move back to Texas. That, and wanting to find Mr. Right and settle down to have a family once her dress shop was well established. Why not start by seeing if she and Damon Adams might be compatible? Or was that too farfetched even to consider?

While he tugged lightly on the material, having unbuttoned one button and moved on to the next, she looked up, expecting to meet a sultry gaze, but his attention remained focused on his handiwork.

Her arms twitched when a warm knuckle brushed the sensitive skin inches above her breasts. Surely, she should be doing something of her own, but what? She was still too new at being a take charge kind of person. She didn't think she had the courage to move right to undressing him—never having been quite as bold about these matters as he obviously was.

"Looks like you buttoned your blouse wrong," he finally commented in a voice not exactly thick with passion. His forehead notched with concentration while he leaned in close. "It'll take just a second more to fix it for you."

Buttoned wrong? She looked down questioningly at the same time her heart plopped at her feet. Sure enough, she'd been in such a hurry to close her blouse, she'd missed a button. Heat crawled into her cheeks, burning her with embarrassment—more because she had actually thought he'd hoped to make love to her than because she had proved herself totally inept at dressing.

Feeling like a first class idiot, she sat stone still, trying not to concentrate on his fiery touch while he slowly but dutifully unbuttoned her blouse so he could then rebutton it correctly. He was not undressing her like she had first thought. He was merely helping her reassemble her clothing.

Even so, feeling the backs of his fingers make feather touches along her skin while she focused on his diligent expression, drove her to distraction. The man was gorgeous beyond belief.

How many hearts had he broken since high school? How many hearts did he have yet to break? With Damon's unbearable good looks and his casual love-them-and-leave-them lifestyle, Paige could well imagine the vast number of willing women he had sampled through the years.

She shook her head at the image of him in bed with some beautiful woman. What did she care how many females he'd made love to in his accomplished life?

"What's wrong?"

Not having expected him to speak, she quickly reined in her thoughts and looked at him questioningly. He must have noticed the heavy breathing. "Nothing is wrong. Why?"

"You shook your head." When his gaze came up to meet hers, his eyes were a darker shade of blue than usual. "I thought maybe there was a problem."

"Problem?" she repeated as she looked down to where he had her blouse again unbuttoned but had not yet begun the process of rebuttoning. A part of her bra was in clear view, and the backs of his warm fingers rested against her bare skin, causing prickly bumps to tighten her nipples— fortunately just out of his sight. "Whatever could be a problem?"

His gaze followed hers to the soft swell of her breasts. "I don't know." His expression turned contemplative. "That's why I asked."

If Paige didn't know better, she might think Damon had paused the task on purpose. She studied his fingers, waiting for him to continue. When they didn't move, she lifted her hands to help.

"Maybe I should finish that," she offered, absurdly disappointed by how readily his hands fell away.

"Maybe so." He scooted away and then stood, looking suddenly flustered as he shoved his hands into his back pockets. "I'm sorry. I didn't mean to do something so forward. It's just that you had buttoned your blouse crooked, and my first thought was to fix it for you."

Feeling uncomfortable to have him standing over her while she rebuttoned her blouse, Paige stood, too. Eager for a little more distance between Damon and her still partly open garment, she took a few backward steps until her calves made contact with the cold surface of her night stand. "Don't worry about a misunderstanding. I know you didn't mean anything forward."

When Damon didn't return a comment, she glanced up from where she struggled with an extremely contrary button, frustrated. Why wouldn't the little bugger go on into its hole like she wanted? It was as if someone held one side of the button hole pinched shut so there wouldn't be enough room for the blasted thing.

Watching Damon, she continued trying to shove the tiny disk through, fumbling more with each futile attempt. "I'm sure it wasn't even on your mind to undress me or anything like that. You were just trying to help. Right?"

Damon pulled his hands out of his pockets and dropped them loosely at his sides. His shoulders tensed and he turned away. "Well, maybe at first it w—no, I have no idea what I was thinking."

Wanting a closer look at his expression to determine if it was guilt or just embarrassment that forced him to look away, she took several steps in his direction, her hands still working with the contrary button. In mid-step, something caught the toe of her shoe, causing her to throw out her arms as she stumbled forward.

Damon must have detected the movement out of the corner of his eye. He lurched forward just in time to catch her before she fell, pulling her immediately into his strong arms. His hard body blocked her path and kept her from tumbling further.

Stunned to find herself suddenly in Damon Adams' sturdy embrace, she glanced back to see what could have tripped her, but made no move to break free from the protective circle of his arms. Puzzled to find nothing there, she looked again at Damon, who also proved in no real hurry to break apart. It was then she realized how desperately her hands clutched his solid shoulders.

"Sorry, I didn't mean to fall all over you," she explained, then grimaced at how that sounded. She tried not to concentrate on the titillating fact that their bodies had mingled and their mouths were now just inches apart. If so inclined, Damon could bend forward and kiss her easily.

Enough with the childhood fantasies.

Disconcerted to still be thinking of the man in such a way, she made her first feeble attempt to push away, but his arms held her firmly in place. Why didn't he let her go?

"I tripped over something." She offered him a sick excuse for a smile.

"So I noticed," he admitted in a voice low and sexy—and warm against her cheek.

"I looked. But I don't see what I tripped over." She was babbling now and knew it. But what else was she to do in a situation like this? It wasn't often she found herself in the arms of an incredibly handsome man with her blouse already half undone. "You saved me from falling."

"I noticed that, too." His gaze lowered to where their bodies met, her breasts pressed intimately against a solid wall of male chest.

Oh, how good that felt. "But I'm okay now, thanks to you."

A playful grin put adorable crinkles in his cheeks while his grip tightened around her, pressing them closer. "Oh, I noticed that too."

Savoring the heady sensation his touch caused, she fell silent a moment, her whole body having gone on sudden alert. Finally, she decided something else needed to be said. But what? "I suppose you have a logical reason for continuing to hold me like this when it's pretty clear that I'm out of danger now."

"Are you?" A taunting eyebrow lifted over a glittering blue eye while his gaze dipped to her mouth. The light overhead cast blond highlights across his dark hair and gave shadowy depth to his sprite dimples. "Are you clearly out of danger?"

Thinking he meant to kiss her yet, Paige stared into those deep, searching eyes with breathless anticipation, unable to conjure the intelligent yet evasive reply she needed. All she could think of was how delicious he smelled, and how enjoyable his hard body felt pressed against hers. Clearly, Damon had no qualm working right alongside his construction crews. "Evidently not."

Damon's dimples lengthened, shaping deep crescents while he studied her lips a moment longer, as if contemplating further action toward her, until suddenly he jerked his head around to cock an ear toward the hallway door. "What was that?"

·Too bewildered by the chaos churning inside her to be aware of anything else, Paige had no response. It amazed her how quickly Damon had gone from looking like a wily cat on the prowl to a little kid who had just been caught with his hand in the candy jar. "I didn't hear anything."

Who could possibly hear over the blood roaring past her ears?

"It sounded like someone knocked on a door."

Although she would much prefer studying the adorable little notch that had just formed in his forehead, Paige closed her eyes to listen, but heard only the rapid thud of her heart still beating out of control. Seconds later though, she heard Jeri's voice. "Dad? Are you in there? Open up. I need something."

Paige's eyes flew back open. It wasn't her door the girl spoke into, but how long until she gave up on her father's door and tried others?

Paige's insides twisted into a tangled knot. The last thing Jeri needed was to find them alone together. She might think it confirmed what just wasn't true: Paige had come to the Seascape Inn to be with Damon and not her. That would only fuel Jeri's anger, which in turn would make dealing with her that much more difficult.

She and Damon stood listening until another quick knock sounded across the hall. This time Paige heard it, too.

"Dad? You in there?"

Not yet having let go, Damon glanced down at Paige again, clearly debating his options. Finally, he shook his head and stepped away. When he did, Paige's legs nearly buckled.

Suddenly, the room felt very cold.

"Sorry, Paige, but I don't think it's a good idea for my daughter to find out that I'm in here alone with you." He headed toward the closest window. "I'll see you tomorrow."

Without another word, he raked back the green print curtains with one smooth swipe of his arm then gently pushed out the window screen, grimacing when it gave way before he expected and clattered against the wall on its way to the ground below. Had he picked a window along the west wall, he wouldn't have had that problem. A first floor overhang would have caught it.

Glancing back with an apologetic expression, he gripped the sill with the curves of his strong fingers and swung himself outside. Slowly, he slid down, lowering his body inches at a time, until just his head and hands remained visible. Fearing heights the way she did, Paige clenched her teeth while waiting for whatever would happen next.

Damon paused to give her one last, long look then dropped lithely into the darkness, leaving Paige as alone and confused as she had been earlier. Only, now, she nursed a dull, throbbing ache that had not been there before.

❧ *Chapter 5* ❧

Heart racing, Damon hurried toward the front stairs, glad now that Miss Hattie never locked her front door. Quietly as was feasibly possible for a man his size, he darted up the bottom half, taking it two steps at a time and thereby avoiding the squeaky third stair. He slowed to a more normal pace after he rounded the landing to the top half.

His head emerging above the mahogany bannister upstairs, he looked across to his door, relieved to find Jeri still there. She would be far more likely to believe he'd gone for an evening stroll if she saw him return from downstairs. He wanted his daughter annoyed by Paige's presence enough to cause a little chaos, but not be seriously worried by it.

No longer knocking, Jeri stood bent over, peering into his keyhole. The house, built around the turn of the century, had doors with old skeleton-key locks in addition to the newer kind.

Circling through the alcove, he glanced toward Paige's room, but channelled his thoughts away from what had almost occurred on the other side of that closed door. He hoped Jeri hadn't bothered peeking through *that* keyhole. Where they had stood, Jeri would have had a clear view of him holding Paige. But evidently, Jeri hadn't given up on his door yet. She still pressed an eye to his keyhole.

When it was apparent Jeri had not yet noticed him, Damon couldn't resist. He switched to walking lightly on the toes of his cross trainers as he came along behind her. Just when she gave up on the tiny key hole and straightened, lifting her hand to knock on the door again, he bent forward and goosed her in the ribs.

"Jeepers!" Jeri squealed, then spun around, eyes wide. Her hair, no longer in a ponytail, fell tangled across her chest. "Dad! What are you doing out here?" She clutched at the oversized baseball shirt she wore to sleep in. The garment had started out his. "You scared the life out of me."

Damon couldn't help but laugh. Jeri looked about ready to climb the panelled wall. Even her bare toes were knotted into tight little balls. "Why?" he goaded. "Did you think I was one of Miss Beaulah's ghosts?"

"No, of course not." She frowned to show how ridiculous that was. "But I didn't know you were there."

"That's because I wasn't." He patted his pockets for his key, then remembered he hadn't bothered to lock his door anyway. Still chuckling at Jeri's startled expression, he leaned around her and turned the knob. "I just came in from outside." He gestured for her to flip the light switch after she followed him into the room. "It's late, slugger. What do you want?"

"The cellular. The phones here aren't working again."

"They're out again?" Damon glanced at the antique telephone that stood on the old darkwood dresser near the front windows of his room. It was one of those tall, shiny white telephones that reminded him of a fat, brass-edged tulip.

"Yes, and I need to call Frankie. I need to tell her about something."

"Frankie?" Damon checked the clock on his nightstand even though certain it was too late for Jeri to be telephoning her friend. "Sorry, slugger, but it's nearly 10:30. I can't let you call over there and wake up everyone at this hour. You know how early people go to bed around here."

Looking puzzled, Jeri checked her watch, a sturdy sports model with a bright red band that matched her shirt exactly. Or rather *his* shirt. But with red being her favorite color, the watch she was rarely without matched just about everything she ever wore. "But it's only 9:25."

She turned her wrist so he could see for himself, but he now was across the room, slipping out of his shoes.

Instead of waving her closer to have a look, he pointed to the bedside clock, clearly visible from both the dresser where she still stood, and the desk, where he now sat. "Sorry but it's 10:25. Evidently you didn't set your watch forward when the pilot told us we had just entered a different time zone."

"I don't remember him doing that," she admitted, pouting when she saw he was right.

Her pale gaze shifted to the cellular telephone not far from the clock. Having learned how unreliable the telephone system was at the inn, Damon had started bringing a cellular with him years ago. He couldn't chance being completely out of contact with the lumber mart or his construction crews while he was there. Small emergencies were far too common.

"So you won't let me have the cellular to take back to my room even for a few minutes?"

"And have Frankie's folks over here first thing in the morning prepared to use me for fish bait?" He shook his head as he leaned back and wiggled his freed toes, still clad in socks. "Sorry, Jer, but whatever you want to talk to her about will have to wait until morning. It's way too late for you to be telephoning anyone around here. Only an insensitive clod would telephone someone at such an hour."

Jeri looked at the clock again, then sighed as she begrudgingly lifted her wrist to change the time on her watch. "I guess you're right. Okay, I'll wait until morning."

Curious to hear Jeri's opinion of her first evening spent with Paige, and wanting to lecture her for at least part of her earlier rudeness so she wouldn't think he now approved of that behavior, Damon waited for her to finish. But before he could say anything, they were interrupted by the beep-beeping of the cellular. They both looked at the thing questioningly.

"I wonder who that could be," he commented, crawling across the large four poster bed rather than walk around.

"Some insensitive clod, I guess. That means it's gotta be a friend of yours," Jeri said, grinning. She paused working with her timepiece to watch Damon punch the talk button then place the receiver near his mouth.

"Hello?"

"Hi, Damon. It's me. Did my sister arrive safely?"

Damon recognized the deep, sultry female voice right away, having heard it most of his life.

"Oh, hello, Blair." He braved a look at Jeri, who tensed expectantly. Even though Blair was one of his best friends and had been since early childhood, Jeri hated her. "Yes, she did. She arrived here this afternoon safe and sound."

His mouth quirked but he managed not to smile. *Boy, was she sound.* Swinging his legs over to sit on the edge of the bed, he tried not to remember just how sound Paige had felt in his arms only a little while ago. Blair had a peculiar talent for reading his thoughts at the most inopportune moments.

"Good, she's been there awhile. Has she met Jeri, yet?"

"Oh, yes, those two have definitely met," Damon replied carefully. Jeri hung on every word. "And it went pretty much as expected."

"It did? Wonderful." She laughed that perfect, sophisticated laugh of hers. "So, tell me what happened. Was it a total disaster?"

"Yes, I'd say that correctly describes it. She made a comment that may have pretty much put the two at permanent odds."

"Oh, she did? So tell me all about it. What exactly did she say? How did Jeri react?"

Tired of having to carefully word everything, Damon pressed his palm over the mouth section of the receiver and turned to Jeri. "Was there anything else you needed?"

Jeri shook her head, but didn't take the hint. She continued staring at him from over by the dresser.

He nodded toward her room. "Then get on back to bed. This is a private call."

Nose wrinkled, she crossed her arms and glowered at the phone. "Oh? A private call from an insensitive clod?" she asked in a louder voice than necessary, clearly hoping Blair heard her. She stared pointedly at the clock. "What's the matter, can't the clod tell time?"

Rather than debate the issue with her when at the moment he wanted her to leave, Damon pointed to the hallway door.

"Go."

He waited until his scowling daughter had stalked out and shut the door behind her before continuing his conversation with Blair. "Sorry, but Jeri was in here listening to every word." He slid back into the middle of the bed to make himself comfortable. Telephone calls from Blair tended to last awhile. "What did you ask me?"

"I asked to know what it was Paige said to Jeri that put them at such odds." Clearly, Blair was annoyed over having been made to wait like that. Patience had never been one of her virtues. "I want to hear everything that's happened between those two since she arrived. Don't leave out anything."

So Damon didn't. He started by telling her about the ballgame, including Jeri's wild pitch suspected to be right on target. "It took all the willpower I had not to come down on her for that ugly little prank. I couldn't believe she tried something like that."

"You can do your parent thing later—after this is all over. For now, she's acting just the way we want her to act. What else happened?"

Damon went on to tell Blair about the tension-filled walk home, and how Jeri had accused Paige of being their reason for having lost the game. "After that, Jeri managed to calm down some and was fairly pleasant during supper, but after supper, I purposely made myself scarce; and as soon as they were alone, the two got into it again.''

''They did?'' Blair laughed again. ''Wonderful. Tell me all about that, too.''

Not feeling nearly as pleased as Blair obviously did, Damon told her about the discussion between Paige and Jeri and how it had led to Paige pointing out how some of Jeri's behavior might not be as ladylike as it should be. ''Putting it mildly, I don't think Jeri quite appreciated Paige's comments.''

''I can *imagine*. I've tried telling the girl that same thing a time or two, and I've seen for myself how she becomes absolutely livid.'' Blair chortled, clearly delighted, then paused to mull over everything he had told her. Though he couldn't see it, Damon knew Blair was beaming that wide, perfect smile of hers.

''So we are off to a good start then?''

''As far as I can tell.''

''Anything else I should know?''

Damon hesitated, then decided not to tell Blair about the back-to-back incidents in Paige's bedroom. Those had nothing to do with the agreement between them anyway. ''Only that I'll be sure things continue digressing according to plan.''

Blair chuckled. ''See that you do. We have to make sure Paige stops obsessing over the silly fact she isn't married and having kids like her friend, little Susan Carmichael. You and I both know that having a family would just drag Paige down at a time when she so needs her independence. It's bad enough our own mother threw away a promising career, as did my dearest friend, Eve. Both ruined their lives by marrying young and tying themselves down with children. I will not let the same thing happen to Paige, too.''

Having heard it all before, Damon tried to change the subject. Like his ex-wife, Blair had never been very domestically inclined and, therefore, would never accept that some women actually enjoyed having families and taking care of them. Those women did not see it as any great burden. "Don't worry about any of that. I have everything under control here."

"I hope so. I shudder to think what Paige's life would be like if she really did move to Mt. Pine, buy that house, and open up some ordinary little dress shop downtown. Not only would she be throwing away most of the money she's saved these past several years, she'd be throwing away her one chance to be somebody. How could she possibly be happy after she eventually came to her senses and realized all she's lost? How can anyone possibly be happy after throwing away such a rewarding future? And for what? Kids and a husband? Or the life of a store owner in a tiresome little city like Mt. Pine?"

Damon groaned silently. No point arguing with her. Once Blair had worked herself up like that, it was impossible to get through to her. It would be easier trying to put in plate glass during a wind storm.

"I already know your feelings about all this. And after a few more days with Jeri, I'm sure Paige will come to her senses and realize that parenthood isn't always all it's cracked up to be." Though a tiny part of him hoped she didn't. He still kind of liked the idea of having Paige around. Especially after finding out what it was like to hold her intimately in his arms. His body still ached with longing.

"I certainly hope so. Because if you don't come through with your favor for me, I certainly won't follow through with mine for you. By the way, I talked to John awhile ago and he told me everything is all set. The contract is yours, as long as you don't fail to mail him that bid in on time."

"I won't. I've been working on it a little each day. I want to make sure it's fair to both of us."

Blair sighed heavily. "That's the problem with you, Damon. It always has been. You try too hard to be fair to too many people. Why don't you just do what everyone else would do and jack up your prices so you'll make more money? The deal is as good as done. John has already said so, and he's not about to go back on his word to me. Besides, he's looked into it and likes the work you've done for others. So why not buy your companies a little more security by stretching your profit margin a bit more?''

"I can't do that. Before Dad died, I promised him I'd always be fair when running his businesses. And I always do everything I can to keep my promises no matter what they are. You know me well enough to know that.''

"Yes, I do, sweetie. That's exactly what I'm counting on.''

Blair pushed the off-button on her cordless phone, careful not to mar her freshly polished fingernails. Holding the phone with the crooks of her fingers, she leaned back into her bed pillows, pleased with how true to form Damon's tomboy-from-hell daughter had behaved thus far. It sounded like Paige had already been fed an adequate serving of that tedious domestic life she'd so foolishly thought she wanted. Thanks to Damon.

No, she supposed the real thanks should go to John Bolin.

She smiled when she thought about how eagerly John tried to please her. He was such a dear man. And wealthy to boot. Perfect husband material. *If* she were to be so inclined. Which she was not.

Rolling over onto her side, she reached for her day organizer and flipped through it carefully with one hand while gently blowing on the tips of the other. She had the number of the Seascape Inn written down there somewhere, and could hardly wait to hear what Paige had to say.

Humming softly to herself, she ran her finger over the telephone numbers she'd jotted down more recently. All was right with the world again. When Paige returned to New York after having suffered through eleven long days of that willful child's company, it would not be to finish packing her things as planned, but to ask Emilie Teek for her old position back. And *that* certainly posed no problem. Blair had already warned Emilie not to bother finding a replacement just yet—Paige's quitting was temporary only. All Paige needed was a little down time to revitalize, and think things through.

Blair laughed at the myriad thoughts that would cross her sister's mind before that little terror was through with her. After Paige gave up those overly idealistic views of marriage and children, having tried to handle an uncontrollable child like Jeri, one who despised any female old enough to attract her father's attention, Paige would gladly return to the ever eminent MissTeek Fashions. After that, Blair wouldn't have to give up any of those lucrative jobs MissTeek had to offer.

Besides, as gifted as Paige was, she would one day branch off and start her own line of fashions. Blair, of course, would be the spokesmodel for this flourishing new line, giving the apparel a certain flair. She and Paige would climb the fashion ladder to fame and success together. The way sisters should.

And Paige would have her to thank for it.

And perhaps Jeri.

She chuckled again. If Jeri knew how she was helping her by treating Paige the way she did, the little hellion would freak.

Dimpling mischievously, Blair entered the telephone number to the inn. When a sleepy sounding older woman answered, she glanced at the clock beside her bed. When did it get to be so late?

"Paige Brockway's room, please."

There was a pause then, "Just a moment."

After several minutes and she'd yet to be patched through, Blair grew impatient. What was taking so long?

Thinking the old woman must have disconnected her somehow, she glanced over to get the number again but finally heard a ring.

"About time," she muttered, her happy mood from before already gone.

"Hello?"

"Paige? Is that you?"

"Yes, it's me."

"Dear, you sound a little depressed," Blair was quick to point out, happy to hear such pronounced despondency in her sister's voice—no doubt from having had her first sampling of Jeri's nasty streak. "What's the matter?"

There was a short pause then, "Nothing's the matter."

Not at all the answer Blair wanted. "Are you sure? You certainly sound like something is the matter."

Again, a short silence. "I guess that's because I don't think it was such a good idea for me to come up here."

Yes, that was more the answer Blair wanted. "Oh? Why do you say that?"

"Because I'm not qualified to offer the kind of help Jeri needs."

Her nails having had time to dry, Blair ran her thumb around the edges to test for roughness. "And what kind of help is that?"

"Professional help. The girl has problems that go far beyond any you told me about. I think she needs a teen counselor of some sort, or maybe even a full fledged shrink."

Don't I know it? Blair thought with a pronounced roll of her eyes. "A shrink? Are you sure you aren't overstating the situation a mite? The kid is only twelve years old. She hasn't lived long enough to suffer the sort of emotional problems that require a shrink."

"I don't know. I think children can suffer a great many emotional problems in twelve years. Look at what we went through by the age of twelve. Or rather what I went through. At age twelve, not only had I lost my mother, like Jeri, I'd lost you, too. Remember? You went off to modeling school just days after you graduated. I can remember how bitter and alone I felt, what with Dad working all the time. I may not have expressed my resentment quite as vocally as Jeri did today, but it was there all the same."

"Why do you say that? What did Jeri do?"

"What did she do? Well, after having already treated me like dog-meat all day, she suddenly went totally ballistic on me. All I did was point out that climbing on roof-tops in the middle of the night wasn't exactly a ladylike thing to do and the child went utterly ballistic on me."

Exactly what Blair had hoped she'd do. "Ballistic? How so?"

"Well, first she screamed at the top of her voice and slammed her fist into things, telling me I didn't have the right to say such horrible things to her. Then all of a sudden she stopped all that shouting and started crying instead, saying something about how none of her friends had time for her anymore."

"Her friends?"

"Yes, she claims the other children have all turned against her; and I think she thinks I've come up here to lure away the one man she considers to be her last friend in the world—her father. I tell you, the girl is totally irrational. I'm sorry, but I think her social failings go far beyond having lived the past six years with no mother or sister to guide her."

"But that's all normal behavior for a child her age. Trust me. Angry rebellion is a stage every parent has to put up with at least once. You'd have put our parents through it, too, had either of them lived long enough. I know I did."

"You did? When?"

"Oh, that's a long story, and it happened such a long time ago," she answered evasively, her memory a little too hazy to recall any one incident. "It has nothing to do with Jeri's biggest problem, which is that she refuses to grow up. She won't even try to behave like the little lady she should be by now. Paige, don't you see? You really are that child's only hope. She has no mother to influence her. You, of all people, should understand what a hardship that makes for her. You had no mother at that age either."

"But I had you," Paige pointed out, bless her dear heart.

"That's right, you did. But Jeri isn't fortunate enough

to have an older sister like me to fill that void. Jeri doesn't even have any aunts or girl cousins she can turn to, and for some reason she refuses to listen to me at all.'' Which was putting it mildly. ''Because of all that, the girl has no idea what's expected of her. You'll have to show her the sort of behavior that is required of someone her age through setting an example. For her own sake, as well as for Damon's, that girl has to come to terms with the fact that she was born female. She needs to understand that being female isn't as bad a deal as she thinks. Besides, Jeri is not the type to accept professional help. She'll have a hard enough time accepting your advice.''

There was another long silence.

''Paige? Can I still count on you?''

The silence continued.

Time to lay on a little guilt. ''Come on, after all I've done for you through the years, can't you do this one last favor for me? I'd think it's the least you could do, knowing you are about to leave me here in New York all alone. You did promise me, you know.''

''I know. I really should keep my promise.''

''Then you'll keep trying?''

''Yes, I'll keep trying,'' she finally agreed, but without sounding too hopeful about the outcome. ''I'll do it as much for Jeri's sake as yours. The poor kid really could use a woman's touch. I just hope I'm the right woman for the job.''

''Oh, you are,'' Blair assured her, her heart soaring with malevolent joy. ''I know you are.''

''Then wish me luck with her.''

''I do. Of course I do.'' Blair smiled to herself as she sat forward, prepared to hang up. ''I wish you all the luck in the world with that child, little sister.''

All of it *bad.*

Invisible as usual, Tony Freeport drifted out of the Cove room where Paige Brockway had just hung up the telephone, and paused in the hallway near the Great White room where Damon Adams had talked to the same caller earlier.

So that was it. Paige was being set up. She had been sent there so Damon and Jeri could cause her enough trouble over the next eleven days to make her want to give up on her own dreams, and continue to go along with her sister's dreams instead.

Frowning at how manipulative and selfish that was, he continued to mull it over after drifting on outside. Apparently, Damon had agreed to go along with the scheme as some sort of a personal favor to Paige's sister. But why? It wasn't like Damon to be exploited that easily.

Something wasn't right here.

And Tony intended to find out what that something was before it caused a permanent rift between Paige and Jeri. Meanwhile, he would continue to do everything he could to throw Paige and Damon together. If ever there were two guests destined to fall in love with each other, it was those two.

That became evident the minute he'd tripped Paige and Damon caught her. The electricity between those two was so intense, the force had struck him from clear across the room.

Yep, the Seascape Inn was due another match up. He felt that right down to the inner soul. But first, he needed to find out why Damon was so willing to go along with Blair's petty plan. Why humor someone like her? And who was John? What was the contract he offered, and why was it so important?

Until Tony had these answers, he'd never be truly effective at making this match.

❧ *Chapter 6* ❧

After a restless night worrying about Jeri, and at the same time trying to figure out Damon's intentions, Paige did not wake up at her usual hour. It was well after nine o'clock before the chatter of a squirrel outside her window finally lured her awake.

Odd, had there been car horns honking, tires squealing, and people shouting, she probably wouldn't have noticed. But the lively chatter of one tiny squirrel was enough to jar her awake.

Groggy from not enough sleep, and hungry, Paige grabbed a comfortable pair of white pleated slacks and a rose-print blouse from the closet then stumbled across the hall to the bathroom to shower, brush her teeth, and get dressed.

By the time she had showered, finished dressing, and started applying her make up, she was still not fully awake; but she did manage to focus again on Jeri's problems, ready to give helping her another go. Transforming her into the young lady Damon wanted would be a task that required her full attention—and her full attention it would have.

She considered several approaches while finishing her make up then putting it away. It wasn't until she picked up a carelessly discarded hand towel to toss it on into the clothes hamper with her own that she caught an invigorating whiff of Damon's cologne. Her contrary thoughts shifted again to the heart-pounding incident in her room.

Even after hours of trying to decide why Damon had held her in his arms as long as he did after steadying her, she had yet to figure out a logical reason. Instead of releasing her as he should, he had pressed her body closer, all the while focused on her mouth as if he might kiss her. Why was he toying with her? Was he trying to see how many ways he could make her squirm? He had certainly made enough girls squirm back in high school with those same type antics. He and his small circle of friends had often amused themselves with that sort of thing.

"Or could he really be attracted to me?" she asked aloud. The slightest possibility that he might be caused her pulse to sprint forward, but she quickly stifled that. Even if Damon was attracted to her for some obscure reason, that attraction wouldn't last long. It never did—not with him anyway. And certainly not for someone like her. Talk about a relationship doomed from the start.

"It would be better not to go there at all." For both of them. She had a dreadful hunch that she might really start to care about this guy if she let herself—as much as she ever cared about Edward Simmons. After all, her reaction to Damon's touch had been every bit as strong, and every bit as mind-fogging, if not more so.

"Not a good thing."

Wadding Damon's towel with her own, she tossed them both into the hamper, closed the lid, and headed back to her room to put away her things. When she started downstairs, her sleep-deprived brain was still stuck on what sort of problems she would cause if she ever allowed herself to care about Damon.

Experience had already proven how much less it hurt when someone she never cared about lost interest and left than when someone she dearly loved suddenly tossed her aside. Even with Blair's help, it had taken years for Paige to get over the heartache caused by her unfaithful fiance, Edward.

Until someone came along who understood what commitment really was, and who could love her no matter what the future held, it was best not to get involved at all. Besides, she had her new life to worry about. Moving to Mt. Pine and opening her own dress shop would take so much time and energy that finding someone worth sharing that life with would have to come later. Letting herself fancy Damon now that she was older was clearly out of the question. It wouldn't fit into her new life's design. She might as well get that straight in her head right now. True, she'd be in a small city where she was sure to run into him from time to time, but the likelihood they could ever be more than just friends was nothing short of absurd.

When Paige entered the kitchen seeking coffee a few minutes later, she was still lost in unwanted thoughts of Damon. So much so, she didn't notice Miss Hattie sitting in an old red rocker near the fireplace just off to her right until the woman spoke, startling her nearly out of her skin.

"Did you finally decide to come downstairs?" she asked, her voice lively and disgustingly awake as she shoved a needle into a dark blue shirt she mended. Old-time band music drifted out of an antique cabinet radio directly behind her. "I was beginning to think we wouldn't see your pretty face again until lunch. Why it's nearly ten o'clock. You've already missed the best part of the morning."

"I overslept," Paige ground out, finding it awfully hard to process such a cheerful conversation while searching the gleaming white kitchen for any sign of a coffee maker. After the night she'd had, she needed caffeine in a desperate way. But she saw nothing that looked even remotely like it held an ample portion of her lifeblood. "Am I too late for coffee?"

"No, not at all. But you'll find it in the dining room on the buffet, not in here," Miss Hattie replied in a clipped accent common to Maine. She wrinkled the bridge of her nose beneath her wire-rimmed sewing glasses, as if they made her itch. "With the coffee, you'll find a few of my blueberry muffins and a bit of cranberry bread alongside a small pitcher of orange juice still chilling in a dish of ice. You are a couple of hours too late for the eggs and bacon I served earlier.''

"None left?" She wouldn't mind a few strips of cold bacon.

"None at all. I'm afraid Damon proved very hungry this morning and ate up almost everything I cooked." She laughed as she pulled the dark threads taut then shoved the needle back into the material. "I do love a man with a bold appetite."

The mention of Damon's bold appetite sent Paige's unruly mind off again to tempting thoughts of the night before. Yes, he had certainly looked to have quite a bold appetite while holding her close in his arms. Try as she might, she couldn't forget the giddy feeling that had raced through her then. What a rotten shame he was so much like Edward—too handsome for his own good, and too self-involved to ever know permanent love.

Why, just look at how Damon's marriage had turned out. The woman had been the mother of his child, for heaven's sake. That alone should have given him plenty of reason to hold on to the relationship longer than seven years—if for no other reason than to spare Jeri the anguish of seeing her parents go their separate ways. Her mother's death, coming in the wake of that divorce, had to have been all the more traumatic for the child.

Damon could have at least saved her from having to watch her parents split up, but he hadn't.

Annoyed with herself for letting Damon intrude on her thoughts yet again, she shoved all that aside and concentrated again on what Miss Hattie had to say.

"Tomorrow morning, you might want to try to get yourself downstairs a little closer to eight o'clock," Miss Hattie suggested, never slowing her needle. "If you make it down between eight and nine, you can share a hot breakfast with some of the other guests." She stretched her neck forward and squinted, causing soft wrinkles around her green eyes as she pulled at the pucker her last stitch caused. "Today, there was only the Gaddys from out in the carriage house. They arrived early yesterday afternoon and, so far, have kept to themselves more than most; but later next week there will be two more families arriving. One is staying only a short while though usually they are here a week. The other one arrives nearer to the weekend and has never been here before."

Having smoothed the material again, she relaxed her face and glanced again at Paige. "Breakfasts can prove quite lively here when the place is full. I do so enjoy that."

"I'll see what I can do about being down in time from now on." When Miss Hattie looked down again, Paige wondered whose shirt that was since it was obviously a man's, but didn't ask. Hearing the story behind the shirt could delay that still much needed dose of coffee.

Heading back down the hall, Paige managed to keep her thoughts off Damon, at least for the time being. Inside the sunbathed dining room, she found the promised coffee waiting beside a linen draped plate with three fat home-made muffins and several thick slices of cranberry bread. Beside it was a small pitcher of chilled orange juice with beads of moisture trailing down into a bed of melting ice.

Filling the pink stoneware cup to the brim, she quickly drank the steamy brew, feeling the precious fluid coat her throat in warmth and, seconds later, bring her sluggish body back to life.

Not wanting to scatter crumbs on Miss Hattie's spotless white lace tablecloth, she sipped a second cup of coffee while still standing, then traded it for a glass of orange juice. She then carried a small plate with a muffin and two fat slices of cranberry bread through the French doors out onto the veranda. Once outside, she paused to fill her lungs with deep draws of the fresh, sea-washed morning air. There were no automotive exhaust fumes, no industrial smoke, or unwashed garbage bins to offend her.

The day was incredibly beautiful *and distractingly quiet*. Accustomed to the harsh, discordant sounds of the city, she found solace in the ceaseless drone of the ocean. It was a soft, rolling sound peppered with sharp, animated chirps and lively squawks of several different birds, and the distant barking of someone's dog. She closed her eyes and breathed again the wind-stirred scent of cedar and salt. The perfect place for a vacation.

Too bad she wasn't on one.

Hoping to find someplace to eat her muffin and bread that would allow a panoramic view of the ocean with its cloud-dotted blue sky, Paige headed around to the front part of the house. Just as she turned the corner, she heard Jeri's voice. Spotting the girl at the far end of the veranda, slouched across a white, ladder-back rocking chair and with a telephone attached to her ear, Paige decided not to intrude.

Making little sound, she moved a fat, pump-style insect sprayer out of the chair farthest away and sat down. She placed her small plate in her lap and her glass on the worn planked floor, near a grey and white flower box that had exploded with vibrant red geraniums.

"Sure, that's what I think, too," Jeri commented, talking in a voice loud enough Paige couldn't help but overhear. Facing the front yard, the girl had no idea that anyone else was there. "But either Dad has no idea what's going on, or he's playing dumb, thinking I'm too stupid to catch on. Either way, something's got to be done. That's why I came up with the really nifty idea of—"

Jeri's eyes rounded the moment she'd shifted positions and noticed Paige seated just a few dozen yards away, nibbling on a muffin, trying to look as if she hadn't heard a word. But with it so apparent Jeri had spotted her, she smiled and waved. "Good morning."

"I gotta go, Frankie," she spoke, again into the telephone. "I'll talk to you later. Just remember what I said." Glaring at Paige, she pushed the off button and sat forward, her sun-bronzed legs sticking out from under yet another oversized T-shirt, this one bright red with a picture of a half eaten hamburger on it.

"I was talking to Frankie," she commented, her tone defensive even though Paige had not asked for the explanation. "Frankie is my best friend here, and she happens to be just like me, so don't you go trying to change her either." She stood, headed for the door, the telephone clamped tightly in her hand.

Having hoped Jeri would be in a better frame of mind that morning, Paige's spirits sank. She let the comments about Frankie pass. There was enough hostility between them already. To point out how unfair the child was behaving toward her would only make the situation worse. "Where are you going?"

"Inside to put the cellular back in Dad's room, that is if it's okay with you." She froze halfway to the door and turned to scowl at her. The kid effected the kind of icy stare that could freeze an active volcano. "Or do I need your permission to do that?"

"No."

"Good." She started walking again. "Then I'm out of here."

"Jeri?" she called after her, trying to decide the best way to ask why the girl was so angry with her. She'd done nothing to her to warrant this kind of hostility, and wanted to find out what the real problem was.

If only she understood this next generation a little better.

At hearing her name, the girl skidded to a second stop just inches short of the door but didn't turn to look at her. Instead she reached up to scratch her forehead through the adjustment gap of the bright red ball cap she wore backwards, then dropped her arm again sharply. "What is it now?"

Paige's courage left her. She would wait to find out more about Jeri's anger. If she didn't handle the girl just right, that whole situation could blow up in her face. "Are you coming right back out?" She put the half-eaten muffin back on her plate alongside her untouched bread. "Don't forget that you're supposed to spend the day with me."

"Only because Dad says I have to. Believe me, if you

didn't have Dad on your side, I'd already be gone for the day.'' She cut Paige another scathing look. ''Just because Dad likes you, doesn't mean I have to.'' Her dark blond eyelashes lowered, shaping her eyes into ominous slits of blue. ''*Don't* expect to be around very long.''

Then she was gone.

Jeri's parting words hung in the air like an invisible cloud when Miss Hattie stepped outside a few moments later, the dark blue shirt neatly folded over her arm.

Don't expect to be around very long was obviously the girl's way of telling her that if indeed she was involved with her father, it would never become anything more than a short, casual affair.

As if Paige didn't already know that. Short-term, casual courtships had been a way of life for Damon as far back as high school. Unlike Paige, who had found out early on that she was not cut out for such casual affairs. The one she'd had in college had left her feeling disgusted with herself. She had gone to bed with the guy mostly as a way to find out what sex was all about. Robert had been cute, and he'd known all the right things to say, but there was never anything like love involved. Which was why breaking it off a few months later hadn't devastated her like when Edward suddenly broke it off with her. She'd fallen in love with Edward.

''Oh, there you are.'' Miss Hattie said when she finally spotted Paige in the far corner. I was hoping I'd catch you before you left for the village.''

Grateful for the interruption, Paige set her plate with half a muffin and two slices of cranberry bread on the floor beside her orange juice then stood, meeting Miss Hattie part way. ''Am I headed into the village?''

''That's what I've been told. Before breakfast, Damon said something about calling to reserve a pair of bicycles for you and Jeri at Landry's Landing. He commented that while he was stuck upstairs doing paperwork later today, you two could ride over to Crescent Cove where Jeri loves to swim. The water is a little calmer there, and because it doesn't stir as much that far inland, a bit warmer, too. My Tony and I used to enjoy riding over there for a nice swim every now and then. We sometimes carried a picnic. Do you think you two will be leaving early enough for a picnic? Damon didn't say what time you'd go.''

"I'm not sure," Paige admitted, uncomfortable with Miss Hattie's casual mention of Tony. Miss Hattie had already told her the story about how her young fiancé had died a hero in the war, and how she'd never married afterward because he was the only man she could ever love.

Paige thought the romantic tale to be deeply touching, but painfully sad. Hearing it had put a damper on her first meal there. She didn't want more of the same now. She already had enough to depress her. "Damon hasn't told me about any of this yet. I guess he decided on renting the bicycles after going to bed last night. I haven't seen him yet this morning, though I guess I should go try to find him.''

"You haven't seen him because not long after he ate all that breakfast, he decided to walk it off. Last I saw of him, he was headed for the cliffs." She pointed off to the huge, craggy rocks that rose out of a long section of raised shoreline. Twisted cedar and patches of poplar jutted from the jagged crevices.

Having passed near the angular drop of rugged granite during the walk back from the village the day before, Paige shuddered. To someone who detested heights, the stark gray cliffs looked dangerous. Why anyone would voluntarily walk near them was beyond normal logic. Not even to go down to the sandy strip of beach below. "Damon takes strolls along the cliffs?''

"Aye, lots of people do." Miss Hattie reverted her attention back to Paige while she reached into her apron pocket with her free hand. She came out with a lace-edged white handkerchief and dabbed lightly at her temple, then returned it to her pocket. "It's beautiful there with cozy places to sit and watch the ships. People just have to be careful and not get too close to the edge. But then there are plenty of warning signs posted to remind them of that.''

She patted her pocket shut. ''And, too, I think maybe Damon has business problems worrying him this trip, which explains why he brought so much work with him. There's something about walking along the cliffs that helps a person to think more clearly. Just ask any of the local Mainiacs. They'll tell you.''

Returning her attention to the shirt folded neatly over her arm, Miss Hattie smoothed the material with a light hand. ''That reminds me, I came out to ask if you'd mind carrying this shirt by Jimmy Goodson's garage before heading out for the day. You remember Jimmy. He's the one who led you out here yesterday. It's his favorite Sunday shirt and he'll need it in the morning. His garage is just two doors down from where you'll go to get the bicycles, and it would save him a trip up here on what is usually his busiest day.''

''If swimming at the cove is what Damon has planned for us today, then I'll be glad to take the shirt by,'' Paige said. Smiling, she held out her hand for it.

''Oh, don't bother with it just yet,'' Miss Hattie insisted. Go ahead and finish your breakfast. I don't want you to go hungry. I'll just put the shirt on this chair here so you don't forget it.'' She bent to place the folded garment on one of the straight back chairs, then stopped. ''No, better not put it in this chair. Candy might think I put it there for her. This is her favorite chair when she visits here.'' She moved one chair down. ''I'll put it here so it doesn't end up with black fur all over it. Thank you for doing this for me.''

Beaming happily, she reached back into her apron pocket and this time came out with a small pair of scissors. ''I think I'll cut a fresh bouquet of gladiolus for the dining room. And maybe a big bouquet of red roses for the parlor.''

Humming softly, she headed for the steps, leaving Paige to finish her breakfast.

Having lost her appetite, Paige stared at the mangled muffin and untouched bread with disinterest then carried them and her glass still half-filled with orange juice back into the house. Not knowing where else to put them, she hauled them into the kitchen and set them in the sink. She noticed the coffee cup she had left in the dining room already there. Miss Hattie was amazingly efficient for someone her age.

Turning back around to face the cheery kitchen, she wondered what to do with herself until either Damon returned from his walk along the cliffs, or Jeri came down from upstairs. She was not used to having so little to do. At work, there were always at least a dozen details awaiting her attention at any given time.

Too bad she didn't think to bring a novel with her. It had been months since she'd had time to read.

Remembering all the books in the alcove upstairs, she hoped one would interest her. Stepping out into the hall just as an elderly woman dressed quite unfashionably in purple and orange entered the front door, she nodded a greeting but didn't stop to chat. Clearly the woman had thought she might, but Paige just wasn't in the mood for an idle conversation with strangers. She continued on to the stairs and had just rested her hand at the end of the bannister when she caught a glimpse of Damon coming up the front steps.

Her heart did an immediate flip-flop. He looked so good dressed in a pair of cut-off jeans with a teal green pullover shirt. The muscles in his legs flexed admirably as he moved across the veranda.

"Paige, wait."

Struggling with an erratic heartbeat, Paige dropped her hand back to her side and turned to face him just as he grasped the handle on the old-fashioned screen door. "Yes?"

"Have you seen Jeri?" He continued toward her.

"Yes, I saw her earlier, just before she went upstairs to put the telephone back in your room." She glanced at the stately old grandfather's clock across from the stairs. "That was about fifteen minutes ago." To keep from blocking his way, she stepped to the side. "I haven't seen her since then."

"But she's still here?" He paused near the foot of the stairs, his hand where Paige's had just been. "She hasn't tried to sneak off?"

Paige blinked at the thought. It hadn't occurred to her that Jeri might try to sneak off. "Why would she do that?"

"Because she's not altogether pleased with how I plan for her to spend most of the day with you."

So *that* was why the girl was in such a foul mood again this morning. She didn't want to go to the cove after all. No problem. They could do something else to pass the time. "But I thought she liked to go swimming at Crescent Cove."

Damon looked surprised by that comment. "How do you know that's what I plan for you to do today? I haven't even told Jeri yet. I wanted to wait until I was sure Jacky had a couple of bikes free to rent first." He nodded in the direction he was headed. "That's where I was going just now. Upstairs to tell Jeri the final plans for the day."

"I know about it because Miss Hattie told me about it just a little while ago. She brought it up while asking me to take a shirt to a friend of hers beforehand. According to her, this cove is a popular place."

"It is for the locals. Not too many people *from away* know about it. The only reason we found out was because one of Jeri's little friends from around here took her there several summers ago. Aaron Butler liked to go there because it's so secluded and quiet. He called it his thinking hole. When his family decided to move back to California last year, he told everyone that was one thing he was really going to miss, his thinking hole." He darted his gaze to the stairs again, as if something had caught his eye, then smiled. "Isn't that right, slugger?"

Paige, too, glanced up and spotted Jeri on the landing, wearing the same oversized red t-shirt and the same pair of white shorts, but she'd changed ball caps. This one was dark blue.

"He said he'd miss that and Batty Beaulah's wild tales of ghosts and goblins," she put in, headed down the stairs. "Oh, and I'll bet he misses those big fat cookies at Miss Millie's. She always let him have however many he thought he could eat." Showing none of the hostility Paige expected, Jeri returned her father's smile, sinking a dimple deep into her right cheek while she trailed a finger down the bannister. Evidently, she wasn't all that opposed to a short trip to the secluded cove. "Of course, now I feel it is my duty to eat his share whenever we stop by there so none goes to waste."

"Of course." He chuckled, then glanced past her to where two portraits hung on the wall above the landing. "How long were you standing up there?"

"Long enough to hear where we're headed." Having reached the foyer, she hurried to slide the desk telephone away from the wall so she could use it. "I'll call Frankie and let her know."

"Wait." Damon stepped forward and took her finger out of the old-fashioned dial before she could twirl it. "Sorry, slugger, I guess I didn't make myself clear earlier. Frankie's not invited this time. Today, it'll just be you and Paige."

Jeri's jaw dropped, making her look as if she'd just been slapped. "But, Dad, you know I *always* ask Frankie to go do whatever it is I do when I'm here."

Damon arched a reproachful eyebrow. "Always?" He tilted his head to one side, as if daring her to continue with that exaggeration.

Paige wanted to chuckle at how quickly Jeri recanted.

"Well almost always." She met his knowing gaze a moment longer, then drew in her shoulders. "At least, more times than I don't."

Damon's expression turned instantly sympathetic when

he touched her on the tip of her downcast nose, causing her to look up at him again. "Well, today, you aren't inviting her to go along. You two have seen enough of each other these first few days."

Jeri's mouth hardened as she sliced Paige an indignant look. "Isn't it bad enough I have to spend the whole day having her as my keeper?" The harsh look held just a second then curled into a sad, beseeching expression when she again lifted her face to her father. "Can't I at least have Frankie along to make it better?"

Thinking it the perfect opportunity to score points with Jeri, Paige leaned forward enough to catch Damon's notice, interrupting whatever he was about to say next with a light wave of her hand. "Hey, if she wants to invite a friend along, I don't mind."

Jeri blinked hard, as if unable to believe Paige had just come to her aid. Her eyes lit with renewed hope. "See? Paige doesn't mind."

"But I do."

Jeri's face plummeted again. "But why can't Frankie come along?"

Damon paused for a short breath, his expression grim when he finally answered, "Let's just say I have my reasons."

"But that's not fair! I really need for Frankie to come along with us. We've got important plans." She cut Paige a worried glance. "Besides, I already told her she could come do whatever it is we end up doing today."

"Your problem is I don't have to be fair." He touched her nose again. "Because I'm your father. And you'll see Frankie again soon enough. Go upstairs to cool your temper a few minutes, then call Frankie and tell her your plans with her will have to wait. You won't be seeing her again until late this afternoon."

"But that's not fair either. We don't get to play on the same team this time, so I won't get to talk to her much at all."

Paige was amazed at how calm Damon remained *con-*

sidering. Despite Jeri's trying behavior, he didn't raise his voice once. "Still, you will get to yell at her from the mound. That's something you always enjoy," he reminded her, then continued. "After you're through calling her, get ready to head on out so Paige will have time to deliver something for Miss Hattie first. I told Jacky Landry you two would stop by the Landing for those bicycles about eleven o'clock, and it's nearly that now. Jacky is also supposed to have ordered boxed lunches for you from the Blue Moon Cafe, and will have those ready when you get there, too."

When Jeri didn't immediately obey, Damon crossed his well-shaped arms and narrowed a steely blue gaze. "Go."

Paige watched the surly child march stiff-armed up the stairs, pausing to cast her and her father one last angry glare before finally stomping out of sight. It looked like Damon may have won that particular skirmish, but the revolt was far from over.

Curious to see Damon's reaction to his daughter's angry retreat, she shifted her gaze back to him. When she noticed how intense he looked while he, too, watched his daughter's dramatic exit, she shook her head in wonder. Why did he let that child get away with such brazen behavior? Paige couldn't imagine.

She might not know that much about children in general, but she did understand when there was a real need for discipline. If that had been her acting like such a spoiled brat, her father would have made sure she couldn't sit down for a week. Blair would have, too.

Absently, Paige rubbed the area of her body that would have been affected the most.

The movement drew Damon's attention back to her the second after Jeri's door slammed shut upstairs. He glanced down to where her hand suddenly froze, then up again to her face. "You do remember how to ride a bicycle don't you?" he asked. His expression revealed none of the parental annoyance that should be there. Nor did he look puzzled about why she might suddenly feel inclined to fondle her own rear end. "I didn't think to ask you that before."

"I guess I remember how." She crossed her arms self-consciously, afraid of what they would next do to embarrass her. "I haven't ridden a bike much since I was a kid, but that's supposed to be one of those things a person never forgets how to do."

Damon nodded his agreement, then offered that woefully handsome smile of his, the one that set her insides to reeling. "That's what Jacky said, too."

He slid the old-fashioned dial telephone back against the wall then moved away from the registration desk. "By the way, she told me she has a nice white one for you to use, but I'm afraid it doesn't have pink and purple tassels."

Pink and purple tassels? Paige stared at him, mouth gaped. "I can probably make do without the tassels." How odd that he remembered something like that.

Still smiling that incredibly sexy smile, he stopped again a couple of feet in front of her. "Just don't try to make do without your swimsuit. Though the place is pretty secluded, you never know when one of the locals will drop by for a swim. Especially this time of year." His gaze drifted downward. "You might want to remember a towel and suntan lotion, too."

A jolt of electricity tingled Paige's skin. Was he imagining what she might look like swimming nude? If so, she hoped his imagination proved charitable. "Anything else?"

"Just be careful." Slowly, his gaze drifted back to meet hers. "I wouldn't want anything bad to happen to either one of you."

"We'll be fine." She swallowed around a sudden mass lodged in her throat and tried to force her heart rate back to a more normal level. She couldn't let him continue affecting her like that. Since last night's encounter, he'd kept her libido way off kilter. "What time do you want Jeri back here?"

"About five o'clock will be fine. I promised I'd put

aside my work later this afternoon long enough to go play another game of baseball down by the church about five-thirty. If you leave the cove by three forty-five, you should be back here in plenty of time.''

''Three forty-five? How far is this cove?''

''Six miles. Easy trip. Don't worry, Jeri knows the way.''

Six miles? Easy? *Was the man insane?*

❊ *Chapter 7* ❊

Paige struggled to keep up. She still didn't understand why they couldn't have made at least part of the trip in her rented car. According to her bicycle's odometer, they'd traveled three miles before Jeri finally veered off the winding, tar-patched road onto the wide, rugged woodland trail. They could have saved a lot of pain and effort by strapping the bicycles to the car and driving as far as the trail. They could have parked at the little country craft shop only a couple of hundred yards up the road.

"Come on, slow poke," Jeri called out, glancing over her shoulder to find Paige lagging behind *again*. Her blond ponytail bounced with lively rhythm while she continued on. "We're never going to get there if you don't stick it in high gear."

"This *is* high gear," Paige muttered between short, desperate gasps for air. At least it was for her. When had she allowed herself to get this much out of shape? Focused more on the leaf-strewn trail directly in front of her than on what might lie ahead in the brushy distance, she glanced up in time to see Jeri's back wheel disappear around the next sharp bend. Good grief! It seemed like the harder Paige pumped those pedals, the further behind she fell. Where'd that kid get all her energy?

She pedaled harder.

"I thought your father ordered you to go slow," she

called out, though no longer sure the girl was still within ear shot. It could be the little demon was in the next county by now.

"I *am* going slow," came the annoyed reply from deep in the woods ahead. "If I went any slower I'd have to get off this thing and carry it. Catch up, or get left."

Not wanting to fall too far behind on the unfamiliar trail, Paige continued to pedal as fast and as hard as her aching legs allowed. "Obviously, your idea of slow isn't the same as mine," she tried again. "How far to the cove?" Maybe her odometer wasn't working right. Surely they'd traveled six miles by now.

"We've gone about three miles. We're just a little over halfway. Come on, will you? I still want to have some time for swimming after we get there." She was far enough away now that Paige could barely make out the next words over her own brutal heartbeat. "Gee, whiz, this is only a six mile trip. What if Dad had wanted us to ride all the way to Indian Point? What would you have done then?"

Paige did not care to know how far Indian Point was. This six mile trip was bad enough. How did she let him talk her into something like this? Why hadn't she done the sane thing and refused? Wasn't one of her new goals to take charge of her own life again? Was letting someone talk her into taking a six mile trek to some obscure cove accomplishing that? *Hardly.*

Damon's words continued to haunt her, each set getting louder and stronger with every gasping breath she sucked through clenched teeth. *Six miles. Easy trip. Don't worry. Jeri knows the way.*

Well and good. But where was Jeri? A good half mile up the trail by now.

Clearly left behind, Paige pulled to a stop and bent over the bicycle to pull huge burning breaths into lungs that suddenly seemed too small. The forest was not quite as dense in this area as where they first entered. But there were still heavy patches of bunchberry vines and spotty tufts of hawkweeds and spiked ferns growing in tangled gnarls beneath the towering evergreens.

The bike trail they followed was wide enough that the underbrush didn't tug at her clothes, but an occasional fallen limb did cause her to veer off the dirt part of the path long enough to go around. Having had such light use, the trail wound through the spiky black tree trunks and shaded patches of dark green moss like a long, thin, gray ribbon. Up ahead, it divided.

Too guilt ridden to concentrate on his work like he so desperately needed, Damon pulled off his reading glasses and tossed them on top of the papers scattered in front of him. How could he have done it? How could he have sent someone as naive and innocent as Paige off into the woods with someone as angry and as cunning as his daughter? Especially when that anger was partly his fault. He'd certainly fueled it enough these past few days by purposely making Jeri's life miserable, knowing full well she would blame Paige for anything that went wrong. Exactly like she had blamed Paige yesterday for having lost that ball game.

Like most kids her age, Jeri rarely took responsibility for her own misery. Her misfortunes were always someone else's fault, usually an adult's.

Rubbing away the tiny indentations his glasses had pressed into his upper nose, Damon glanced first at the front windows then at the clock. It was not even one o'clock yet and already he spent half his time watching the main road for signs of Jeri and Paige. He would not get much work done at this rate.

"What's the point?" he asked aloud. Shoving back from the old desk, he glanced idly about the room, and spotting one of Jeri's favorite baseball caps on his dresser, rose to get it. It was the cap she'd earned the day she made all-stars earlier that year—having been the only girl in all of Mt. Pine to advance from regular play that year.

He smiled proudly as he plucked a long blonde hair

from the adjustment clasp. Jeri had always been quite the individual, never balking when faced with a challenge. Unlike her old man who had given up his childhood desire to be a high school teacher and a baseball coach to run the family businesses for his father, Jeri knew exactly what she wanted, and went after it. Until recently, she had never allowed anything or anyone to get in her way. Nothing kept her down.

How he hated the insecurity he'd noticed in her these last few months. All because the other kids had started to mature, and she hadn't.

"Poor kid." It had to be rough watching all her friends' interests change while hers stayed the same. But eventually the time would come for Jeri's hormones to kick in, too, and she would finally realize that she, too, had a feminine side.

Damon sighed to himself as he hugged the dirt-streaked ball cap against his chest. How he dreaded the day when Jeri finally noticed boys and started to appreciate them for something more than their batting averages, or their abilities to make a soccer goal. When that happened, he would involuntarily become less important in his daughter's life, making him fight for whatever scrap of time she might set aside for him. That was the main reason why, for now, he was quite happy to let her continue being the outspoken little tomboy she wanted to be.

Smiling appreciatively, he slapped the undersized cap on his head and tugged it down as far as it would go. It was Jeri's outspokenness that would eventually help win him that big contract he so gravely needed. After Jeri made Paige realize that parenthood was not all warm fuzzies and loving hugs, Paige should willingly give up her sudden notion of wanting a family. After that, life in a lackluster place like Mt. Pine should become a lot less tempting.

Blair was counting on it.

So was he.

Reluctantly, he headed back to the desk. He had until

the end of the following week to get that bid in the mail, and he wanted it to be a fair one.

Propping the bicycle against a large rock at the top of the slope, Paige made it as far as the sun-baked beach where Jeri sat munching on an overloaded sandwich, then collapsed face first in the sand. She sucked in several long, needed breaths before turning over onto her side. "You did that on purpose, didn't you?"

Jeri darted her tongue out to capture a bit of mustard stuck just beyond her mouth. "Did what?"

"Left me behind on the trail, knowing I didn't know how to get here. Nor did I know how to get back to the main road." If she hadn't eventually left the trail to follow the bank she'd found around to the cove, she would still be lost. Those trails went everywhere.

"What if I did?" She took another big bite of her sandwich then reached into the white box open on the towel beside her for a potato chip—clearly unconcerned with how near death Paige was.

Too exhausted to gather the energy needed to be as angry as she should, but still determined to know the girl's motive, Paige rolled back onto the sand and stared up into a cloudless blue sky. Water stirred gently nearby. "But why? What have I ever done to you to make you want to do something like that to me?"

She turned her head to watch Jeri take several hefty gulps of her soft drink and, for a moment, Paige was distracted by the thought she probably had a soft drink just like it in her boxed lunch. Forcing herself into a seated position—not easy for someone who'd had no feeling in her legs for the last fifteen minutes—she pivoted so she faced the girl.

Ignoring her thirst, she continued, "First, you tried to hit me with a baseball, then you accused *me* of having been the reason you lost the game, and now you try to get me lost in the woods. Why would you want to do all that to me?"

Jeri took another long gulp of her drink, tossed the empty can into the box with what few potato chips remained, then popped the last of her sandwich into her mouth. "What does it matter?"

Thinking she detected more hurt than anger in the girl's voice, Paige leaned in to have a closer look at her expression. There was clearly more to this than she'd first realized. "It matters a lot. I'm worried about you. That's why I am trying so hard to understand what's go—"

"Get out of my face," she shouted, interrupting. Suddenly, she scooted away. Clearly, she did not want to hear anymore of what Paige planned to say. "I may have to spend some of my time with you, but I don't have to listen to you—and I sure don't have to tell you anything I don't want." Springing to her feet, she peeled out of her t-shirt and shorts, then adjusted the legs of the dark red one piece she had worn underneath. The swimsuit revealed the trim body of a budding young woman. "I'm going swimming."

Grimacing, she slung her hat onto her towel, then ran several steps down the sandy slope. A little over halfway to the water's edge, she stopped to look back, her expression now unreadable. "You coming in?"

"What? And give you an easy shot at drowning me? I don't think so." Besides, she'd need every ounce of her energy for the long ride back.

Waiting until Jeri was neck deep in the sand-lapping dark blue water, her hair drifting behind her like spilled gold, Paige climbed the slope back to her bicycle to scavenge through her box lunch for that soft drink.

Rather than return to the hot sun, she sat in the shade of an ancient oak and watched while Jeri dove down into the water repeatedly, each time bringing up some new prize from the inlet floor. Sometimes it was a shell, other times it was a soggy piece of driftwood, and once it was a small child's shoe. But no matter how insignificant the treasure, she examined it thoroughly before tossing it back into the deepest part and diving again for something new.

After a couple of hours of this underwater treasure hunt, Jeri grew tired of her game and clamored up on a pile of large, smooth rocks that jutted out of the water along the far side of the cove. There she stretched out on her stomach and rested, lifting her head every now and then to look in Paige's direction—as if worried she might have started back without her.

Fat chance of that, Paige thought, knowing it would take hours to find her way out of that confusing forest without help. The girl had the clear advantage in this situation. So, why did she keep looking over at her with a notched forehead? And how much longer until time to leave?

She glanced down at her watch. Only two-thirty. An hour yet. She tilted her head back against the tree trunk in an attempt to make herself a little more comfortable, but that turned out to be a bad idea.

Having ridden well over eight miles by the time she'd finally found the cove, and having had only a few hours sleep the night before, Paige did not even know she had dozed until her head rocked forward and she nodded herself awake. Startled, and a bit panicked, she quickly scanned the area for Jeri and found her still enjoying the sun's warmth, lying on the rocks across the cove.

Relieved, Paige shifted positions, thinking that might help keep her awake. It didn't. Lulled by the warm sun splashing through the breeze-tossed oak leaves overhead, and the subdued sound of water gently lapping across the gray sand and rocks, her eyelids again grew heavy. But she did not dare give in to her drowsiness a second time. Not when falling asleep could mean being left behind again. Or worse. With the tide now easing in, she had drowning to worry about, too. The water level had risen steadily, until the surface was only inches away from Jeri's towel. Having little knowledge of oceans, she wasn't sure how much higher the water could rise. She tried to decide if she should get up to rescue that towel.

Shifting positions again, she glanced at her watch first,

surprised to discover an hour had passed. Thank goodness.

"Jeri, it's three-thirty," she announced, then stood to stretch her legs, and grimaced at the tightness in her muscles. How she dreaded the long ride back to the inn. "We should go ahead and start back."

Jeri didn't answer, but did sit up. She glanced across the water, studying Paige for a long moment before finally diving into the water and swimming in her direction.

"Did you enjoy your swim?" Paige asked, standing at the water's edge with Jeri's towel in her hand.

"Yeah, I guess." She took the towel and dabbed at the water dribbling down her taut, sun-tanned skin. "But I would have had more fun if you'd have come in, too."

That comment caught Paige off guard. "You get that big a kick out of drowning people?"

Jeri paused with the towel pressed against her cheek, staring at Paige a long moment, then grinned. "Only those worth drowning."

Paige arched an eyebrow, not sure if that was intended as a slight or a compliment. But judging by the playful grin, Jeri had said it in fun.

Not trusting this sudden change in attitude, Paige continued to be wary of the child's intent when following that last comment with a quip of her own. "Then I'm sorry to have put such a damper on your fun. It just so happens, I am well worth drowning."

Jeri laughed.

It was an amazing sound. One Paige had heard only once, during the baseball game, when Harold Baker had acted up while playing outfield.

Jeri waited until she'd finished drying her legs and arms before she slung the damp towel over one shoulder and headed for her clothes. "Come on, let's get going."

During the return trip to the inn, whether because Jeri had worn herself out from swimming, or because she had already pulled the getting-her-lost scheme once, and felt it would be overdoing it to try to lose her yet again, Jeri took a much more leisurely pace back. Paige fell behind only once during a steep uphill climb, but to her relief, as well as disbelief, Jeri had paused at the top of the hill, pretending to gaze out at the ocean.

Although the girl didn't say much to her during the trek back, Paige sensed far less hostility toward her. Something about their afternoon at the cove had mellowed the child. Enough so as to have made the painfully long trip well worth it.

Jeri had a lot to think about during the ride back to the inn. For the first time that she could remember, an adult other than her dad had looked at her like she really did care. As weird as it seemed, there had been something about Paige's face when she asked why she'd purposely lost her in the woods that made Jeri think that maybe this time someone else really did care about what was going on inside her head. Paige had said right out loud that she was worried about her. Said she wanted to understand her.

But why? Because of her father? Did Paige think that by showing she cared about his daughter, she would then win big with him? Was that her game? But if that was the plan, why would she bother with working the scam when he wasn't even there to see it?

No, something about Paige's eyes when she'd said she was worried about her had made Jeri think that maybe, just maybe, this lady really did care. That was probably what had scared her half to death back there—the thought that someone she did not even know might care about her. That sort of thing just didn't happen. Geez, her own mother hadn't even cared about her. Why should this lady?

Entering Sea Haven Village from the south, she glanced back at Paige, now only about a soccer field's length behind, still trying to decide if what Paige had said to her was in any way true. The thought that it might be made her wonder more. Could she possibly trust this woman? Or was she just like her mother, who'd tossed the word trust around like it was some cheap, over-inflated basketball. *Trust me.* Empty words her mother used often. *Trust me* usually meant her mother had just told a bald face lie.

The only person Jeri found she could really trust was the one who had never once said the words 'trust me.' Instead, her father had gone about earning her trust by doing exactly what he said he would do, and by always being honest with her. People like that didn't have to say the words *trust me*. They knew trust came automatically when the person deserved it.

"You making it okay?" she called back to Paige, then slowed down again to let her catch up. Since the road got wider there in town, might as well let her catch up to ride side by side.

"I'll live," Paige shouted between deep breaths, then added at a not so understandable volume, "Unfortunately."

Jeri had to chuckle at that. It was pretty clear that this woman wasn't used to riding bikes long distances like that. Man, was she ever going to be sore tomorrow. "You look pretty thirsty." She waited for Paige to pull up beside her. "Do you want to stop at the Blue Moon for a cold Coke? If not for a Coke, then maybe for an ambulance?"

Paige cut her a look that made her laugh louder before she glanced down at her watch without letting go of the handlebars.

Was the woman afraid the bicycle would go off on its own if she didn't keep a death grip on it?

"No, better not. It's after four-thirty. You and your father have that baseball game at five-thirty, and I'm sure he'll want you to eat something first."

"You aren't going with us?" Why? Because she was too tired? "We usually walk, but we could go in the car Dad rented if you want to."

Paige cut her eyes at her again. She looked like she didn't know what to think of that offer so Jeri explained quickly, before Paige got the wrong idea and thought maybe she wanted her there for personal reasons. "The more people we can get to play with us, the more fun the game is. We always try to round up everyone we can."

Paige's forehead notched a second before she looked ahead again. ''We'll see.''

Jeri sighed, disappointed. 'We'll see' usually meant 'no' whenever it came out of an adult's mouth. 'We'll see' meant Paige wasn't planning to go with them at all. But that didn't make much sense. Going with them would be a good way for her to spend a little more time with her dad. Even though there would be other folks around, Paige could still give him the eye and smile at him whenever she wanted. Just how tired was this lady?

Jeri thought more about it. If the woman was too bushed right now to want to grab at the chance to be with her dad again, but did for some reason end up going along with them later, Jeri would need to remember to make sure she played on the *other* team.

She grinned at the thought. Frankie would just *love* her for that.

❧ *Chapter 8* ❧

One short nap and two extra-strength Advil later, Paige allowed herself to be talked into joining Damon and Jeri at the ball field. Though she missed supper—having been dead to the world at the time—she did manage to gobble down a couple of still warm cupcakes Miss Hattie had baked that afternoon, and now looked forward to the ice-cream sundaes Damon promised for after the game.

She refused to think about the lecture her sister would give for eating such fattening snacks, but after the workout she'd had earlier, she needed the energy boost. Besides, Blair was a fashion model who had to stay trim if she wanted to continue drawing in those high profile jobs. Paige didn't have that worry. A few ounces here or there wouldn't put her career on the skids. But then again, Paige no longer had *a career* to obsess over like Blair did. She'd gladly given that up just this month. It was that, and knowing what lay ahead for her in Mt. Pine, that made it so much easier for her to put up with all she'd had to put up with since arriving there.

Paige smiled as she slid her hands into her jeans back pockets, waiting to see whose team she would play on. How good it felt knowing she did not have to go back to that big stress pit to do anything more than pack her things and say goodbye to a few friends. Just as soon as she was through here, she could make her move from that big,

flashy apartment in New York City to the small picturesque one she'd found in Mt. Pine—*guilt free*.

"Looks like Jeri lost the draw of sticks." Damon
nudged, pulling Paige's thoughts back to the activities
around her. Everyone except Ricky and Johnny Thomas
had gathered at the pitcher's mound to find out which team
ended up with what new player. Ricky and Johnny sat in
the grass—in that slouchy way only teenagers can—
munching on some of their grandmother Millie's home-
made cookies.

Damon looked disappointed at the outcome. "That
means you are on the other team."

Because this was to be a rematch from the afternoon
before, both sides remained the same except that Frankie's
team just added Paige while Jeri's team took on Jimmy
Goodson, the young man Miss Hattie repaired the shirt for.
Jimmy had closed his garage early after being invited to
play ball with them.

"Of all the rotten luck," Jeri commented, looking duly
contrite.

Frankie, on the other hand, studied the short stick between her fingers suspiciously, then glanced again at the
even shorter stick between Jeri's fingers. Finally, she
turned to Paige, a grim expression on her young face while
she looked her over. It was as if Frankie had already made
up her mind not to like Paige. But if that was so, why
would she have picked her for her team? After all, she had
come away with the longer stick. That had given the girl
her choice.

"It looks like you get to be on the winning team,"
Frankie said, tilting her head while gazing up at her. Like
Jeri, Frankie wore her blonde hair in a ponytail to keep it
out of her way, but unlike Jeri, Frankie's baseball cap was
dark purple and she wore it bill forward.

She also had a streak of what looked like automotive
grease across her jaw and several more on her shirt, making Paige wonder if Frankie might be an even bigger tomboy than Jeri. No wonder Damon looked for ways to keep

the two apart. He would never make much progress with Jeri while she was influenced by this obvious grease monkey.

"So what position do you play best?" Frankie asked, poking one knee out while she continued to study Paige.

While awkwardly flexing the oversized leather glove Damon had borrowed for her from Mayor Horace Johnson, Paige thought back to the few times she had played baseball as a child. "Bench-warmer."

Frankie blinked, frowned, then grinned. "Leastwise you're honest. Do you think you can handle left field? With Ricky Thomas moved up to shortstop and Ross Rutledge still on third base, not too many balls should make it out that far anyways."

Paige cut her gaze to where Damon discussed something with Jeri and Jimmy only a few yards away. She tried to decide if he had overheard any of that, and was now laughing royally inside.

"Thanks loads for that vote of confidence," she said wryly, then chuckled. "Yes, under those circumstances, I should be able to handle left field just fine." If the third baseman and shortstop were the ones to be of help to her, she gathered left field meant it was left to those looking out at the field and not to those actually playing the field. Rather than ask to be sure, and thereby show just how baseball ignorant she was, she headed in that direction. When no one called her back, she figured she had guessed right.

All went well during the first inning of play. No balls made it past the two teenage boys playing in front of her, and three teammates batting before her struck out, saving her from early disgrace. It was Frankie and the preacher who managed to get good, solid hits, bringing in their first point.

With the early score one to one it wasn't until the second inning that things started to fall apart for Paige. First, when Damon hit a pop-up fly straight to her and she missed it, swearing it went straight through the glove they'd borrowed for her. And later, when it came her turn to bat.

Gripping the bat in the way that made the most sense to her, she stood near the plate about where little Barney had stood a minute before.

When Jeri looked at her with a perplexed expression, Paige was certain she'd done something stupid. Rather than come off looking like a total fool, she gave up her goal of ignoring Damon as much as possible during the game. Her body hadn't yet come to terms with what happened last night. She hadn't wanted to throw it even more confusion. "What am I doing wrong here?"

Damon rose from his squatting position, a grin tugging at the outermost corners of his mouth. His blue eyes sparkled with mirth when he came around to stand in front of her. "I take it you haven't played much baseball."

"Why do you say that?" she asked, a death grip on the little bulb at the end of the bat propped on her shoulder— ready to swing with all her might.

"Educated guess," he said, then grasped her gently by the shoulders to move her back several inches. "If you stand over the plate like that, not only will you miss the ball entirely, you're gonna get creamed."

As focused on the tiny little power surges electrifying her shoulders as she was on what it was he'd said, she sucked in a quick breath. Her pulses still raced wildly when he backed away again and she looked down at her feet. "But I was exactly where Barney stood, and you didn't push him back like that." Granted he did help the boy with his swing again. But he hadn't bothered actually moving him.

Damon clasped his hands, still clearly fighting the urge to laugh. "That's because Barney's a good foot shorter than you are. That reduces his range quite a bit. If someone your height swings from that close, the wide part of the bat is going to end up way out of the strike zone. Especially if the batter happens to be holding the bat by the hand-stop instead of the neck."

Paige looked at the bat questioningly. The thing had a neck?

"Do you want me to show you how to bat?"

Remembering how Damon had put his arms around Barney from behind while demonstrating how to swing level, Paige's mind raced ahead to the inner turmoil she would face. That might be a bit more than her body could take at this time.

But, then again, if she did not let him show her how to bat correctly, she would never be able to make up for having dropped that fly ball. She owed it to her teammates to do her level best while at bat. "Yes, I do."

Obligingly, Damon moved around behind her.

"Not *again*," little Bobby from first base cried out when it became obvious there would be yet another delay in the game. "Jeri, why can't your dad figure out whose team he's on?"

For once, Jeri didn't respond. Instead, she stood on the mound, her glove tucked under her arm, patiently waiting.

Though surprised, Paige tuned that and everyone else out. She was determined to concentrate solely on what Damon had to show her, not on what Jeri might be thinking or on the effect Damon's touch would undoubtedly have on her. She sucked in a deep breath and held it tight while a pair of incredibly masculine hands came around her from behind to grasp her arms firmly just above the wrists.

"First thing you'll have to do is relax," he told her, his voice low and instructive. "You are as stiff as a brand new brass hinge."

Relax? With Damon's arms around her and fourteen other players impatiently waiting for the game to get back underway? Who was he kidding?

"Here, let me help." Damon freed her arms so he could massage her shoulders with the tips of those long, strong fingers.

Paige slowly released the breath she had held far longer than was healthy. After all she'd gone through that day, the slow manipulation of her tight shoulder muscles felt downright decadent. Unable to resist the tiny shivers of pure pleasure, she closed her eyes and lolled her head back, wishing she could lie down for a full body workover.

"Um, you don't have to get quite *that* relaxed," Damon commented, his soft breath falling very near her ear. The intoxicating scent of his cologne drifted up to tempt her nose about the time he abandoned her shoulders. "Just loosen up enough to be able to make a full swing with the bat."

Snapping out of it, Paige pulled erect again. *Loose, but not too loose.* Somewhere there was a happy medium. Paige wiggled her upper body in an effort to find it while awaiting her next instructions.

Moving closer, Damon grasped her upper wrists again, enveloping her in a body heat so sensual, and so arousing, she felt guilty to have so many children around watching them. One of them, Damon's own daughter.

A quick glance at Jeri revealed the girl didn't look all too happy over what was happening at home plate. Yet she didn't complain either. Odd, that.

"Now what?"

He shifted his weight. "Grip the bat about two to three inches from the end with your left hand, thumb to the top," he told her, again very near her ear. "Then place your right hand on top of that."

Eager to impress him, she did exactly as told. But again he chuckled. "I didn't mean cover one hand with the other. Both hands are supposed to be solidly gripping the bat, butted up against each other." He wrapped his fingers around her right hand to move it into place. "There, like that."

"Oh." Funny, she had never really noticed how a batter held the bat before, but she supposed this was the correct way. "Now what?"

Damon left his hands snugged around hers a moment longer than necessary, then slid them again to her upper wrists, his body still pressed against hers. How solid he felt.

She took another quick breath when that last thought sent her heart rate vaulting again.

"Okay, now you turn your head to face the pitcher."

She did. Jeri still stood with her glove tucked under her arm, eyes narrowed while she patiently gripped the baseball. She looked as if she wasn't quite sure what to make of her father's instructions.

"Now bring the bat back carefully, so you don't conk me in the head, then crook your elbows out just a little." Guiding her by her wrists, he helped her bring the bat back to the correct angle, inches above her shoulder. That caused his foot to move closer while his arms drew tighter. The muscles in his chest rippled against her back with each new movement.

Two more quick breaths. "Okay, now what?"

"Now bend forward slightly at the waist, allowing your weight to shift to the balls of your feet."

She did, then gasped when she realized what part of his anatomy now pressed firmly against what part of hers. She swallowed hard. "N-now what?"

"Now you need to bend your knees just a little and bring your shoulders back so we can take a practice swing. Let me continue to guide your arms so you'll get the angle right."

When Paige twisted into the ready stance, his body shifted against hers. Suddenly it became terribly hard to concentrate on the angle of the swing. Or anything *else* for that matter.

"While you bring the bat around level like this, you need to move your front foot slightly forward so that you step into the pitch."

When she proved too distracted to respond correctly to that last command, he slid his knee between hers and nudged her right leg forward about the time the swing followed through. *How erotic.*

"You have to remember to step into the pitch," he repeated. "You didn't do that. Let's try it again."

"No, no, no," Paige responded quickly, afraid she would break into a cold sweat if they tried that a second time. It didn't feel quite right to be so extremely aroused with an ordained minister just a few yards away preparing to bat next. "I think I've got it. Let me try it on my own."

Damon hesitated before letting go, but finally stepped back out of the way. "Okay, let me see your stuff."

When Paige readied the bat, she couldn't believe how it felt every bit as erotic having Damon watching her from behind as it did to have him touching her.

"How was that?" she asked after what she hoped was a perfect swing. Bravely, she glanced around to see his expression, and her heart skipped two full beats when she noticed how dark his eyes had grown.

Rather than voice his reply, he drew in a sizable breath and nodded his approval.

"Looks good to me, too," little Bobby shouted from first base, clearly ready for the game to resume.

"Yeah, it was nice and level, Mr. Adams," Andy agreed from third base. "That oughta do it."

"It certainly did it for me," Damon finally commented, then cleared his throat after he cut a widening gaze to Reverend Brown. He took a far more serious tone when he quickly returned to his position behind home plate. "Just keep your eye on the ball and don't swing at anything higher than your shoulders or lower than your knees." Paige committed that advice to memory.

When Jeri shot that first pitch in right at waist level, she made a hard, level swing at it, but missed.

"Strike one."

Damon made a leap for the ball and barely caught it. "You also shouldn't swing at anything farther away than your bat can possibly reach."

Now he tells me. Paige moistened her lips in preparation for a second attempt. She watched apprehensively while

Jeri slowly wound her right arm, readying for the second pitch.

Okay. Nothing higher than her shoulders, lower than her knees, or farther away than her bat can reach. Stay loose. Swing level. Step into the pitch. And don't ever let the preacher know how very much you enjoyed that bending at the waist.

The next pitch zinged right over the plate, again waist high. But Paige was too distracted by that last thought to swing at it.

"Strike two."

Jeri shook her head, and waited expressionless for the ball's return. A few moments later, she rocked back on one leg, winding her arm for the third pitch.

Again, she sent the ball in right over the plate, waist high. Paige took a mighty swing and yelped when the bat made contact, jarring her arms right up to her teeth. She stood with the bat still in her hands, dumbfounded, while she watched the ball sail high into the air and drop down again just behind where Fred Baker lay sprawled, having tripped in a clumsy attempt to run backward and catch it. *How about that? She hit it.*

"Run!" Frankie was first with the command, but it was quickly followed by half a dozen others screaming, "Run, Paige, run!" Suddenly, Paige felt like the lead character in somebody's first grade primer. "Run, Paige, run!"

Meanwhile a half dozen other voices chimed in, these shouting, "Get up! Get up, Mr. Baker, and go get that ball!"

Paige had never felt an adrenaline rush quite like the one that charged through her when she rounded third base and glanced over to see Fred rearing his arm back to fling the ball home—that was, until she looked toward the ball's destination. There stood Damon, masculine legs braced on either side of the baseline, his glove up, and his attention on Fred.

"Run, Paige, run!"

She remembered from an earlier incident involving

Bobby that the runner had to stay in the baseline, but how the heck was she supposed to get past Damon when his whole body was in the way like that? The only thing she could figure was that she was supposed to plow right over him.

"Run, Paige, run!"

Digging her shoes into the sandy soil, she picked up speed again, urged on by the rising shouts of excitement from her teammates—the words no longer discernible. She prayed her stay in the hospital would be a short one as she closed her eyes and plunged headlong into that solid wall of flesh.

She saw stars only briefly after the impact and again when she landed on her stomach with a jolt. It was not until she opened her eyes a few seconds later that she discovered where she had wound up. Instead of lying face down in the dirt like she expected, she rested directly on top of Damon, their unblinking eyes barely inches apart.

She groaned the moment her breath returned, having pulled her gaze free of his and discovered she was a good two feet from home plate. She had failed to score her point—or rather the point she had hoped to score for her team. Judging by the devilish sparkle in Damon's blue eyes as his arms came around her to keep her from sliding off, she had just scored a mega point with him.

She offered a sickly grin and, as was her habit during awkward times like this, rather than make some profound excuse, she stated the obvious, "You were in the way."

"No, duh," he commented, his grin widening while waiting for whatever was to come next. He seemed in absolutely no hurry for her to stand.

"You got me out, huh?"

He shook his head no, his eyes glittering all the more. "I don't happen to have the ball." He let go to show her his empty hands. "Fred threw wild."

It was in that moment that Paige realized her teammates were still shouting at her. The message was to scramble home. Hoping she might yet earn that point and make up for the dropped ball, she did just that.

Never had scrambling been so pleasurable.

By the time the game ended with Jeri's team winning by one point, Paige was happily exhausted. Since most of those who'd played did so solely for the opportunity to tease and taunt each other, she had never had such fun while playing sports. She couldn't understand why Blair hadn't allowed her to be a little more athletic while in school. Competing like that had been great fun.

Everyone was in an exceptionally chipper mood when they came away from today's game. Even Frankie, who'd tried her level best on the pitching mound, wasn't all that concerned over the loss. "Looks like we've both won one," she said to Jeri after the two groups blended together near the street. "Since Ricky and Johnny have to leave Tuesday morning to go back to Georgia, I think we need to play one more time Monday afternoon for the championship. That's the only way we can find out which team is really the best."

When it was agreed that everyone but Fred Baker could be there at 5:30—and after his daughter, Nolene, reluctantly consented to take his place—most of the players retired to the Blue Moon Cafe three doors down for ice cream sundaes and soft drinks. Even the losers, who decided it was a good way to drown their sorrows.

Lucy Baker, Fred's wife, had walked over to the field earlier and, therefore, expected the rush. There were a dozen dessert glasses lined up in front of her when they entered.

"So who won the baseball game?" she asked Damon and Jeri, first to reach the tall wooden counter where she stood scooper to the ready. The slender redhead adjusted the dark red apron she'd slid on over her tight white jeans and red-and-white checked blouse. Judging by the slow, soft drawl, the woman hailed originally from the South. "Or dare I ask?"

Waiting her turn, Paige stood a few feet behind Jeri and Damon, as did Jimmy and Frankie. Fred's three nephews had already piled into one of the red-vinyl booths near the old-fashioned juke box and started fiddling with the condiments.

The only other customers at the time were two older men: one pale, wiry and bald, and the other more weathered looking with stark gray hair and his cheeks covered with long gray stubble. They sat at one of the smaller tables sipping coffee from heavy white mugs with two empty dinner plates still in front of them. A large stuffed marlin hung on the rustic wall directly behind them, looking almost as if it had an interest in their conversation.

With her usual youthful exuberance, Jeri had hopped up on one of the padded stools that looked like they came straight out of a 1950's soda fountain. Leaning on her knees to peer over the counter at the flavor choices, she chose to be the one to answer Lucy's question. "We won, of course—but with very little help from your husband." She cut a playful glower at Fred, who'd stopped at an old, cluttered bulletin board near the end of the counter to check something pinned there before heading on around. "He overthrew to home plate twice, letting a score come in each time. If it weren't for Dad, Barney, and me playing so good today, we'd never have won."

Damon shook his head at his daughter's cavalier assessment while he neatly tucked his folded ball cap into his waist band. "Modest, she isn't."

Grinning, Lucy watched while Fred strolled cautiously toward her. "You overthrew the ball twice?"

"Wasn't my fault." Fred muttered then bent forward to give her a loving peck on the cheek, careful not to let the pencil tucked behind her ear catch him in the eye. "Damon is obviously shrinking."

"How unfortunate," Lucy replied, then looked at Damon with a look of mock sympathy for only a second before her grin returned.

Finished tucking in part of his cap so he wouldn't lose

it, Damon arched a playful eyebrow and leaned forward to catch Fred's eye. "Odd that my daughter had no problem getting the ball right to me." He tugged lightly on Jeri's ponytail. "I don't see why you should have."

"She stood a lot closer than me," he quipped, reaching for one of the red plastic glasses stacked near the soda fountain. "Besides, I forgot my sunglasses again." He pouted. "I had the sun in my eyes. She didn't. She had her cap to turn around when the sun got too bad for her."

"But, Mr. Baker, the sun was behind you," Jeri pointed out, then elbowed her Dad as if she could not believe Fred had even bothered with such a lame excuse. Damon responded by dropping his arm around her shoulders and giving them a light squeeze.

Paige couldn't miss the loving gesture. How heartwarming to see such love between a father and daughter. Perhaps she'd misjudged him somewhat when thinking he could never commit to a relationship. He'd certainly committed himself to this one. Not all fathers did. So maybe he wasn't as much like Edward as she first thought. Perhaps it wouldn't be quite as grand a mistake to fall in love with Damon as she first thought.

"You don't really need sunglasses when the sun is behind you like that," Jeri continued, then laughed when that made Fred wrinkle his nose at her.

"Oh, but Fred has eyes in the back of his head," Lucy offered quickly, in ready defense of her man. "Just ask Nolene. She'll tell you." Her smile faded for a moment while she quickly scanned the restaurant. "Where *is* Nolene?"

Fred darted a concerned look in Jimmy's direction, as if hesitant to answer that question in the young man's presence, then looked again at the soda machine where he filled his glass to the brim.

Paige also glanced at Jimmy who now looked out the window as if suddenly more interested in the late afternoon shadows than in the topic of conversation. What did he have to do with where Nolene had gone?

"Nolene is with Andy," Fred finally answered, bending forward to sip part of the drink before picking it up. "Andy fell and tore his shirt, and she went with him to explain to Lydia that it wasn't the boy's fault. You know how she hates him playing sports like that."

Obviously not as concerned about Jimmy's presence as Fred was, Lucy peered through the front window to a building across the street. "It's summer. Is the boy supposed to study all year long?"

"Either study or work for them at The Store."

"That's too bad. I really thought Lydia had started to get over all that last summer." Lucy shook her head, then with Jeri pointing to a container of chocolate ice cream, bent forward to dig out a generous portion. "Do you want a pile of whipped cream on top of that?"

"Just chocolate syrup, chocolate chips, and nuts."

Shifting his weight to one well-muscled leg, to allow him to slip his billfold out of his back pocket, Damon grimaced when he watched Jeri take her first gooey bite a few seconds later. "Isn't that a little too much chocolate?"

"Are you kidding?" Jeri asked. She licked her upper lip where some of the dark syrup had caught, not missing a drop. "You can never have too much chocolate."

Paige agreed and when her turn came, she asked for the same. She tried not to think about what Blair would have to say about ordering such a sinful concoction. She was again free to choose what she wanted to eat.

After getting their ice creams and soft drinks, Damon, Jeri, Frankie, and Paige sat at one of the longer tables in the center of the room while Fred joined his nephews in the booth. Jimmy, Johnny, and Ricky took their food and headed outside to eat on the tables out on the roof.

The room filled with laughter and loud voices as different plays of the game were discussed and re-discussed. Paige enjoyed the camaraderie while she held her dessert glass in front of her and slowly relished the contents. It amazed her how in just the few hours she had known these people, they had allowed her to feel very much a part of the group. She hoped life in Mt. Pine would be like this.

When she looked at Damon, who was busy stirring his strawberry sundae into bright pink mush while Frankie made a game of dropping gooey globs of nut-sprinkled vanilla ice cream into her mouth from six inches away, Paige couldn't help but smile. It felt good knowing she already had at least two friends in Mt. Pine: Susan Carmichael, her friend since elementary school—and now Damon.

Her heart fluttered like a bird wanting to take flight, making it hard to concentrate on the next bit of conversation. All she could think about was how exciting life would be with Damon as her personal friend. And if progress continued, she might have Jeri for a friend, too. That thought warmed her every bit as much as having Damon for a friend—although in a decidedly different way.

"Why aren't you eating?" Frankie asked, pointing to the way Paige sat with her spoon poised but not active.

"No reason," she answered, embarrassed to have been caught woolgathering. She shoved the spoon into her mouth when Damon stopped stirring to look at her, realizing only after she'd done that, she had just finished taking a bite. The spoon was empty. "I guess I just don't want to run out of ice cream before anyone else."

"As slow as you are eating, I don't think that'll be a problem," he pointed out, waving his spoon at her. Seated to Paige's right, with Jeri and Frankie directly across from him, he scooted a little closer in to have a better peek at her ice cream dish. When he did, his knee brushed hers. "I'd say you need to eat that sundae pretty quick, or you'll end up having to drink it."

Aware how truly pleasurable that whisk of male warmth had felt, Paige kept her leg exactly where it was with the hope he'd brush against her again.

After a few minutes watching the two of them from behind the counter, Lucy ambled over to the table. Without announcing her intentions, she dragged over another chair and joined them, sitting at the end closest to Paige.

"I hear Barney hit a home run." She glanced at the booth where the boy chattered excitedly with some of the others, then winked at Damon who had paused massacring his sundae long enough to hear her out.

If it hadn't been such a sassy wink, Paige would have thought the woman was flirting with him right there in front of her husband. Even so, she slowed her eating to keep a cautious eye on Lucy.

"That must have been something," Lucy continued happily. "Fred's nephew has never done that before in his life."

"Oh, yeah, it was something all right," Jeri put in, "Barn hit that ball a real good lick right after Dad showed him how." She set aside her spoon just long enough to take a long draw off her straw, draining over half her root beer in seconds. "Dad's always been pretty good at being a coach." She looked at him proudly. "He was one of the biggest reasons the Red Sox did so good this year."

"He was?" Lucy asked, glancing at Paige while encouraging Jeri to continue her praises.

Damon shifted uncomfortably in his seat.

"He sure was. Dad would come to the practices to help Coach Settles as much as he could. And one week, while the other coach was sick, Dad took over entirely." Shoving her drink back, she picked up her spoon again. "Barney's problem was that he kept dipping the bat every time he swung it, sorta like my friend Jody Jackson used to, so Dad showed him how to keep it level all the way through."

"Sounds like your daddy makes a very good coach's assistant," Lucy commented. She lifted up the knob style salt shaker, as if trying to decide how much was salt and how much was the rice put in there to keep the salt from clumping in the humid ocean air. "I'd say he's a daddy to be proud of."

"Thanks," Damon commented, then looked at Paige, his pale eyes sparkling as if bearing some unspoken message. "I do enjoy coaching—even when those needing my help are members of the other team."

Reminded of her own brief session with "the coach," Paige's face flared hot. She could still feel his strong arms around her, his body pressed intimately against her back. Dang, if that didn't make swallowing suddenly impossible.

"Yes," she added, unable to leave his comment hanging. "I have to admit Damon is very good at that sort of thing. He also helped me to get my first hit ever."

"That's right," Frankie piped in, talking around the big glob of ice cream she had just popped into her mouth. "Miss Brockway scored our second point for us." She gulped the contents in her mouth then stabbed her spoon into her ice cream again. "Of course, it would have looked a lot more cool if she'd run across that home plate on her feet instead of crawling across it on her hands and knees the way she did. But, hey, our team was happy to get whatever kind of point it could get."

"You crawled in home?" Lucy asked, turning her attention to Paige, clearly amused. She lifted a hand to pat at her red hair, making sure it was all still wound into a loose twist. "Rather unconventional, wasn't it?"

Paige smiled weakly. How could she explain having crawled across home plate without it sounding totally inept? Fortunately, she didn't have to. Jeri saved her that embarrassment by introducing another.

"Right after crawling over my dad," she stated bluntly, clearly not all that impressed with Paige's scoring technique.

"Crawling over him?" Lucy lifted a questioning brow to Damon. "How'd that happen?"

"I was flat on my back at the time." His amused gaze again held Paige's, apparently enjoying her discomfort. "That pretty much made it easy for her to crawl all over me."

"Oh?" Lucy's other eyebrow came up. She assessed Paige in a way that made Paige want to crawl out of sight, then grinned again, "It appears I missed an interesting game." Her green eyes twinkled as if pleased with the information she'd just earned. "Sounds more like you guys switched over to playing football instead of baseball. A lot of personal contact going on, hmmm?"

Paige's cheeks flamed hotter while she tried to figure out the easiest way to change the subject—before her ice cream melted into hot chocolate soup, and her heart rate soared well beyond its limit.

As it turned out, she didn't have to. Lucy changed it for her. "How long have you known Damon?"

That was an innocent enough question. So why did it make Paige feel yet more self-conscious? Was it because of the provocative way Damon continued to stare at her? "I've known *of* Damon since childhood. But I've known him individually for only a day."

Lucy appeared to be surprised by that. "And how long have you been here in Maine?"

"Also only a day. I arrived yesterday afternoon."

Lucy looked lost to new thoughts when she commented, "Only a day and already there's all this contact going on?"

Without explaining why, she stood and headed over to the bulletin board where first she surveyed the different scraps of paper, then bent over the food counter to write something on the back of a page torn out of her order pad. Her eyes narrowed with concentration.

Paige watched this odd behavior until Damon cleared his throat and brought her attention back to his incredibly handsome self. For an endless moment he just looked at her, as if he, too, were lost to thought. Finally he spoke. "She's placing a bet," he explained, as if having read the question in Paige's mind.

"A bet?" Paige looked again at the sprightly redhead who now pinned her piece of paper to the bulletin board with vigor.

"I'll explain later," he promised, then cut his gaze to Jeri as if it would be something he would rather not discuss around her.

Taking his cue, she changed the subject to one they could safely discuss despite the girls. "I forgot to ask earlier today but when do we return the bicycles to the Landing?"

She nodded through the window toward a weather bleached wooden building across the street bulging with curios and fishing needs. She had expected to leave the bikes there on the way back, but Jeri had told her they were supposed to keep them awhile longer.

"We'll return them the end of next week. I told Jacky that you two would want them for the next several days. There are a lot more fun places to visit around here. Jeri's favorite cove is only one of many."

Paige longed to ask if most of these 'fun places' weren't also accessible by car; but she refrained for fear she would sound lazy and unappreciative. Instead she tried to look mildly pleased while he continued.

"Since you two had such fun today, I thought you might like to pedal out to Indian Point on Monday. You could see the lighthouse, that little museum, and visit some of the shops. Make a whole day of it. Just the two of you."

"Just the two of us?" Jeri frowned immediately. "But I wanted to hunt for shells with Frankie on Monday. Then maybe dig for a few fishing worms after that so we can try our luck later. Plus, we have that ballgame at five-thirty."

"If Frankie doesn't have plans, you two can hunt for shells and dig for worms tomorrow as soon as church is over and everyone has finished lunch. On Monday, I want you to show Paige around Indian Point. There will be plenty of time for you two to see most everything there before coming back here for the game."

Remembering from a comment Jeri made earlier that Indian Point was even farther away than Crescent Cove, Paige stifled a groan. "Maybe if we went there in my rental instead of riding those bikes, we could manage to get back that afternoon in time so the girls could still go out and dig up a few more worms together, or hunt for a few more shells before the game.'' She tried not to picture what it must be like to dig for worms when she said that. The process had to be disgusting.

Damon studied Paige a long moment, then shook his head. "I'd rather she get her exercise."

Like the kid didn't get enough? She was healthy as a horse and her muscles solid as a rock.

"But, Dad, what if I don't want to ride out to Indian Point Monday?" Jeri whined, her happy mood gone. She and Frankie now shared a scowl.

"Maybe you'd rather we did something else," Paige put in, hoping to get out of that yet. "Maybe you'd like to go shopping in New Haven instead?"

"*Shopping?* Are you nuts? I hate shopping."

"Okay, what about taking in a craft show? I hear there's one all week long over in Brunswick and another over at New Harbor."

She wrinkled her face with disgust. "That's even worse."

"Well, then, what would you like to do Monday?"

"Hunt shells with Frankie."

The muscles that shaped Damon's strong jaw hardened. "Which you are not doing. On Monday, you're going to Indian Point with Paige."

Seeing he meant it, and thinking to help, Paige forced a smile she did not feel, "Besides, we'll have a great time riding out to the point together, just the two of us." She'd managed to say that with far more enthusiasm than she felt. When Jeri continued to eye her father dubiously, Paige stretched that strained smile a little further. "Trust me on that."

Frankie shot a worried look at Jeri, who paused eating in mid-bite. Without putting the ice cream into her mouth, she tossed her spoon back into the fluted glass, looking first disappointed, then angry. "I'm finished. I want to go over to Frankie's for awhile."

She lifted Paige a bitter glower. "*Alone.*"

Chapter 9

"Don't you see what she's doing?" Jeri said to Frankie after the two girls had settled onto their favorite spot near the end of the floating pier, legs dangling in the air over the side. "She's trying to get to my father through me. She thinks that if she could just fool me into thinking she's my friend, then I'd do what I can to help her get my father to like her, too."

Frankie brought one leg up so she could turn to face Jeri, and propped her back against a piling. With the other leg left hanging, she rested both hands on her bent knee. "I don't get what's happened. I thought you told me just awhile ago that maybe she was all right after all. Isn't that what you said on the way over to the Blue Moon? That you'd gotten a chance to think more about it while you guys were at the cove and that you decided she might not be so bad?"

Jeri tightened her upper lip, disgusted with herself for having been so easily fooled. It was true, in a moment of stupidity, she'd thought that woman might really care about her. She should have known better. After women reached a certain age, all they ever cared about was themselves. That and getting themselves a husband. Which explained why Paige was desperate enough to follow her dad all the way up to Maine. She'd told Miss Hattie she was twenty-seven. That meant she should have been married years ago.

Why didn't Frankie understand all that? Was it because she was a couple of years younger than her?

"But don't you see? I thought all that *before* she said to trust her awhile ago."

Frankie shook her head, but her expression showed she was trying to understand. "No, I don't see. Just because your mother used to say that to you all the time, and never once meant it, doesn't mean this lady is doing the same thing. To tell you the truth, I kinda like Miss Brockway."

"Paige," Jeri corrected her. She kicked her feet hard. "Dad thinks we'll all be better friends if I feel important enough to call her by her first name. And the only reason you are starting to like her is because she *wants* you to start liking her."

Frankie wrinkled her forehead. "Yeah?"

"Don't you see? She's trying to get to me through you, and she's trying to get to my dad through me. It's all a part of a big plan to win my father over. That's why she came here. Not to be with me, but to be with him. Don't you get it? That's why I gotta do something really bad to send her running back to where she came from. Something worse than I ever did to anyone before. Even worse than I did to that airline stewardess who followed him out here last summer after she'd just met him."

Frankie flattened her bent leg out, letting her hands drop into her lap. "But you nearly gave that woman a heart attack!"

Jeri grinned at the memory. "It sent her packing, didn't it?"

"Heck, Jer, it nearly sent *me* packing and all I did was watch! What can you possibly do that's any worse than that?"

Jeri lay flat on her back and screwed up her face since that always seemed to help her brain work better. "Let me think. What can I do to make sure those two don't end up together?"

Frankie slid further down the piling, resting her chin against her chest, and waited. She was being extra quiet so Jeri could continue to think out loud, and Jeri appreciated that. "So, what can I do to make sure Paige Brockway knows what she's up against here? Something that will send her a clear message but if she told Dad about it, he'd never believe her—"

Frankie slumped even further down the piling, but still said nothing.

"Something really, really bad."

Suddenly, Frankie sat up. "What about setting him up with somebody from around here to make her jealous? Lucy Baker's sister is due to come in on Monday. She's about the right age. If not her, maybe there's another guest staying out in the carriage house who'd work out. Heck, people are always getting matched up at the inn." Her eyes rounded. "Nobody would ever suspect we set it up."

What a dumb idea. She met Frankie's gaze in disbelief. "And chance Dad falling for whoever we set him up with? No way." She sat up, too. "No, it's gotta be something that keeps him safe out of the clutches of any woman."

Leaning forward so she could readjust her shirt, Frankie asked, "Why are you so against your dad dating at all?"

Jeri took a deep breath. "You wouldn't understand if I told you. Your parents are still both alive and still both married to each other. And they both love you, too. You've got it made. Me? I've only got my dad. He's all I've ever had. Even when Mom was alive, he's the only one who loved me. And I plan to keep him. That's why I can't let him and that woman be together. Not now. Not ever."

Frankie tapped her fingers together then glanced off toward the village. "Then why'd we leave the cafe like we did?"

"Why not?" She shrugged while she, too, looked toward the village. From there, they couldn't see much more than the back of Landry's Landing, a corner of The Store, and the church steeple. "There were lots of other folks still there. It's not like they're going to smooch or anything like that right there in front of everybody.''

"But they have that long walk back together. A walk they could make even longer if they took the ocean trail. A walk they'll now have to make all alone since you're no longer with them.''

"Oh, Geez, Frankie. Why didn't you say something before now?'' Her heart now about to pop wide open, she clamored to her feet. "We gotta go find them.''

"Not we. Mom isn't going to let me run off like that, not with it nearly dark. She'd slit my throat if I walked you any farther than halfway to the inn.''

Jeri glanced skyward, and scowled. There was a faint pink color tracing one side of the clouds. It *was* getting dark. Not only did they have that long walk back to the inn alone, they'd be taking that walk in the evening shadows. She had seen enough television to know that evening shadows made things more romantic somehow. Probably because you didn't have to really look at whoever it was you were kissing. *Kissing?* Geez!

"Well, I've got to go find them right away. If I don't call you before then, I'll see you tomorrow in church.'' She shook her head one last time before taking off down the pier. "Geez, Frankie. You really coulda said something sooner.''

"Why do children have to be so difficult?'' Damon said as a way to start a conversation. Neither he nor Paige had spoken since leaving the cafe, and the silence had started to unnerve him. He braved a glance in her direction, knowing full well the impact that would have on him. Every time he looked at her while they were alone, it set off something inside him that he had a hard time controlling.

Looking surprised he'd spoken, she slowed their already leisurely pace. "What did you say?'' She dampened her lips in that most enticing manner of hers. "I'm sorry; I was thinking about something. I didn't hear what you said.''

He shrugged, too interested in the way the soft shadows hugged the smooth lines of her face to care about anything but watching her. What was it about this woman that drove him to total distraction like this? It was more than the obvious fact she was beautiful. There was just something about the way she moved, and talked, and smiled at him that drove him insane.

"It wasn't that important. All I asked was why children have to be so difficult. Sometimes Jeri's obstinate behavior really gets to me and makes me want to reach up and pull out my hair."

Her gaze drifted to the top of his head, as if considering what he might look like snatched bald. Subconsciously, he raked his fingers through the sides. He wanted to be sure the warm breeze hadn't made a total wreck out of it, though the air stirred with a lot less vigor in the wooded areas. Suddenly, it was no longer all that important to drive Blair's message home. He was too curious about what had so completely captured Paige's attention. "What were you thinking about?"

Facing ahead again, Paige looked uncomfortable as she crossed her arms over her well-shaped breasts. Breasts he'd caught quite a glimpse of the night before.

Pulling his gaze off her, he let out a sharp breath and hoped her answer would lead his thoughts away from that dangerous distraction.

"I wasn't thinking about anything much. I was just going over a few things in my mind. I'm sorry I wasn't paying better attention. It's just that I seem to have so much more to think about these days." She fell quiet and continued to walk at the slower pace, already lost in thought again.

Damon wiped suddenly damp hands on the backs of his jeans. Why did being alone with her leave him so utterly speechless? Never had he had such trouble trying to think of something intelligent to say. "Did you have a good time this afternoon? Did you enjoy the baseball game?"

Paige's brown eyes stretched wide, as if he had just

caught her at something he shouldn't. Was *that* what she was thinking about? The baseball game? Was she remembering that big hit of hers, the one that earned her first home run? Or was she maybe thinking about the little coaching session she'd had just before that big hit? Could it be that Paige was just as affected by all that close contact as he'd been?

He let out another sharp breath at the memory of what it had felt like holding her in his arms yet a second time, her soft body pressed back against his while he showed her the fundamentals of batting. *The things that woman did to his libido!* If he hadn't had a darn good reason to squat down and place his glove up in front of himself right afterward, he might have embarrassed everyone out there.

Fearing a similar response now, he curled his fingers around the edge of his baseball glove and sent his thoughts in a different direction.

"Yes, I enjoyed the game," she finally answered, then slowed further still. "It was a lot more fun than I expected."

"Then you're glad I talked you into coming along?"

"I am now. I'm not so sure I will be all that happy about it in the morning. I had already used up most of my energy during the bike ride to the cove. After adding that game, I'm very near exhaustion."

But not too exhausted to smile, obviously. His insides did a little jig at the mere sight of it. She truly had one of the most perfect mouths he had ever seen on a woman. Wide and full, showing just the right amount of teeth. What he wouldn't give for the courage to pull her into his arms and kiss that perfect mouth right then and there. It was something he had longed to do since last night.

Insides curled tight, he recalled the incident in which she had tripped and fallen into his arms. Oh, how he'd enjoyed that. But he couldn't very well count on something like that happening a second time. Too bad. The memory of how very close he'd come to kissing her right in her own bedroom made him ache inside. If he closed his eyes, he could probably still feel the heat of her body in his arms.

But he didn't dare.

She might not think of him in exactly the way he wanted if he were to stumble blindly over some loose rock or a bulging tree root. But then again, if he did stumble, it was possible she would return his favor from the night before and catch him in her arms before he fell. He stifled a naughty grin, thinking maybe he should unbutton his shirt first sort of like she had.

Absently, he rested an empty hand over his chest and fiddled with one of the buttons.

"What's wrong?" Paige wanted to know, glancing at his hand curiously.

Damon noted they were about halfway through the trees now, where no one from the outside could see them.

"Do you have heartburn?"

His mouth twitched, traitorous thing that it was, then he nodded. "I guess you could say that." He could hold back his grin no longer. Nor his laughter. "Yes, I definitely think you could say that."

Looking at him as if he might be a power tool come unplugged, she stopped to face him. "Do you have any medicine for it?"

Oh, yes, and I'm looking at her. "I'm sure I'll figure out something to help the burning go away." He continued to focus on her mouth. Only one thing could stop the blazing inside his heart. He took a tentative step toward her, his racing heart just inches from hers.

As if second guessing him, she blinked several times and looked away. "I wonder what caused it? The root beer maybe?"

"There's only one thing I know of that could cause an ache like this." He waited for her to ask what, his mouth parted in readiness for the kiss. When she didn't comment at all, his mood soured.

Instead of following the course of conversation he'd hoped for, she changed the subject. "It's getting late—"

She started walking again. She acted almost afraid to be alone with him. What was he? Some sort of ogre? "—and after the day I've had, I'm hoping to get to bed early."

Alone, no doubt.

He followed along sullenly.

Already dressed for church, Jeri showed Frankie where to hide. "Stay right here and don't make a move until you hear the attic door drop shut. When you do, sneak up the stairs and lock it." She handed her the old-fashioned skeleton key she had swiped off the front desk. "But be real quiet about it. I don't want her knowing what you've done."

Frankie stood in the narrow stairwell that led up to Miss Hattie's bedroom, her eyes so wide Jeri worried they might pop. As expected, Frankie didn't ask her any questions. She had decided long ago it was just a lot safer not to know everything that went on inside everybody's head—especially Jeri's.

"All this because you think your dad wanted to kiss her last night on the way home?" Frankie wanted to know. "Don't you think you are overdoing it a little?"

"No. As soon as you have locked the door, go back downstairs, put this key in the little ceramic cup on the desk, the one with the blue chickens painted on it, then wait for me in the parlor."

Ever faithful, Frankie slid the key into her skirt pocket then nodded that she understood. Clearly, it was Sunday morning. Like Jeri, the only place where Frankie ever wore a skirt was to church.

"You stay put." She rubbed her eyes until they had to be all red, then pinched her nose till it ran. "I'll go get her." She nodded one last time to Frankie, then scampered away.

Paige was still in her dressing robe when Jeri knocked on her door and she finally answered. Jeri sniffed loudly the minute she looked down at her.

"What's wrong?"

"I forgot to pack my Bible, and I can't find the one

Miss Hattie told me was in the attic. And she's already left so she could put all those flowers out before everybody gets there.'' She sniffed again. ''I have to have a Bible. We always read verses in Sunday school. Do you have one I could borrow?''

Paige shook her head and knelt, grimacing as if that had caused her all kinds of pain. Sore from yesterday, no doubt. ''No, I'm sorry, but I don't have one.''

Didn't think so. She sniffed again. ''But I have to have a Bible.'' She paused for added effect. ''Maybe you could go up into the attic and help me find the one Miss Hattie said was up there. She said I'd find it in the trundle. But I don't even know what a trundle is.''

Paige looked like she was completely taken in when she explained, ''A trundle is something made so it rolls. They make trundled beds. Was there a bed up there?''

Jeri nodded vigorously. ''But then why would she put a Bible in a bed?''

''You're right. That doesn't make sense. Maybe there's a trundled trunk up there. Were there any trunks?''

Again Jeri nodded vigorously. ''More than one.''

''Any of them have wheels?''

She shrugged, then sniffed again. ''I never noticed.''

Paige glanced at her watch, then out into the hall, clearly worried she wouldn't have time to finish getting ready to go with them to church. ''Where is the attic?''

As soon as she'd asked that, she gripped the door frame with both hands to pull herself back up, acting more like someone close to eighty years old than twenty-seven.

''Come on. I'll show you.'' Jeri headed immediately for the narrow stairs that led up to the room that had once been Anthony Freeport's bedroom. They were stairs similar to the ones going up to Miss Hattie's room at the other end of the house where Frankie now hid, only these were steeper.

Paige followed without further question. It wasn't until they were both inside and she noticed the setup that she said anything else. "Are you sure this is the attic?"

"Yeah, Miss Hattie said that when her fiance and his family lived here a long time ago, that this was his room. He liked it up here where he could look out the window and see every bit of Sandy Cove." She pointed to the only window low enough that a person could peer out of it.

"Sandy Cove?"

While Paige's attention shifted to the window, Jeri dropped the door into place. If Paige thought that was strange, she didn't say.

"Sandy Cove is that gated cove over near the village. Want to see it?" She crossed over to the tall, narrow window that was never used anymore. It had been so long since anyone had opened it at all, it didn't even have a screen; and it took her five minutes and a kitchen knife to break the seal. As soon as that was broken, she hurried to open it, hoping the sounds from outside might help drown the click of the lock as Frankie turned the key on the other side of the door. "See? Over there. Just the other side of Jimmy's garage. That's Sandy Cove."

Paige stood beside her for a moment looking out, then finally turned to survey the room. She noticed the bed first, and frowned. "That's definitely not a trundled bed."

"It's not?"

"No. But that is a trundled trunk." Paige moved slowly over to the trunk nearest the dresser. It was in the area of the L-shaped room that received the least light.

"But that trunk is always kept locked." Jeri sat on the bed and waited for her to give up looking for a Bible so they could move right on to the next part of her plan. "That can't be where it is."

Pained, Paige gave a tiny whimper when she knelt before the large, dusty leather bound trunk, then to Jeri's surprise, lifted the lid. There on top was a Bible. "Here it is."

Jeri sat forward, unable to believe that not only had she opened a trunk no one had opened in years—not since

Miss Hattie had misplaced the key—she had found a blessed Bible right on top. Did Miss Hattie find the key and not tell anyone?

Reluctantly, Jeri accepted the small Bible from Paige. She felt guilty as could be when she spotted the name Anthony Freeport in gold letters at the bottom. This was that dead man's Bible. The one who was supposed to come back from the war and marry Miss Hattie but had died a hero instead. She shouldn't be bothering with a dead man's personal things. It wasn't right.

But she'd gone too far with the plan to turn back now. If she admitted what she'd done just so she could put the Bible back, Paige would use it against her. Then she'd never get the woman to leave. There was nothing to do, but go through with it.

Continuing forward, she glanced at her red sports watch that didn't exactly go with the dark blue skirt and blouse she had on, but it was the only watch she'd thought to bring. "And, look, you still have time to go back downstairs and finish getting dressed."

Setting the Bible down gingerly on top of an old Army trunk, she bent to open the door. Sure enough, Frankie had done her job. It wouldn't open. "Something's wrong." She put just the right amount of panic in her voice. "I think maybe the door is stuck again."

"Again?" Paige had just now managed to get back to her feet and cross the room.

"Yeah, sometimes in the summer this door sticks for some reason." She gave it a really hard yank for effect. "And I think maybe this is one of those times."

"What'll we do? Should we try calling for your father?"

Oh, no, don't do that! "No point in it. He wouldn't be able to hear us if we did. This house is built like an old fort. Looks like I'll have to climb out the window and go down the tree and get help."

"The tree?"

Paige walked stiff-legged back to the window, like one

of those mummies in an old horror movie. Was she really that sore from yesterday's bike ride? Or had that tumble she took on top of her father hurt her in some way? *Or* was God just getting even with her for being such a weasel? Imagine, trying to use a nice little girl like her just to get at her father.

"But that can't be safe," Paige interrupted, bringing her thoughts back around.

"Sure it is. I've climbed down that tree lots of times. Just because you are a big scaredy-cat afraid of heights doesn't mean everyone is. Just watch."

Having said that, Jeri slid out the window, walked across the sloping roof to where a tree limb grew within a few feet of the house, and kicked off her Sunday shoes. Tossing them to the ground along with her footie socks, she sat down at the roof's edge, then reached out to grab the sturdiest part of the limb.

"Come back here. You'll hurt yourself."

"No I won't. I'll be right back." Then, as easy as could be, she swung herself over onto the limb and started shimmying down. She grimaced when she realized there was one little detail she had overlooked. The fact that she'd never climbed down this tree in a dress before. She gritted her teeth against the sandpapery feel of the bark against her skin.

Within minutes, though, she was on the ground and had her socklets and shoes back on. She plucked off the leaves and sticks she had collected along the way, then waved at Paige, who stood at the window pale as the ghost that Batty Beaulah swore haunted Seascape.

Looked like the woman really *was* afraid of heights. Good. *That* oughta keep her right there in that attic all day. Or at least until Miss Hattie returned late that afternoon.

Shaking her head at how much trouble a faulty memory could get a kid in, she grinned while she hummed the same hymn Miss Hattie had been humming earlier, all the while trying to figure out all the ways she could keep her dad gone. She stopped at the parlor just long enough to tell

Frankie they'd be leaving in just a minute, then hurried upstairs to knock on her father's door.

"You ready?"

"Almost. Come on in while I finish tying my tie."

He leaned in toward the mirror and made all kinds of weird faces while looping the tie this way and that until finally, it slipped right into place. As soon as he snapped the clasp in place, he reached for his water blue coat. "Go tell Paige it's time."

He gave the mirror one last glance.

"Don't have to. I already talked to her. She's not feeling too well right now." Still had to be pretty pale after watching her climb down that tree. "She's going to have to skip church today, but she wants to meet us at the cafe for lunch afterward." Wants to, but won't get to. "If she doesn't make it there by twelve-thirty, we are to go ahead and eat without her."

"She's ill? I wonder if there's something we can do for her." He closed his door and, instead of heading for the stairs, headed toward Paige's door.

Jeri's heart slammed into her ribs with a solid force, as she hurried to head him off. "I already asked that. There's not much anyone can do for her. She just needs to stay in awhile." She tugged on her father's arm. "Come on. We need to get on downstairs. Frankie is already here waiting on us."

Damon hesitated a moment longer, then finally went with Jeri. If he suspected anything was up, he didn't show it when he greeted Frankie a few minutes later.

Jeri felt little remorse while the three of them took the ocean trail toward the village. After seeing the way Paige had lured her father into nearly kissing her yesterday on the trail back to the inn, Jeri knew the big faker had gotten exactly what she deserved. Paige never should have come there wanting to horn in on her Dad like that, and she never should have lied to her to do it. A person like that deserved to be outsmarted.

Quite pleased with herself, Jeri crossed her arms proudly

while walking between her father and her friend. She'd sure put one over on that lying witch.

"Life is good," she couldn't help but say aloud.

"Yes it is," her father agreed, taking a deep breath. "We couldn't ask for better weather." He glanced up at the sunshine trickling through the trees. Except for a few clouds off over the ocean, the sky was one big patch of bright blue today. "It's a shame Paige has to be stuck indoors on such a beautiful morning."

Jeri blinked at his choice of words. "Yeah, too bad she's stuck like that."

Frankie coughed. Twice.

"I hope she feels better in time to join us for lunch. I thought maybe while you two kids were off looking for new shells, or digging for worms, or whatever it is you plan to do this afternoon, I'd show Paige the view from the top of the Seascape lighthouse. On a day like today, we ought to be able to see most of the islands." Dropping his gaze back to the path ahead, he frowned, as if he thought something just wasn't quite right. After that, he slid his hand up under his coat tail and patted his back pocket. "Uh-oh."

He slowed to a stop.

"What's wrong?" A crawly feeling slithered through Jeri's stomach. She didn't need any uh-oh's right now.

"It looks like I forgot my wallet." He studied his empty hand, baffled. "I could have sworn I picked it up and slid it into my pocket right before I put on my watch. But if so, it would still be here. The pockets in these pants are way too deep for it to slip out unaided."

"Are you sure it's not in the other pocket?" Jeri asked, praying it would be. If it wasn't, he might suggest going back for it. By now, Paige had probably figured out she'd been left behind and would be making all kinds of noise.

Still frowning, he checked the other pants pockets, then patted those inside his coat. "Nope, not there either." The notches in his forehead folded deeper. "I was certain I'd picked it up." He turned, glancing down the trail behind them, then at his watch. "I have to have money for the offering, and money to pay for lunch." He sighed with frustration. "You two go on ahead to Sunday school. I'll be back in plenty of time to join you for the main services."

"*No, Dad, you* go on to Sunday school. *We'll* go back and get your billfold. I know right where you keep it," Jeri insisted, her blood pumping at such a fast rate, it made her heart hurt. "I'd hate for you to miss even part of Reverend Brown's lesson. He said it was going to be a real good one, remember?"

"Sorry, Frankie's parents wouldn't like that. You two go on. I'll be back as quick as I can." Smiling at what he probably thought was her generosity, he patted her lightly on top of the head, then took off walking swiftly back the way they'd just come.

"What's wrong?" Frankie asked in a harsh whisper, keeping her voice low even though Jeri's father was already far enough away he wouldn't have heard her even had she talked in her normal voice. "You look scared to death. Just what did you do to that woman?"

Jeri didn't have time for explanations. "We have to follow him."

❦ *Chapter 10* ❦

"Paige?" Damon heard her cries for help long before he saw her. "Where are you?"

"Here."

Having come up the front drive rather than cut across the damp, grassy field where he might have ruined his polished shoes, he didn't spot her until he'd rounded the front corner of the house. When he did, his heart twisted. Paige was up inside the massive branches of the largest of the ancient oak trees shading the south side the house—hanging on to one of the stouter limbs for dear life.

"What on earth are you doing up there? And dressed like that?" All she had on was a white dressing robe and one bedroom slipper—and whatever items might be underneath. He hurried closer.

"Falling," came the shaky, one word response.

Not with that death grip, she wasn't. But obviously she didn't know that. Seeing the stark fear that paled her, he already looked for ways to help her down. There were no limbs low enough on this particular tree to give himself a boost up. Nor any chairs in the garden or on the veranda that were tall enough.

He peered up at her again, as puzzled as he was panicked. Why was this woman outside wearing a flimsy dressing robe while climbing a mammoth tree like that in the middle of a Sunday morning anyway? Blair had never once mentioned that her sister might be just a'tad insane. "Didn't you tell me you were afraid of heights?"

"I am. Very." She whimpered.

Well, that certainly made this all the more logical. Still looking for a way up, he circled beneath the tree. Could he reach any of the limbs by jumping? He doubted it. "How did you ever get up there?"

"Don't ask so many questions." She spoke those words through clenched teeth. Whether they were clenched out of anger or fear, it was impossible to tell. "Just get me down."

Still looking up, he shook his head, amazed by her dexterity. It would take someone born part monkey to scale that tree without a ladder or spiked shoes. He had once seen Jeri wiggle up it inch-worm style, but he doubted his own ability to do the same. "I don't think I can get up there on my own, and even if I could, I doubt I'd be able to get you back down the same way. I'll have to have a ladder."

"Find one."

That time it was obvious. The fear in her voice was starting to give way to anger. Knowing that made him want to chuckle. It wasn't *his* fault she'd climbed up a tree and gotten stuck. It would serve her right if he called the volunteer fire department in to help. Old Robert Rutledge would get a big kick out of this one, not having had a good, hard laugh since the time Sheriff Cobb got his bottom stuck in the Blue Moon's bathroom window while trying to escape from the ever-persistent Miss Beaulah.

"But I'm not really sure where one is." He stroked his chin while he studied what he could of the two long, slender legs wrapped deftly around a sturdy tree limb. He didn't know which had a tighter grip, her legs or her arms. Both were folded nearly twice around. "I'm not even sure Miss Hattie owns a ladder."

There was a moment's pause, then, "Would it encourage you to go look for one if I told you that I'm bleeding?"

"Bleeding?" Suddenly all humor left him. He squinted to get a better look through the branches. He didn't see any blood, but that didn't mean there wasn't any. "Where?"

"My thumb. It has a big splinter in it and it's bleeding all over the place."

Relieved the injury was small, but still faced with the problem of getting her down, Damon glanced toward the garage. That's where most people kept their ladders. But then, Miss Hattie wasn't most people.

"I'll be right back," he assured her, already on his way.

"Now where have I heard *those* choice words before?" she muttered in a voice barely loud enough to be heard.

"What was that?" He paused, not sure he had heard right.

"Never mind. Just go find a blasted ladder."

To Damon's relief, the garage indeed held a ladder. Within minutes, he was back at the tree with the device extended and propped into place.

"I'm coming," he told her unnecessarily. Her gaze hadn't left him since his return. Quickly, he tugged out of his coat and folded it. No sense ruining a perfectly good dress coat. Nor his new shoes. "Just hang tight up there."

"Cute."

Despite the continued seriousness of the situation, he chuckled again when laying his coat over a nearby bush.

Paige didn't share his amusement. "You find this all very funny, don't you?"

"Well—" he started to give an honest answer, then thought better of it. "Of course not." He quickly stuffed his socks into his shoes and placed them on the ground near that same bush, then tucked his tie into the front of his shirt. "I'm coming."

"Good, I'm in pain here. My arms are giving out and I'm starting to slip."

When Damon glanced up again and saw that she was right, all laughter left him. She really had started to slip.

Her strength was playing out. "How long have you been up there?"

He didn't wait for an answer. He hurried up the ladder then swung over to the limb just under her. Wrapping his legs around the sturdy bough and hooking them at the ankles, he stretched his arms as far as they would go. When he couldn't quite reach her waist, he grabbed hold of her hips instead. "I've got you now. On the count of three, you can let—"

Before he finished his instructions, her strength gave out. She dropped like a baby chicken flapping its useless wings in a futile attempt at flight. Damon was astonished he had the strength to pull her onto the limb with him where she again latched on for dear life. *Amazing what a guy could do when thoroughly panicked.* It was almost as if he'd had help pulling her over.

"Paige?" He waited until he was certain she wasn't going to fall again before offering her further instructions.

"What?"

"You can let go of my ear now." When she didn't respond right away, he tried again. "Let go of the ear in your right hand so I can sit up and get us the rest of the way down."

Finally she did as she was told. After he was upright again, and while the blood returned to his earlobe, he reevaluated the situation. Paige now had the limb in front of him in a tight bear hug with her beautiful butt hiked up and just inches from the trunk, like a playful kitten ready to pounce. During the fall, her robe had come open enough to reveal the top of a torn shimmering-beige slip underneath. What possible reason could she have to be outside up an oak tree so scantily dressed?

"We're just a couple of feet up from the limb where the ladder is. Do you think you can let go of this one long enough to reach for the other one?"

She turned to see what limb he meant, then lifted her head an inch to look at him. Nothing else about her moved. "Maybe."

Not yet having recovered from Paige's near-plunge to the ground, Damon waited until his own heart rate had settled more, then showed her how to move from one limb to the other without falling again. It took a lot of coaxing, but eventually he managed to persuade her to switch limbs.

"We're nearly there." Sitting, he scooted to where the ladder was still propped against the limb and, again, showed her exactly what to do to climb the rest of the way down to the ground. "Do it just like that."

He made sure she saw him safely on the ground, then climbed up again part way so he would be there to catch her should she slip.

"Come on. I'm here to help you the last of the way."

Although not willing to sit up like he had, she did manage to inch her way over to the ladder, her robe parting more with each movement. Once there, he helped pry her fingers off the limb so she could grip the ladder rails instead. Eventually, he talked her onto the ladder directly in front of him, and together they worked their way down one rung at a time.

He tried not to concentrate on the most obvious benefit of being her hero, which occurred each time he moved down a rung and then she slid into place in front of him. That felt far better than it should. Too bad he couldn't have found a longer ladder so they could have started at a higher limb. How he hated for this part of the rescue to come to an end.

But end it must.

The moment Paige's foot hit solid ground, she spun around to face him, all wide-eyed and grateful. He still had his protective arms around her, gripping the ladder rails. That kept them in very close proximity.

"Thank you," is all she said before suddenly she kissed him.

Not having expected it, Damon tensed, nearly bringing the ladder down on top of them. He managed to give the thing a last minute shove to one side, not really caring when it landed right on top of one of his favorite dress shoes then bounced over onto the other one.

Finally, he was having that kiss he'd longed for last night. And what a kiss it was.

Even though Damon had known Paige for ages, always before it had been as that skinny little kid who had once lived three blocks over. He hadn't known Paige to be the sexiest woman alive but for a couple of days. Still, it felt to Damon like he had waited for this particular kiss all his life.

Folding his arms around her, he accepted her offering eagerly. He pulled her hard against him as he pressed his mouth more hungrily to hers. His body absorbed all the warmth hers offered while he devoured her sweetness for the first time, filling himself with a need so strong and a passion so instantly vital, he felt its growth inside him.

Overcome with a virile desire too powerful to ignore, he darted his tongue past her soft, pliant lips to sample the more intimate areas of her mouth. When she allowed this sampling of the warmer, sweeter regions inside, he was like a man starved. He had to have more.

Continuing to hold her body pressed hard against his with a splayed left hand, he risked censure by sliding his right hand first across the gentle curves of her back then around to the front, where he tugged gently at the sash of her robe. It gave way easily, allowing him to push the torn white fabric away from her body, yet permitting it to hang loosely around her, cloaking her. Underneath, he discovered only a slip, panties and bra, all perfectly fitted to a firm, receptive body.

When she didn't pull away after having had her robe opened, his hand trembled only slightly when it slid back over the thin outer garment. Deftly, he searched for the clasp of the bra, hoping to work it right through the silky fabric. Then it occurred to him they stood out in the open where anyone passing might catch a glimpse of them through the trees. But he so wanted to feel her heated skin beneath his hand. So wanted to touch those parts of her that might eventually help him make her his. Yet he dared not. Not here.

But having gotten this far with a kiss bestowed out in the open like that encouraged his hope. Would she allow him to carry her inside and claim her as his? Or would the attempt jolt her away? If it did not, would she allow him to carry her all the way to his bedroom? Or should he take her only as far as the parlor? Which would she prefer? With no one home, it didn't matter to him where in the house he made love to her—as long as he did indeed make love to her before he exploded from his own need.

Still devouring her with hot, hungry kisses, he slid his hand back around to her rib cage where he paused while continuing to work up his courage. Testing her level of need, he slowly edged his hand upward, easing it toward one of the breasts he so longed to touch. His hope rose every higher with each inch his hand moved closer, then sank like lead when suddenly she tensed, as if he had just touched off some silent alarm inside her. Instantly, she gasped and pulled away. Her dark eyes were just as wide as before when she broke free of his grasp.

"Thank you," she told him between hard swallows. Turning away, she quickly tugged the robe back into place and retied the sash. Clearly, she hadn't meant to kiss him. Nor had she meant for him to try anything so forward as a result.

Not certain if that second thank you was another for having saved her from a dangerous fall, or a new one for how ardently he had responded to her kiss, he answered in a not too steady voice, "You're welcome. Anytime."

Both still dazed, they stood a foot apart staring at each other, until finally her attention darted off toward a section of forest just beyond the small pond, near where Seascape land divided from the neighbor's.

When she scowled at what she saw there, he turned in time to glimpse someone darting out of sight. "Who was that? Miss Beaulah?" Had to be. "Odd that she'd still be out there at this hour. She rarely misses church."

He thought about that more, then chuckled. With Paige dressed in a white, flowing dressing robe, Beaulah Favish must have thought she had finally found one of those ghosts she constantly stalked. The woman wouldn't leave her post for anything, even church, if she thought she might finally have her proof.

"I can't be sure who it was from this distance," Paige answered a bit too quickly—likely furious that someone had seen her during her moment of indignity. Her dangerous bout with the tree had not left her in the most jovial of moods. "But I think I know who it was."

Still recovering from that brief but volatile moment of passion, Damon gave the forest a second look. Nobody. Whoever it was had already left. Probably to go tell anyone who would listen about the ghost she'd just witnessed him pull down out of Miss Hattie's oak tree. What fun the folks at the Blue Moon would have with that.

Returning his attention to Paige, who had just bent to pick up a stray bedroom slipper, he admired the view a moment, then broached the question that had been nagging at him since he arrived there. "Are you ready yet to tell me why I came back here and found you stuck up in that tree?"

"How should I know why you came back here?" She straightened, her lost shoe in hand. Unlike him, she already had her breathing back under control. "I'm just glad you did."

She was dodging the issue. "You don't want to talk about it, do you?"

"No," she answered honestly, dropping the shoe so she could shove her foot back inside. "I usually try to avoid subjects that cause me to come away feeling like a total idiot."

He turned his attention to the tree again, then nodded. "Yes, I could see how this particular situation might have that tendency."

When she laughed at that, it surprised him. Just seconds

ago, she had looked ready to explode with anger. "The explanation would only disappoint you."

Her smile was back. Warming him to his very toes.

He tried not to be worried by that. "Try me."

"The simple truth is, I managed to get stuck in the attic after everyone was gone and, when I couldn't pry the door open, I decided to give climbing down the tree a try."

He glanced up at the window to the attic and saw that it was indeed open and screenless. Next he noticed the windows to her room. They, too, were open, though not screenless. "Why didn't you just climb down to your room and go in there? All you would have had to do is pop off one of the screens like I did the other night, and climb inside."

Her mouth flatlined the moment she looked up at the windows and saw them still open, a light breeze tugging at the curtain sheers.

"I didn't think of that." She turned to glower at him.

"And you aren't too happy with me for having pointed it out to you either," he surmised, disappointed her smile hadn't lasted longer.

She let out a heavy breath. "Right now, I'm not too happy about anything." She gestured to her tattered, dirt-streaked white robe. "I need a bath. I itch all over, and I still have a splinter lodged in my thumb."

"Want me to help?"

She glanced down at her thumb apprehensively. "Getting the splinter out?"

He couldn't resist. "No, getting rid of all the dirt and the itch. I remember once being pretty good at helping people with their baths. When Jeri was little, I used to have to help her sometimes. Especially with the getting undressed."

She cut him a look of warning. "I do think I can handle the bath part just fine."

"Even with an injured thumb?"

"Yes, even with an injured thumb." Already she headed for the front of the house, limping slightly. Evidently, she'd strained something during her brief affair with the tree.

"Can I at least help you get rid of the splinter?" he called after her, running to grab up his coat, socks and dented shoes so he could keep up with her.

She paused on the veranda and glanced back at him. "Yes, if you can find a clean needle, you can help me get rid of the splinter."

"There should be one in Miss Hattie's sewing box in the kitchen. I'll be right up as soon as I've found one. Be sure to leave the bathroom door unlocked."

She cut him one more scathing look, then disappeared inside the house.

Paige did not trust the mischievous gleam she'd detected inside the brilliant blue of Damon's eyes. Not yet having recovered from that amazing kiss, she was very careful to lock the bathroom door before slipping out of her clothes and into a soothing tub of hot, soapy water.

Leaning back slowly, for every muscle in her body screamed in protest, she rested her shoulders against the large, oval tub. She stared first at the small windows overhead then at the chest high cabinets that divided the raised bathtub area from the sink area while still contemplating the explosive kiss she'd shared with Damon.

She hadn't meant to kiss him, but something about the situation had prompted her to do just that. Was it gratitude for having just been saved from danger? Or was it something more?

Her blood sped at the memory of the passion they'd shared. How embarrassing that she had prompted such provocative behavior from him. She certainly hadn't meant to. Or had she? Why else would she have responded so enthusiastically to his touch?

Mortified by what she'd done, she shook her head to try to erase that memory while next she recalled what had caused her to end up in such a vulnerable position to begin with. At first she was furious with Jeri for what she'd done, and could hardly wait to get the little imp alone so she could tell her exactly what she thought of her little prank. She plotted ways to give the girl a good strong dose of her own foul medicine by doing something equally dreadful to her.

Blair or no Blair, she'd put up with that child's antics long enough. It was time for some good old-fashioned revenge. But before she could decide just how to go about getting even, the hot water had slowly worked its wonders on Paige's sore muscles, and her outrage gradually gave way to concern.

It was pretty clear now that the child viewed Paige as a far worse threat than imagined. First, Paige had suffered that angry outburst in the parlor because of it. Then, Jeri had purposely left her behind on the winding trail to the cove knowing she would become lost. And today, this. Paige bent to examine the splinter in her thumb. Although she had pulled part of it out with her fingernails, a fragment remained deeply imbedded. Putting gentle pressure on the area with her mouth, she leaned back again.

What made today's little incident as disappointing to her as it was confusing was the fact that she thought she and Jeri had made such headway the day before. During the long ride back from the cove, Jeri remained withdrawn, but the anger she had shown Paige earlier had dissolved.

Or so she'd thought.

What had triggered this latest incident? What could she possibly have done to make the girl try something as cruel as locking her inside the attic, then leaving the house? It couldn't have been anything she'd done after their return from the village last night. She had been too exhausted after her long day. She had gone on to bed almost immediately, leaving Damon and Jeri to share their evening alone. Jeri should have enjoyed that, what with the way she loved to monopolize her father's time—and with good reason. Damon was a great father to Jeri, and gave her his undivided attention when they were alone together. Something that continued to amaze her.

Still trying to figure it all out, Paige thought back farther, to the incident in the cafe. After several hours of getting along with everyone, Jeri had exploded in anger simply because her father had made it clear that she and Paige were to spend Monday together. Was *that* what had caused Jeri to lock her in the attic? Did Jeri blame *her* for what clearly was someone else's decision?

That was hardly fair. But then at twelve years old, it was hard for a girl to know what was fair and what wasn't. Jeri didn't even know the proper behavior for a twelve year old. That was the whole reason Paige was there.

Sighing, Paige sank lower into the gently caressing warm water. How could she ever teach the girl to act like the young lady her father wanted her to be if she was so violently afraid of growing up? Didn't Jeri understand the changes lying ahead for her were perfectly normal? Obviously not.

"Poor kid."

Although Paige's own youthful fears had been of a different nature, she fully understood the confusion Jeri felt inside. Twelve was such an emotional age. It was a shame the kid had to stumble through that without a mother's support. Paige knew only too well what *that* was like.

"So now what?"

She slapped at the water in frustration sending tiny ripples in all directions. Before she could hope to convince Jeri to do any girl-type things with her, she first had to find some way to *make* that child like her. Jeri had to accept her as a friend, even if it meant Paige forcing herself to do some of the incredibly loathsome things Jeri liked to do. And possibly include her friend, Frankie.

"That's right, Brockway. Time for a whole new approach." Instead of forcing Jeri to go shopping with her, or attend a local craft show, or talk about such things as upcoming fads and fashions, she would let Jeri take the lead. For awhile, Paige would do whatever disgusting thing Jeri wanted to do—whether Damon fully approved or not. Once a pattern of sharing time together was established, she could start slipping in the things she wanted to do, discreetly bringing the child around. The best way to bring out the budding woman in a girl like Jeri was for Paige to ease her way in after it.

Too late now for church, Damon changed out of his torn trousers to a pair of jeans with an open-neck pullover shirt—*very* careful to slip his wallet deep into the right hip pocket. He still had a hard time believing he'd left it. If it weren't so absurd, he'd think someone picked his pocket and returned his wallet right back to where it had been before. But then again, he was approaching the age where the memory started to go. And as bad as he hated it, he was having to use his eyeglasses more and more. What would go next? His hair?

He shuddered at the thought. Once the looks started to go, and having fallen so short in the personality department, he would have nothing left to attract people to him. Especially people like Paige, used to being around fashion model types all day. Life would sure get lonely when the only folks left who paid any attention to him were those who worked for him. Overloaded with his usual insecurity, he slumped his shoulders and headed back downstairs to find that needle in Miss Hattie's sewing basket.

After singling out one the appropriate size, he notched it through a corner of his ribbed shirt collar so he wouldn't lose it then headed back upstairs to check on the attic door. It could be awhile before Paige came out of the bathroom ready for him to remove that splinter. He might as well make good use of his time.

Walking along the second floor hallway, headed for the narrow staircase that led to the attic door, some little devil stirred inside Damon, making him walk out of his way to give the bathroom door handle a playful jiggle. He had only wanted to give Paige a quick cause for alarm by making noises at the entry, and was surprised when the handle turned easily and the door came open.

After the frightened way she'd retreated from that kiss

outside, he had expected her to lock the thing and seal it shut.

"Damon!" The shriek came from somewhere back in the tub area the second he took his first faltering step inside. He then heard a sharp splash followed by a strangled, "What do you think you are doing?"

Dumbfounded, he stood in the sink area staring in her direction but unable to see her over the tall cabinet divider. The door had been left unlocked. Was she expecting him to come in? If so, was it so they could take up where the kiss outside had left off? "I-I'm not sure."

"How'd you get in here?" Her head rose high enough to allow her to see him over the top of the cabinets. Her brown eyes looked stretched to their limits.

"I, ah, turned the handle then gave the door a little push." He pointed in the direction of the still open entry, though he continued to meet her startled gaze. What was with that look of alarm? If she didn't want him there, why hadn't she locked the fool door? Especially after he had hinted to her he might try something.

"Well, you can just close it right back. Now."

Wanting to help, he quickly obliged.

"Da-mon, I meant with *you* on the other side." She rolled her eyes and sank back out of sight. "How did you manage to get a key to the door?"

"Key? Why would I need a key? It was unlocked."

"Oh, no it wasn't." There was that head again. "I was very careful to lock it before I took off any of my clothes."

He glanced at the referenced pile of clothing only a few feet from where he stood, particularly interested in the lacy scrap of material she used for a bra. Hardly enough garment to make it worth the effort. Nor was the matching scrap of lace-edged silk panties so flimsy it wouldn't hold up against a hard sneeze.

So that was the kind of underwear a New York fashion designer wore. He quirked a devilish grin and looked toward her again. Would she be at all interested in seeing what kind of underwear a struggling building contractor wore? "Looks like you weren't careful enough."

Intrigued by her predicament, he stretched his neck and took a tiny step in her direction, wanting to chuckle at how quickly her head dropped back out of sight and was followed by a soft muttering. Maybe she really did think she'd locked the door.

He took another step.

"Don't come over here! I'm naked."

"I'm *not*."

She popped her head back high enough that he could see her eyes again. She looked more worried than ever. "What does that have to do with anything?"

"Nothing. I just thought you were wanting to point out our various differences. You're naked," he spoke calmly, pointing in her direction. "I'm not." Gesturing to himself, he took yet another tiny step forward. "You're wet. I'm not."

He continued pointing to her first, then to himself, each time taking another tiny step forward. "You're squeaky clean by now. I'm not."

Again, he stretched his neck to catch a better glimpse over the cabinets. He was close enough now, he saw down to the tops of her smooth shoulders. "And you're mad as hell." Grinning, though he tried not to, he pointed to himself again. "I'm not."

"Damon, I'm warning you." She ducked out of sight again, water swishing. "I don't have a towel over here. Don't you dare come any closer."

"Or what? You'll scream? I don't think there's anyone around close enough to hear you." He ached just knowing he was in the same room with her nude, and she had nothing to use for cover. "I could be wrong, though. You might try it."

His blood raced hotter and faster with each tiny step forward. Just the other side of those cabinets was a very beautiful, very naked woman with a sexual presence powerful enough to make his knees buckle. Why, he'd barely survived that kiss outside. What man in his right mind wouldn't try to take a peek?

He heard water splash again. Was she getting out? Without having been given a towel to cover herself? Surely not.

Close enough to the cabinets to rest his hands on top, he tiptoed forward again just in time to see her turn around and pop up out of the water as high as her dimpled behind—then a curtain disappeared back into the water with her. Submerged again, she didn't turn to face him until she had the pink material wrapped securely around her.

She met his interested gaze with an angry glower. "Now, will you please explain to me again what you are doing in here?" If looks ever turned physical, Damon would be on a critically injured list.

In an attempt for quick redemption, he pulled the needle out of his collar and held it up so she could see. "I've come to remove your splinter like the helpful hero that I am. Remember? You said I could."

She didn't have to know he was as shocked as she was to find that door unlocked.

Paige didn't look too impressed with his valor. "Can that possibly wait until I'm through with my bath?"

"Sure, it can." Pressing down on the top of the cabinets with the heels of his palms, he lifted himself high enough to sit on top Indian style. "I can wait till you are through."

When she shifted to her knees, as if debating getting out, Damon swallowed hard with anticipation. Apparently Paige had no idea that water made that pink material practically transparent. While she kept one hand bent around behind her holding the gap in back closed, she used the other to push herself the rest of the way out of the tub. Water sheeted down her body, molding the thin cloth tighter against her supple form.

What Damon saw before him then was almost too much for a mortal man to bear. It was a good thing he sat with his legs crossed in front of him.

Chapter 11

Paige could not remember ever being more angry, or more turned on in her life. There she stood with only a wet, ruffled Pricilla curtain panel around her, all alone inside a warm, cozy bathroom with the very man she'd fantasized about for most of her life sitting just yards away, staring glittery eyed at her.

How much more adrenaline could one body possibly pump without causing some sort of permanent damage?

"You could at least turn your back," she told him as she stepped onto the crescent shaped white mat. While she studied him cautiously from only a few yards away, her heart thumped so hard and fast against the walls of her chest she feared it would self-destruct. Why didn't the man at least blink?

"I'd rather watch."

With one arm still behind her, Paige pulled the edges of the wet material tighter while she looked around for a towel. Yesterday there had been one on the rack near the tub. Today, though, there was none. She should have thought to bring one with her from her own closet. After all, she'd been told that was what they were there for.

"But I would rather you didn't watch," she countered, even though it wasn't altogether true. If she weren't so sore from all that exercise yesterday, she just might be tempted to put on quite a show for him. But titillating him was out of the question. Not just because every muscle in her cried in agony with each tiny movement she made, but also because of where such a spectacle could lead.

No, titillating Damon from a distance as a cruel way to torture him was out of the question. There had to be a better way to retaliate against his brash behavior.

"Therefore, if you would just turn around," she continued, keeping a deceptively calm voice. "Or better yet, you could step out of the bathroom for a few minutes."

Damon's gaze remained riveted to the sopping wet curtain as if silently wishing the pink material away. "Oh, but I'm quite comfortable right here, and I like facing this direction."

Again she resisted the dangerous urge to retaliate. Instead, she slipped her other arm around behind her to make sure there would be no telltale gap in the material when she walked past him. "Okay, then you can continue to sit right there facing that direction while I move over into the other part of the room and slip my robe back on."

His mouth curled into an adorable pout. "Party poop."

Captivated by that boyish pout, Paige's blood shot hot trails through her, urging her to move closer. Instead, she pooled her resolve with a quick, unsteady breath, and limped quietly on past him.

Twice before she had made the mistake of giving her body to the wrong man. Once for all the worst reasons, and once for what had seemed like all the best reasons. She didn't need to make that sort of mistake again—for *any* reason. Especially when the partner in question was one well known for using women for his own pleasure, then tossing them aside—including his own wife, the woman who'd given him his only child.

A man truly had to be self-serving to do something like that. Paige would do well to keep that in mind. She certainly didn't want to end up as devastated as Damon's poor ex-wife must have been when suddenly she became little more than yesterday's news.

No pleasure was worth that.

She sighed as she glanced at her discarded clothing. If only there were an easy way to convince her rebellious body of that fact. Never had she felt such an aching desire to make love to a man. With Damon's many years filled with experience, he had to be one fantastic lover.

"It'll take me just a minute," she said, still watching him closely, making sure he didn't turn around at the last minute to see her peel off the wet curtain and slip into her robe. "Promise you won't turn around."

"I'm now on my best behavior," he vowed. Obediently, he sat with both hands resting in his lap, still facing the bathtub. His back was stiff while his breaths came in quick, shallow bursts. Obviously, he'd recognized how very close she had come to forgetting herself.

Determined not to be affected by the unexpected fact that he obviously desired her, she turned her back to him.

Still clutching the Pricilla curtain as tightly as her tender muscles allowed, she caught a glimpse of herself in the large wall mirror above the twin sinks as she prepared to bend down and pick up her robe.

She sucked in a sharp breath, horrified.

What was the point of making him stay turned around when he had already seen everything about her? The wet material she held so tightly around her body revealed every private detail.

No wonder his eyes were about to bug right out of his head. With her arms bent around behind her to hold the material together like that, her shoulders had arched to give a proud display.

"What's wrong?" he asked without turning around to look. "What made you gasp?"

"You could have told me," was all she could answer, still staring at her reflection, mortified.

"About what?" He sat with his back just a little straighter than before. Was that supposed to make him look guiltless?

"About the effect water had on the curtain."

"Oh." His shoulders shook. *The scoundrel!* "That?"

"Then you did notice." How could he not?

"Sure I noticed. Fine view." He drew in a long, slow breath, then forgot his vow to behave himself and turned to face her again. His eyes glistened with far more than amusement when he dropped one leg and let it dangle. "Damn fine view."

Startled by how profoundly she had affected him, for it was evidenced in his eyes, and his jeans, she dampened her lips and again regarded the possibility of making love to this gorgeous hunk of male right there on that thick, white bathroom rug. Who would ever know? Certainly not Jeri. After what that girl had done, it would be awhile before she dared show her face again. And not Miss Hattie. She wasn't due back at the bed and breakfast until mid-afternoon.

If only she weren't so sore.

Or so terribly afraid of reopening old wounds.

"Well, that's it." She bent to snatch up her clothing with one hand while still holding the practically worthless curtain in place with the other. "You've had your eyeful."

Spotting the empty shower stall, she marched inside and pulled the glass door closed with a bang, wincing at the pain that shot through her injured thumb still needing attention. "The show is over."

"Are you mad at me?"

"Yes." Turning her back to the glass, she peeled the cold, wet curtain away from her damp skin, annoyed to find the air inside the small chamber even colder. Her nipples tightened rock hard.

"But are you going to forgive me?"

"No."

Not about to try to wriggle her still damp body into her thin undergarments, Paige hooked the lingerie over the shower head long enough to shove her arms directly into her robe.

"Does this mean you'll never consider marrying me?"

"Damon?" She paused just long enough to tie her sash. "Do you truly enjoy annoying me?"

"Yes."

Securely in her robe again, she opened the shower stall where Damon now stood only a few feet away. Apparently he'd moved just so he could watch her shape through the cut-glass door. "Don't you have any scruples at all?"

"Nope," he answered, his playful grin back. "I used to, but I had myself vaccinated." His dimples sank deeper. "I'm now completely rid of the pesky things."

Moaning, she grabbed her remaining clothes and returned to her room, aware he followed as far as the hall, carefully watching her every step.

"So how come you didn't tell Dad about what I did to you yesterday?" Jeri asked Paige shortly after the two had arrived at the small pond in the grassy field just south of the inn. Carrying with them a tin bucket and two trowels, they had both dressed in denim shorts and sleeveless shirts. Jeri also wore a backwards bright red ballcap that didn't quite match the strawberry red in her shirt, and a pair of battered-white, marine-style canvas shoes. Paige, on the other hand, wore wide-strap white sandals that brought out the white design in her mostly yellow blouse, and a pair of brown-rimmed sunglasses designed to accentuate her heart-shaped face.

What a mix-matched pair they were.

"I didn't see any reason to tell your father anything." She waited for Jeri to set the bucket down and tell her where and how to dig. "What happened yesterday happened between us."

As repugnant as digging for worms and then fishing off a nearby floating pier sounded to Paige, if that's what Jeri wanted to do that day instead of riding out to Indian Point, then that's what they would do. By going along with the sort of activities the child truly enjoyed, Paige hoped to make Jeri finally like her. Besides, Paige didn't think her still achy muscles could take another extended bike trip so soon after that last one. She'd told Damon she'd much rather give fishing a try.

"I don't get it."

"What's there to get?" she asked. "The way I see it, you were the one who played that dirty trick on me. Your father wasn't involved in it." Though he had certainly played a few of his own dirty tricks since her arrival. Her heart drummed a fierce rhythm at the memory of that embarrassing incident in the bathroom. She had avoided Damon ever since. "So why should I bring him into it? Even though I'd appreciate an apology, I wouldn't enjoy one you were forced to make."

Jeri glanced at Paige briefly then, as if not understanding why there should be an apology, knelt to one knee to take a plug out of the damp ground with her trowel. She dug her fingers through the loose dirt, looked disappointed, then tried again. The second time, her fingers came out of the clingy dirt holding a big, fat, brown, wiggling worm. After a quick inspection, she tossed it and some of the dirt into the bucket. "So you don't plan to tell him ever?"

"Not unless he comes right out and asks how I came to be in the attic in the first place. I won't lie to him. But I also won't volunteer unsolicited information."

Jeri's blue gaze turned distant as if mulling that over while she dipped her fingers back into the freshly turned earth and a second later came out with yet another fat worm. Without looking at this one, she tossed it in with the first.

When all Paige did was watch the procedure, repulsed, Jeri sat back on her heels and pointed to the trowel still dangling from Paige's hand. "Aren't you going to help?"

Paige looked first at the trowel, then at the chosen ground, and then into the dented bucket where the two fat brown worms writhed. "Of course I am."

Having vowed to make Jeri like her, she, too, knelt to the ground not far from the water's edge. After whimpering from the sore muscles she still had, and from the uncomfortable feel of the damp earth sinking under her knees, she took a plug out of the ground and turned it over. She prayed for a barren hole as she raked a crooked finger through the sun warmed soil. "I also don't plan to tell your father that I know you didn't go on to church like you indicated you did."

"How do you know that?"

"I spotted you off near the woods soon after he helped me down out of the tree." Paige cringed when the tip of her finger came in contact with a soft, moving, wet object. Surrounding it lightly with her finger and bandage-covered thumb so as not to squish it, she pulled the tiny creature out of its hiding place and held it away from her. It wiggled indignantly in front of her. *Gross.* "And Frankie was with you."

"Is that why you kissed my father like that? Because you knew I was watching and you wanted to get back at me for what I did?"

So jealousy *was* at least part of the kid's problem. "No, I did it because I was grateful to him for having helped me safely down from that tree." She quickly tossed the worm into the bucket of then wiped her icky fingers on a nearby patch of grass. "I was terrified when I tried to climb down the same way you did and found out I couldn't. He saved me from falling and hurting myself. I never would have kissed him if it hadn't been for that."

Jeri's cheeks tightened. "So it was my fault?"

Afraid the child was about to go on the defensive and clam up, Paige jumped topics in mid-conversation. "What happened to make you do something like that?" she asked, careful not to sound accusing. "I thought for awhile there we had started to get along."

"I thought so, too. But I was wrong."

She waited for her to explain, then prompted, "So what went wrong between us?"

"Nothing." Jeri glowered as she eased her trowel into the earth again. "I don't want to talk about it. All I want is for you to go home."

Trying hard to keep in mind what it was like to be a

frustrated twelve year old, Paige studied Jeri's angry expression a moment, then resumed digging, turning the
earth one messy clump at a time. She poked at each one
with the tip of her finger. "Sorry, but I'm not leaving just
because you say you want me to. I promised your father
that I'd spend this coming week and part of the next with
you, and I will. The truth is we can't always have everything we want. If we could, my life would sure be a lot
different." She would have moved back to Mt. Pine ages
ago and already have a successful dress shop and maybe
even her own family. Had that happened, then perhaps she
would be having this thought-inducing conversation with
her own child instead of someone else's.

She glanced again at Jeri. What would it be like to be
a mother and have a daughter that age? *Challenging* was
the first word that entered her mind. But *fulfilling* occurred
second.

"Well, I happen to like my life just the way it is," Jeri
muttered, scowling so hard by now that her mouth puck-
ered nearly out of sight. "I don't want any part of it to
change."

Within that statement lay the crux of the child's problem. Jeri was afraid of change. Afraid of what would happen to the fixed pattern in her life should she become more
like her friends.

"I'm sorry, kiddo, but change is inevitable. And so often it turns out for the better." To Paige's chagrin, she
found another worm. This one fatter than the last. *What
luck*, she thought dismally. "Life would be pretty dull
without some kind of change every now and then, don't
you think? Change is what brings us tomorrow's little
treasures."

"Okay, if you are so all-fired hot about there always
being changes, then do me a big fat favor and *change* the
subject," Jeri muttered just before she, too, unearthed another worm. This time she stopped to play with it. "I'm
tired of listening to all this garbage about change and it
being good."

Glad the child hadn't ruled out talking to her altogether, Paige felt encouraged. Believing progress had been made, however small, Paige carefully extracted the worm she had just found, letting it dangle for a moment. This one didn't appear quite as outraged as the last. "So what would you rather talk about?"

"You leaving."

Paige sighed and tossed her worm on into the bucket. Talk about beating oneself against a hard wall. Suddenly, she understood what a racquetball felt like inside.

Later, she understood what an idiot felt like for, unlike Jeri and Frankie, who had mastered all the nuances of fishing that helped them bring in fish after fish, Paige had never fished a day in her life. To her discouragement, the first thing she caught was herself. In the rump. Twice. While trying to learn to cast off the end of the Co-op's pier.

The first time Paige snagged herself, Jeri and Frankie had proved merciful. Frankie had patiently extracted the hook while making soothing comments like, "That's okay, everyone does something like that at least once."

But when Paige hooked herself again only minutes later, this time yanking on the line so hard that she ripped a small hole in the back of her denim shorts, Frankie was no longer feeling magnanimous and had a field day with the duplicated blunder. She burst into a fit of giggles every time she caught sight of the jagged tear that exposed Paige's poor choice of bright pink underwear.

Following that embarrassing episode, Paige spent a full six minutes trying to reel in her first and only real catch of the day. When it turned out to be a tiny fish five inches long—barely larger than the fishing lure she'd used in lieu of a worm—Frankie couldn't ignore it. She had to tell everyone who came within earshot all about Paige's big catch of the day and how masterfully she'd reeled it in by nearly falling backward on her butt.

Being from a village whose livelihood came from the sea, everyone found Paige's obvious lack of skill remarkably entertaining. Everyone except Paige, who eventually stumbled while trying to liberate her treble-hook from a nearby boat and landed belly first in the brisk, salty water.

It was after she'd climbed back out of the water and gone right back to fishing that Frankie decided Paige was okay and kindly told her so. "Most folks I know would have given up after hooking themselves in the butt twice," she admitted, now grinning more with admiration than amusement.

Dressed in a pair of loose-fitting periwinkle-blue over-alls with a contrasting dark-blue, short-sleeve shirt under-neath, Frankie sat parallel to the uneven edge of the pier, her back hunched against a piling. Her knees were bent for comfort, and her bare feet pressed flat on the sun-baked pier. "You've got what my friend Hatch calls gumption."

Paige paused reeling in the borrowed lure she had man-aged to tie onto her broken line all by herself.

She stood only a few feet from where Frankie had gin-gerly unhooked yet another fish and dropped it back into the sea. They'd agreed early on to keep only those fish large enough to cook—although they'd kept Paige's fish in a small bucket for awhile just to point and make fun of it.

"Who's Hatch?"

"He's the old man who takes care of the old Seascape lighthouse." Frankie gestured to the quaint white and black structure that stood sentinel over a rocky finger of land that spilled out into the ocean. From the pier, only part of the adjoining house could be spotted through the dark evergreens and jagged boulders. "Hatch says you have to respect people who have gumption."

Paige smiled while she tugged a clump of cold wet hair off her cheek with a crooked finger. She liked the idea of having gumption. "He sounds like a very wise man."

"Oh, he is." Frankie glanced up at her and chuckled. She had stopped fishing long enough to pop open a can of grape soda, and turned it up for a quick swallow. "Even Hatch himself will tell you that. He once told me that nobody knows as much about life as old sea-dogs like him, and Hatch would never josh about something like that."

Laughing along with the sprightly little girl, Paige glanced over at Jeri hoping to find a similar glimpse of emerging admiration, but was sorely disappointed. Seated high atop a set of weathered pilings with her suntanned legs crooked around them for balance, Jeri kept her scowl while she continued to work her fishing reel like an expert. The child gave no quarter.

"What about you, Jeri?" Paige encouraged while she pulled uncomfortably at her still soggy clothing. She supposed the salt in the water was what made the blouse feel so icky against her skin. Now she wished she hadn't listened to Frankie and voted down fishing in the pond just so they would not have to use those worms she and Jeri had gathered earlier. Had she'd fallen into a fresh water pond, she wouldn't feel so sticky now. And her dry-clean-only blouse might have at least a small chance at survival.

"What about me?" Jeri asked, in one of her best how dare you bother me tones.

"Do you think Frankie is right? Do you think maybe I have gumption?"

"No. Not when I know *why* you haven't quit." She gave Frankie a look that clearly accused her friend of being a traitor. "I'm not as easy to fool as some people seem to be. I've seen your kind too many times."

Paige rested the end of her rod on the weathered planks of the floating pier. Was there more to Jeri's antagonism than simple jealousy? "And what kind is that?"

Jeri didn't answer. Instead, she swung her rod back and recast her line immediately after having reeled it in.

Paige studied the child's quick, forced movements, paying little attention to the soft sound of footfalls coming up behind them. The Co-op's main pier was a busy one and she knew so few of these people that she'd quit looking hours ago to see who walked by them. It wasn't until the footfalls stopped directly behind and the person spoke her name that her heart jumped up and introduced itself to her

Adam's apple. *Damon was supposed to be back at the inn still working.*

"What on earth happened to you?" he asked.

Though Paige had not yet turned around, she was pretty certain that question was directed at her. But unable to maneuver her Adam's apple with her heart still lodged in her throat, she couldn't answer right away. Instead, she closed her eyes a moment, well aware of what she must look like with her dark hair hanging in wet strings and her salt-ruined clothes a matted mass against her skin. Damon sure had a special knack of catching her at her worst. First in her bedroom while acting like a twelve year old, then next up a tree too petrified to move, then in the bathtub with only a curtain for cover—.

That last thought caused even less room inside her throat. Reminded of the embarrassing effect water had on certain materials, her eyes popped back open so she could check her wet clothing. Relief flooded her to see that, although the expensive blouse and the flimsy bra underneath were both plastered to her, the clothes together had not become transparent.

That gave her the courage needed to turn around. "Whatever do you mean?" She tried to sound casual while she kept a death grip on the rod she'd borrowed from Frankie.

Damon stood only a few feet away dressed in a pair of soft-textured faded blue jeans that cuffed over a pair of old, worn white with black cross-trainers. He had on an unbuttoned cotton shirt worn loose with the warm wind tugging at the pale blue material. And no belt. That allowed the jeans to ride dangerously low on his extremely masculine hips. Judging by the tan line peeking out from behind the waistband, Damon usually went without any shirt at all. Probably while working construction jobs, which also explained the sleek muscles that sculpted two very strong shoulders.

Studying how the smooth, rounded contours of his chest gave way to the solid, flat planes of his stomach, she noted the expanse of dark, springy body hair and how it narrowed as it trailed downward. Thinking of where that hair ended, Paige's stomach vaulted hard and fast, jamming her pulsating heart even further against her poor, defenseless Adam's apple. When he shifted his weight to one leg and casually hooked his thumbs into his front pockets, the white strip above his waistline widened. How much darker that body hair looked when contrasted against such pale skin.

Did the man not realize how erotic he looked standing there like that? Goodness, how she'd love to see him without that shirt—or those jeans.

"I mean you are soaking wet. What happened?" He cut a questioning glance to Jeri, as if he suspected her to have had something to do with Paige's current state.

"She fell in," Jeri stated, in ready defense. "I had nothing to do with the fact she now looks like some stupid drowned rat."

"Not all drowned rats are stupid," Paige said inanely and she quickly raked her fingers through her matted hair, wishing she'd gone on back to the inn to change. But then Damon wasn't supposed to surface again until nearly 4 o'clock. Thinking it quite unfair of him not to keep to his own schedule, she glanced at her watch. Just a little after three-thirty.

Or was it?

It was that exact same time the last time she checked. Peering more closely, she saw why. The second hand no longer moved. Her fall into the water had frozen her watch. She tried to catch a glimpse of Jeri's bright red watch, but couldn't with the child waving her arms wildly like that.

Having let Paige's comment pass so she could argue further with her father, Jeri asked, "Why is it that whenever something goes wrong around here, you always suspect me?"

"Because so many times, when something does go wrong, you have had at least some small hand in it. It's just your nature to act first then take time to think it through later, long after you've done your deed.''

Jeri narrowed her blue eyes. ''Well, I didn't do anything to Paige.''

This time, Paige thought while awaiting a chance to fit in a word of her own.

''I was sitting way over here when she fell in over there. Isn't that right, Frankie?''

''That's right, Mr. Adams. Jeri's innocent on this one. This time, Paige did it to herself.'' Her eyes rounded the second those words had left her mouth. Clearly aware of the implication, she hurried on so Damon wouldn't have as long to think about the slip. ''Paige was trying to unsnag her line again, and got a little off balance. It could have happened to anyone.''

Damon studied Frankie a long moment, then looked briefly at Jeri before finally returning his attention to Paige. ''You'd better go on and get cleaned up. We have that baseball game in just over an hour and I'm sure you won't want to wear a pair of torn, wet shorts for that.'' He held out his hand. ''Come on, I'll walk back with you.''

Paige wasn't sure if it was the thought of touching Damon again or the reminder that a small part of her carnation pink panties was exposed that caused her such a jolt. Probably a combination of both.

Choosing to avoid physical contact with the man for fear she'd melt right into the puddle of water at her feet, she pretended she hadn't noticed the proffered hand and turned to look at Jeri instead—Jeri, who might have gone ballistic had she taken that hand. The girl had made it perfectly clear she didn't want her around her father.

''But, Dad, I wanted to show you all the fish we caught.'' Jeri interrupted and gestured to the old, beat-up ice chest that Frankie had brought and filled with sea water for the keepers. ''Paige can go back by herself.''

''Not when I feel partly responsible that she's standing here soaking wet with that big rip in her clothes. If you hadn't insisted the two of you go fishing with Frankie instead of riding out to Indian Point together, she never would have shown how little she knows about fishing, and never would have fallen in.''

''How do you know she doesn't know anything about fishing?''

Damon lifted an eyebrow and looked at Paige again, water still trickling down the backs of her legs, spilling across the expensive leather sandals slowly tightening at her feet. ''I'd think that much was rather obvious.''

''Well, she could have said no,'' Jeri pointed out, not ready to take any blame for Paige's predicament. She curled her hands tighter around the rod.

''The point is, she didn't say no. And the reason she didn't is because you wouldn't let it go. You wanted to go fishing with Frankie and refused to accept any other option.''

He offered his hand to Paige again and, having had time to prepare herself for an intense response, and not wanting to be rude to a man championing her cause, she decided to chance Jeri's outrage and accepted it. Her pulses raced madly when his warm fingers closed around hers, stirring far more inside her than just her blood.

Stark images of what it had been like to kiss him yesterday fluttered about inside her head like butterflies undecided on their destinations. Still embarrassed, since she hadn't meant for anything like that to happen, she tried not to remember just how very much she'd enjoyed the kiss, or how very far she had allowed the kiss to progress. If she hadn't spotted Jeri's subtle movement over near the pond, there was no telling where that kiss would have led.

The thought of it both thrilled and terrified her. She was not ready to make that same heartbreaking mistake again. Damon was not the sort of man she would look for when the time came. He was more like what she'd vowed to avoid. ''Here's the rod your folks let me borrow.''

Frankie quickly stood and took it from her just as Damon gave Paige's arm a light tug and led her away.

''Dad, wait up,'' Jeri called after them before they'd gone far. ''I'll go, too.''

"No, you need to help Frankie put away the fishing supplies and carry that cooler of fish inside," he called back to her, glancing over one shoulder briefly. "And don't you usually stay and help clean them, too?"

Paige didn't hear an intelligible response, but gathered by the growling tone in Jeri's muttering that Damon had struck a nerve—and she knew just which one. Jeri was furious. Damon had just chosen to be alone with someone else instead of letting Jeri tag along. Oh, the repercussions *that* choice would cause.

When Jeri didn't try to follow anyway, as expected, Paige concluded that the girl usually did stay to help clean the fish, although Paige did not even want to consider what all *that* might entail. The mere thought of what it took to make those fish look like the ones bought in a supermarket made her wet toes curl.

To Paige's surprise and relief, Damon didn't speak again until after they had climbed the slope to the main road, well out of the girls' earshot.

"I came down to see if there was any talk about me going around, but found out all the talk was about you."

"Me?"

"Yeah, I figured Miss Beaulah would have started some really wild stories about how I'd wrangled her ghost down out of a tree yesterday; but when I stopped by the Co-op to chat with Frankie's mother, I heard that you were the one providing today's entertainment. Not me." His grin widened while he paused to look for traffic, then proceeded across, her hand still neatly tucked in his. "I arrived just in time to watch your not too elegant climb back out of the sea."

Wonderful. Now he had *that* image of her to carry around along with how awful she had looked as a gangly twelve year old. "Yeah, well, those rope ladders aren't exactly all they are cracked up to be."

Away from the constant noise of the water splashing onto the rock lined shore or against the wide, wooden pilings, the sound of her squishy sandals caught his notice and his smile shifted to a thoughtful frown. "Sorry you ruined your shoes and probably that blouse. Someone should have hinted that maybe you were just a tad overdressed for fishing."

Paige looked down at what had been a billowing, soft-textured blouse—now limp and sagging. Chances were Damon was right. The new blouse was ruined. She should have paid closer attention to what Jeri and Frankie had on. But then, those two always dressed in plain, unkempt clothing and who knew that fishing was such a messy, dangerous sport? Even before she fell in, she had torn her shorts and gotten her blouse wet twice. "I agree, someone could have warned me. But I have a feeling those two wanted me to learn my lessons the hard way."

He shook his head and looked forward again while they continued up the slope toward the Seascape Inn. "Just be glad you don't have any children of your own or you'd find yourself having to face that sort of thing every day. Having to deal with it every day certainly gets old in a hurry."

"I can imagine." She looked down again at her ruined blouse and tried not to think about what her hair must look like.

He waited till she'd braved another glance in his direction, then grinned again as he trailed his shimmering blue gaze over her sloshy, sodden form. "I must admit, you certainly do wear water amazingly well."

❧ *Chapter 12* ❧

"Crud! No matter what I do to that woman or how good I do it, she always manages to come out the winner." Disgusted, Jeri tossed her rod to the pier with a clatter. "How does she do that?"

Frankie pulled her gaze away from the shore. "Well, if hooking yourself in the butt twice and then falling in the water with all your clothes on while a half dozen people are watching is the same as coming out a winner, then I'd say she manages to come out that way by being a grade-A klutz." She picked up the rod Jeri just dropped and added it to the other two still in her hand. "You ready to call it quits?"

"No." Jeri's gaze narrowed while she stared after the two adults, now crossing the main road together, her dad dressed in his jeans, shirt and shoes, and Paige plodding along beside him in sopping wet clothes. Why her dad would want to hold hands with someone who looked like that was beyond her. It'd be like holding hands with the Swamp Thing. "I'm not giving up until she's gone."

Frankie sighed, temporarily returning Jeri's attention to her, and gestured to the ocean. "I meant the fishing. Are you ready to put all this fishing stuff away and clean the fish? Mom said she'd cook them for tonight's supper if we cleaned them before heading off to play baseball. Of course, you're invited to help us eat them."

"Can't come." Which was a shame, considering Frankie's Mom sure knew how to cook fish right. "I have to stick with those two as much as I can. You know I don't like it when they're alone together."

Frankie didn't try to argue her into coming. "After what happened yesterday, I can see why. Even from as far away as we were, I could tell that was some kiss. Definitely a PG-13. It maybe could have even been R rated."

Jeri cringed at the memory. Paige had squashed herself against her dad. And he'd let her. "How would you know?" She readjusted her ballcap. "You're only ten years old. Your Mom never lets you see anything like that."

"You forget. My cousin in California has cable," Frankie told her, grinning while she secured the hooks so they wouldn't swing out and catch anything. Unlike Paige, Frankie had learned the danger of a fishing hook a long time ago. "Remember, I was just out to see her a couple of weeks ago. Want to hear some of what I saw?"

"Not now." Jeri had seen enough R rated movies herself over at Amanda Harper's house to last her a lifetime— maybe two. Never could understand the interest in all that. "Right now, I want to hurry and get those fish cleaned so I can go on back up to the inn."

"So those two don't have too much time alone?"

"Right. I want to be up there by the time Paige gets cleaned up and into dry clothes. It bothers me enough that he's walking back alone with her—even though she looks like something a dog dragged out of the ocean during the worst part of low tide. I sure don't want them being alone together after she's had time to change her clothes and dry her hair again."

"I can sure understand that. Paige is what Hatch always calls a real looker. I figure she's one of the prettiest women I've ever seen."

Jeri scowled, then bent to get the two tackle boxes and the bucket of live bait they'd brought with them but hardly used. "Why is it that no matter what I do to the woman, it backfires? The whole reason I finally gave in and agreed to let her come along with us today is because what I wanted to do was keep her away from my Dad for the afternoon, and what happened?''

Frankie must have understood there was no need to answer as Jeri stood again and waved her free hand toward the inn, where for the time being her dad and Paige were hidden by a patch of trees. ''Somehow I ended up throwing them together instead. Just like when we locked her in the attic to keep her out of our hair yesterday. I don't get it. Where did I go wrong?''

''I don't know. Maybe where you went wrong was in hating Paige to begin with.'' Frankie frowned when she attempted to toss her long blonde braid off one shoulder with a quick flick of her free hand, but with so much force it slung all the way around and landed on the other. Rather than give it another try, she let it stay. ''You said at first that she was out to change you, but I don't see her doing anything like that. If anyone is trying to change anyone around here, it's you trying to change her. Could it be that the woman isn't as rotten as you think? She seemed like an okay lady to me.'' Gripping the three rods with both hands so they supported each other, she started toward the Co-op.

''Why?'' Jeri hurried to catch up. ''Because the woman didn't give up after falling in the water?'' What kind of reasoning was that anyway? ''Or do you think she's okay just because she pretended to like us first?''

''Pretended?'' Frankie shifted the rods to one hand so she'd have the other free to work the back door.

''Yeah, pretended.'' Jeri repeated in a quieter voice since there were always a few grown ups hanging around inside the co-op building that time of day. She didn't like the idea of anyone else listening to their conversation. ''Paige doesn't have me fooled like she thinks. Not like she does my dad. I happen to know that lady was just *acting* like she likes us because she thinks it will make Dad like her more.''

"Acting?"

Jeri nodded. "Women are always doing that sort of thing with Dad, pretending to like me just to score extra points with him. Paige is no different than any of the rest of them. It's just that she's hung in there a little longer." Jeri had to give her credit for that. "Most of the others would have tucked tail and run after being left to rot out in the woods, much less after then being locked in an attic filled with a lot of a dead man's personal things. But, no, Paige is after Dad and his money just like all the others were. She doesn't really care about me at all."

Afraid she was about to cry even though there was no reason to, Jeri put down the tackle boxes and took several steps back the way they'd just come. "No woman has ever cared about me. Not even my own mother. But then, you already know all about that."

"I care about you." Frankie propped the rods against a sign nailed to the wall, wiped her hands on the backs of her overalls, and followed. "That's why we're such good friends."

"You're not exactly a woman." With the threat of tears now gone, and thinking they might as well go on back for the fish since they'd both emptied their hands, she headed that direction. "And you won't be for years yet."

"But my mom is a woman and she cares about you."

"Good try, but your mom cares about *you*; and because I'm a friend of yours, she's nice to me. Kinda like Paige is trying to be nice to me because she cares about my dad." She waved her hands just before she came to a stop beside the old ice chest. "Adults are like that, especially women."

"Will we be like that?"

While looking down into the murky water and finding most of their catch looked like it was still alive, Jeri thought about that. "Geez, I hope not." She bent and poked at the two fish floating on the top to figure out if they were really dead or just playing like it. One splashed and disappeared behind the other fish while the other bobbed on the surface without flicking as much as a fin. Might as well clean that one first. "Maybe because we found out about this so early in life, we can do something to somehow keep ourselves from one day turning out like that."

Frankie bent to grab the handle on one end of the cooler then waited for Jeri to do likewise. "So what are you going to do about Paige?"

"I'm not sure. I've got to find some way to make her show Dad that she's faking." Jeri grunted when she picked up on her end. Those fish were heavier than she thought. "I've got to make Dad see for himself that the woman is just here to impress him with how good she can get along with me." Slopping water along the way, they headed for an outside wooden table where they could clean the fish then hose the mess into the water. "She probably hopes to con him into marrying her by pretending she'd make a good step-mother. I can't let that happen."

"But what if she isn't faking? What if she really is okay?"

"She isn't okay. She's a fake, and I am going to find some way to prove it to both you and my dad. Just you wait and see. I'll trip her up somehow."

As expected, Jeri did little more than glower at Paige all through the baseball game. When it came Paige's turn to bat, the girl's expression was rock-rigid while she pitched them hard and fast, twice coming very close to Paige's shoulder. Paige might have been more annoyed by the child's mean-spirited behavior if it weren't for the fact that when she didn't bother to swing at all those wild throws, she was allowed to advance to first base with very little physical effort on her part.

Since she was still a little sore at the tops of her calves from that bike ride two days earlier, being allowed to walk instead of run didn't bother her one bit. Nor did the fact that she had yet to work up a sweat like some of the others. Besides, with the game running so close—the score at the start of the last inning an even six to six—Paige was willing to accept any advantages given.

The only downside was that it seemed to bother Jeri more and more when she ended up walking her each time. Even though a few of the wilder ones were just a bit suspicious in nature, it was clear Jeri desperately longed to strike her out, especially that fourth time.

With Ricky following Paige in the batting order, there was a very good chance he would come along behind her and claim yet another good, solid hit. If he did that this time, Paige might have time to make it around for what could end up being the winning point. Paige's heart raced excitedly over that thought when she dropped the bat to one side and hiked straight to first base as it did when she glanced back at home plate and noticed Damon smiling at her.

"Oh, *man*, Jeri, you're giving it to them," little Bobby on first base complained, scrunching up his freckled face to show just how annoyed that made him. He let out a sharp breath when the disgruntled pitcher refused to look at him. "Shoot, what's wrong with you today?"

"Nothing." She still didn't bother to look at Bobby. Could be because Paige was over there, too. "Take a chill-pill, will you? So what if I let that one get by me? It's not that big a deal. I'm going to strike out this next one. Just you watch."

She waited until Millicent Thomas's thirteen year old grandson had finished making a few hard practice swings and stepped up to the plate before she took a careful wind-up and pitched one right over.

Ricky took a swing, but missed.

"That's a little better." Bobby nodded, but kept his pensive expression. "Maybe you haven't lost us this game after all."

"Me?" That comment must have struck a vital nerve. Jeri spun to glare daggers through the eight-year-old. The wind blew loose strands of blonde hair across her angry face. "Hey, I'm not the one who overthrew third and let them get that last point."

"I didn't overthrow. Andy wasn't watching. He was too busy looking back at someone who didn't even have the ball to see the throw coming from the person who did." Bobby nodded toward Nolene, who paid no attention to the exchange. She stood with her head tilted slightly to one side, smiling prettily at Andy on third base. Unlike the other two girls who had used sturdy rubber bands to bind their long hair, Nolene's was tied back with a pretty floral pink scarf and she had on enough hair spray, her puffed bangs lay perfectly in place.

Paige had to grin. The teen was clearly smitten with the handsome young man on third.

"Children, children," Reverend Brown called from where he and the rest of Frankie's team sat on the grass, waiting a turn at bat. He rubbed at his neatly cropped beard with a bent knuckle. "This is only a neighborhood game. We're supposed to be here having fun, not blaming each other for silly little mistakes made."

Damon nodded in agreement.

Jeri cut an impatient look at both, then nodded her own agreement. "Here comes another one, Ricky. Get ready to strike out and take the field."

After waiting for her dad's hand signal from directly behind home plate, she pitched this one a little high, but not too much. Paige's breath froze when Ricky acted like he wanted to take a swing at it, but didn't.

"Strike two," Damon verified needlessly. He stood to toss the ball back to his daughter. The afternoon breeze lifted his dark hair away from his always sexy face as he called out, "Good pitch, slugger. Toss him another one. All we need is one more out."

Even though the preacher was right, this was only a neighborhood game, Paige's heart continued to pound fast and hard inside her chest while she waited for that next pitch. Part of her hoped Jeri would get her strike so she'd feel better about the game, and about herself—for the child had enough frustration to deal with right now. Any more and the child might explode.

But another part of Paige hoped Ricky knocked that ball all the way into the next county.

She held her breath again, and waited. Ricky had come very close to connecting with that last pitch. Wanting to see if others looked as anxious as she felt, she glanced over at Frankie, whose keen attention shifted from Jeri to Ricky then back to Jeri.

Even the preacher sat with his hands clenched in fists. "Knock that ball straight to heaven!"

No one moved but Jeri when the wind up finally came. Then the pitch.

This one sailed far too high. But Ricky took a swing at it anyway, picking it right out of the air above his head to send it sailing in Nolene's direction.

It took Paige a moment to realize he had really hit it. When she did, she took off toward second base as fast and as hard as her sore legs allowed. When Nolene backed up to try for the rebound rather than run forward to catch the ball in mid-air, Paige took advantage of the extra few seconds and headed on around to third. She managed to plant her foot on the base just seconds before Andy stretched out and caught the ball in the very tip of his glove.

"Safe on third," Frankie called out, jumping excitedly. "Look at that. She's safe on third."

It was now Frankie's turn to bat. And what a turn at bat she had. When Jeri sailed the ball low and inside, Frankie swung hard and popped it over Jimmy Goodson's head. Nolene wasn't prepared to run for it, making Jimmy have to desert second base to rescue the ball.

By the time he snatched it up and sailed it high over Jeri's head, straight to Damon, Paige and Ricky had already crossed home plate with what turned out to be the winning two points.

Later, when Jeri's team came up to bat for the last time, Damon did manage to get one more hit, but it was caught in the air by Ross Rutledge on third base. After that, Andy

and Nolene struck out. Barney was so excited when Nolene took that last swing and missed, and little Bobby was
so disgusted, that the brothers threw their gloves into the
air at the exact same moment, but for far different reasons.

"All right!"

"Oh, shoot!"

"Gimme a gun and I will."

By the game's end, Fred Baker had finished up with the
Planning and Zoning meeting next door, and even though
it was his own daughter who Frankie had so determinedly
struck out there at the very last, he invited everyone to the
Blue Moon for complimentary sodas.

The offer of free soft drinks lifted even little Bobby's
spirits and there was no more mention of murdering his
brother. Jeri was the only one still brooding when they all
headed as a group around the front of the post office toward the Blue Moon. She walked with her shoulders
slumped, slapping her glove against her bare leg with
every other step she took.

Paige understood the reasons behind Jeri's glum mood.
Not only had the child just lost a baseball game—something to which she clearly was not accustomed—but only
a couple of hours earlier her father had opted to walk Paige
back to the inn rather than stay at the pier with her. That
couldn't have set well with a daughter who already felt
threatened. Paige should have insisted Damon stay. But
there was just something about seeing Damon's hand held
out to her at the same time he had valiantly defended her
that had made her want him to come along with her.

Even though all they'd done was walk hand in hand to
the front door of the inn, at which time she went up to
bathe and change while he returned two telephone calls
he'd gotten in the short time he was gone, Paige had truly
enjoyed those minutes spent together.

Damon had behaved himself the entire time. She hadn't
had to squirm once.

Still, Paige wasn't sure that short dalliance was worth
the anger it had obviously caused Jeri. Hoping to avoid a

repeat of the indignant outburst that had followed that last neighborhood game, Paige now treaded lightly. Waiting for when they were alone again to talk out any problems with the girl, she tried not to monopolize the conversation at the table while awaiting the hamburgers and french fries they had decided to have to complement their free sodas.

To lighten Jeri's sullen mood, she let Jeri and Frankie control the topic—as did Damon, who spent most of his time staring out the window, clearly lost in thought. He looked worried. Was he concerned with Jeri's behavior that day? Or was something else bothering him? Business maybe? Did one of those returned telephone calls bring unwanted news from Mt. Pine?

Experience had proven to Paige how hard it was to keep certain kinds of work problems from becoming a constant burden. She had spent many sleepless nights worrying over a certain design, or whether or not production would finish an important job in time for a showing. And she wasn't even the one in charge. Being a boss like Damon had to make such worries all the more profound. But then, that was something Paige hoped to find out for herself very soon.

"Oh, good grief, Frankie, will you look over there at that?" Jeri said, pulling Paige's thoughts back to what went on around her. The kid's nose wrinkled with disgust when she leaned toward her friend at the same time she hooked a thumb in the direction of the food counter.

Paige and Frankie both turned to see what Jeri found so repugnant. Nothing unusual caught Paige's notice. Several patrons sat on the swivel stools along one side while Nolene and Lucy served food to them on the other side.

"Look at what?" Evidently, Frankie had no clue either.

"At Nolene Baker." She bent low and spoke to Frankie in hushed tones, but loud enough everyone at their table heard her easily. "Behind the counter."

Damon stroked his jaw thoughtfully while he, too, studied Nolene. She had just served Andy Johnson and Ross Rutledge their french fries and now toyed with the tips of her scarf while she laughed pleasantly over something Andy had just said.

The easy movement of Damon's hand drew Paige's attention away from the activity around the counter and back to him. Even though he had shown improved behavior today—gallantly curbing his more provocative tendencies—he still remained the most distractive man she'd ever met. Disturbingly so.

All through the baseball game, she had caught herself ignoring the game's progress, and admiring him instead. It didn't matter whether he was catching behind home plate, batting, or standing to the side, cheering his teammates—every action appealed to her in some way. She was even captivated by the playful look of parental precaution he displayed when he finally said, "Okay, slugger, I'll bite. What's wrong with Nolene?"

"What's wrong?" Jeri cut him a quick look of disbelief. "Just look at her. Look how stupid she's acting. She was just like that all through the baseball game today. That's got to be part of the reason we lost. Nolene was too busy laughing at every stupid thing Andy said. What's her problem? Why does she do that? Why does she laugh so loud at anything Andy Johnson says?" She tossed her hands at the illogic. "I happen to know the guy. He's not *that* funny."

Damon's eyes glittered above a barely suppressed smile, as if he were extremely pleased Jeri had noticed something like that. Probably because he was so eager for Jeri to grow up and start behaving more like a young lady. "Nolene doesn't have a problem, slugger. That happens to be perfectly normal behavior. It's called flirting, hon." His dimples dipped when he looked briefly at Paige, as if to make sure she had caught the significance behind Jeri having noticed Nolene's behavior.

Paige worried Damon was reading too much into Jeri's declaration. Just because she had noticed the behavior, didn't mean she was anywhere near ready to emulate it.

"Flirting is something older girls tend to do whenever

they are around older boys they like," he continued. "It's how they attract the attention they want."

Jeri lifted an eyebrow, showing how ludicrous she thought that comment. "If all she wants is Andy's attention, why doesn't she just go ahead stand on her head? That would be sure to get his attention, wouldn't it?"

"Give her a minute," Frankie put in with a chuckle as she turned back to face her plate. "She just might try that next." Not as concerned as Jeri over the teenage girl's antics, Frankie took a large bite of her hamburger, chewed four times, and swallowed. "Nolene has been trying to make Andy like her for as long as I've lived here. But he's too close a friend to Jimmy Goodson."

Jeri scratched at the edge of her red baseball cap. Clearly, she didn't follow any logic. "And?"

Frankie slid her soda closer to her, scowling when her straw shifted around to point the other direction. "Jimmy has had a crush on Nolene since she was about fourteen and Andy knows it." Rather than simply pull the straw back around to face her, Frankie climbed onto her knees and bent over the plastic glass. Having changed from her overalls into a pair of loose fitting blue shorts, she folded her grass streaked legs up under her. "In fact, if Jimmy was still here, he'd be acting worse than Nolene is right now. The guy acts like a real goofball around her, and he does it on purpose."

"That is just so dumb." Jeri's expression turned speculative, her attention on Frankie while she chased the meandering straw with her mouth until finally she captured it. "I don't see why anyone would want to waste good time flirting."

Frankie shrugged as soon as she released the straw again. She'd used all that effort for one quick sip. "Mom says it's an art. She says one day even I'll want to try it, though she doesn't think I'll ever be all that good at it."

Clearly amused, Damon pressed a paper napkin over his mouth to keep from laughing over Frankie's forthright comments. Or perhaps he was afraid if he didn't clamp something over his mouth, he'd join in and say something he shouldn't. But either way, all Paige noticed above the rumpled napkin were his sexy blue eyes.

If Jeri thought it odd her father now breathed through a napkin, she didn't show it. "Well, I sure won't be trying nothing like that. I can't think of anything that is any more stupid." She swiped a fat french fry through a puddle of ketchup. "Except maybe for kissing on the mouth."

Damon's gaze darted to Paige, his blue eyes still glimmering when he finally lowered the napkin. "What about you, Paige? You sure are being quiet through all this. What's your opinion of kissing on the mouth?"

Paige nearly strangled on her hamburger. She hadn't expected such a question. Nor did she have any idea what to answer. Had he asked just two days ago, she might have agreed in part with Jeri. Kissing had never quite been what it was supposed to be. But that kiss yesterday had altered her opinion dramatically. Even with Damon being exactly the sort of good looking, woman-using man she'd sworn never to fall in love with again, she had truly enjoyed that kiss. And had wanted more.

Her heart sprinted at the memory of what it had felt like to have her mind sent reeling and her pulses soaring at levels she'd never experienced before.

"I can't really say what my opinion is," she finally answered. In this case, honesty appeared to be the smartest as well as the easiest way out.

Unable to continue gazing into Damon's questioning eyes and still keep breathing, she focused on the mustard stain on Jeri's strawberry red blouse instead. "Kissing has both its advantages and disadvantages."

"Well, I can't see any advantage to it," Jeri muttered, not accepting any of this as fact. She gave Paige a telling look when she leaned forward and sucked the last of her drink through her straw. "I think it is something we should *all* try to avoid. Seems to me kissing on the mouth like some folks do could end up being some sort of a health hazard. So why bother?"

Paige decided not to venture into an explanation about love to a girl who clearly did not want to understand. "I guess to some people kissing is a good kind of bother. Some people truly enjoy it."

"I don't see why." Jeri grabbed up her empty glass and headed for the counter. Frankie cut Paige a look that let her know she had no idea what Jeri's problem was as she, too, scooted her chair back and lugged her glass over for a quick refill.

As soon as the girls were far enough away not to over-hear, Damon leaned across the corner of the red-checked tablecloth toward Paige. "Interesting."

His pale eyes glittered even more when he asked his next question with feigned innocence. "Would it be all right, you think, if a little bit later this evening I *bothered* you for further discussion on all this?"

Chapter 13

By the time they all went up to bed that night, Damon had managed to introduce the word *bother* into nearly every conversation he had participated in—each time locking his gaze with Paige's in a most unnerving manner. It was as if he had decided to make a ceaseless game of torment out of it.

And torment her it did. Even after Paige bathed and changed into her night gown, all she could think about was how hot and *bothered* he had made her with his overuse of that particular word. When she crossed the hall to her bedroom to find a note taped to her door, she didn't know whether to laugh at his unyielding antics or scream aloud her frustration.

The note read: *"Warning: I think I may have to bother you at least once before I go to bed. Damon"*

What was with him? she wondered, glancing at his door, relieved to find it closed. Was he annoyed with her because she hadn't taken the opportunity during their cafe discussion about Nolene to impart a little feminine wisdom to Jeri? Or was he trying in some weird way to tempt her into kissing him again, since *that* was the association Jeri had placed on the word?

Or did he just derive great pleasure from tormenting her for some reason? Maybe it was all part of that be-in-control thing men so enjoyed.

Clutching both her dirty clothes and her toothbrush in her left hand she pulled the note off the door with her right, folded it over twice, and carried it inside. Her first thought was to toss it away, but she ended up placing it on top of the baseball glove she had forgotten to return to Horace Johnson and had left on the table beside the door so she wouldn't forget it the next day.

She thought she might want to reread the note before going to bed. Though she wasn't sure why.

After carefully locking the door then testing it, since the doors in that inn seemed to have a will of their own, she turned out the lamp on that side of the bedroom then hesitated with her fingers resting on the top button of the only robe she had left, having ruined the other one.

A prickly sensation washed over her during the walk to the other lamp, as if her body wanted to warn her of some-one else in the room. Nerves poised, she changed her mind about removing the robe and scanned the dimly lit room instead. Nobody.

"You're being silly," she chided herself the entire time she was on her hands and knees checking under the bed, and again under the hanging clothes inside the closet. At the same time she turned the light back off inside the closet, she thought she heard her bedroom door open, but a quick look revealed it still closed. *Her imagination had run amuck.*

"There's no one here," she said aloud, eager to con-vince herself of that. With nowhere else large enough for a human to hide, she shook the eerie sensation and pro-ceeded to take off her terry cloth robe.

With restless thoughts of Damon and Jeri yet to be dis-sected, she carefully folded the fluffy white garment over once and laid it across the back of the desk chair, then glanced at the neatly made bed. Should she lie down and try to go on to sleep, and risk her fitful thoughts taking over an even larger degree? Or should she relax a moment by looking out of the window for awhile?

Hardly a choice. Hoping to sort through some of her

nagging concerns before lying down, she left the desk lamp on for now and headed to the window just right of it. Parting the sheers, she lifted the bottom half as high as possible to let in fresh air. With arms crossed over the white Grecian-style night gown she'd bought to wear with her other robe—now scuffed and torn beyond repair—she breathed the heady night scents and gazed out over the gated cove beyond the village.

Entranced by the view, she pressed a bare shoulder against the window frame and stared idly at the different lights sparkling across the dark water. Wishing she also had a view of the local lighthouse, she considered going out to the alcove to sit for awhile, but quickly dismissed that idea due to her skimpy dress.

Instead, she stayed up and watched the warning lights blinking atop the cove gates. They were pretty enough to calm her frazzled nerves and help put the events of the day into better perspective. Not certain what to make of either Jeri's or Damon's behavior that day, she leaned closer to the black screen, staring absently at the night view until the creaking sound of a door out in the hall caught her attention.

Paige's already harried heart rate bounded forward with the frivolous hope that Damon had come out of his room hoping to torment her one last time before going to bed.

Listening carefully, she heard soft footsteps across the way, then nothing. Trying to figure out who was out there, and where that person was headed, she hurried to press her ear against the smooth door, and jumped nearly out of her skin when someone knocked lightly on the other side barely seconds later.

Stepping back so her voice would come from further into the room so whoever it was wouldn't guess she had been listening, she called out in a not at all too steady voice, "Who is it?"

"Me."

Damon. Hurrying to get her robe, she pressed a hand

against her rampaging heart to keep it from bursting right through her chest. "Coming."

Without taking time to put the robe on for fear he might give up and go away, she hurried back across the room to let him inside. She clutched the garment in front of her, surprised when a few seconds later he entered the narrow portal inside her door carrying a baseball glove.

Bewildered, she glanced at the clock. Nearly midnight. Did he expect to get up a game at that late hour? Or was he as restless as she was and, to work off some of that, hoped to go outside and play a little catch with her, like he sometimes did with Jeri? Didn't he know how much of that time would be spent trying to find all the balls she had missed? They'd end up in the bushes more than anywhere else.

Her next breath lodged in her throat. The thought of being alone in the bushes with Damon on such a gorgeous night exhilarated her at the same time it terrified her.

But then, if going outside was his intention, why had he come there barefoot, wearing nothing more than a lightweight pair of summer blue pajama bottoms?

Distracted by the same sleek body that had snared her attention earlier that afternoon, it took Paige a moment longer than it should to find her voice again, shaky though it was. "Why do you have that glove?"

When she didn't immediately close the door behind him, he did, ever so quietly. Then he moved further into the room, his bare feet caressing the polished floor with each agile step. For some reason, his smooth, easy movements reminded Paige of a cat stalking its prey. That analogy distracted her more.

"I came to return it to you," he answered finally. "But I don't really care to wake Jeri in the process." He held the glove out to her. "Not at this late hour."

"Return it? But that's not—" Her voice wavered again when she gestured toward the table nearest the entry and saw only the folded note Damon had left on her door. The baseball glove was gone.

"Not what?" His gaze followed hers, as if hoping to figure out what had cut her sentence short.

Certain the glove had been right there just a few minutes ago, she blinked twice then looked at the door—far too baffled to respond to his query. She remembered having to unlock her door to let him in. How could he possibly have opened the thing when it was still locked? Even if he did have some way to get around the locks in that house, how could he have slipped several yards into her bedroom and snatch something out of there without her noticing it? If nothing else, the crisply folded paper on top would have made noise.

Dumbfounded by the impossibility of it all, she stuck out her empty hand and let him place the glove there.

"I'm not sure how that thing ended up in my room," he went on, returning his acute attention to her eyes. It was as if he had decided to memorize every tiny detail about them. "But I found it on one of the nightstands beside my bed."

"In your room?"

If he was anywhere as confused as she was, he didn't show it. "All I can figure is that you must have left it there earlier when you came by to give me that message from Miss Hattie about the cookies."

Paige thought back. She couldn't have left it in his room then. She'd already put the thing in her room. She was sure of it. *Or was she?*

Suddenly doubting her sanity, she turned the glove over and ran her fingers over Horace Johnson's initials. It certainly looked like the same glove. And it also felt like the same glove. Her mouth flattened when she glanced again at the table. With no duplicate lying there, she had nothing to prove it was otherwise.

Had she imagined leaving it on the table? Or was old batty Beaulah right and there really were ghosts inside the Seascape Inn? She shook that last thought. She had enough cause to worry about her powers of reason—or lack thereof. It was far more likely she had picked up the glove again without realizing it earlier, before heading downstairs to find out what that delicious smell was. She only *thought* she saw it still on the table later, when she put the note down. She'd certainly had enough on her mind that evening to distract her.

She looked again at the main source of that day's distractions.

While Damon waited for her to do something with the baseball glove, he glanced around the room until his roving scrutiny fell on the folded piece of paper on the table. "I see you found my note."

Still too preoccupied over what had happened with the glove to foresee what was coming, Paige did her usual and gave the obvious answer. "How could I miss it? You taped it right to the middle of my door."

"So you read it?"

"Of course I read it." While still clutching the wadded robe to her ribs, she set the glove on the desk then anchored it in place with a book she'd borrowed from the alcove. For good measure, she set a metal paperweight, a tablet of paper, and a plastic ink pen on top as well before turning to face Damon again. When she did, she found that he had followed her halfway. "Why wouldn't I read it?"

"Oh, I don't know. I thought reading it might have been too much of a *bother*." Tiny, adorable lines formed at the creases of his eyes, making him look very mischievous—and every bit as dangerous. He took a cautious step in her direction. "You know how much some people hate to be bothered."

After she retreated just one step, he took several more, halting directly in front of her. His azure eyes narrowed in thought, bringing her attention to his incredibly long, dark eyelashes. She took a deep, quivering breath. Why wasn't there a law against men like Damon having such sexy-looking lashes? The eyelashes only added to his dangerous appeal.

"Fortunately," Damon's rich, male voice deepened into

an almost hypnotic sound, "I don't happen to be one of them." He moistened his lower lip with a maddeningly slow, sexy stroke of his tongue.

She mimicked that movement with one of her own, dampening both her lips, then tried futilely to swallow. "Oh?"

Her tongue brought his attention fully on her mouth. "As I recall, you didn't seem too adamantly opposed to being bothered while we were outside yesterday. At least not at first."

If there were any coherent thoughts left inside Paige's brain, they frolicked just outside her grasp. She pressed the fingers of her free hand against the top of the desk to steady her equilibrium while he bent sideways, reaching through the sheers to pull down the nearest window shade. While stretched to one side, his pajama bottoms slid lower on his taut hips.

She glimpsed the white skin hidden there.

"Just in case Beaulah Favish is out there watching," he said as a way to explain his actions when he faced her again.

"At this hour?" She scowled at how foreign her voice had sounded.

"As batty as that woman is, you can never know when she's out there watching this house."

Which would explain Paige's feeling of being watched earlier. If only she could explain away why she'd thought she'd laid his note on top of a baseball glove that obviously wasn't there.

His note. Tiny shivers cascaded over her.

His note had warned her he might try something like this.

She swallowed past the constriction in her throat, and tried to figure out how she'd gotten herself into this predicament. She never should have let him close that door.

"But surely Beaulah has gone to bed by this hour." She pointed to the clock without actually looking at it. She didn't dare take her gaze off Damon even long enough to be sure of the time. He could be all kinds of tricky when he wanted to be. "It's after midnight. All good people are in bed by now."

"Hmm, I notice *you* aren't in bed yet," The soft glow from the only lamp burning caught the silvery highlights in his blue eyes when he darted his gaze in the direction of her untouched covers.

"Are you insinuating that I'm not a good person?"

"Not insinuating—just hoping." Dimples that had dallied at the corners of his seductive mouth sank suddenly deep. "Just like I'm hoping you will let me kiss you again."

"Why?"

"*Why?*" His eyes widened. He clearly hadn't expected to have to give a reason. "Because I want to."

Being questioned out of the blue like that had clearly distracted him. "But why?"

His gaze probed hers, as if to figure out her reason for asking so many questions. "I guess because you are a beautiful woman who drives me crazy with desire, and has since that first moment I set sight on her—as a woman that is."

Reminded of what his opinion of her as a twelve-year-old had been, she asked, "Are you telling me that you no longer view me as that skinny little kid who used to follow you and Blair around when she'd let me?"

"How could I now that I've seen how agreeably you've filled out in all the right places?" His eyes released hers a moment to take in a lower view. "There's nothing skinny about you now."

Uncertain if that was a compliment or a well hidden dig, Paige was just about to ask him to qualify that statement when the ringing of two telephones caught her attention. The one downstairs rang a quarter second before the one upstairs. Twice. Then stopped.

But Damon didn't. Having had to lean away from her to pull down that shade, he quickly shifted back into place.

Now he stood close enough for Paige to breathe in the invigorating scent of his cologne.

Unfortunately, the movement of her deep breath drew his attention to that area beneath her wadded robe where her heart still hammered out of control. "When Blair told me that you were perfect, I thought she meant for taking care of Jeri. I had no idea she meant you were perfect in every aspect imaginable."

Paige lifted an eyebrow—that comment had carried it a bit far. She fought an errant urge to check his tongue for traces of silver. "Damon, nobody is perfect."

She tried to manage a couple of rapid steps backward to put a little more needed distance between them, but the desk chair stood in the way, causing her to stop. She didn't remember pulling the chair out, but evidently she had. Chairs didn't move themselves.

Before she could decide an alternate plan of retreat, the robe pulled out of her grasp almost like it had been jerked. She reached out to try to catch it, but Damon's arm got in her way and she grabbed his sleek, strong wrist instead.

He looked pleased by that mistake while he continued with the absurd conversation. "Don't call yourself no-body."

Quickly, he kicked the robe up under the desk, out of their way as he brought his free arm around her and pulled her body closer. The heat from his smooth, bare skin pierced the thin material of her night gown in a most erotic way as his attention dipped to her mouth. His blue eyes darkened with intent.

The moment of truth had arrived for Paige. Did she want Damon to kiss her again, knowing how profoundly she would respond? Or should she push him away to save her heart from the painful consequences that would undoubtedly follow?

At that moment, Paige honestly didn't know what she planned to do—and would never know because while she still tried to decide, the telephone on the desk beside her rang, rattling her right out of her skin.

Damon glowered at the offending device. "Who'd be calling you at this hour?"

With the main part of the small chair still planted against the backs of her trembling legs, Paige bent at the knees and sank gratefully onto the ruffled, bow-tied cushion— weak now from the effect of her own adrenaline. "I'll give you one guess who."

Not knowing whether to curse her sister or praise her, Paige reached for the receiver, answering on the third ring. "Hello?"

Damon waited to hear her verbally verify the caller was indeed Blair before heading dejectedly for the door. He stopped to look back at Paige a long moment, then quietly let himself out, obviously aware a phone call from Blair meant Paige could be tied up in conversation for quite some time.

As disappointed as she was relieved, Paige's heart continued to hammer at twice its normal rate for several long, breathless minutes after he'd left. She tried to concentrate on her sister's conversation, all the while waiting to hear the real reason behind the late night call. But if Blair phoned for anything other than an update of Paige's activities, she never said. After a fifteen minute conversation about the miserable weather New York was having, and about a few of the more minor things that had gone wrong for Paige since her arrival last Friday, Paige hung up wondering why that couldn't have waited until morning.

If not for the interruption, there was no telling what might have happened with Damon.

As frustrated as Damon, Tony drifted back and forth between the turret and the dresser, following his every step. There had to be some logical way to get this man back in Paige's room. But what? The glove trick sure wouldn't work again. If he pulled that stunt a second time, it would spook them both. Once spooked, they'd start worrying about how a baseball glove clearly changed rooms on its own, which would eventually lead them to fretting over

Miss Beaulah's ghost—as Damon liked to refer to him. After that, they would lose all focus on the important matters at hand. Land-sakes, it wasn't every day mortals discovered they had a helpful ghost like him actively meddling in their affairs.

No, only as a last resort did he dare let his existence be known. So what could he do about these two short of locking them in the cellar? Which wouldn't work anyway, what with Jeri always one step behind one or the other.

The next several days proved very trying for everyone, but for no one more than Jeri. Since realizing Paige's true nature, she had tried several times to get the woman to lose her cool in front of her dad, but so far everything Jeri had set up had gone wrong. It was almost as if the lady had a guardian angel looking out for her. Even the old frog-in-the-shoes trick hadn't worked, because when Paige went to put her shoes back on, the frog had disappeared. How, Jeri didn't know, since she'd been careful to put the frog in face first; and everyone knew frogs didn't have enough sense to back up on their own.

Even those tricks that hadn't fallen apart at the last minute never worked out like she'd planned. A lot of the time, either her dad came out of nowhere to the rescue, or Miss Hattie did—even when Jeri was certain nobody else was around. It was as if somehow they knew when trouble was afoot. Even when they didn't get there in time to rescue her, they were johnny-on-the-spot with a comforting shoulder to take the edge off what she had done.

But this time, Jeri had it made. Everything was perfect. The guests that were there earlier had left hours ago, and the ones that were supposed to have arrived that morning had called to say they'd be a day or two late because of car trouble. Cora, Miss Hattie's part time kitchen help, had called right after that to say she had hurt her ankle and couldn't work that day; and Jeri had heard her dad say that Pete Pilgrim was supposed to call him at four o'clock with some prices he needed for that important bid he was working on. He would wait for that call in his room so he'd be where he could write the figures on paper.

And because it was Wednesday afternoon, Miss Hattie would stay gone at that Historical Society meeting Paige just drove her to for the next few hours. Normally, Miss Hattie would have taken that old 1932 Ford of hers to the meeting, since she was head of the food committee this year and couldn't just walk over. But after Frankie had showed Jeri how to pop off the distributor cap and loosen the rotor, the old car just wasn't running well enough to get her there.

"Imagine that." Jeri chuckled. Miss Hattie had had little choice but to ask Paige to take her and all that food over to Miss Millie's.

Everyone was gone at the moment, except for her father, who was upstairs in his room on the other side of the house seated at a desk that faced in a whole different direction. No one even knew Frankie was coming back over.

Jeri waited beside some bushes near the road. This time, she would be very careful to make sure nothing went wrong. Then when Paige got mad and accused her of having had a hand in what happened to her, she would smile and admit to her she was right. When Paige then marched back up to the inn to tell on her, still furious about it all, her father was sure to get real angry at his daughter for what she'd done, but he would also see what a big faker Paige Brockway really was.

"Oh, yes." It would sure be worth whatever punishment she got when everyone, including Frankie, saw for themselves how Paige had only been pretending to like her all this time. And the reason why she'd been pretending such a thing would be obvious, even to her dad.

Jeri could hardly wait for Frankie to show up with the paint.

Chapter 14

Slipping out of his shirt to get more comfortable, Damon took a short break while still waiting for Pete's call. It was pointless to try to work around those numbers he needed, not with his thoughts being so equally divided between his many pricing figures and that kiss he very nearly stole from Paige a few nights before. If only Blair hadn't called when she did.

His pulses revved at the thought. He'd come within inches of sampling that sweet mouth of hers again. *Inches.* Then was not given another opportunity to be alone with her again. How much frustration could one man be expected to bear?

Having just moved to the turret where he could stretch out on the soft window seats while waiting for Pete's call, Damon wondered where the object of a good majority of his thoughts had gotten off to when he first spotted his daughter and Frankie walking quickly across the field toward the grassy pond carrying something between them. He'd expected Paige to be with them.

From the open guillotine style windows, he had a partial view of the tranquil little pond where Paige had gotten her shoes stuck in the mud the day before. From there he could also see the tall, leafy oaks that grew at the water's edge and the little white gazebo near them—which turned out to be the two girls' destination.

Moving the cellular phone from the blue cushion beside him to the sun washed window sill where he'd be less likely to knock it off, he shifted sideways to make himself more comfortable while watching the girls set down and bend over whatever it was they'd carried.

"What are those two up to now?" Something else to Paige's disadvantage, no doubt. With it pretty much being his duty not to let them go too far with their aggravating pranks, he studied their actions carefully, trying to decide if the end result would be something he should save Paige from, or let happen so he could sympathize with her afterward.

Either way, he came out ahead. When he saved Paige from impending doom and she knew about it, she was grateful to him. Maybe not grateful enough to kiss him again like he so wanted, but grateful all the same. When he didn't come to the rescue, and Jeri got away with whatever she tried to do to make Paige want to leave, then Paige witnessed for herself just how trying kids could be. Or at least that was what she was supposed to do, but Paige seemed to be little affected by Jeri's pranks. Much to Damon's amazement. And Blair's chagrin.

It was why Blair was starting to grow antsy. These last five days had gone by with Paige hardly mentioning to her that Jeri had become quite a handful. With what few problems Paige did relay to her being so minor in nature, Blair worried Jeri wasn't living up to her fullest potential for some reason, and that Paige might not leave there as disillusioned as she wanted. To Blair, that wasn't good. She was counting on Jeri to help Paige see what a mistake it would be to move to Mt. Pine, and in time to keep her from blowing most of her savings. Blair thought it important that far worse events than getting a pair of expensive shoes stuck in the mud or falling fully clothed into the ocean needed to happen. And soon. Paige was scheduled to return to New York and finish packing her things sometime Tuesday morning.

Jeri had only six more days to do her worst and thus

prevent Paige from getting what would prove to be a very expensive lesson in life. Blair feared that six more days might not be enough time at the rate matters progressed now, and had asked if there might be some way to encourage Jeri to behave a little more badly.

Damon tapped the tips of his fingers together while he tried to decide how he felt about it all. With such a drastic slowdown of new construction in his area, he needed that building contract for the new health resort to salvage not only his father's businesses, but also the jobs of many of the people who'd worked for them all these years.

Even so, he hated having to target Paige like that. True, it might be as much for her own good as it was his and Blair's—because from what he'd viewed so far, Paige wasn't quite cut out for small town life anymore—but for now it was hard not to see the harm they caused.

Did the three good ends truly justify the means in this case? He wasn't sure anymore. Not only was Jeri being allowed to get away with antics that deserved swift punishment, Paige had been set up from the start and didn't deserve any of whatever Jeri tried to do to her.

And this time, it looked like paint was to be involved. Either that or the two girls had had such a strong bout with their consciences, they'd decided to put their energies toward something constructive for a change. At the moment the two worked like possessed demons putting a fresh coat of white paint on the bench style seats inside the gazebo.

Closing his eyes, he tried to remember what Paige was wearing. He couldn't let her ruin any more of her good clothes on his account.

Why was it that woman seemed to overdress for everything?

Jeri and Frankie barely had time to get the seats painted and hide the half-empty can and the paint brushes before they heard Paige's car headed back up the main road toward the inn. With so many trees between there and the village, at first they caught only glimpses of shiny blue as the car moved closer.

"She must not have stayed to help Miss Hattie set up all the food after all," Jeri commented, glancing around to make sure there was nothing lying around that might tip her off as to what they'd just done. "Grab that stick we stirred the paint with and get on out of here."

Frankie, who hadn't really wanted to help out with this particular prank, ran over to where they had opened the paint can and snatched up the stick. While still there, she ripped up a patch of grass that had paint on it, too. "You sure you want to go through with this?"

"Of course I'm sure." She crossed her arms over the front of her bright, Pepto-Bismol pink T-shirt with the words "Born to Greatness" emblazoned across the back. "It's her own fault that I'm having to do this. If she wasn't so blamed stubborn about staying no matter what, I wouldn't be forced to stoop this low."

Squinting, Frankie kept up with the car's progress while she stuffed the paint matted grass into her shorts pocket rather than take time to try to sink it in the pond. "Just you remember which seat it is we didn't paint."

"Don't worry. I know which one. Now get out of here. If she knows you're around, she might suspect something is up before she ever comes over here. Don't forget, when she left with Miss Hattie, I told her you had too much to do this afternoon to come back over to play."

"That was true enough. I didn't come back over here to play," Frankie agreed. Bending low to be less detectable now that the car was out in the open and not blocked by trees, she headed for the long, low stone wall that divided Miss Hattie's property from Miss Beaulah's.

It wasn't until she'd squatted down on the other side where they had hidden the paint and the brushes that it dawned on Jeri. Miss Beaulah might be out there watching them. Her heart jumped at the thought of Miss Beaulah hurrying out of the forest in time to warn Paige about the wet paint.

While Paige's car slowly ground its way up the narrow graveled drive in front of the inn, Jeri quickly studied the woods for the sight of those big old binoculars, but she saw nothing but shadows among the many trees, bushes, and ferns. Miss Beaulah had probably taken her binoculars and gone over to Miss Millie's to watch what went on in one of those Historical Society meetings she was never allowed to attend after that falling out between her and one of the ones who started the group.

Or at least Jeri hoped that's what she had done.

As expected, after Paige parked her rental car around back of the green house, right where it had been before, she headed toward the gazebo. Paige hadn't wanted to leave Jeri there to begin with and sure wasn't going to let her be alone much longer than she'd already been. Probably too worried she'd get into trouble.

Chuckling, for nobody deserved what was about to happen to her any more than Paige did, Jeri hurried to sit down on the only unpainted spot, her heart racing like a wild wind before the storm. Spotting white paint splattered on her left leg, she gasped then quickly tucked it up under her so Paige wouldn't see it and ask questions.

Staring off toward the pond with the saddest expression she could muster, she pretended not to know that Paige had returned and was already headed her direction.

"What's wrong with you?" Paige asked just before she reached the gazebo. "Are you still upset because Frankie had to go home early?"

Jeri didn't answer on purpose. It always drove grown ups nuts whenever they asked a question and nobody answered it. Instead, she continued to stare out across the water, her shoulders sagging while her insides turned board stiff. She silently waited for Paige to come closer.

Which she did. "Just because your friend had to go home for awhile to take care of a few chores for her mother is no reason to sit out here all alone, letting this beautiful afternoon go by."

When Jeri heard her step up onto the gazebo floor, she

finally turned to face her. If she looked just sad enough, Paige would more than likely come over and sit down beside her while pretending to be concerned. Right on all that wet paint. The explosion of anger that followed should be totally awesome.

"But there's nothing for me to do with Frankie gone." Nervous that something could still go wrong, she pulled her blond ponytail forward so she could play with the ends of her hair.

"Sure there is." In the shadows now, Paige slid her sunglasses back, anchoring the earpieces in her dark hair. "You like to go wading, don't you? Why not kick off your shoes and splash around in the water for awhile?" She narrowed those dark brown eyes of hers only a little. "Just avoid that area over there by the yellow flowers so you don't get bogged down in mud like I did."

"I don't feel like getting wet," Jeri answered in her sulkiest voice. Her heart thudded hard and fast while she waited for Paige to sit down somewhere. It didn't really have to be right beside her. All the other seats had wet paint, too. "I don't feel like doing much of anything with Frankie gone. I just want to sit."

"But sitting is no fun," Paige continued, again headed toward her, but stopped to notch her forehead after a few steps. A soft breeze ruffled both her blouse and her hair as she took a couple of strong whiffs from the air. "What's that smell?"

"What smell?" Jeri blinked, hoping not to look at all troubled by that question. She hadn't thought about the fact that wet paint gave off a smell.

"That chemical smell. What is it?" She glanced around, probably trying to figure out where it came from.

Jeri's stomach felt like a heavy rock. "Oh, that. Weed killer probably. I think maybe Jimmy Goodson came by earlier to put some new kind of weed killer around the gazebo so it would be easier to mow next time."

Jeri's blood nearly burst out of her veins with relief when instead of questioning the smell anymore, Paige finally turned, positioning herself to sit down beside her. The moment of truth was finally at hand.

"Isn't there something you can think of to do without Frankie that might be fun?"

"No. Besides, I don't want to have any fun without Frankie. She's the best friend I've got here." Jeri watched intently. Paige's knees finally started to bend. Only a second more and—

"Oh, *look*. A ladybug." Instead of sitting down the rest of the way, Paige straightened and headed for the brightly colored bug that had just landed on a nearby bannister.

Jeri's heart fell against her rock hard stomach with a silent splat. "What are you getting so excited over? It's just a bug."

"Oh, but seeing a ladybug land in the sun is supposed to bring good luck."

Jeri scowled. "You don't really believe that, do you?"

Shrugging, Paige bent to have a closer look at the dainty creature. When her sunglasses fell forward as a result, she pulled them out of her hair, folded them, then tucked them into her front pocket. "I don't see any reason not to believe it."

Jeri stared at the backs of Paige's light pink slacks and floral top, knowing she was about to make a real mess out of both. Well, ruining such good clothes would be her own fault for thinking she always had go around looking like some fashion model. The lady should have packed more than one pair of jeans and one pair of denim shorts when coming to a place like Seascape. "That sure is a mighty pretty outfit you have on there."

"Thank you." Paige spun around, clearly surprised. *Talk about being eager for compliments.* "I designed the blouse myself. It was part of MissTeek's spring collection this year."

With Paige's attention finally away from that stupid bug, Jeri pretended to be impressed—although she had never heard of anything called MissTeek before. "It looks expensive. Is it?"

Nodding, Paige finally moved back into place, right in front of the bench beside her. "All MissTeek fashions are expensive because of all the careful detail. That's why they are sold in the most exclusive shops only."

This time, nothing drew Paige away and she sank smack dab in the middle of all that wet paint. It took her a moment to realize what she'd done.

Jeri nearly cackled when those brown eyes of hers stretched to the size of half dollars. "What's wrong?"

Paige didn't move. She didn't even blink. "Something doesn't feel right."

"Why? Because of the wet paint?"

"Wet paint?" Paige pressed a fingertip to the bench beside her and sucked in a loud, hard breath when it came back with white paint all over it. As expected, she jumped to her feet and tugged at her clothes so she could get a good look at the backs of them. "Why didn't you warn me I was about to sit in wet paint?"

Her heart near bursting, Jeri curled her hands in her lap. *Here it came. The moment of truth.* "Didn't want to."

"Then you really knew about the paint before I sat down?"

"Of course I did. I'm the one who put it there." She glanced off toward the main house to figure out how long it would take Paige to march up there to tell her dad all about what all his daughter had done, and was surprised to see her father on his way there. Judging by his eager steps and how he still adjusted his shirt as if having just put it on, he figured he'd gone a little too long without Paige's sickening-sweet company. Again.

That meant Jeri would be witness to all the fireworks when they happened. She unfolded her bent leg in preparation to move in closer.

"But why on earth would you do this?" Paige wanted to know, seemingly unaware anyone else was headed toward them, even though she mostly faced that direction. If all went right, Paige would start screaming at her long before she realized who was nearby to see it happen. She hadn't quite raised her voice yet, but unlike the incidents at the cove or in the attic after which Paige never really showed much anger, Jeri knew this time she would.

This was far more serious than being left behind on a dark forest trail or locked into the attic for awhile. Far more. Real damage had been done this time. More than just getting a pair of nice shoes stuck in some mud. This time her whole outfit was ruined; and this time it clearly was not an accident.

"You'll find out why." Jeri stood so she could face the entry her father would use when he joined them inside the gazebo. She didn't look forward to having him as angry at her as he would be, but she could hardly wait to see his expression when Paige suddenly let loose on him, too. Sorta like that stewardess did the last time. "Hi, Dad."

"What's going on here, slugger?" He narrowed his blue eyes as if trying to see what about Paige's clothes had her so alarmed.

"Nothing," Jeri answered on purpose. That was the sort of answer sure to make Paige blow her stack all the more. Remembering Frankie, she glanced quickly at the wall to see if her friend was still out of sight, or if she'd let her curiosity get the best of her and now peeked over the wall. There was no sign of a blond head at all. *Smart girl.* Now was not the time to let on she was anywhere near there.

"Nothing?" Damon repeated, already scowling. The man was no fool. He knew something was wrong. "Jer, if that's true, why does Paige look so upset?"

"I guess because she just did a dumb thing and sat in some wet paint." She took a deep breath and held it, giving Paige plenty of time to tell them both exactly what she thought of that. When it didn't happen, Jeri prodded her a little more. "She probably thinks it's all my fault because I forgot to warn her."

"You admit knowing about the paint?" he asked, as if needing to have that fact separated from the others. He crossed his arms, an action that pulled the back of his blue plaid shirt tight across his bunched shoulders. It was easy to see how upset he already was.

Jeri nodded and thrust her chin forward to indicate no cause for remorse. "Yes, sir, I do."

"And do you have a reason for not telling her?"

"Yes, sir, I do." Jeri nodded again, but this time took a tiny step back. Although Paige had not yet shown her temper, her father was about ready to explode. Jeri could tell that easily enough by the way that hard muscle down the back of his jaw had started to pump in and out. Why wasn't this working out the way it was supposed to?

"You do have one? Well, do you mind sharing that reason with us?" He gestured to Paige, who stood to the side silently watching him, hardly any anger visible.

What was wrong with the woman? She'd just sat down in wet paint and ruined her nice clothes. Why wasn't she as angry as her dad was? Or more?

Jeri curled her fingers around the hems of her red shorts. This was not going at all like she'd planned. Why wasn't Paige at least yelling at her? "I might tell *you* about it later, but I'm not telling her anything. Ever. Not with her standing there thinking I'm the biggest brat she's ever met." *There,* Jeri thought smugly. *That gave Paige the perfect start.*

Falling silent a moment, Jeri waited for Paige's angry agreement. But all the woman did was stand there, hands clenched at her sides. Not saying a blasted word.

Too bad her father wasn't as inclined to be silent.

"If you ask me, I'd say she has darn good cause to think that." Damon signalled for Paige to turn around with a quick twirl of his hand. When he saw the damage done to both the pants and the blouse—even the curled tips of her dark hair had blotches of paint on them—he closed his eyes and groaned. "I'm sorry about the outfit, Paige. Of course I'll reimburse you whatever it is worth." He glowered at Jeri. "And my daughter will later earn enough through doing odd chores to repay me that same amount."

Paige still didn't say a word to anyone. She merely nodded her agreement.

Nobody had that much self control.

"What's with you?" Jeri finally screamed, having had enough of this phony composure. "You know good and well you are angry at me for doing this to you. Why don't you just come out and tell Dad what you really think about me? Why don't you tell him how I get on your nerves and have since the first day but that you pretend to like me so he won't think bad about you? Why don't you finally just come out and show him what a faker you are?"

When even that didn't get a rise out of Paige, she threw up her arms. She was so frustrated she wanted to hit something, but had few choices that weren't covered with wet paint—or that couldn't strike back. "You think you have me fooled with your big act to be nice to me, but you don't. I'm way too smart for that. I know your game, lady, and I know what kind of liar you really are."

When even that didn't get the angry response she wanted, Jeri shook with rage. Paige was staying calm on purpose to make herself look good while making Jeri look bad. "How can you stand there like you have no idea what I mean? You know right what I'm talking about. Man, I hate you!" With tears threatening to embarrass her, she took off running toward Frankie's house, hoping her friend would circle around and meet her there. She needed someone to reason this out with.

To Jeri's surprise, her father came after her. She had expected him to stay with Paige so he could say nice things to her and offer that big, comforting shoulder of his like he had the day before.

"Stop right there, Jerina Louise!"

Jerina Louise? Oh, God, she *was* in trouble.

Not about to push his anger any further, she froze in her tracks, her legs suddenly as achy as her throat was strained.

He continued toward her in a hard march. "Where do you think you're headed?"

"To Frankie's," she answered hopefully, though she

pretty much figured that destination was now no longer an option.

"Oh, no you're not. Not after what you just did." He jabbed a finger in the general direction of the inn while glowering at her. "You are going straight to your room to cool off and think about the rotten things you just said. After I'm through talking to Paige about all this, I plan to bring her to your room so you can apologize to her."

Jeri had a feeling now was not the time to tell him she had no intention of apologizing to that woman—ever. "Don't do your talking in the gazebo. At least not sitting down," she warned, then changed directions and headed for the house.

Too angry to care that the telephone in her dad's room was ringing when she passed by, she marched straight into her room and climbed across the bed to get to the only window with a good view of the pond.

Scanning the tree-pocked countryside to the southeast, she caught a glimpse of Paige and her father walking together toward the ocean. She was barely able to make out their shapes before they disappeared through a patch of trees—no doubt headed for the metal stairs that led down to the beach. This time of day, with the sun so warm and the wind hardly stirring, the beach would be a nice place to talk. *Too nice.*

With the beach usually vacant in the late afternoon, Paige would probably end up finagling another kiss out of her father.

"Well, that sure didn't turn out like it was supposed to," Jeri muttered. Falling backward onto the mattress, she stared up at the ceiling a long moment.

Trying to make Paige blow her stack in front of her father hadn't worked any better than having tried to make Paige want to tuck tail and run away from them. She had given it a go several times now, and had failed each one. The woman was way too good at hiding her true nature from those that mattered.

"That means it's time for a new plan of action," she muttered dismally.

Not sure what to try next, she rolled over onto her stomach to give it deeper thought. "Whatever I come up with, this time I need to be darn sure it is completely fool proof—" She snorted. "—or rather completely *Paige* proof."

What would work good against someone like her? The woman had to have a weak spot. Everyone did.

Having run out of path, Paige stared idly down across the glistening blue waves that teased the edges of the secluded white-gray beach below, still too stunned by the hurtful words Jeri had flung at her to say much of anything. She had accepted Damon's apology and, needing his comfort, allowed him to walk with her while she tried to get over the terrible things Jeri had said to her.

There'd been no point changing her clothes before setting out. They were already ruined. Even if she had put them in water to soak right away, there was little chance she could ever get that much latex paint out of such delicate fabric.

But it wasn't the loss of yet another set of clothes that set her stomach to churning. It was what Jeri had said to her. And how she'd said it.

The child hated her. Truly hated her. While Paige had grown to care about Jeri, despite all that obstinate behavior, the girl had come to literally despise her. Paige had thought the two were becoming friends, giving her yet another reason to look forward to her move to Mt. Pine, and all the while Jeri loathed her.

Paige gripped the stair railing. The words still stung like a fresh stab through the heart. No one had ever said anything like that to her before. Even when Edward dumped her for someone else, he had never once said he hated her.

She never should have let herself become emotionally involved with the child. She knew better than that. Just like she should not allow herself to become emotionally involved with Damon. How foolish she'd been to kiss him the other day. And how stupid to have daydreamed about that kiss ever since.

This trip to Maine was not turning out like Paige planned. Not at all. She was supposed to come there for eleven days, do what she could to help a misguided child, and then leave, having done one last big favor for Blair. That was it. Nothing more.

She dug her fingernails into the palms of her hands. It wasn't supposed to be something that could hurt her like this. If only there were some way to turn off all these painful emotions. Some way to ignore the deep hurt they caused her.

"Are you ready to talk yet?" Damon asked, having walked quietly beside her or behind her for the past fifteen minutes. "If so, I'm ready to listen."

Paige wasn't sure she *could* talk about it yet. Not after having tried so very hard to make the girl like her. "I just don't understand what went wrong. What makes your daughter feel so much hatred toward me?" Forcing aside her fear of heights, for at the moment nothing could hurt her more than Jeri just had, Paige started down the metal stairs that ended at the edge of the small, pebble strewn beach. With Damon following one step behind her, she waited until both feet were safely on the ground below before turning to face him again.

It touched her to see how concerned he looked, but even that didn't ease her pain. If anything it frightened her more. Clearly, he too had entered her heart, leaving her all the more vulnerable. "Being jealous of me is one thing. That I could eventually have coped with. Just like I've managed to cope with her ever changing moods that have ranged from pleasant to obnoxious. But having her suddenly call me a liar and tell me that she hates me was something I was not at all prepared for. Why did she do that?"

Damon studied the water lapping gently at the coarse gray sand nearby for several seconds, then glanced off to where that same ocean pounded a huge finger of rocks with far more force before finally he answered. "She didn't mean it. At least not in the way you think she did. She's just angry right now because she thinks of you as an intruder. For two reasons. I don't know if Blair told you or not, but this place is special. Jeri and I have been coming here for quite some time. Ever since the first summer following the divorce."

Paige detected a bitterness in Damon's voice at the mention of his divorce that she hadn't expected. She looked at him questioningly. He even looked a little bitter. "Yes, Blair did mention that coming to this place had become some sort of a vacation tradition for the two of you."

"Coming here is more than just that." When he faced her again, his lash-fringed eyes reflected emotions so deep and so varied, Paige didn't dare try to identify them all. "Coming here has grown into an important part of our father-daughter relationship."

He gestured to a large, lone rock that stuck out of the sand, about the size of a child's bed. It had not yet been overtaken by afternoon shadows and, with little worry that the rough surface could do further damage to Paige's slacks, it offered an acceptable place to sit. "To understand part of why Jeri is so upset at having you here, I think you should know that Jeri and I came to Seascape our first time at the suggestion of a good friend of mine—a doctor who used to visit here himself a lot. He told me about this place after seeing for himself what an emotional shambles the divorce had left us in."

There was that bitter tone again. Clearly he was not at all happy about the divorce. Could it be Damon wasn't the one who'd left the marriage like she thought? Having made herself as comfortable beside him as was possible, Paige marveled at the thought while he continued his explanation.

"After Westworth told me how quiet and restful this town is, he suggested I bring Jeri here for a couple of weeks of emotional healing. It helped us so much to get away and spend some time together in a place where everyone acted so caring toward us, and where there were no reminders of what my wife had done, that we have continued to come back at least one week each summer ever since. Usually, we try to come for two weeks. Nothing rejuvenates us more.''

Paige could certainly understand that, having felt the same legendary magic of the Seascape Inn the first day she arrived. There was something indescribable about the place, something that encouraged a strong feeling of hope and well being. It had made her want to set aside all her other troubles and simply enjoy the quiet wonder of it all. Too bad she hadn't known about Seascape in those months immediately following her break up with Edward. Her pain would have eased a lot sooner in a place like this.

No wonder Jeri was upset with her. Not only did the child fear her as a contender for her father's affections, Paige had unknowingly trod upon Jeri's personal little haven. A haven she'd shared only with her father—until now. ''Blair never told me that part of it.''

Blair also had never talked to her about Damon's divorce, but then why would she? Paige had always been careful not to show an outward interest in Damon simply because she didn't like the old emotions and disappointments that always stirred to life whenever her sister discussed him. Now she wondered just whose fault the divorce was. Could she have misjudged Damon on that level, too?

She had certainly misjudged him in other areas of his life. Like with his devotion to his daughter. When she first came there, she had expected a father who not only wanted someone to keep his daughter out of his hair, but he at the same time wanted that daughter to grow up and act more adult so he wouldn't have to deal with a child's immaturity anymore. Instead, she found a man who truly enjoyed whatever time he shared with his daughter. So much so, he had made it a point to spend at least part of every summer here with her.

Since it wasn't his own selfish need at work, Paige no longer understood why it was so important for him to hurry and see his daughter grown up. Why not just let her mature at her own rate?

"The way your sister likes to talk, I'm surprised you don't know everything there is to know about me," Damon said, with a good natured smile. Clearly, he hoped to change her solemn mood. His dimples prominent again, he leaned over to tweak her lightly on the nose.

It was a simple gesture that sent a network of sensations coursing through Paige's body, which she had no time to analyze. It was enough for now to know they were there and caused by him. "Ah, but only if the topic of conversation has something to do with herself," Paige added, laughing along with him. How good that felt. Moments ago, she'd doubted she'd ever laugh again.

"True." Damon pushed further back onto the small boulder to bring his feet up in front of him. The sun slanted across his dark hair, bringing out the golden highlights. "She does like to talk about herself. I'll agree with you there." His eyes sparkled a brilliant blue that even the North Atlantic couldn't match. "She's been that way all her life—though there have been a few times she has allowed me to talk about my own problems. She is probably the only person alive, other than Jeri, who knows me. Really knows me."

A twinge of jealously tugged at Paige's heartstrings. Although she knew Damon and Blair were never romantically involved, they had been close friends for as long as she could remember. That was because their own fathers had been such close friends before their deaths. Paige might have been a close friend, too, if she hadn't been so young when she had to move to Dallas to be with Blair as a result of their father's death—and if she hadn't been far too infatuated to think of him as anything beyond the man of her dreams. "You two have been buddies a long, long time."

Damon nodded, then chuckled as he shifted around to

sit Indian style, facing her. "Sometimes I think maybe too long. It starts to get dangerous when someone else knows a person as well as Blair knows me." As if that statement had wrought some deep, dark troubled thought, Damon's playful expression fell serious a moment. "Sometimes I think Blair knows me even better than I know myself."

"I doubt that." Wanting to be as comfortable as Damon, Paige pushed further back and, turning to face him, also sat Indian style. With a bent knee touching his, she couldn't help but notice the resulting warmth it caused her as she leaned forward, her hands resting on her thighs.

She tried not to let the physical contact affect her more than it should. She had enough problems to deal with at the moment. She didn't need to add being attracted to the wrong man to the list—a man whose daughter literally hated her. She'd suffered enough heartbreak in the past few years. "You two don't even see each other but once or twice a month when she's working some of the shoots her agency gets for her in Dallas."

"True, but you add that up over years and years, factor in all those late night telephone conversations, and there's plenty of opportunity to keep up with what's inside the other person. Heck, your sister is one of the few people who knows just how bad I wanted to become a high school coach way back when I first started college."

Paige remembered some mention of that earlier.

"So why didn't you become one? You were young, smart, and healthy. Still are for that matter." *Darn healthy.* Images of what it had been like to have her own coaching lessons flashed through her thoughts, stirring an already unruly libido. Her attention dropped briefly to those strong arms, now basking in the late afternoon sun.

"I couldn't. Dad needed me to help him run his businesses. I ended up taking managerial courses and architectural courses instead of liberal arts and sports." His smile returned, but not as profoundly as before. Still, the beauty of it caught Paige's notice. "Turns out, I'm pretty good at both."

When she didn't comment right away—too mesmerized by that heart-stopping smile—he shrugged as if having had to give up his one true dream wasn't all that important. "Isn't that really all that matters? That you be good at whatever it is you do?"

"I used to think so," Paige admitted, relating everything he just said to her own life. A pang of sadness blended in with the many other emotions vying for her attention. "I became a fashion designer for similar reasons. It's what Blair wanted me to be. I had the talent, and she had the drive. I remember thinking 'why not?' when I agreed to take the courses she had selected for me. The next thing I knew, I'd skyrocketed to the top of the fashion world in New York City."

"But it's not what you truly wanted to do with your life," he stated with more understanding than Paige ever expected.

"No it's not."

He tilted his head, his soft hair shifting while he studied her. Like most men as handsome and imposing as Damon, his emotions remained largely unreadable.

That reminded her again of Edward. She pulled her knee away from his, suddenly needing a little distance. She had too much going on inside her as it was.

Damon glanced at where her knee no longer pressed against his before locking his gaze with hers again. "So what is it you wanted to do with your life? I mean back when you first went to college, what did you want to become?"

"That's just it. Back then I had no idea. That's why it was so easy for Blair to place a hand in it. I had several talents that I could have easily cultivated, but Blair, being so much older, was already well involved in the fashion world. She wanted me to develop the flair I had for designing. She saw it as a complement to her modeling."

Never having admitted this to anyone other than Susan Carmichael, Paige fiddled nervously with a crease in her pink slacks. She hoped Damon would be discreet enough not to tell Blair. She'd already hurt her sister enough by announcing her plan to move back to Mt. Pine. There was no reason to hurt her more by letting her know just how unhappy she'd been all these years. Despite the love and loyalty she felt toward Blair, Paige had truly hated living with her in New York. "Since I had no real dream of my own at the time, none I was aware of anyway, I followed hers instead. It wasn't until much later that I realized what a serious mistake I'd made."

Damon shifted uncomfortably, dropping his gaze to her fidgeting hand. "How so?"

"I don't like New York. The truth is, I despise it more and more each day." When he arched an eyebrow and looked at her as if he found that difficult to believe, she explained further. "Oh, it was exciting enough at first, all those bright lights and bustling streets, but the flash and constant activity grew old in a hurry for me. I'm just not cut out for the quick pace of Blair's glamorous life."

"But I hear you make good money doing what you do."

"Darn good," she agreed, noting his somber expression. Why did he look so bothered by that? "But no amount of money is worth the daily aggravation, or the sheer ruthlessness I faced. Although I enjoyed the designing part, I just couldn't take the greed and the treachery that's become a very big part of the fashion world. It didn't take long for me to figure out I'd much rather have married the right man and settled down somewhere peaceful to have children while pursuing a more sedate career. I suppose I'm just like a lot of other women my age."

Having already told him that much, she decided to tell it all. "I almost did marry someone once, though I think had I done so then, it would have been for all the wrong reasons. At the time, all I could focus on was the fact he wanted to live somewhere other than Manhattan, and he thought having kids and a house would be great."

"You're talking about Edward Simmons."

Paige blinked at hearing Damon speak the name. "I should have known Blair would have told you."

A corner of his mouth crooked, making him look a little less troubled than he had just moments before. A glimmer returned to his blue eyes. "Well, for awhile there, hunting that man down and strangling him with her bare hands was about all Blair could talk about. She never did like the idea of you marrying him and moving off to California without her, but she absolutely hated the thought of him writing you that Dear Jane letter from L.A. telling you he'd found someone else when he was supposed to be getting things ready for you to join him. According to Blair, she was pretty much willing to risk a little jail time to get back at the guy for what he did to you."

Paige laughed at the thought of Blair inside some jail cell, dressed in designer coveralls no doubt. Within hours, she would have the tiny cubicle decorated in ultra-modern and would have all the male jailers at her beck and call. "You gotta love her."

His smile widened. "At the same time, you really wish you could hate her."

Amazed at how very alike they thought, Paige studied Damon a long moment. It seemed so strange that they both could be as close as they were to her sister and not have had a reason to cross paths again before now. "She's one of a kind. And I owe her a lot for taking such good care of me both after our mother's death, and again after Dad died. Blair can be a bit flighty at times, and she's very self-centered, but she has always been there for me when I needed her most. I love her dearly, and because I do, I'm willing to do just about anything for her." Including stay right there in Maine, as promised, and give another try to helping Jeri understand and accept the changes that lay ahead for her.

"Anything except stay in New York," he commented. He unfolded one leg so he could lean closer, as if it was important for him to see her expression clearly.

"That's true. Anything except stay in New York. I just can't take that sort of lifestyle any longer. Not even for Blair." Although not certain why, she shuddered beneath his close scrutiny. "I'm now twenty-seven years old. It's time for me to take charge of my own life. I've followed someone else's dream long enough. Now I want to follow my own. I no longer see that as selfish."

Damon's expression remained gravely pensive when he gazed out across the active water glittering in the late afternoon sun. "And nothing can make you change your mind?"

"About living in New York?" She shook her head. "I'm far too excited now about moving to Mt. Pine and opening up a dress boutique. It's the sort of thing I should have done with my life from the very start." Although she wouldn't dare admit it, she'd grown equally as excited over the prospect of living in the same area as Damon. Now that they'd become friends at last, she was eager for the chance to get to know him better. Even if it put her heart at risk. "I made my decision, and there's no turning back."

To her surprise, and delight, Damon leaned forward and captured one of her hands. He held it a long moment, studying her long fingers, then just as abruptly let go of it. When he slid off the rock and gestured toward the stairs, no semblance of a smile remained. Suddenly, he looked as if he'd just lost his best friend. Or worse.

Paige couldn't imagine what she'd said to bring on such a somber mood. What could she do to make him smile again? "What's wrong?"

He didn't reply right away. "Let's go on back to the inn. I have some serious thinking to do." He waited until she'd pushed herself off the rock, too, then grimaced at the tiny white streaks of paint she'd left behind, clearly a reminder of what had brought them there. "And Jeri has some serious apologizing to do."

❀ *Chapter 15* ❀

Paige stared at Jeri with disbelief. After the girl's staunch refusal to open the door to her father upon their return from the beach, the last thing Paige expected when opening her own door an hour later was to find the child standing in the hallway, her blond head bent and hands folded in front of her.

"I've come to say I'm sorry."

Paige glanced out into the hall, expecting to find Damon standing off to one side, coaching her. But, evidently, he thought Jeri needed to face this one alone. Good for him. It was high time he took a firmer hand with the girl.

"So you finally let your father in to have a talk with you?" she asked, nodding that she understood the reason for this sudden display of contrite behavior. She stood back and gestured for Jeri to come inside. Might as well hear the girl out.

Still dressed in a bright pink T-shirt and red shorts, Jeri walked as far as the mixed-green braided rug at the foot of the bed. "No, he gave up on that about half an hour ago. I think maybe he's talking on the cellular telephone with Pete right now. I'd planned to stop by and tell him I was coming over here to apologize, but when I heard him inside talking, I decided not to bother him. I figured it would be better if I did this alone anyway."

Damon had nothing to do with this? Paige's heart took

a tentative step toward hope. "You came here of your own accord?"

"If that means I came in here because I wanted to, then yes." Standing stiff as a board, she waited until Paige had closed the door and turned to face her again. "I want to apologize for what I did to your clothes. That was real mean of me, and if you'll let Dad give you what the clothes were worth like he offered to, I'll work odd jobs for however long it takes to pay him back."

Paige was far too dumbfounded to respond right away. It was like watching a poorly orchestrated dream unfold before her. What could possibly have caused such a dramatic change of heart if not a lecture from her father? Was she truly sorry for what she'd done? "If you'd rather, we could leave your father out of it altogether and you could pay me directly instead."

Paige set aside the comb she'd used to liberate most of the paint from her hair, then feeling awkward about the unexpected situation, she ran her hands over the delicate pleats in her linen slacks. If her jeans had dried yet from having had to wash them again after yesterday's mud escapades, she'd have worn those instead. She'd seen no sense putting her favorite tan slacks and brown print blouse in the same jeopardy as some of her other clothes. "You could work off part of the debt by helping me move into my new house in a couple of weeks. That is if the purchase goes straight through like it's supposed to."

"You'd let me do that?" Jeri's forehead notched in exactly the way her father's had earlier when they'd discussed her dreams. "Even after everything I've done to you these past five days you'd let me work for you like that?"

Paige had to smile at the child's perplexed expression. "I'm willing to forgive, forget, and start over if you are. Besides, I'll need the help. I've accumulated a lot of stuff over the years."

"I can't believe you are being this nice to me after all that I've done to you." Jeri studied her a long moment then finally smiled, too. "Okay, it's a deal." Her shoulders visibly relaxed. "Instead of making Dad pay you back for whatever those clothes cost, and then me having to pay him that same amount, I'll pay you back myself by helping you with some of the work when you move to Mt. Pine. Let's shake on it."

When Jeri stuck out her hand, Paige leaned forward to make sure she didn't have something hidden inside, then accepted the firm handshake.

Jeri looked as pleased as Paige was by this turn of events. "By the way, how much does that outfit I ruined sell for?"

"The slacks and blouse together sell for just over two hundred dollars." When Jeri's pale blue eyes bugged nearly out of her head, Paige hurried to add, "But because I'm the one who designed the blouse, and I designed it to go with those particular slacks, I only had to pay what the material was worth. I think it cost me about fifty dollars for both garments. I'd think ten hours of work ought to call us square." Also, it should give them ten extra hours to get to know each other a little better. Ten hours not forced on them by either Damon or Blair. Paige could hardly wait.

"Ten hours it is." Jeri's smile widened when she gestured to the clock beside Paige's bed. "It's almost time to go downstairs and eat supper. You hungry?"

"Yes." Suddenly, Paige was very hungry. Happy, too, even though still a little leery over everything that just happened. "Let's go see what Miss Hattie and Cora have prepared for supper. Then if you feel up to it, I challenge you to a game of checkers down in the parlor."

"Checkers?" Her face lit with eagerness. "I happen to be a pro at checkers. You're on!"

Damon glanced at his watch, then dropped his arm back to his side and headed back toward the inn. He'd missed supper, but wasn't really all that hungry.

Still unable to concentrate on his work, even though he

now had most of the figures he needed, he had taken a walk along the rocky cliffs overlooking the gated cove where he'd promptly lost track of time. Since having found out how very unhappy Paige was living in New York, he felt far too guilty about the promise he'd made Blair to continue working on the very bid that was to gain him his reward for having kept that promise.

Torn now between hoping Paige succeeded in bravely following her own heart after all these years, and still wanting her to change her mind about leaving New York so she'd stay at Blair's side, he had sought time alone to think. Time to decide what, if anything, to do about Paige. About Jeri. And about Blair.

Nothing was clear to him anymore. Instead of helping Paige arrive at what Blair had told him was the right decision for everyone including Paige, it could very well be that by doing what he could to change her mind he was merely helping Blair sentence her sister to a life filled with yet more unfulfilled dreams. Much like his own.

He didn't know what to think about it all. Blair had clearly misrepresented Paige's situation to him. But whether Blair had done so on purpose, he didn't know. It could be that Blair, in her own blind, self-centered way, truly believed Paige would be far more happy there in New York while continuing to do the same thing she'd done all these years, than were she to move to Mt. Pine and open a dress shop—and maybe settle down and have a family. It was too hard for someone like Blair to see that kind of life as anything but a drudgery.

But it was what Paige wanted to do. Needed to do.

And yet he was supposed to try everything within his power to stop her.

God, how he hated himself for having made Blair that promise. Even if he chose not to follow through, he hated himself for ever having thought it right to try to alter someone else's choices. And why? So he could save his father's businesses. Save his father's lifelong dreams.

"Noble reason for an ignoble cause," he muttered

against the evening wind as he shoved his hands deep into his jeans pockets.

So whose dreams were more important anyway? His father's? Or Paige's? Now he hated himself for another promise he'd made. This one to his father—to do his level best to carry out the family business in an honorable yet profitable manner. Having made that promise, it became his duty to carry forward with the construction and lumber businesses.

Damon's heart felt like cold lead pressing hard into his gut while he proceeded up the dark, desolate path toward the inn. Both his promise to his father and the one he had made Blair worked against what he really wanted to do. Which was to support Paige in her belated decision to follow her heart.

He knew too well the misery she would face if she didn't follow through and do what she really longed to do with her life. Who was he to sentence her to such grief? Besides, he liked the idea of having Paige nearby. Especially when he considered that one day Jeri would grow up and leave home. Then where would he be? He'd be alone, and probably wishing he'd found some way to include Paige in his life. Just the thought of what it would be like to have Paige around always made his pulses race.

If only that contract weren't so blasted important.

"There you are," Miss Hattie called out as soon as he'd neared the front steps.

Damon had been so lost in thought, the voice startled him. He glanced down the dimly lit veranda until he spotted her sitting in a spindle-back rocker near one of the lantern style hanging lamps with a dish pan of fresh-picked peas in her lap.

"You missed supper," she commented, not glancing down while continuing to work the small white peas out of their dark green shells. "I put a plate in the microwave ready for you to heat up. Two minutes should do it. It's there when you're ready."

"Thanks." He took a short, determined breath. "I'll

come back down and eat after I've had a word with Jeri about something.'' It was high time he put his daughter's behavior above his promise to Blair and take charge again. Jeri would apologize to Paige for having ruined her clothing if he had to carry the child over to Paige's room kicking and screaming.

"Oh, but Jeri's not upstairs."

"She's not?'' He paused to listen for the television. He heard none. Surely she hadn't run off to see Frankie after he'd told her not to go there. "Where is she, then?"

He glanced in the direction of the co-op and saw only the lights on the pier remained lit. The co-op building itself stood dark against the deepening gray sky. That meant Frankie and her family had already gone home—twice as far to walk and retrieve his daughter.

"She's in the parlor playing checkers with Paige. Seems that checkerboard I keep set up in there became too much of a temptation.'' She glanced at the locket-watch dangling from her neck and squinted to see in the soft light. "They've been at it for over half an hour now."

Damon froze with one foot on the top step and the other on the planked floor, uncertain he'd heard her right. "Jeri and Paige? Inside together? Playing checkers?"

"And having a lot of fun at it. So much so, you might want to go in and join them. Ask if you can play the winner. Although I'm not sure who that would be. They looked pretty evenly matched earlier when I took them some lemonade to sip.''

Damon stepped over to the nearest lighted window to have a peek through the lacy sheers. Sure enough, Paige and Jeri sat on either side of a small table, laughing over something Jeri had just said. He couldn't have been more shocked had he stuck a wet finger in a live electrical socket.

"By the by, Damon, you've had a couple of telephone messages in the past few hours.'' She lifted the flat pan high enough with one hand to feel around inside her apron pocket with the other. "I think maybe she tried calling your number first, because I heard that little telephone of yours beep-beeping when I was upstairs earlier. But she must have given up on that and tried calling you on the Seascape line instead."

She? Damon's heart grew heavier still while he waited for Miss Hattie to finally produce the little pieces of paper. Undoubtedly, it was time for him to give another update.

"They're from someone named Blair." She watched him carefully for a reaction. "The voice sounded familiar to me, though I'm not sure why. I suppose she's called here for you before, but without giving her name. Is she the woman you've been dating lately?"

Dating? Oh, right. He'd told Miss Hattie he had finally started dating again as a way to keep her from trying to match him with Paige. He had known early on what a lousy idea it would be to let himself become romantically involved with Blair's little sister.

Too bad he didn't always allow his own common sense to rule.

"No, Blair is just a friend," he replied, looking down at the rectangles of paper handed him rather than at Hattie herself, uncomfortable over the lie he'd told. He patted his pocket to see if he still had his eyeglasses with him, then frowned when he realized he'd left them on the desk upstairs. He would have to wait until he had his glasses or better lighting to read the tiny scrawl. "Did Blair happen to say what she wanted?"

"Just for you to call her before ten o'clock. Said something about going out to a party then, and she's also not going to be around tomorrow." Miss Hattie shook her head and returned her attention to her peas. "Ten o'clock seems awfully late for a person to be heading off to a party. It's more the time for folks to be heading off to dreamland."

Not wanting to face a conversation with Blair on an empty stomach, Damon tucked the messages into his front pocket. He'd wait until after he ate to call her. Right now, he still had too much to think about concerning Paige. And Jeri.

What could possibly have happened to bring those two back together? He hesitated with his hand on the curved screen door handle to glance again at Miss Hattie. "This place does have a way of working small miracles, doesn't it?"

"Hmmm?" Clearly, Miss Hattie had already dismissed him from her thoughts. "What was that?"

"Nothing," he smiled. "I was just thinking how nice it is to hear Paige and Jeri in there having such fun."

"Especially after that little incident out in the gazebo," she agreed, pausing in her work. "You'd think something like that would have put the two at each other's throats for quite some time."

"You know about that?" But how could she? She was in town at the time.

"Aye, they told me all about it during supper."

"They did?"

"Aye, they did that so I wouldn't be too surprised when I looked out tomorrow morning and found the two of them painting the rest of the gazebo. They seemed to think the thing looked rather odd with only the seats inside freshly painted." She took a deep breath of contentment. "So they've decided to paint the rest of it. Inside and out. And if they have any paint left over when they finish that, they plan to paint some of the chairs out in the garden. How truly sweet they are."

Damon stared at her a moment in utter disbelief, then went on inside. Not wanting to intrude on his daughter's fun, and not ready to be in the same room with Paige, who attracted him like no other woman ever had, Damon walked hurriedly past the parlor, barely taking the time to glance inside as he passed by.

Having just entertained thoughts of what it might be like to have Paige a more permanent part of his life, he didn't want to be reminded that he and Jeri were supposed to be turning her off to the idea of marriage and children. Let the two enjoy themselves for awhile. Tomorrow would be soon enough for them to find reason to dislike each other again. Plus he had other reasons to want to avoid Paige for now. In the past half hour, it had become clear to him that she was the type woman he could fall for in a big way. If he allowed himself to become any more involved with her than he already was, he'd end up devastated when he eventually lost her. Which was exactly what would happen. The women he cared about always left him, usually not too long after the novelty of having conquered him wore off.

He suspected it was his appearance that drew them to him in the beginning, but those good looks of his had never been enough to keep them interested for very long. Sad, but true. He had never been able to hold on to anyone important to him. No matter how hard he tried, he couldn't seem to make any relationship last. In the end, even Trana had left him for grander pursuits.

Paige would too. He never should have let her kiss him after he'd saved her from that tree. It had only stirred to life emotions that had been better left stagnant. He should have kept her out of his heart. By not doing that, he courted trouble. And he knew it.

Battling the insecurities that had plagued him since his youth, Damon headed on back to the kitchen to eat his meal alone. Then, he'd go upstairs and call Blair. If he didn't, he risked having her angry with him and he couldn't afford to let that happen.

There were still his father's businesses to worry about.

For the second morning since the ugly incident in the gazebo, Jeri greeted Paige in the dining room with a cheerful smile. Today, she had given up her usual sloppy reds and pinks for a pretty yellow blouse and white, cuffed shorts. Having chosen not to wear her usual ponytail, her long blond hair fell down her back and across her shoulders like a shimmering curtain of spun gold. For the first time, Paige saw Jeri as the beautiful young lady her father so wanted her to be.

It both thrilled and unsettled her.

"We're having French toast for breakfast," Jeri said after glancing up from a full glass of orange juice to spot Paige entering from the main hall. "Miss Hattie's already gone to get it."

"With strawberries again?" Paige asked, already looking for and finding the small cut-glass bowl that contained large, red-rimmed slices of the chilled fruit. Pulling out her chair, she settled in her usual spot directly across from Jeri, careful to take her linen napkin and spread it neatly across her white slacks. It surprised her again, when Jeri did likewise. No prompting this morning?

"And lots of powdered sugar, too." Jeri gestured to a lidded silver bowl with a shifting spoon beside it. "Of course, some people like plain old maple syrup on their toast; but I'm like you, I can't see passing up another shot at those really fat strawberries they have up here. You just can't beat them."

"That's true." Glancing at the place beside Jeri where Damon usually sat, she noticed it still perfectly set, a napkin tented around his juice glass. "Is your father sleeping in again?" She tried to keep a casual tone.

Jeri nodded, having finally taken a sip of her juice and needing to swallow first. "I think he's already back at work on that bid he has to get out next week. I stopped by to see if he was ready to come downstairs and, even though he was dressed and all, he said he'd wait and eat later. He probably won't come down until after we've already left for Boothbay."

Paige's fingers rested around her own juice glass while she thought about the decidedly feminine day they had planned. First a craft fair near the harbor, then lunch at a cafe famous for its salad bar. How odd to have such a day planned with this child.

Remembering the ugly outburst from just two days ago, and all the incidents preceding that, Paige continued to be rightfully distrustful of the overt change in Jeri's attitude toward her, but decided not to analyze it any longer. She was tired of worrying all the time. About Jeri. And about

Damon. "Your father certainly has kept very busy these past couple of days."

"Yeah, if I didn't know better, I'd think Dad was trying to avoid us on purpose."

Paige couldn't argue that. Lately, she had noticed Damon watching from a distance, but rarely bothering to join them. It was probably just his way of allowing her a stronger effect on Jeri now that the pendulum had finally swung and the girl enjoyed being with her. Even so, Paige wished Damon would find a reason to visit with them on occasion—more than during the evening meals and once or twice in the afternoons. She enjoyed being around the feelings of warmth and family she sensed between those two and wanted to experience more of that.

But then, like she'd told Jeri more than once, people couldn't always have everything they wanted. If they could, her own life wouldn't be so off target.

A soft rustle just inside the hall door caught Paige's attention and brought it spinning back to what went on around her.

"Here they are, straight from the kitchen," Miss Hattie chimed, entering with her usual soft smile. She wore a sea-green cotton dress gathered loosely at the waist, and carried a small platter of steaming French toast. "Better eat them while they are still hot."

Distracted by the delicious aroma and the conversation that bantered between Miss Hattie and Jeri, Paige managed not to think or talk about Damon again until they had all eaten their fill. "Jeri, as soon as you've brushed your teeth, you need to stop by your father's room and tell him we're leaving. You might also mention that we probably won't be back until at least mid-afternoon."

Jeri hurried away from the table, eager to comply.

"That girl is certainly changing in a hurry, isn't she?" Miss Hattie said, leaning back in her chair to sip the last of her coffee. "Growing up."

Paige smiled, hoping she had at least something to do

with that. "I think maybe you're right. She has started to grow up, at least a little."

"It sounds like you care about that child a good deal."

Miss Hattie's mention of caring caused Paige a moment's concern. She well remembered what had happened earlier when she'd allowed herself to care about Jeri. "I do care about her," she replied, choosing honesty over caution. "I've found it far too hard not to care about her."

"And her father? Do you care about him, too?"

Paige's heart skipped a full beat when she glanced at Miss Hattie again. The woman studied her like a hawk. "Of course I care about her father." She smoothed a nonexistent wrinkle out of her maroon and gold jungle-print blouse. We're friends."

"Close friends?"

Paige shook her head adamantly. Having been told about the betting that goes on at the Blue Moon in which the locals try to decide which of the Seascape Inn's guests will end up making a love-match and in what amount of time, she decided to discourage Miss Hattie from placing any senseless wagers. There'd be no wedding announcements this go'round. "No, not close friends. But we are friends."

To Paige's surprise, Miss Hattie looked extremely pleased by that response, then made no more mention of Damon. Nor about caring. Nor about friendships. Perhaps she'd wagered against the two of them making a match because, instead of prying further into Paige's relationship with Damon, she abruptly changed the subject. "It's a shame Frankie has to stay home again today. She does so enjoy being around Jeri, but her mother thinks she should help Hatch repair that gate today. Especially since she's the one who forgot to latch it back the night that storm blew through last month and broke it."

Paige didn't comment. Truth was, she was glad to have Jeri to herself another day. They'd had great fun painting the gazebo yesterday morning then helping Miss Hattie transplant all those geraniums in the afternoon. She'd learned a lot about caring for gardens, which would help her when it came time to do something with her own yard.

"Oh," Miss Hattie continued, having already dismissed her thoughts about Frankie. "I heard on the radio that today's supposed to be a hot one. I hope you two remember to put on plenty of sunscreen and insect repellent before you start wandering around all those craft booths. There's not much shade to be had in that part of the harbor and you already know what pests some of these insects can be."

Grateful the conversation hadn't returned to Damon even though she sensed that's who Miss Hattie really wanted to talk about, Paige agreed to make sure she and Jeri both put on sunscreen and repellent, and also promised to leave off a cook book with Mrs. Hayz, a friend of Miss Hattie's who had a booth at the craft fair where she sold all manner of gourd art.

By the time Jeri returned from upstairs, Miss Hattie had toddled off to the kitchen with her tray of dirty dishes, and Paige was ready to push aside all thought of Damon to start her day long adventure with Jeri.

❧ *Chapter 16* ❧

With Damon having made himself so scarce during the past couple of days, Paige had found it much easier to control the physical longings she felt toward him. By the time Friday afternoon rolled around, she had all but forgotten how trying it was on her emotions to be near him.

She and Jeri had enjoyed their day wandering about the craft fair, purchasing a few items they thought would look nice in her new house. It wasn't until they'd returned, changed into their swimsuits with plans to cool off down at the beach, and then discovered Damon already there that her libido shifted back into high gear again. Reminded just how deeply he affected her and how addled it left her, she did what she could to steer clear of him. For sanity's sake.

And for Jeri's.

When they first arrived to find Damon sitting on the same rock where he and Paige had talked days earlier, Paige noticed that Jeri, too, became suddenly very tense—as if not sure she wanted her father and Paige to be around each other again. But when Paige purposely didn't do much more than tell him about girl-type fun they'd had earlier and how much help Jeri had been picking out decorations for her house before heading out to swim, Jeri relaxed again. After only a few more minutes chatting with her father, she joined Paige in the deeper water of the inlet.

Delighted at how well she and Jeri were getting along,

almost like sisters, Paige climbed up onto a small island of clustered rocks to sit and talk with her new friend awhile longer. She had hoped Damon would give up his vigil from the beach and join them, but when she finally braved a look in his direction, he'd already gathered up his cap and his towel and was halfway up the stairs. He paused near the top, turning to glance back at them briefly, then continued on out of sight.

Disappointed more than she should be for she had no important reason to want him to stay, Paige returned her attention to Jeri who sat on the rock beside her, exploring the inside of a large sea shell. Paige noticed the girl didn't sit sprawl-legged like she usually did. Instead, she sat with her legs together, ankles crossed. She also held her back and shoulders erect. *Far more ladylike.* Paige warmed at the realization progress had been made, however small, and wished Damon had stuck around a little longer to witness some of the changes. A compliment from him would carry far with Jeri, who truly adored her father.

''Where'd you find that?''

''This shell? It was caught between those rocks there,'' she gestured to a separate island where the low tide sloshed around the base of several jutting boulders. Big blue eyes, much like her father's, looked up from the shell briefly. ''I noticed it because of the way the sun hit it.'' She turned the thing over then back again. ''It's not broken anywhere so I thought I might use it to make a jewelry bowl like that one we saw at the fair today. I figure all I need is some of the clear stuff they coated it with.''

Surprised she would think of something like that, Paige smiled. Hating to see such a beautiful face hidden behind wet hair, she reached over to pull a clinging strand away from Jeri's cheek and was surprised when Jeri didn't try to thump her hand away like she would have a few days ago. ''Well, you just never know where you will find one of tomorrow's little treasures, do you?'' Sometimes they came in the unexpected form of a sprite twelve-year old. ''Do you have much jewelry to put in it?''

Jeri's mouth quirked to one side, then flattened. "Not much." She dropped her gaze back to the smooth white shell with pink and grey traces. "Just some of my mother's jewelry that my other grandmother came by and gave to me a few weeks after Mom died. Grandma had no use for it and thought I might want to wear it someday."

Paige considered that. Jeri was of an age now a little jewelry might help her to feel a bit more feminine. "And do you ever wear any of it?"

"No!"

The answer came a little too abruptly. Was that anger in Jeri's voice? Were they back to that already? Paige's hopes plummeted. "Why not? Don't you like to wear jewelry?"

Jeri shrugged, refusing to look up while she ran her wet fingers back and forth over the smooth inner wall of the sea shell. "Some jewelry is okay, I guess. I like tiny gold chains with pretty charms on them. Sort of. But Mom's jewelry isn't like that. It's way too big and—" she struggled for just the right word, "—colorful."

Sounded like perhaps gaudy was the term the child wanted. "So you don't wear it at all."

"No. Don't plan to either. Wouldn't feel right if I did." She cut Paige the briefest of glances. "Just because Grandma gave the jewelry to me, doesn't mean Mom ever intended for me to have it."

What an odd thing to say. Why wouldn't Jeri's mother want her to have her jewelry? "I don't know, I think if your grandmother gave it to you rather than keep it for herself, she did so because she knew your mother wanted you to have it."

"Think so?" Jeri's expression brightened with what could only be hope—but only for a moment. Just as abruptly, her sad expression returned. "No, I don't think Mom ever said nothing at all to Grandma about wanting me to have anything she ever owned. Mom never really liked me much."

That was a horrible thing to say. But what would be

even more horrible was if she believed it. Something chewing at Paige told her that she did. "I'm sure you are wrong about that. I'm sure your mother loved you a lot. Just like your father loves you."

Jeri buffed the tip of her tongue back and forth between her lips while she considered that, then looked at Paige with a crinkled brow. "Did your mother love you before she died?"

"Of course she did. We were very close during the time she was still alive."

"Lucky you." Dismissing the conversation, Jeri tucked the large shell into the top part of her swim suit and, without another word, dove back into the water. When her blond head broke the surface again, she was a good distance away, too far to continue an earnest conversation.

Paige watched, deeply concerned about the grim feelings the child harbored as Jeri avoided looking back at her. From where Jeri swam, she could see part of the marina and the apex of land that held the lighthouse so that's where Jeri landed her gaze. After a moment, she gestured to the rocky peninsula with a quick lift of her wet chin. "Can I go see if Frankie's finished with that gate yet? If she is, maybe she can come swimming with us."

Paige didn't know what to answer. Part of her wanted to find some way to resume their telling conversation about the girl's mother and in the process learn something about why her parents divorced, while another part worried she had monopolized Jeri's time a little too much already.

Finally, she did the unselfish thing and waved her on. "Warn her we only have another half hour or so to swim. I have an important telephone call coming in about six o'clock and your father has already said you aren't to go swimming without me here to watch you. So when I go in, you two will have to go in, too."

While Jeri headed for the beach to put on her sandals and grab her towel, Paige glanced in the direction of the inn, even though she couldn't actually see it from there. Time to give Blair another update. Only today Paige looked forward to it. A lot had happened since she and Blair last talked Tuesday night.

Finally, she had some very real progress to report. She could hardly wait to hear Blair's happy response.

As it happened, she didn't have to wait long. When she finished showering and changing into a breezy salmon pink sundress, the phone in her bedroom was well into a third ring.

"It turns out you were right all along, Blair," Paige admitted cheerfully after the usual exchange of hellos. "And for once I am very glad that you were." Holding the phone to her ear with one hand, she worked a comb through her freshly washed hair with the other. "It's true. All Jeri needed was someone to fill the big gap in her life that having no mother and no sister had left her with. At first, she didn't want me acting like either one toward her, but she's come around now. You wouldn't believe the progress I've been able to make in these last two days. It's amazing."

"What *sort* of progress?"

Paige wanted to laugh at how hesitant Blair sounded. "I know, I have a hard time believing it, too. But you should see Jeri. The girl has started wearing her hair down, giving herself a much softer look, and today she left all her baseball caps up in her room. Plus, she's started tucking her shirts in. The girl actually has a nice waistline. Oh, and this morning she did something else that nearly blew me away. She put her napkin in her lap without being prodded. Then, today at lunch, she thought to ask me which fork to use, and then used the one I told her to. It's amazing how hard she's trying and how much she's changed in so little time. What gets me is that I don't even know what happened to make her change her attitude toward me so quickly."

"You sound pleased by all this."

"Oh, I am. In these past couple of days amazing things have been happening to me, too. You might find it hard to believe, but Jeri has begun to fill a need that, until recently, I only suspected I had.''

''What kind of need?''

Good question. ''It's hard to explain. It's like there was an emptiness inside me that I'd disregarded. A void I hadn't noticed existed until suddenly I'd started to fill it. Funny thing is, when I came here, I'd vowed not to let myself care about Damon or Jeri. But with Jeri, that proved impossible. I couldn't help myself. We are too much alike.''

''*Alike?*''

''Yes, in a strange way we are very alike, yet obviously different. After all, until I met Jeri, I'd never touched a worm, or dug for crabs, or gotten a home run in baseball. Yet, she does that sort of thing all the time. There's nothing Jeri won't try. Nothing she'll back away from. She's truly an amazing child.'' Paige's heart swelled with the unexpected joy the child had brought her, and a very deep sense of pride. ''I am so happy that Jeri and I have finally become friends I could burst. And to think, I owe this all to you.''

''What does Damon have to say about all this?''

''Damon?'' Her heart twisted. Though ecstatic over the progress she'd made with Jeri, she ached at the thought of Damon and how he'd suddenly distanced himself. Even though that distancing was undoubtedly best for all of them, it left her wishing things could be different. That Damon himself could be different. ''Not much. He's still too busy with that bid he has to have done by the first of next week. But surely he's noticed some of the changes in what time he has been downstairs. He would have to be blind not to.''

''Then I guess he's blind because he didn't mention a word of any of this to me earlier when I asked him how things were going up there.''

''You called him for a report on me?'' Didn't Blair trust her to do what she'd promised to do? ''Why?''

''I wasn't after a report. I called him this afternoon

about four o'clock to find out where you were, and why you were not answering your telephone.'' Her voice rose with typical Blair annoyance. How she hated petty inconveniences. ''After we wound up today's shoot a little earlier than usual, I was free to call much sooner than I'd thought I'd be. But a lot of good that did when I couldn't get you to answer your blasted phone.''

''At four o'clock? That's about the time Jeri and I were off swimming.'' And having their first little heart to heart. Her thoughts drifted to the yearning she'd heard in Jeri's voice when the child had mentioned her mother. How Paige longed to know more about that.

''So I heard.''

Paige set her comb down and leaned back in the chair, confused by Blair's tone. ''What's wrong? You sound angry about something. I would think the fact that I was off getting to know Jeri better would make you sound a little happier than that. I think it is my having spent so much time with her recently that finally allowed me to break through some of those barriers she's tossed up. Once I'm through those, I should be able to make an even bigger difference in that child's life.'' She could hardly wait.

''Sorry. I've had a very trying couple of days. And they seem to be growing more and more trying as they go along. *Nothing* has gone right for me lately.'' She fell silent a moment, but Paige didn't try to fill the quiet. Blair just needed time to evaluate exactly what it was she wanted to say. ''The truth is, I'm not so sure I believe everything you've told me about Jeri.''

''You think I'm making it up?'' She'd never lied to Blair in her life. Avoided the truth maybe, but never once had she purposely lied.

''No, I think you truly believe everything you told me.'' She paused again. ''Paige, I don't like to be the one to dampen your spirits, but I think that the little imp is probably pretending to like you just to throw you off guard for some reason. Nobody changes that much that quickly.''

''But why would she pretend something like that?''

Paige wanted to know, an uneasy feeling creeping into her stomach. She well remembered the angry tirade just two days earlier when Jeri had blurted out how much she hated her, and how Jeri thought she was a liar. But they'd gotten past that. "No, I think we've reached a very real turning point here. Although she was very reluctant to accept my company at first, we're actually becoming friends now."

"Are you sure?"

"Of course I am." Paige heard far less conviction in her voice than had been there a few minutes earlier. Her sister's negative attitude had affected her more than it should. "Why do you always have to be such a worrier?"

"Because, dear sister, if I don't worry about you, no one will. It's obvious you never concern yourself with what all could go wrong in a situation, or you wouldn't make so many mistakes all the time. Sweetie, I've known Jeri all her life, which is exactly why I don't trust her." She fell silent again, giving Paige a chance to worry she might be right.

"But she's changed."

"I'm sorry, but I don't buy it. I think that child is up to her usual no good."

"You're wrong this time, Blair. Jeri just needed someone to reach out a friendly hand to her. Someone other than her father. She may have been cautious of me at first, imagining I came here to trap Damon, but I think now she understands that fear was unfounded." Holding the receiver to her ear with her shoulder, she dropped both hands to her lap, studying how pale and water-logged they looked against the deep salmon color of her dress. "I know better than to go around harboring fantasies that include someone as handsome and carefree as Damon. It's a self-destructive thing to do. I learned that lesson. Remember?"

"I miss you, Paige," Blair said, suddenly switching issues. "I'm ready for you to come back here."

Paige closed her eyes, steeling herself for what would follow that. "I know. And I will be back. For a few days anyway. I do have to finish packing. Plus, I'll visit when

I can, and you can visit me when you do the shoots your agent gets you in Dallas.''

"No, I mean I'm ready for you to come back here to stay. I'm ready for you to forget all about moving to Texas and stay right here in New York with me.''

"I know you are. But I can't.'' A familiar pang of guilt wrenched through Paige while she listened to Blair's long, melodramatic sigh. How she hated hurting her sister like that.

"I talked to Emilie Teek yesterday,'' Blair told her, already switching tactics. "She misses you, too. She told me to tell you that she still hopes you'll change your mind about moving and come back to work for her. That's where you belong, you know. In New York, coming up with extraordinary designs for MissTeek Fashions. Not in Mt. Pine, throwing your life away like Mother did.''

Okay, time to end the conversation. Paige had heard enough of that before she left for Maine. "Blair, it's six-thirty. I have to go or I'll be late for supper.'' Before Blair could comment again, if about nothing else than the ungodly hour they ate while at the inn, Paige offered a sugary sweet goodbye then hung up. Her hands still trembled when she scooted the telephone back where it had been. The last thing she needed was to take off on yet another deep guilt trip. It was bad enough she now fostered fresh doubts about her budding relationship with Jeri.

With Frankie and Jeri off running an errand for Miss Hattie, Paige found herself at loose ends the following morning. She was still a little troubled over some of what Blair had said to her the evening before about suspecting Jeri to have ulterior motives, but not enough to be paranoid about it.

Already dressed in her favorite loose-pleat white shorts with a white-stitched lilac blouse, she didn't want to sit around her room worrying about what might or might not be, and knowing Damon had not yet finished that bid he was working on, she decided to take a short walk and headed off toward the marina.

Having grown accustomed to the feeling that someone was watching her, she didn't bother to scour the area for a glimpse of Beaulah Favish, whom she had yet to meet. If the woman was out there, so be it.

With plenty of time to kill before the girls' return, she continued beyond the marina on toward the lighthouse. In the eight days she'd been there, she had yet to venture onto the small, rocky peninsula northeast of the inn, and was curious to have a closer look at the quaint little structures there.

When the shell-strewn path she followed passed through a newly repaired gate, she was close enough to see that a small door at the base of the tower stood open. But instead of heading there, she continued on toward the little house attached off to one side.

"Hello?" she called out after entering the tiny side yard where bright yellow daisies bloomed in the full sun. Wanting permission from whoever lived there to climb up to the top and have a look, she had started around to the front door when she noticed a note taped to one of the windows.

"Gone to New Harbor to get paint for the fence. Back soon, Hatch."

Remembering Hatch as Frankie's colorful old friend who thought people like her who showed "gumption" were to be admired, Paige decided he wouldn't mind if she went on inside and had a look around.

"After all, what else would one expect of someone with gumption?" Smiling at the thought, she walked back to the open door and, finding it was not at all dark inside, hurried up the winding stairs. To her surprise, she rested only once during that long flight up, being in better shape than usual as a result of all the exercise she'd done lately.

Pleased by that, she crossed through a gleaming white, glass-lined room filled with brass instruments and, surprised herself when she stepped out alone onto what was labeled the cock walk. Further exhilarated by the ocean scents carried on the warm wind, she breathed deeply the intoxicating air. Although more than a little intimidated by the height, she felt lured to the sturdy black railing.

Gripping the iron band, she refused to look down. Instead, she stared off toward the ocean where several white terns flew suspended in the sun-warmed breeze, then beyond to the many islands visible to her now—two covered with fat, lazy harbor seals. With the squawking birds, barking seals, and the thrashing of water against the craggy shore a few hundred feet away, she barely heard her own foot tapping against the rail when she next turned her attention to the Seascape Inn, nestled in all those colorful flower gardens and surrounded by blankets of dark green grass. Wanting a better view, she moved to that part of the cock walk.

With the wind stirring behind her now, she pried one hand off the railing to hold her hair back away from her face while she studied the plush scenery. Her heart skipped a full beat when she noticed how tall the trees were that shaded the inn, and recalled having gotten stuck in one of the larger ones. But, whether she'd responded like that from the memory of her stark, white fear or from the embarrassments that followed, she wasn't sure. "I should have known better."

"Known better about what?"

Not having heard Damon's approach, Paige gasped and turned to face him. With one hand pressed over her heart and the other still gripping the rail, she shouted to be heard over the many noises. "I thought you still had work to do."

He shaded his eyes against the morning sun. "I do, but Miss Hattie asked if I would be nice enough do her a little favor. She's such a dear woman, I hated to tell her no when I knew all it would take is maybe fifteen minutes of my time. Especially when I'm almost finished with my work anyway."

Paige watched how the wind tossed his hair first into his face, then away, wondering how he managed to look handsome even then. She could well imagine what her own ratty hair made her look like at the moment. "Why? What was the favor?"

"She found out she had some mail for Hatch. Somehow two letters had gotten mixed in with her own, and because one was from the Coast Guard, she was afraid it might be important. Since he has no telephone right now, she asked me to bring them over and hand them to him personally rather than simply put it in his mailbox by the road since he probably won't check his mail again until Monday. She wanted him to know he had it now. When I saw the note on the window and found that the door to the house itself was locked when usually it's not, I decided to come up and put it the only other place where I knew he wouldn't miss it."

"And where's that?"

He gestured to the glass wall behind him. "In the light chamber, over there near the compass. Hatch is a creature of habit. He ends almost every day up here smoking his pipe and watching the ships pass."

Feeling awkward to have Damon only a few feet away, especially when she'd thought herself alone, Paige turned and looked out in the direction she thought Hatch probably saw those ships. When she pivoted toward the ocean again, the wind that had felt exhilarating to her moments earlier plastered her clothing against the front of her body in a disconcerting way. She pulled at the lilac material self-consciously. "I guess then it's not always this windy up here."

"No, there's usually a pretty stout wind out here across the point," he corrected, clearly noting the way her clothes adhered to her form, despite her futile efforts to remedy the situation. His own standard-cut cotton shirt, barely one shade bluer than his eyes, whipped tight around his stout muscles, though the wind made little difference in the snug fit of his jeans.

"Then how does he smoke his pipe?"

"He does that inside the light chamber. Not out here at the rail. He usually watches the ships from in there, too."

Thinking that also a better place for them to stand and talk without having to shout at each other, or worry about her clothes and hair, she pushed away from the metal railing and headed back inside. As expected, Damon followed.

Her heart, which she'd hoped was racing from the fear of where she'd just stood outside, continued to beat unmercifully beneath her breast when she relocated to a few feet away from the huge metal-encased lamp that had in its time warned many a ship in the night. Seeing her disheveled reflection in the gleaming glass cover, she quickly raked her fingers through the tousles to make herself a little more presentable.

Damon stood several yards away. "Need a comb?"

Adding to her distress, he closed the distance between them to hand her a small black comb he'd slipped out of his back pocket and used on his own gorgeous hair. She'd much rather he stayed on the other side of the small chamber. There was something about being alone with him while surrounded by such majestic beauty that both intrigued and alarmed her.

"Yes, thanks." She accepted his offer and quickly worked the comb through her hair a few strands at a time. Once she had it looking adequate, she handed the comb back.

He studied her a long moment before slipping it back into his jeans pocket. "I explained what I'm doing here. But what are you doing here? I thought you, Jeri, and Frankie had plans for today."

"We did—*do*. But Miss Hattie needed the girls to run an errand for her, too. She'd accidentally left one of her good cooking pots over at Miss Millie's house the other day and needed it back. She also wanted the girls to take the preacher a magazine she thought he should see, and to stop back by The Store to get a gallon of milk and a couple of cloves of garlic. I figured it would take them at least forty-five minutes to do all that so I decided to spend some of that time coming here to see the view from the inside of the lighthouse. I've been here eight days and haven't had a chance to see any of this. I've been too busy."

"Putting up with Jeri," he commented, his expression thoughtful.

Paige couldn't tell if he was troubled by that notion or pleased by it. She hoped pleased.

"Oh, I don't mind," she hurried to assure him, just in case it was troubled he felt. "Especially not when you consider the progress that I've made these past couple of days. I truly treasure the time Jeri and I spend together. I've learned a lot about myself from that girl. I'm so glad she's finally letting me be her friend."

Damon looked as cautious as Blair had sounded on the telephone last night while he ran his hands down the front of his pale blue cotton shirt. "You've learned something about yourself? Like what?"

"Like what all I'm missing by not having a family of my own. In the past few days, I've had such fun being with Jeri and watching the different changes taking place, that I now understand what a true joy she can be. You are very lucky to have her in your life."

Damon's gaze shifted to the ocean. "I can't argue that. She's what's kept me going all these years. If it weren't for Jer, I don't think I could have handled half of what I've had to handle these past several years." His blue eyes narrowed slightly as if maybe he'd spotted something questionable on the horizon, then widened again. When he brought his attention to Paige again, his expression was tense, as if something alarming had just occurred to him. "But don't get the wrong idea. Parenthood has its problems. Believe me. Plenty of problems. There are times I've been tempted to pull out every last hair on my head."

"Oh, no, don't you dare do that," she blurted out without thinking. Embarrassed, she hurried to add, "that could hurt."

He chuckled, his arms relaxing. "I'm sure it would."

Mesmerized by the dimples now flanking that wide, always-sexy smile of his, Paige grappled for something else to say. Something that might make her feel more at ease in his strong presence. What was it about this guy that made her insides turn into jelly and her brains to worthless mush?

An awkward silence stretched between them. Wishing desperately for something to say, she stared at the sensual shape of his mouth as his smile slowly abated. His glittering expression grew intent just before he took a tentative step closer.

For some reason, Damon suddenly planned to kiss her. That much was obvious. Should she risk her heart and let him? Or play safe and turn away? But how could she play it safe when she so longed to experience his provocative kiss at least once more? The truth was, she yearned to kiss him again as much as he obviously yearned to kiss her. So why not allow it? Just one more kiss to carry in her memory?

Paige's mouth parted in anticipation while Damon bent forward to press his lips warmly against hers. At first, that's all about them that touched. Just their lips. But that simple contact was enough to send Paige's senses spiraling and make her legs suddenly weak. By the time he'd drawn her body hard against his and she felt her breasts flatten against the hard, smooth planes of his chest, the weak feeling had spread to every inch of her body and her breaths came in short, needed gasps. Then, when his tongue dipped inside to tease her inner mouth, her heart thudded with such unexpected force she feared it would burst.

She'd longed for another kiss like this—ever since the one they'd shared last Sunday. And now she had it.

Eager to experience more, she pressed closer, confused when instead of taking further advantage of her, he suddenly pulled back, the kiss ending as abruptly as it started. For the next few strangled seconds, neither spoke. It was just as well, for Paige needed time to curb her racing heart before trying to act like nothing had happened.

"You're right about the changes taking place in Jeri," Damon was first to speak, beating her to that next scrap of conversation. There was just a hint of distraction in his voice while he tried to act as if that kiss had never occurred. "In the past couple of days that girl has shown a complete turn around where you are concerned." He studied her a moment before returning his attention to the ocean again. "I'm not so sure I trust her ability to change that dramatically that quickly, but as long as it results in this temporary calm, I'm all for it."

Still not fully recovered from the abrupt ending to that kiss, Paige crossed her arms, annoyed. Did everyone think her incapable of establishing a true friendship with the girl? "Why would you care if there's a calm or not when you've been avoiding us whenever we're together for days now?"

"Avoiding you?"

"Yes, I've seen you watching us from your room, or from the veranda, or wherever." She locked gazes with him, daring him to deny that. "It's obvious you aren't working at the time, but you also don't bother to join us. At first, I thought you stayed back out of the way so I could have a stronger effect on the girl, but now I'm not so sure that's the reason." She paused to draw a breath around the constriction suddenly tightening at her throat. She was confused. "Is it something I've done? Is there something wrong with me?" Is that why he ended the kiss so quickly? "Are you avoiding me for some reason I don't know?"

Damon didn't need to answer her. His startled expression did that for him. She'd just hit the nail right on its flat little head. He *was* avoiding her. But why?

Rather than stay to discuss the matter like Paige desperately hoped, Damon stepped away from her. The air around her grew suddenly cold as he distanced himself.

"I need to get back."

"Why?" she couldn't stop herself from asking. Her

heart ceased beating beneath her crossed arms while she held her next breath in wait.

"To avoid certain risks," is all he had to reply before disappearing down the metal stairs.

❀ *Chapter 17* ❀

Damon walked past Miss Hattie without speaking. At first, he didn't see her behind the desk, scribbling on a note pad. His mind was still on Paige's concerned expression, and how he'd longed to pull her back into his arms and assure her she had done nothing wrong. Assure her that the problem between them existed inside him and not her. But he didn't dare. He had his father's business to worry about. And all those construction workers whose jobs hinged on him getting that contract from Blair's friend. He couldn't let everyone down just because he'd foolishly allowed himself to fall in love with Paige Brockway of all people.

The sad truth was, without the contract, there would not be enough work for everyone in his employ. Nor would he be able to keep his father's dreams sound.

Many a livelihood depended on him, including his own and Jeri's. He couldn't let his personal needs get in the way of that, bad as he wanted to.

Hating himself for getting caught up in such a mess, he pressed his lips together and tried not to visualize the hurt and confusion he'd noticed in Paige's beautiful brown eyes. He had enough concerns tugging at what little remained of his tattered heart. He had that bid to finish and get copied. He wanted it in the overnight mail first thing Monday morning. Blair couldn't do a darn thing to help his cause if John Bolin didn't have that bid in his hands by Thursday noon and with the way the mail was these days, even sending overnight wouldn't assure that.

"Did you give Hatch the letters?" Miss Hattie startled him as she laid down the pen and folded her soft, wrinkled hands neatly over the smooth page. While awaiting his answer, her gaze shifted from the foot of the stairs where he'd come to a faltering halt at the parlor door.

Out of curiosity, Damon turned to see what had attracted her attention and spotted Jeri and Frankie sitting on one of the settees not far from the open windows. It stunned him to see that they sat, heads together, both dressed in cotton shorts with companion blouses tucked neatly inside. Jeri had chosen a red outfit, while Frankie wore mostly dark purple. The fact that neither had on her favorite ball-cap was distracting enough, but seeing them both with their long blonde hair neatly combed and their faces freshly scrubbed was downright mind-boggling.

"Hatch wasn't there," he finally answered, diverting his attention back to Miss Hattie. "But I left them both where he'd be sure to see them today." He cut another quick glance toward the girls, hard pressed to believe the changes in them.

"I agree," Miss Hattie offered, as if he had spoken his thoughts aloud. "It is so strange the way those two girls have started behaving these past couple of days. Why, they've been acting almost like sweet little girls instead of the prank-loving tomboys they've been for so long."

Damon moaned at having his fears verified. *That* was all he needed. On top of everything else plaguing him right now, he certainly did not need to have his daughter outgrowing her tomboy stage and leaving him behind. *Great.* Even though her coming of age was something he always knew would happen, he just wasn't ready to face it yet.

Looking at Miss Hattie again, then at where his rapidly aging hand still gripped the banister, he swallowed around the sickly feeling claiming his throat. Not only was Jeri getting older, he was, too. Soon, he'd lose the only female who'd stuck by him for any true length of time—to *fate* of all things.

He ran his free hand over his face wearily. There'd soon come a day he'd be all alone. "I suppose it's time Jeri realized she was a girl."

"Aye, but you don't sound too happy about that."

"I'm not," he answered honestly. "I don't think I'm quite ready to start worrying for Jeri about things like boyfriends, and dating, and broken hearts. I'd hoped for a few more years yet before having to face any of that."

Miss Hattie chuckled. "A few years wouldn't have helped. I don't think any father is ever ready for that sort of thing. I remember how worried my own father was when I first hinted I might be in love with Tony Freeport. I don't think he slept for weeks after that."

"Oh, great, so now I have weeks of going without sleep to look forward to," he muttered. "As if I haven't already lost enough sleep here lately." Worrying about his business. And about Paige. Again, her sad image tugged at his heart. How he wished he could do something to take that sadness away without, in turn, jeopardizing his situation. Just like he wished he could keep Jeri from the heartaches that lay ahead. The teen years were the most emotional of all, filled with far too many road blocks and turning points.

Facing forward again, he started back up the stairs, wishing there was some way to turn back time and then keep it there. At least a little while longer. He'd lost too many people in his life. He wasn't ready to lose Jeri, too.

Unaware Jeri and Frankie were already inside the house, Paige still wondered about this risk Damon claimed to avoid after she'd walked as far as the front veranda then sank into one of the cushioned chairs out front. Just what sort of threat did she pose for him? Surely not the threat of falling in love. She wasn't even his type. Never had been. So what was he so afraid of? Was it something else?

Perhaps the risk he worried about was the risk of spending too much time away from his work. He'd mentioned how important that contract was to his business several times. Maybe he was worried he wouldn't get it ready on time if he stayed away from his room too long.

But if that was his problem, why would he spend so much of that precious time he needed for the bid watching them from a distance? Why wouldn't he spend it locked inside his room, his head bent over his work instead of pressed against a window? Wasn't that why he brought her there, to keep Jeri occupied and at the same time do what she could to change the child's attitude about life?

Paige dropped her head back against the top slat of the ladder-backed chair. There would be no figuring out that man. And no time to try—even if she thought she could. As soon as the girls returned, the three of them were supposed to go over to Lydia Johnson's and find out what kind of materials to buy for the decorations Lydia would eventually make for Frankie's cousin's wedding. Because Frankie's aunt wanted to have the wedding there in Sea Haven at the church where she herself had been married, Frankie's aunt and mother had asked Lydia to help out with some of the arrangements.

At the urging from Frankie's mother, who like Damon longed for a more refined daughter, Frankie and Jeri had eventually agreed to help out and did so by volunteering Paige to take them into New Harbor to buy the materials needed.

Never having been involved in a wedding herself, not even one that would take place weeks after she had left, Paige looked forward to the afternoon filled with shopping for pretty materials, and spiced with small talk about matrimony and romance. Anything to get her mind off Damon and his nebulous comments inside the lighthouse.

It was while Paige sat there, forcing her thoughts away from Damon yet again while watching the main road for the girls to return, that she first heard Frankie's voice through the open window behind her.

"So how long do you plan for us to keep it up?" Frankie asked, her tone low but not whispery.

Surprised, Paige turned toward the sound. Judging from the direction and clarity, Frankie was just inside the windows, but a glance through fluttering sheers didn't reveal anyone.

"I don't know. For as long as it keeps her away from my father, I suppose. That's the whole reason I decided to get along with her in the first place, remember? To keep her busy and away from Dad."

Paige's heart wrenched under the sudden weight of Jeri's words, their implication obvious. Blair and Damon were right, and she was wrong. Jeri hadn't really changed at all. She was just pretending to have done so as a completely needless ploy to keep her away from Damon. But then the girl had no way to know her efforts were unnecessary, that Damon had no desire to be around Paige anyway. Jeri obviously thought it was her ability to keep Paige preoccupied that prevented the two from being together, and was darned proud of it.

With her thoughts suddenly in a tumultuous whirl, Paige sat numbly listening for Frankie's response. The hurt crushing her was too much to allow her to do much more than grip the arms of her chair.

"But look at all we're having to give up for us to go through with this," Frankie complained. "This is Saturday morning for pity's sake. We shouldn't be sitting here in our good shorts waiting around to go buy material for some frilly little doodads Mrs. Johnson is going to make for my cousin Karen's wedding. Why should we have to spend your last Saturday here off shopping? Mom's headed into New Harbor next Monday. She could get all that stuff then."

A shadow moved within view of the window. Judging by the way her voice grew louder, it was Frankie coming closer. "This morning we should be down there on the beach seeing what that last tide brought in and left, or over at the wharf watching the boats unload. Not sitting here waiting to spend yet another day play acting for a woman who probably isn't anywhere near as bad as you seem to think anyway. This isn't fair."

Further heartstruck, Paige blinked back a blur of tears while waiting for Jeri's response to that, although she already had a pretty good idea what that response would be. *How could she have allowed herself to be so completely taken in?* Why didn't she listen to Blair?

"I don't know, Frank. I've kinda gotten—"

"Uh-oh." Frankie's voice grew weak.

"Uh-oh, what? Oh, no!"

Aware she'd been spotted through the curtains, and not wanting to face them with what she had just heard, not yet anyway, Paige pushed out of the chair and virtually flew down the front steps toward the graveled drive.

"Paige!" Jeri called after her through the window. "Come back here."

Oh, sure, so you can cause yet further damage to my heart? Paige thought as she increased her speed rather than slow it. She had to get away. She didn't want them to see her tears. Didn't want them to know just how completely and painfully they'd fooled her.

"Paige! Stop."

Darting in and out of the tall, fat evergreens that lined the drive, she tried to decide which direction to run, not certain where she'd find the privacy she so suddenly needed. Finally, she thought of the cliffs. As much as she hated to go anywhere near them, that would be the last place they would look for her. And with the trail leading to them low enough not to be seen from the house or the front yard, she had a very real chance of making it there undetected. She ran toward them as hard and as fast as her legs allowed.

With emotions raw and strained, she scrambled down the rocks to a small, grassy cubby-hole just a few feet below the trail's end where she'd be safe from most people's view. Anyone strolling near the mouth of the cove a half mile away would be able to see her, otherwise the place was concealed to view. She herself would never have known about the site if Jeri hadn't lured her out onto a tiny bluff near the edge of the village. At the time she'd thought Jeri was just trying to help her get over her nervousness when around heights. But now she understood that Jeri was more likely having fun watching her fidget while standing as close to the edge as she dared creep.

Refusing to look down, for the grassy ledge where she sat was set high above the water and not terribly wide, Paige glanced behind her and to both sides. She saw nothing but rocks, bent trees, and tufts of hawkweed beyond her grassy little haven. She'd found the perfect place to sit and think about what she'd just learned. A place that would conceal her long enough to decide how to get over it. Or even *if* she could get over it.

If only she hadn't given Jeri such a prominent place in her heart. If only she had listened to her initial gut instinct and not allowed herself to care about the child. Or about Damon.

Paige pressed her head back against the rock wall behind her and stared vacantly into the cloud-dotted blue sky. Blair had tried to warn her. Tried to make her see how foolish she was to believe she had started to make a real difference in Jeri's life. Blair was right. Jeri had only pretended to need her. The girl had played her for a fool from the beginning.

But, as usual, Paige had been too blind to see any of that. Too eager to believe that Jeri had started caring about her as much as she'd started caring about Jeri. Why hadn't she listened to her sister? Why hadn't she seen the situation for what it really was?

She closed her eyes against the pain still plucking at her heart. If Blair was so right about Jeri, was she also right about how foolish the decision was to move to Mt. Pine? Was she chasing rainbows? Would she be making just as grave a mistake to leave New York and follow a dream that had no logical place in her life?

Maybe she should cut her losses now and forget the

move. It certainly wouldn't be worth the pain of living in a place where she was sure to run into Jeri often, and be reminded of what a fool she'd been. It would have been hard enough seeing Damon from time to time and remembering how shamelessly she'd responded to his kiss. She didn't need the two constant heartaches.

"Paige? Where are you?" Jeri called from somewhere overhead, probably from the trail that skirted the larger rocks. "Paige, I need to talk to you."

Paige didn't answer. She was tired of the girl's manipulations. All she wanted was to be left alone.

"I don't think she came this way," Frankie said in not as loud a voice, obviously following along. "I think she probably headed off toward the lighthouse. Even if she didn't, we'd have a better shot at spotting her while up there."

Panicked, Paige turned her gaze toward the lighthouse. From the ledge where she sat, her back pressed against a solid rock wall, she couldn't see the lighthouse or the peninsula of land beneath it. They could search all they wanted from there and would never spot her. The large hollow she'd chosen was just deep enough into the rocks to give her visual protection from that protruding area.

"Well, we gotta get to her before she talks to Dad. I don't want her telling him something that might not even be true."

Paige shook her head. Even now, the girl considered herself first. She was afraid of the trouble she'd face with her father. Knowing that, Paige bent her forehead to her knee and wept.

Miss Hattie backed away from the front door when she spotted Jeri coming up the flagstone walk that led down to the beach and off toward the marina. She didn't want the girl to know how concerned she'd been to see the two girls tear out of the parlor like their shorts were on fire, calling out after Paige.

Having seen what a good head start Paige had on the

girls, she pretty much knew they would come back without having found her. Only for some reason Frankie was no longer with Jeri. Damon's daughter was alone when she entered through the screen door and looked up to find Miss Hattie back behind the registration desk.

Miss Hattie's heart went out to the child the minute she spied her red-rimmed eyes. The dear girl had been crying. "Did you catch her?"

Obviously too emotional to speak, Jeri shook her head in answer. Her lower lip trembled.

"Do you mind me asking what happened?"

Jeri looked at her a long moment, as if trying to decide if she trusted her with such secrets, then shook her head again. She turned her eyes toward the floor and took a couple of steps toward the desk. "I did something awful."

"You?" Miss Hattie encouraged as she came back around the desk to take the child's hand in her own. If her knees would have allowed her to get back up, she'd have knelt down so she could see better into the young girl's watery blue eyes.

Jeri nodded while she continued her study of the foyer floor. "I hurt Paige something fierce."

When Miss Hattie tugged on her hand to lead her into the parlor where they could sit together on a settee, Jeri didn't resist. "But surely you didn't do it on purpose, did you?"

A full minute after they'd seated, Jeri finally answered. "What I did to hurt her, I did on purpose. But I didn't do it so much to hurt her. I did it to keep her away from Dad. I don't like the way he looks at her when she's around. And I sure don't like the way she looks at him, too. It makes me worry."

"So you devised a plan to keep them apart?"

"I just didn't realize it was something that would hurt Paige like that." Finally, she lifted her gaze to meet Miss Hattie's. "I had no idea she really cared about me."

"But now you realize she does."

Jeri nodded vigorously, her eyes straining with concern.

"You should have seen her face when she accidentally overheard me and Frankie talking about it. She looked like she wanted to cry, not because she was angry at us. It was because she was hurt."

"Why would you doubt that she cares for you?"

Jeri pulled her hand out of Miss Hattie's and folded it with the one already in her lap. "I'm just not used to being around adults who really care. Oh, there's been plenty of women who have told me how much they care about me, and who've told me how much they want to be my friend, but that's never been true. They just want to get on my good side so I'll say nice things about them to my dad. I thought Paige was like them. So when I couldn't make her admit it to anyone, I decided to pretend she'd suckered me in, just to keep her busy doing things with me instead of with Dad."

"And Paige overheard you admit this to Frankie? Oh, my." Miss Hattie turned her attention to the windows. The poor dear.

"We were standing right over there while we were talking about it," Jeri pointed in the same direction Miss Hattie now looked. "And she was just outside there, sitting in one of those chairs. We just didn't see her."

Miss Hattie clasped her hands together. What a mess. What a mess.

"Miss Hattie, what am I going to do?" Jeri suddenly wailed. "I tried to find her so I could explain things to her, but she wouldn't answer me when I called."

"Maybe she's run off too far to hear you."

She pressed fisted hands against her stomach and bent forward while she continued to look to Miss Hattie for answers. "But how am I going to explain things to her if she's done that? I gotta have a chance to explain."

"And just what is it you want to explain?"

"That I didn't mean to hurt her." The words were so painful to the child, they came out punctuated with loud sobs. Tears streamed down her cheeks. "And, how I was starting to like being with her. Some of the things she likes

to do aren't so bad. I had fun helping her pick out stuff
for her new house. I might have started out thinking I hated
her, but that was back when I thought she was just like all
those other women. Before I got to know that she's nothing like them—or my mother.''

Miss Hattie blinked. *Her mother?*

''Turns out that Paige was okay and really did want to
be my friend. Why else would it have hurt her so bad to
hear what we said?'' She hiccupped, then sniffed. ''A
woman I could really like finally took a liking to me, and
I blew it.''

''What about your father's new lady friend back in
Texas? Don't you care for her?'' Miss Hattie handed her
a handkerchief as she leaned closer, hoping to get the answer she needed to be able to proceed with a clear conscience.

''What lady friend?''

''The one your father's been dating recently. The one
he told me about over the telephone when he called to
make Paige's reservation.''

Jeri looked confused by that. ''Dad isn't dating anybody. I know that for a fact. He spends his spare time with
me. Either that, or he spends it doing work around the
house.''

''There's no lady friend?''

Wiping away the remnants of her tears with a corner of
the handkerchief, Jeri's expression creased more, as if
thinking the question bizarre. ''No.''

Well, that certainly put a new spin on things. ''What
about this Blair who calls every now and then?'' Damon
had said she was just a friend, but with Damon one could
never be sure of his definition for friendship.

''That's Paige's sister.'' Disgust burdened the child's
voice. ''She's a friend of Dad's and I think maybe she has
something to do with Paige being here, but I'm not sure
what that is.''

''So I'm mistaken about there being someone special
waiting for your father back home?'' There was no inno-

cent woman who could have suffered a broken heart were he to return there suddenly feeling differently about her? But why would Damon have told her there was? To keep her from meddling in his affairs? *Hmmmmm.*

"What are you smiling about?"

"Me?" She glanced toward the television set to catch her reflection in the dark screen. She was smiling, wasn't she? She supposed Tony and his parents were all smiling about now, too, that is if ghosts did that sort of thing. Having never actually seen them in all this time, she wasn't sure of the particulars. "Oh, nothing. It's just that I'm so pleased to hear how much you and Paige care about each other." That would certainly be a blessing later on—should there be a match.

Miss Hattie could hardly wait to tell Jimmy this turn of events. He had refrained from putting his money on these two simply because she'd told him there was someone back home waiting patiently for Damon's return. Knowing now that there wasn't made all the difference in the world.

If Hattie didn't miss her guess, the dry spell at the Seascape Inn was about over. It had been four long weeks since they'd had a pairing. It was high time they broke the tedium.

Reaching out to run her fingers along the curve of Jeri's still damp cheeks, she could hardly wait. "Don't you worry about Paige. I'll see to it you get a chance to talk with her."

"You promise?"

"Oh, you can bet on it." Just like everyone at the Blue Moon could now bet that there was about to be another match made at the Seascape Inn. She could feel it in her bones. "Why don't you go upstairs and wash your face then come back down to the kitchen and get yourself a glass of lemonade or some fresh apple cider? I think sipping a nice cool drink will help you feel better."

Jeri stood as if about to leave, then suddenly leaned over to offer a hug that warmed Miss Hattie to her very toes, then took off for the main stairs at her usual quick speed.

Several minutes later, when she rushed by the registration desk on her way to the kitchen, Miss Hattie noticed she'd indeed washed her face and had pulled her hair back into a bouncy ponytail again. Also she wore her favorite ball cap again, backwards like the children these days tended to do.

Shades of the old Jeri, she mused, turning to greet the family that had just pulled up out front. The Osborns had finally arrived.

"So between the car giving out on you and the broken water pipe in your house, you've had quite a delay," she commented minutes later, while watching Carolyn Osborn sign the register with neat penmanship. Her two children stood near the front windows watching their father check something in the trunk of their car. One son was a short, inquisitive three year old with black curly hair and the other a tall, handsome fifteen year old with light brown hair, who had already informed her he'd rather she call him Richard than Ricky.

"Quite a wide difference in your sons' ages," Miss Hattie commented, poking around the ceramic bowl that held all the keys to the carriage house, including those to the two upstairs bedrooms. Noticing movement out of the corner of her eye, she glanced toward the back of the house and saw Jeri slowing to a halt, her attention on the children at the window.

Carolyn Osborn laughed at the comment about her sons' ages. "Well, after having had a child who enjoyed getting into trouble as much as Ricky did, it was quite awhile before my husband and I decided we wanted another."

The older boy spun around, his pale green eyes narrowed. "My name is Richard," he corrected her, his Wisconsin accent a little more pronounced than his mother's.

Carolyn winked at Miss Hattie. "I do keep forgetting. He's decided he's too old for us to call him Ricky anymore."

"Aye, most kids go through that," she agreed, then laughed along with her. When Jeri then took a couple of tentative steps in her direction, Miss Hattie noticed the girl carried two lemonades instead of one. How sweet. The child had thought to bring her one, too.

"Mrs. Osborn, I'd like for you to meet one of our other guests." She gestured to Jeri, eager to make the girl feel included. "This is Jeri Adams. She's in one of the rooms upstairs."

"Jerina," Jeri corrected quickly, then gave Richard a furtive glance, her blue eyes suddenly as wide as antique doorknobs. "Jerina Adams."

"Oh?" Miss Hattie turned to see what Richard's reaction was to that. He stared at Jeri a moment, then turned back around to gaze out the window again. Seeing Jeri's hurt expression, she quickly continued with the introduction. "Oh, yes, of course. *Jerina* Adams. I keep forgetting how much you've grown up here lately." She offered a look of encouragement. "Jerina, this is Mrs. Osborn and those are her two sons, Austin and Richard."

Austin spun about upon hearing his name, but said nothing when it became obvious no one really needed him. Richard hesitated a second, then turned around, too. "Hi," he finally said, then shifted his attention to his mother. "Mom, do you know if Pop remembered to pack our swim fins?"

"You'll have to ask him. I wasn't the one in charge of getting together the swimming gear."

Richard cut his gaze to Jeri once more then headed for the door.

Miss Hattie noticed how Jeri's unblinking blue eyes missed not one movement the boy made while he crossed the veranda to the steps, headed toward his father. Clearly, the dear girl was rattled by the young man's presence.

Hmmmm. Were these two young folks the ones destined to fall in love this summer and one day marry? It had happened with guests far younger than these two.

Dividing her attention between Jeri's slack expression and Richard's confident swagger, Miss Hattie tapped her fingers against the smooth surface of the desk. Now, she wasn't sure who was meant to be the Seascape Inn's next match.

Had she misread the feeling she'd had in her bones?

❧ *Chapter 18* ❧

Worried about Paige's emotional state, Damon left the lighthouse a second time, headed toward the Marina. Hatch had seen Jeri and Frankie earlier. They'd left his place just as he returned from New Harbor; but he hadn't seen anyone who matched Damon's description of Paige.

"I'd sure be rememberin' it if I had seen someone as pretty as all that," he had replied with his usual deep chuckle and a knuckle rub of his paint-splattered gray beard. His eyes had twinkled with untold thoughts while he watched Damon turn and head dejectedly back the way he'd come.

After checking the marina, which was teeming with lots of noisy fishermen but no beautiful brunettes with big brown eyes, Damon next stopped near the trails leading off into the forest. There the only fresh tracks he found belonged to a large dog, probably Walter, Jr., the community mutt.

His next stop, the village.

His concern growing, he hurried back the way he'd come, cutting across a grassy field rather than stay to the winding paths. He had glanced out the window as soon as he'd detected the panic in Jeri's voice when she'd shouted Paige's name, and knew something had gone dreadfully wrong between the two. Paige had lit out of there like a scalded cat with Jeri and Frankie following only a few minutes behind.

Having no idea where she'd gone, he wished now he had stayed put long enough to gauge her path. But fearing the worst at the time, he had put his shirt and shoes right back on and taken off several minutes behind the girls. Judging from what Hatch said, the children never found Paige, and with Frankie having to return home, Jeri had given up looking. That meant it was up to him to figure out where Paige had gone. "And try to find out what on earth went wrong this time."

Planning to detour by Beaulah Favish's house on his way into Sea Haven, thinking the village snoop might be able to provide him with Paige's general direction, Damon strode with long determined strides toward the main road. When he neared the black-patched edge, something unseen tugged at his clothes, as if willing him to go a different direction.

With the morning wind now a light breeze and no one else around, Damon couldn't explain the feeling of being led away from the road, but decided to go with it. Perhaps it was a gut instinct tinkering with his mind.

Ending up at the tallest cliffs, unable to go any further, he searched beneath many low-branch trees and the clusters of rocks scattered about, but didn't find Paige. Thinking fate had pulled a fast one on him, he turned back toward the road just seconds before he heard a faint sob, followed by a loud, undignified sniff.

"Paige?" Not knowing the direction of the sound, he glanced again under the trees and scanned the crevices between the odd shaped rocks. "Paige, is that you?"

No one answered, but that peculiar feeling of being guided came back, pulling him closer to a modest slope. There, he heard another sniff. This time, he distinguished its direction and seconds later, to his amazement, he found Paige sitting cross-legged in a small, grassy area that overlooked the water a dozen yards below, her beautiful face drenched with tears. Had he been a betting man like most of the patrons of the Blue Moon, he'd have willingly wagered good money that Paige would go nowhere near those cliffs. He'd seen her skirt them often. She truly had to want her privacy to come there.

"You're crying," he stated the obvious, trying to decide whether to stay and comfort her, or leave her alone like she obviously wanted.

Paige shook her head adamantly in answer, as if to deny her tears, paused, then reluctantly nodded. His heart went out to her when he saw just how distraught she really was. "What's wrong?"

She sniffed, then patted her pockets and sniffed again. Figuring she searched for a handkerchief or a Kleenex, he felt of his own pockets, but all he had was a comb, an ink pen, and the small felt patch he sometimes used to clean his eyeglasses. With nothing better to offer her, he handed her that.

She nodded her thanks and sniffed again, though not quite as indelicately as before. "It looks like you and Blair were right all along," she finally said, her voice high and wavering. "And, as usual for me, I was wrong."

"About what?" Staying, he sank down into the soft, wind-bleached grass, facing her. He considered taking her hands in his, but she seemed to need them fisted at the moment. "Are you talking about the mistake you'd make moving to Texas? I don't remember ever having voiced an opinion about that one way or the other."

"No, not about that. About Jeri." She dabbed first at her tear-clumped eyelashes, then at her dainty, pink-rimmed nose. "I am quite aware that you as much as told me to be wary of all the changes I thought I saw in Jeri; but did I listen? No. Fool that I am, I went right ahead and believed that I had started to make a very real difference in your daughter's life. I truly believed that we'd begun to form a genuine friendship."

"What happened to change your mind about that?" Damon swallowed hard, not too sure he wanted to hear the answer. He couldn't bear seeing her so hurt.

Paige didn't answer right away. First, she dabbed again at her eyes, then took time to absorb some of the wetness off her cheeks. What the felt patch didn't get, Damon knew the warm breeze curling up the cliff would eventually dry. Still, he couldn't resist and reached out to collect a shimmering tear off her jawline with the tips of two fingers.

When that caused her to pull away from him, his heart sank like a rock in the ocean. Paige no longer wanted any comfort from him—undoubtedly resulting from their little exchange awhile ago in the lighthouse. He had ducked out on a conversation that very well may have been important to her. All because he was afraid of where it might lead.

Paige waved the felt patch back and forth several times, as if to dry it, then finally answered, "Shortly after I returned to the inn, I overheard the two girls talking about me. From what I heard, I found out what they've been up to these past couple of days. Jeri admitted that pretending to enjoy spending so much time with me was her way to keep me busy and away from you." Paige's voice grew even more strained, causing her to grimace and look away again. "Jeri never considered me a friend. It turns out everything I bragged about to you in the lighthouse was a lie."

Damon closed his eyes to block out the unbearable sight of Paige's tears. He was to blame for all the pain Paige now suffered. He'd maneuvered Jeri into thinking Paige was romantically interested in him when that just wasn't true. Paige had no interest in him at all—romantically or otherwise. If she did, she wouldn't have turned her back on him so many times in this past week. But he'd let Jeri believe otherwise.

He clamped his eyes tighter while anguish and guilt played tug-of-war with his gut. "I'm very sorry Jeri hurt you."

The unexpected touch of Paige's hand on his forearm caused such an intense jolt to his system, his eyes flew open again. It surprised him to find her now leaning toward him, studying his expression.

"But there's no reason for you to feel bad, Damon. It's certainly not *your* fault Jeri hurt me. It's to your good that you tried to warn me." Even after she lifted her hand away and rested it again on her thigh, the warmth of her touch lingered. "*You* tried to tell me how unlikely it was Jeri could have changed that much that quickly. *I'm* the one who refused to accept that." Her eyes clear again, though her dark lashes were still damp at the corners, she offered a genuine smile. One Damon didn't deserve, but treasured all the same.

"If anything," she continued her unsettling attempt to comfort him, "you should be demanding my thanks for that. It's certainly not your fault I was too stubborn to listen to you."

Damon nipped at the outer edge of his lower lip, debating whether to admit the truth to her or not. The pain she suffered *was* his fault. And Blair's. But what good would it do anyone for Paige to know that—other than to clear his conscience?

His stomach clenched when Paige continued heaping the blame on herself. "Blair also tried to warn me. But I didn't listen to her either. Oh, I should have. She was certainly right about me. I am obviously *not* very good at seeing the whole picture. Which is why I now think maybe I should give up the foolish notion of moving to Mt. Pine. Blair has warned me about that, too."

Many times, no doubt, Damon thought, his heart shattering to hear Paige ready to cast aside her long-held dreams. Odd that Paige had just said exactly what he and Blair had both longed to hear, and all he wanted was to argue with her. But if she didn't move to Mt. Pine, there was little chance he'd ever become part of her life. How unfair that her moving there meant he'd lose everything else.

"Don't jump to any hasty decisions—either way," he commented, at least giving her that. "Whether you choose to return to New York, or move to Mt. Pine, it deserves your full consideration. It's certainly not something you should decide while still so upset over what Jeri has done.''

"Thanks. That does sound like good advice." She tilted her head and studied him with those dark, fathomless brown eyes a moment. The ends of her hair dipped to caress one shoulder, making his hand long to imitate.

"I just don't want you making a wrong choice."

"And I don't want to risk making anymore big mistakes in my life either." A tiny notch creased an otherwise flawless forehead while she continued studying him. "I sure wish you would tell me why you've been avoiding me these past few days. If I've done something to upset you, I'd like to know about it."

Damon groaned. Back to that again? "It's nothing you've done. But you are right, I have been avoiding you."

She blinked, clearly as surprised as he was he'd just admitted that. "But why?"

Aware of the serious damage he'd do if he told her about Blair's plan, Damon considered changing the subject. But in the end, he decided to tell Paige at least half the truth. "Because I happen to be a big coward."

"Coward?"

Her mouth parted while she thought about that, bringing his attention to the soft fullness of her lips. His heart rate doubled then tripled at the vivid memory of how good it felt to kiss those very lips. When his gaze dropped further, to the part of her covered with a tear splotched blouse, he also recalled how good it felt to hold her close in his arms. "Yes, coward."

"You mean you are afraid of me?"

He started to answer no to that, but in the end said, "Yes. In a way I am. I'm afraid of what could happen to me were I to follow these strong impulses I have and try to get to know you a lot better." He rubbed his damp palms over the rough texture of his jeans. "The thing is that the women in my life never stick around long. That's why I've found it to be a lot easier on my battered heart, as well as my psyche, when I avoid any situation where I could end up falling in love again.''

Paige sat absently watching him. She gave no indication she had caught the implication hidden inside what he'd just said. Didn't she understand, the way he felt now he could very easily end up losing every shred of his heart to her? Truth was, he may already have.

Otherwise, he would never risk telling her any of this. ''I've discovered that life is much more bearable when I don't give people much chance to hurt me.'' He continued meeting her gaze, wishing she'd blink or at least wrinkle her brow. Anything to indicate she understood, or at least wanted to.

Finally she spoke. ''You've been hurt often?''

He frowned. There was no clue to her thoughts in her voice either. ''As you might recall, back when I was still in high school I suffered one relationship break up after another. Girls were willing enough to catch my attention, but as soon as they were certain they had it, they moved on to their next conquest, caring little how that might affect me. I reached the point, I refused to let my heart become involved in my relationships any longer.'' He clamped his hands over his knees in an attempt to brace himself against the bitter memories. ''It became a ·matter of self-preservation, especially when it turned out I wasn't the kind of guy who could keep any of them interested for very long.''

''It sounds to me like maybe you associated with the wrong kind of girls.'' She looked almost annoyed over that.

''Maybe.'' He paused to consider the possibility. ''But my problem grew a lot worse until, later, anytime a particular relationship lasted more than a few weeks, I simply quit taking chances. I quickly moved to end it. That way *I* got to be the one to say goodbye. It didn't take me long to figure out that my dignity came out far less bruised that way. That's pretty much why not letting myself become too emotionally entangled and then being the one to break it off became a way of life for me. It was the only way I knew to protect the two most vulnerable traits about me, my pride and my heart.''

Paige focused on her hands, as if not sure what to think about such a revelation. Evidently, it bothered her to find out he had such a cowardly streak in his character.

"But eventually you married," she pointed out, still not looking up. "Surely your heart was involved then."

Nodding, for indeed it was, he considered those turbulent years. "I'm not sure how I let Trana get past the barriers I'd so carefully built to protect myself, but get past them she did. And destroy me, she did—shattering Jeri's young heart in the process." He curled his right hand into an angry fist. It was the damage Trana did to Jeri that scarred him worst of all. "I can't believe I left us both wide open for that."

"So now you've vowed never to fall in love again," she commented rather than asked and lifted one hand to massage her temple. It sounded as if she understood that logic perfectly. "You plan never to let yourself be hurt like that again."

"Which explains why I've been steering clear of you so much these last couple of days. For some reason, you affect me more than any other woman ever has—even Trana." *Well, at least that pricked her interest.* She blinked in surprise. "At first, I thought what I felt was nothing more than a profound sexual attraction, but later I realized my attraction to you was more than that. It had shifted at some point, and grown, until I'm no longer sure what it is I feel toward you."

"And you don't like that." Her hand fell limply back to her lap where she again gave it her undivided attention.

For some reason it bothered him that she seemed so willing to accept his decision not to fall in love with her. "It's not that I don't *like* being affected by you, it's just that I'm not prepared to put my heart on the line. I have too many other things going on in my life right now. I don't need further complications."

"I understand." She twitched her pretty nose in a way that made him want to reach out and touch it with the tip of his finger to see if maybe it would tweak again. He clasped his hands together instead.

"Do you?"

"Yes, really, I do. And, now that you've explained it to me, I don't blame you one bit for wanting to avoid being near me. Especially after the way I so blatantly threw myself at you."

"When was that?" Had he missed something?

"After you helped me safely down out of that tree."

His blood stirred at the memory. Having relived the aftermath many times, he'd forgotten who instigated that amazing kiss. "Well, I didn't exactly mind that."

She looked at him questioningly, but then returned her gaze to her slender hands folded neatly in her lap. "Still, it caused you enough concern to start avoiding me."

Damon came close to denying that, then realized it was true. It was shortly after that he had perceived the very real danger she posed. And not just to his heart, but to his whole way of life. He was supposed to be making her think ill of marriage, and family, and small town life; then suddenly he'd wanted to convince her the opposite was true. Rather than doing all he could to send her running back to Blair, he'd started to daydream what it would be like to come home and find Paige waiting for him everyday. Or if she had to be the one to work late, to be able to greet her at the door with a warm welcoming kiss.

Paige was right. It was indeed right after that heart-stopping kiss that all those splendid fantasies started. If memory served, it was about then he spoke the word marriage for the first time since his divorce. He had said it to her in jest, eager to get a rise out of her since at the time she'd so effectively gotten a rise out of him; but the tempting thoughts that word had aroused had stayed with him a long time after that.

Even now, he wasn't fully opposed to the idea.

If only that contract he so desperately needed didn't continue to ride on that absurd promise he'd made Blair. Oh, how he resented Blair for this latest ploy of hers, for somewhere along the way it had taken a nasty turn.

Uncertain what else he could say to Paige, and aware she needed more time to think, Damon sat quietly a moment, then finally stood. "I believe it's time I had a long talk with Jeri. Her cruel behavior toward you has gotten out of hand. Expect another apology upon your return to the house."

"No." Paige looked up, her beautiful brown eyes wide with alarm. "Don't. I'd rather have no apology at all than to listen to one someone else forced her to give." Her tears gathered again, burning right into the very core of Damon's heart. "I'd rather talk to her about it myself. When I'm ready."

"Okay, when you're ready," he repeated softly, then quietly left.

Paige would have stayed hidden along the ocean's edge for several more hours had her head not started to throb like some growing beast against her skull. She needed aspirin. In a bad way.

After carefully abandoning her little haven among the cliffs, still a little leery of its precarious location, she noticed a car parked beside the carriage house with its trunk and doors open. The new guests Hattie had told them about had finally arrived. They'd no longer have the inn to themselves like they had since the Gaddys left.

At first, Paige thought she would walk over to offer a friendly greeting to the four making multiple trips from the car to the guest house, but her head pounded harder with each step taken. By the time she finally neared the inn, she was in no mood to say hello to anyone, not even Miss Hattie who stood on the veranda watching the new arrivals settle in.

With hands curled into tight balls, she trudged up the steps. Two aspirin and a soft pillow awaited her upstairs.

"Paige, dear, what's wrong?" Miss Hattie hurried toward her. She'd obviously recognized the pain tightening her expression.

"I have a killer headache," she answered in as few words as possible, never slowing her pace. She had to make it upstairs. Before she passed out from such intense pain. "I'm headed to my room to lie down."

"Oh, dear. Do you have anything to take for it?"

"Yes."

Miss Hattie followed as far as the stairs. "Can I do anything for you?"

"Just see that I'm buried near the ocean," she muttered beneath her breath, then answered in a voice meant for Miss Hattie to hear, "All I need is some peace and quiet."

"Oh, dear." She commented again, then hurried away.

Paige's pain was so fierce by the time she entered her bedroom, later she barely remembered taking the aspirin, pulling down her shades, or climbing into bed.

She recalled having cried herself into some major headaches in the past, but nothing like the one that had sent her burrowing under all six of her pillows. Experience told her what she needed most was darkness and rest, and although still tormented by what Jeri had done and the heartbreaking admission Damon had made out by the cliffs, she somehow managed to drift off to sleep. But her dreams proved to be far less than restful.

Images of the unattainable drifted through her head, giving her tiny glimpses of what it might have been like to have Damon and Jeri become a permanent part of her new life in Mt. Pine. Fitfully, she caught snatches of different scenes in which she and Damon were obviously a couple, or in which she and Jeri laughed in the sun and shared wonderful secrets.

The most disturbing of her dreams was one in which she was locking up a dress shop for the day and her husband, the beloved high school baseball coach that he was, slipped up behind her to kiss her lightly on the ear. The dream had felt so real, she'd taken a playful swipe at him, only to thump a pillow that had fallen off those piled on top of her head.

Drawn fully awake again, her restlessness returned, only now her heartache had grown until it far surpassed the headache.

How could she bear never having such happiness?

If only, like her, Damon hadn't pledged never to risk his heart in a relationship again; because suddenly her own such vow meant nothing to her. She was finally ready to fall in love.

She smacked one of the many pillows covering her head in frustration over such a hopeless situation.

Big mistake.

Her tears followed immediately.

Jeri sat as straight as she could in the oversized booth, hoping to impress Richard yet. She had wanted to return to her room to take the rubber band back out of her hair and brush it full again, but never had the chance. So she tried to make do by remembering to put her napkin in her lap like Paige had showed her—right after she took her baseball cap off and placed it on the vinyl covered seat beside her. But neither effort had any effect.

What did it take to make this guy notice her? she wondered, discouraged. Maybe if she laughed harder at some of his jokes. But then Richard hadn't told her any good jokes yet. Fact was he hardly talked to her at all. If Miss Hattie hadn't suggested they go into the village for a couple of sodas at the Blue Moon, he would probably still be sitting on the veranda grumbling about his father's decision not to go snorkeling until late Monday. *Wait, that's it.* "You know, Richard, if you need someone to go snorkeling with you today, I'd be willing to go with you." Truth was, she'd give her right arm to do that.

"Huh?" He pulled his attention away from the cash register where Nolene Baker rang up a customer's charges. "What was that about snorkeling?"

Jeri scowled, trying to figure out what Nolene was doing

that interested him so. "I said that if you still need someone to go snorkeling with you, I'd go."

"Nah. I'll wait and go later." He returned his attention
to the register. "Who's that?"

"Which one?" There were two people standing near the
register where he'd pointed before dropping his arms back
down on the table.

"The girl taking the money."

"Her? That's Nolene Baker," Jeri answered reluctantly,
not sure why it bothered her that he wanted to know something like that. "Her folks own this place."

He lowered his chin to his arms while continuing to
watch Nolene's every little move. "Oh, man, what a hot
number she is. She got a boyfriend?"

Jeri felt a sharp stab of something in her stomach. "Yes,
sort of. She likes Andy Johnson whose folks own the store
with the gas station across the street." For some reason,
she thought it imperative Richard be told Nolene's age.
"Since she's nearly seventeen, she'll probably want to
marry Andy just as soon as she turns eighteen."

"Too bad." A grin stretched up one side of his mouth
while his thoughts looked like they had just taken off for
outer space. "Because if I were only a year or two older,
I'd sure do what I could to give that Andy guy a run for
his money."

Jeri clutched her hands under the table and pounded
them silently against her legs. She couldn't understand
why hearing him say such things hurt as much as it did.
He was just some boy for heaven's sake. One she'd just
met at that.

Maybe the problem was in the way he treated her—like
she was just another guy. But, no, she was used to that.
The boys on her baseball team treated her that way all the
time. So that made no sense.

She pressed her fists together when she looked at Richard again, still trying to figure it out. With him staring at
Nolene like a little hungry puppy waiting for supper, she
couldn't help but notice how big and green his eyes
looked, or how thick and blond his hair was. Even blonder

than her own hair, and cut so it fell forward some before dipping straight back in a soft wave. And what was it about the shape of his nose and cheeks that made her want to memorize their form?

"Yeah, man," he continued. "If I could be just a year or two older, I think I might maybe have a chance with her. Don't you?"

Considering Jeri thought him tons handsomer than Andy, she pursed her lips into a tight pout and leaned back hard against the booth. "Yeah, I suppose you would."

"It's too bad about this Andy though. He's sure one lucky fellow to have someone like her liking him. Someday, maybe I'll get as lucky."

Jeri fell silent while she, too, studied Nolene. What was it about her that appealed to Richard so much? She wasn't any prettier than most girls that age, not that Jeri could tell anyway.

"Look, she's headed over here," Richard said, straightening. "I'll bet she's going to be the one to take our order."

You don't have to sound quite *that* excited about it, Jeri thought grimly while she waited for Nolene to slide the pencil out of her shiny hair and stroll over to their table. Sure enough, Nolene was the one to take their order, and when she left to go get them their soft drinks and Richard his potato chips, he all but licked the table between them.

Jeri sank dismally in her seat. This was all too weird to understand. She sure wished she could talk about it with someone who probably knew about this sort of thing. Frankie sure wouldn't be of any help. Neither would her dad. Not with this. Paige might be able to help her figure out some of this. But then Paige was still mad at her. She hadn't come out of her room all day because of it. She even missed lunch.

"Here you go," Nolene said in an extremely bouncy voice as she placed their orders in front of them. She looked first at Richard, then at Jeri, then smiled.

"Thank you," Richard responded with an awfully cute wag of his head.

Jeri wasn't sure why but she downright resented the wink Nolene then gave them. She had seen both Nolene and her mother wink a dozen times at practically anyone who entered the place, but for some reason Jeri felt like taking that particular wink as an insult.

"You got something in your eye?" Oh, how she longed to tell Nolene Baker to step outside. She'd show her who should be winking at Richard and who shouldn't.

To increase Jeri's resentment, Nolene never answered her. She merely looked at her as if she had no idea what she was talking about then headed back to the counter with her tray tucked neatly under her arm.

Richard seemed oblivious to Jeri's annoyance while he watched Nolene cross the room. "Oh, yeah, she's something else."

Tears stung inside Jeri's eyes, adding to her confusion. Determined no one saw them, she looked down at her hands and vowed to find some way to make Paige forgive her. She needed someone to talk to about this. Someone who'd had experience in such things and could tell her what to do.

If only she'd realized sooner how important Paige's friendship would be to her one day. She sure could have saved them both a lot of grief.

Right now, Jeri cared not one lick that her father obviously liked Paige plenty. Truth was, she wouldn't care at all if her dad decided to make Paige a regular part of their lives.

It might make both their lives a lot happier.

292   *Regina Hamburg*

back spring... Paige wasn't going to be all right either. His...

❧ *Chapter 19* ❧

When Paige didn't come down for supper that night, Jeri felt terrible, and decided it was because she was still too angry over what she'd done. Way too angry to come downstairs and give her a chance to explain what she'd done. Which was the whole reason Jeri had climbed out onto the roof shortly after it turned dark and now stood outside on top of the overhang. It was also why she'd brought a table knife with her.

She had to talk to Paige and did not want to give her the chance to tell her to go away. Popping off one of the window screens to Paige's room as quiet as she could so the noise might not be heard through the open window, she set the insert neatly aside then tugged on the light green window shade to make it ease back up.

When she saw the only light came through louvered doors across the room, she worried for a moment that Paige had gone off somewhere. She edged closer to the stripes of light stretching across the bed where a lot of pillows were piled in a heap, but with so much darkness, she couldn't tell if Paige was in there among them or not.

Could it be that Paige didn't bother to come down for supper because she wasn't even there? Only one way to find out.

"Paige?"

The suddenness of how all those pillows went flying

scared the next breath clean out of Jeri. It took her a second to recover enough to follow with, "It's me. Jeri."

By then Paige sat bolt upright in bed, looking around as if she'd probably just woke up. Her right hand went first to her chest then to the back of her neck, where she poked around gently a few seconds.

"Paige, I need to talk to you."

Light flooded that half of the room, making them both blink. "How'd you get in here?"

"I—uh—I sorta came through the window."

Blinking harder, Paige sat with her hand still on the bedside lamp, staring at her. Makeupless, her brown hair was tousled in all directions and she was dressed in rumpled white shorts and a wrinkled purple shirt. Not exactly the way Jeri was used to seeing her. Maybe Paige wasn't the right one to talk to about all this after all.

"You scared me right out of my wits, girl. Why would you do that?" She blinked several more times, still trying to come better awake.

"I needed to talk to you. In person." Jeri stood several feet away, fingers curled at her sides, waiting to see if Paige intended to order her on out of her room—or let her stay.

Prodding her forehead with her fingertips, Paige slid on off the bed and headed for the small vanity in the outermost corner of the room. There, she picked up a hairbrush and started brushing. Only after she finished did she finally look at her through the mirror. "So what is it you wanted to talk to me about?"

Jeri let out the breath she'd held, so afraid Paige wasn't going to forgive her enough to even talk to her, and hurried closer. Within minutes she'd told her everything. About how she hadn't meant to hurt her, at least not these last few days, and about how she'd even started to really like being around her, which had been a real surprise to her. Then, after she was sure Paige understood all that and had accepted her tearful apology, she told her all about what else had happened to her that day.

Paige didn't interrupt once while she first described what Richard looked like then tried to explain what it was she'd felt when she was around him. "At supper tonight, I could hardly swallow my food. It was like his just being in the room had clamped my throat shut."

"I see." Paige was no longer watching her through the mirror, but had turned to face her.

"Do you? Do you see?" Jeri asked, hopefully. "Because I don't see any of it. All I know is that when Richard is around I want him to notice me that same way he noticed Nolene when we were at the cafe, but he won't."

For some reason, Paige found that funny. The smile she'd been holding back stretched wide when she leaned back in her chair. "I see."

Jeri dropped her arms in frustration when Paige still didn't bother to say what it was she saw. Maybe Paige wasn't really going to forgive her for what she did after all.

"So are you going to help me or not?" she finally asked, impatient to get on with it. The sooner the better.

"Help you out how?" Paige's expression grew more serious when she sat forward again.

"By showing me how to be more like Nolene so Richard will notice me instead of her. Today, all he did was treat me like I was just some other boy."

"And you didn't like that."

"No, because I want him to think I'm a girl."

"You *are* a girl."

"Yeah, but that's my problem. He doesn't seem to notice that." She jammed a fist to her hip. "Not even after I finally pulled the rubber band out of my hair and left my baseball cap in my room."

Looking thoughtful, Paige's eyes glittered with light from the bedside lamp across the room as she bent forward to turn on the lamp on her vanity as well. "Let me see if I understand. That very same person who grew so angry when she told me just last week that she had no desire to become a young lady, ever, now wants me to demonstrate

a few tricks that will make her seem a little more feminine?''

''Okay, so I'm sorry about that, too.'' Geez, did she plan
to bring up every little thing she'd ever done to her? ''It
wasn't right for me to yell at you like that anymore than
it was right of me to trick you into ruining your clothes
every other time you turned around. I'm sorry I was that
dumb. But you said you could forgive all that. If that's so,
will you please now show me what I need to know?''

Paige studied Jeri's pensive expression a moment more,
then nodded. She couldn't allow the child to suffer any
longer. Jeri had now apologized for what she did, admit-
ting how wrong she was, and for the first time had sounded
truly sincere. ''Let's start with the way you stand most of
the time. Like now.''

Jeri looked down. ''What's wrong with the way I'm
standing?''

''Nothing, if you happen to be out on the pitching
mound getting ready to toss your next pitch. It's just not
all that attractive to stand there with your hand on your
hip, one leg locked stiff, and the other jutting out at an
angle like that with the knee bent.''

She quickly straightened her knee and dropped her hand
back to her side. ''So how should I stand?''

''When your goal is to make a certain young man notice
you, you should stand more like this.'' She stood to demonstrate.

Jeri paid close attention to everything Paige had to show
her, and practiced putting part of it to use right away. At
some actions, she was a natural, but at others, she proved
awkward at first. Still, she didn't give up.

After over an hour of careful instruction, Jeri sat in front
of the mirror where she'd just practiced her laughing,
wanting to sound just like Nolene, and quietly studied herself. She turned her chin first one way, then another. ''I
know you said I'm not quite ready for make-up yet, but
what about maybe a different hairstyle?'' She wet her lips
in anticipation. ''Something really daring.''

''Jeri, you do know that you don't have to change everything about you in order to attract a boy, don't you?'' Paige asked. In the past half hour she'd started to grow uncomfortable over just how much and how fast Jeri hoped to change. Even though Paige had finally been handed the perfect opportunity to sway Jeri's impressionable young mind in the direction Damon wanted her to, she decided to slow her down a bit. Damon was wrong to want his daughter to grow up faster than she should.

Maybe Paige should tell him that.

''You don't want to mess with my hair?''

''That's not what I meant. What I don't want is for you to think that you have to change what's inside your heart just to attract this Richard you're suddenly so fond of. No boy is worth that. If you are to be truly happy when you're older, you will need the young man you eventually fall in love with to accept you for what you are deep inside. Not for what you appear to be on the outside.''

When Jeri continued to look confused, she knelt beside her. ''Try to understand. You are a good person. True, you get a little frightened at times and lash out at those you think have threatened you, but deep inside, you are still a good person. I'd hate to see you alter that in any way for anyone.''

''So what are you telling me?''

''To always follow your instincts.''

''My instincts?'' Her nose wrinkled.

Paige nodded, then explained, ''It was your instincts today that made you aware that you wanted to behave a little differently around Richard. And it will also be your instincts that will eventually tell you if he's worth the effort.'' She tried to simplify it more. ''If you feel a desire to be soft around Richard, then by all means be soft. But if that's not how you feel when you are around him, then be however it is you think you need to be. I can show you how to be soft and how to come across as a graceful young woman, but the one thing I can't *show* you is how to decide what's right for you. Promise me that no matter what we do here tonight, no matter what I show you how to do, you will always follow what's inside your heart.''

Jeri blinked several times, then suddenly threw her arms around Paige and hugged her tight. ''I promise.''

Paige felt such an overwhelming rush of joy, she thought she'd burst. ''I'm so very glad we're friends again.''

''Me too,'' Jeri said. Several more seconds passed before she dropped her arms, sniffed, and pushed herself away. ''Now, will you help me do something with my hair? Maybe cut it off and make it look more like yours?''

''Mine?'' Paige's gaze flew to the mirror, horrified at the thought of cutting that much of the child's hair. She'd have to chop off a full foot to make those golden tresses shoulder length like hers. ''Oh, my goodness. You want to cut your hair?''

''Please? I think having this hair makes me look stupid.''

''No-no, how about I show you how to style it differently instead?'' She stood again. ''I think a French braid might be just the thing to make you look older.''

''A French braid?''

''It's a much wiser choice than cutting off that beautiful hair. Besides, guys like long soft hair.'' She rested her hands on Jeri's shoulders. ''Trust me.''

Jeri's back turned ramrod stiff.

''What's wrong?'' You'd think by her expression that someone had just slapped her. ''What did I do?''

Nervously running the tips of her fingers across the edge of the vanity, Jeri stared hard into the mirror, as if debating how to answer that.

The strange reaction worried Paige. She knelt again so she could better see into Jeri's wide blue eyes. ''Hey, what's wrong?''

''Nothing.'' She continued to stare straight ahead but dropped her gaze to the bottom of the mirror. ''It's just what you said.''

''What? To trust me?''

She nodded, her expression more pensive. "I have a hard time doing that with grown ups. Especially with those who say it to me out loud. That's what made me so angry at you that day at the cafe. You said to trust you and I knew right then I'd better not."

"Why?"

"Because the grown ups who tell me I can trust them always turn right around and do something to let me down." She dropped her hands to her sides, letting them dangle past the green cushion of the small vanity chair. "The only adult I trust is Dad, and there for awhile I wasn't even sure I could trust him anymore, what with the way he was looking at you yet all the while telling me he brought you here to help entertain me." She darted her tongue between her upper lip and her front teeth then finally admitted, "Why, I couldn't even trust my own mother. Anytime Mom said the words trust me, it usually meant she'd just told me a lie."

Her chin trembled but her eyes were dry. "Mom was always telling me lies. She told them to Dad, too. I guess 'cause it was easier for her to hand us a bunch of lies than face up to the real truth."

Able to see the tattered remnants of Jeri's deep emotional scars, Paige's heart splintered into a dozen pieces. "And what was the real truth?"

"That she didn't love us." She dropped her gaze. The first hint of a tear collected near the corner of one eye. "That she loved somebody else instead. That's why she left us, you know. Because she'd fallen in love with some man she'd met in Dallas. She tried telling me she couldn't help it that she'd fallen for this other guy, and that she still loved me and always would. But she never came to see me again after that. She didn't even bother to send me a card on my birthday."

For the next several seconds Jeri stared unseeingly into the mirror, her thoughts somewhere in the dark past. "About a year later, Grandma called to tell us Mom had been killed in a train wreck over in France. The man who stole her from us was with her, but he didn't die. He brought her back and had her buried in a big fancy cemetery in north Dallas just like she would have wanted. Dad made me go, but all I really remember about that day is how much I wanted to get out of there.''

"So that's why you said your mother might not want you to have her jewelry." Paige had wanted to know her reason, but hadn't realized it would be anything quite this heartbreaking.

Jeri nodded, her face twisted with the hurt she'd felt just from talking about it. "My mother never loved me. And she never loved my Dad. She married him because she thought he was a lot richer than he really is. Dr. Westworth told me it wasn't our fault, that there was something wrong with her.''

Aching inside for what Jeri and Damon both must have gone through, Paige squeezed her eyes shut. It felt like a dozen tiny hands had reached inside her soul and now slowly squeezed the lifeblood right out of her. "Dr. Westworth was right." She slid forward to cradle Jeri in her arms, wishing she could pull her right into her heart and protect her there forever. "Your mother was a fool to give up someone as precious as you are.''

Accepting the needed comfort, Jeri pressed her face deep into Paige's blouse and shook violently. Though no sobs tore from her throat, Paige knew the girl wept bitterly. Giving her time to wash some of the long held misery from her heart, Paige did nothing to stop her.

Instead, she bent her cheek to the top of Jeri's trembling head, and joined her in her tears.

The sun had barely made an early morning appearance when Jeri showed up at Paige's door with her clothes in hand, anxious to get started. It being Sunday, breakfast would be served promptly at eight so Miss Hattie could leave for church in time to set out the flower arrangements she'd made the day before.

Far more wide awake than a child who'd had only six

hours of sleep should be, Jeri skipped inside and suggested they get started.

Pushing aside her need for coffee, Paige turned her attention immediately to the child's needs. With Jeri being only a couple of sizes smaller than her, Paige started by loaning her a frilly blue print blouse to go with that same dark skirt she'd worn to church the Sunday before. Or rather that Jeri *would* have worn to church had she not been sidetracked with other, less saintly endeavors. Not wanting to be reminded of the embarrassing incident in the tree or the kiss that followed, for that kiss was what drove Damon away, Paige set those thoughts aside for a time when she wasn't quite so busy. They had very little time to do everything Jeri wanted done.

Soon, Jeri had changed her clothes, arranging them just so, and Paige had shaped her blond hair into a soft French braid with tiny curls at each temple. By the time Paige had put a touch of perfume behind each ear and slipped a pretty gold chain with a sculpted gold heart around her neck, Jeri grew nervous about heading downstairs.

"What if he doesn't like me when he sees me?"

Paige studied this new Jeri with honest admiration. "Then the young man is an idiot and doesn't deserve a second thought from you."

Jeri considered that a moment then laughed first in her usual way, but quickly refined it to a softer more tingling one.

By the time eight o'clock came, Jeri had completed the transformation and was truly beautiful. Paige then had to hurry to get ready. She certainly didn't want to miss seeing Damon's face when Jeri entered the dining room looking like the perfect young lady he'd always wanted her to be. He'd probably bust a button, he would be so proud.

"You ready?" Jeri asked as soon as Paige shoved her feet into a pair of slipper style shoes. Not wanting to upstage Jeri in any way, Paige had selected a simple-in-design beige business style suit with a basic white tailored blouse. She didn't bother accessorizing with either her maroon or blue scarf.

"As I'll ever be," she replied, hurrying to get the door. "Just remember, follow your instincts and nothing can go wrong."

Jeri wet her lips, took a deep breath, then walked gracefully out into the hall. Paige had never felt more proud of anyone than she did of Jeri that morning while following her down the stairs and into the dining room. It took a lot of courage for Jeri to trust someone enough to make the changes that person suggested, then come down and test those changes on Richard.

"There he is," Jeri whispered, coming to an unexpected halt just inside the doorway.

"You can't back out now." Fighting an errant chuckle, Paige nudged her on toward the table where Richard sat drowning a stack of still-steaming pancakes in a thick pool of maple syrup. When he glanced up to see who'd entered and clearly did a double take, it pleased Paige right down to her very soul. That was exactly the reaction Jeri had wanted. And it was exactly the reaction Jeri deserved.

"Jerina?" he asked, setting the syrup down on top of his butter knife, almost toppling it sideways. Clearly, he wasn't sure he recognized her.

"Yes?" she replied in a cultured tone as she slid gracefully into her chair angled across from his. She smiled sweetly at him at the same time she reached for her napkin.

At hearing Jeri's given name spoken rather than her nickname, Damon, too, looked up from his pancakes and did an even bigger double take than Richard had.

"Jer?" He stared at her, jaw gaped. He was so stunned by what he saw, his cheeks paled until they nearly matched his white dress shirt.

"—ina," Paige finished for him then gave him a meaningful look to let him know he was to use the full name this morning.

"Jerina?" he obliged, his mouth still parted.

The poor man hadn't blinked once since noticing Jeri's

transformation. Neither had Richard for that matter.

Paige couldn't be more pleased. Despite all effort not to care about either Jeri or Damon, they both had found definite places in her heart, enough so that seeing this moment between father and daughter brought Paige feelings of pure joy. If only these two had definite places in her life as well.

She sighed twice, the second time with sadness, for that was wistful dreaming. Damon had been quite clear. He did not want the sort of lasting relationship that would in any way involve risking his heart. He wanted nothing meaningful nor permanent ever again.

How disheartening, since Damon had turned out to be just the kind of man Paige had always wanted in her life. He was nothing like she'd first thought, and never had been. Instead of being the heartless love-them-and-leave them type of guy she'd thought him to be, he had been every bit as feeling and every bit as insecure in his relationships as she'd always been in hers.

She'd misjudged Damon from day one. He had proven to be both kind and considerate to her, every bit as much as he was gentle and loving to his daughter—despite the emotional scars left by the painful marriage he'd suffered. Damon was definitely the sort of man she would like sharing her dreams.

And her bed.

Blushing at that last thought, for although Paige had considered such things in private, she had never dared such bold thoughts with him sitting right there. For some reason having done so now caused her cheeks to flame. She put her hands behind her to keep from fanning her face.

To halt these wayward thoughts, she returned her attention to Jeri, who clearly had Richard dazzled with her shy, dimpled smile and clever comebacks. Even little Austin was duly impressed with her, telling his mother out loud what a pretty lady Jeri was. Paige had to laugh at that. She supposed to someone barely three, a twelve year old appeared down right ancient. Especially a twelve year old as beautiful and poised as Jeri was at that moment. Even Paige had a hard time believing she was the same kid who just six days ago had sunk down on her grubby knees to dig in the dirt for worms.

As for Damon, all through church services, he kept a close scrutiny on Jeri who sat with Frankie and Richard on the pew in front of them. Occasionally he would turn a bewildered gaze to Paige, but mostly he studied every perfectly placed hair on his daughter's prim head.

Later, during lunch back at the inn, when Jeri proved to know which utensil to use for her fruit cup and then held it in a dainty grip rather than clutched in a tight fist like she'd been prone to do before, his expression shifted from befuddled to dark and unreadable. Still, his gaze rarely left his daughter. Nor did his presence. Everywhere Jeri and Richard went that day, Damon went, too. Paige followed only to make sure he didn't do anything to embarrass Jeri during such a sensitive time.

By mid-afternoon it was pretty clear Damon wasn't anywhere near as pleased by Jeri's budding femininity as Paige thought he would be. Whenever she dared brag on Jeri's different attempts to act grown up, he responded with low, indiscernible grumblings.

During the hours they played croquet out in the side yard, Damon spent a lot of time with his hands jammed into his jeans pockets. He also had a hard time calling his daughter Jerina like she wanted. More than once, he slipped the nickname slugger into a conversation. If Paige hadn't known better, she would think that a deliberate attempt to sabotage Jeri's efforts.

Fortunately, Richard paid little attention to anything Damon had to say, and the mentions of slugger went unnoticed.

When Jeri started to loosen up more after the second croquet game, making certain adjustments in her new persona so that she had her natural laugh back and smiled just a little off center again, Damon didn't seem quite as uptight. But, still, he remained on edge. It wasn't a reaction that made sense to Paige. He should be bubbling with delight. *What did it take to make the man happy?*

"Nice shot, Jerina," Paige called when the girl bounced her ball off Damon's right through the final two hoops and struck the goal stick.

"Looks like I win again," she said but in such a way it didn't sound as if she taunted anyone. "I certainly am lucky today."

Damon bent close to Paige. "At least she isn't letting him win. That would be taking it a little too far," he muttered, then headed off in the direction Jeri had just sent his ball.

Paige frowned, still not understanding his foul mood. He should be beside himself with joy, not gripping his croquet mallet like a murder weapon. Was something else bothering him? Had to be. He couldn't expect Jeri to behave any better.

"Ah, but my ball is right behind yours," Richard said, bending to take careful aim. "As soon as I make this shot, why don't we call it quits for awhile so you and me can take a walk down to the cafe and grab a couple of sodas?"

Jeri cut a delighted look to Paige, then smiled sweetly at Richard. "Oh, I'd like that."

Damon cleared his throat, as if determined to make his presence known.

"That is if Daddy doesn't mind," she quickly added.

"Daddy?" Damon paused, as if needing to digest that.

Paige feared Damon was about to tell her she couldn't go simply because he was in a foul mood so she hurried to intervene, "Of course your father doesn't mind. You two go ahead. Have a good time."

Damon looked ready to explode.

After Richard made his shot and returned his mallet to the rack, there remained little reason to finish the game. Paige had fallen too far behind to be any real threat to third place. As soon as the two kids had left, Damon bent to snatch up his ball.

"So how do you like the new Jeri?" she asked him

casually, even though what she really wanted to know was
what had him in such a sour mood. While he picked up
the stray croquet mallets, she started gathering the wire
hoops.

"I'm not sure."

"You're not sure?" She stopped to watch him jam the
mallets into the rack. "Why?"

"I don't know. I guess because it caught me off guard.
It's not exactly what I expected, you know."

"Not what you expected?" she repeated, annoyed that
he wasn't completely satisfied with the progress Jeri had
made. What more could he hope for in such a short time?
"But she was great just now. What exactly are you after?
Miracles?"

"Miracles?" He looked puzzled by that. "No, I don't
think it's a miracle that I'm after. Not when what I want
is the same as what practically every other man with a
daughter wants."

Unable to believe he expected anything more from Jeri,
Paige drew in a long, determined breath. What she had to
say to Damon about that could very well make him furious
with her, but it had to be said. "There's something I've
been wanting to mention for quite some time now."

He stopped helping pull up the hoops and looked at her
expectantly. "What's that?"

Paige hesitated only a second, then plunged forward
with what she had to say. "That I think maybe you're
pushing Jeri just a little too hard. I know you want her to
grow up in a hurry, that you think it is time she behaved
more like a young lady than a wild tomboy, but kids have
to mature at their own rates. As it has turned out, this is
indeed to be Jeri's coming of age summer, but if it hadn't
been, I think it would have been wrong for us to continue
trying to bend her into fitting an older mold before she
was ready."

Damon's forehead pulled into a perplexed frown.
"What on earth are you talking about? Why would you
think I'm in a hurry for Jeri to grow up?"

Upon seeing how truly baffled he looked, Paige, too, became confused. "Didn't you just tell me that you were after the same thing that all other fathers wanted?"

"Yes." He nodded. She had at least that much right. "And that is for his daughter to stay his little girl forever. Certainly not for her to grow up too fast, and *especially* not for her to start showing a romantic interest in boys." He tossed the hoops he'd gathered onto the ground in a display of clear frustration. "That happens to be the last thing I need right now."

"But Blair told me that the real reason you wanted me to come up here was to help you turn Jeri into the proper young lady she should be by now. She explained how you were worried because Jeri wasn't behaving like the other girls her age. That's why you wanted someone like me to take Jeri in hand and help change a few of her tomboy ways by showing her what being female was all about."

"Blair did *what?*"

His blue eyes narrowed with such disbelief, it caused Paige a moment's hesitation. "Blair told me about some of the problems you were having raising a daughter without a mother's help. She said you needed assistance convincing Jeri it was time to grow up and move on into the next phase of her development. Isn't that why you wanted me to come up here and spend some time with the girl? So I could show her what it's like to be female? According to Blair, that's the real reason you asked me here."

"I never said any of that," Damon's gaze narrowed more, then widened again. "Blair is the one who thinks Jeri should be acting a little more like a proper young lady by now. I suppose she thought she'd be doing me a favor by encouraging you to work toward that. But I happen to be happy with letting Jeri be whoever it is she wants to be. There's no reason to rush her into something she's not ready for."

"So we agree on that."

"Oh, yes, we definitely agree on that." He nodded then quirked an unexpected smile as he moved toward her, his gaze locked with hers. "And I'll bet there's plenty more we can agree on."

As startled by this sudden change in behavior as she was affected by his nearness, Paige couldn't think beyond the fact that she hoped when he came closer, he'd put his arms around her. "And what's that?"

"For one thing, that your sister can be quite a meddler when she wants to be."

"That's putting it mildly," Paige muttered, her heart doing sudden flips as he gently gripped her shoulders with both hands.

"As long as we're clear it was Blair's meddling that has caused most of the problems you've had since coming here. Not anything I did." His gaze searched her as if it was very important to him she understood that. "I may have my faults, but being a driving father isn't one of them."

For the moment, Paige couldn't recall one single fault this man had. So far, every bad thought she'd had about him had proved untrue. Even the divorce hadn't been his doing. "I'm sorry I imagined the worst about you. I should have known it was all Blair's doing." Teetering between the anger she felt toward Blair, and a very real desire to be kissed by Damon, Paige tilted her head to study Damon's features. He was the closest thing to perfection she'd ever encountered. "I should have known you were innocent."

"Innocent?" His smile widened, sinking playful dimples in his cheeks. "Not if you consider the thoughts that are going through my mind right now."

"Oh?" That questioning word barely squeezed by the lump suddenly filling Paige's throat. She dampened her lips in hopes those not-so-innocent thoughts included kissing her again. She prayed if that was so, this time he would not pull away.

With only inches between them, Damon studied her a long moment more with those incredibly blue eyes of his. Then just when she thought he was about to bend forward and give her that kiss she so longed to have, he let go abruptly. When he spoke again, his voice came out as harsh as his next actions were brusque.

"No, Paige," he muttered, bending to jerk the last of the metal hoops out of the ground as if for some reason angry at her. "You're wrong. I'm not at all what anyone could call innocent."

Still aching with a very real need to be kissed by this man and not understanding what about her frightened him so, she watched, bewildered, while he quickly sorted the equipment, jammed everything back in the box, then carried it all to the house.

Paige's heart shattered into a thousand tiny pieces. Clearly, Damon still did not want to risk anything that might lead to his falling in love.

❧ *Chapter 20* ❧

"Damon, why didn't you just keep quiet and go along with it?" Blair wanted to know, her telephone voice rising as if it was his fault he'd been caught off guard by what Paige told him. "Couldn't you figure out why I told her that? I knew any attempt Paige might make to try to alter Jeri's behavior would make the child just that much more hostile toward her. Jeri does not like anyone interfering in what she thinks is her business. She's made that clear to me many times. I knew any little nudge Paige gave Jeri would automatically be considered a full-fledged shove by Jeri. And I was right, wasn't I?"

Damon gripped the phone, his anger forcing him to his feet so he could pace beside the bed. "Did it ever occur to you that perhaps I don't want Jeri being nudged in any particular direction?"

"Well, yes," Blair admitted, no repentance in her voice. Clearly, she couldn't see that she had done anything wrong. "And that's really one of your downfallings, sweetie. You are far too lenient with that child. You always have been."

"How I raise my daughter is my business."

"And how I convince my sister to stay in New York where she belongs instead of moving to Mt. Pine where she'll be miserable is my business. As it just so happens, in this case, your business overlapped with mine. Are you forgetting just how important this is to me?''

''No.'' He paused in his pacing when he kept passing through a tiny area in the room that felt so much colder than the rest. It was too disconcerting.

''Then are you forgetting just how important all this is to *you*?''

''No.'' How could he with her constant reminders?

''Then lose the attitude, Damon. I'm only doing what's best for us both. What's best for all three of us. And I'm doing it anyway I can.''

Damon didn't quite buy that middle part. ''But what if you're wrong about what's best for Paige? What if she really would be happier living in a simpler place, leading a much simpler life?''

''Damon, I know my sister. I know what she needs to be happy,'' she returned, clearly annoyed. ''That's why I was so upset to hear that she still plans to make that foolish move. Even after all we've done to try to convince her not to, she's still dead set on throwing her life away—with no consideration at all to how it will affect anyone else.''

Keeping the cellular to his ear, Damon walked over to the turret to look out the windows. He had that feeling he often had there of being watched. This time, closer than usual. ''She has a right to her own dreams, you know.''

''Not when those dreams are all wrong for her,'' she snapped, paused briefly, then asked, ''Are you somehow forgetting that if you don't come through by helping me convince Paige that she's wrong, then I'm not going to feel much like doing what I can to make sure you do get that contract you need? Do you really want to see your parents' dreams go down the tubes after all these years of hard work? Damon, the construction business is pitiful right now. You need that big contract to keep from going under.''

Not spotting Beaulah Favish like he'd expected, Damon turned away from the windows and took a deep breath, hoping to push aside some of the guilt and self-loathing he felt. "I already know how much I need that contract."

"Then quit worrying about the little white lie I told Paige and do something more to help make sure she leaves there completely disillusioned with that domestic sort of life she so thinks she wants. I guess the thing for you to do right now is find some way to put Jeri and Paige at odds again. That way Paige won't think of Jeri's friendship as a positive reason to go ahead and move." She let out an exasperated breath. "Goodness, I wish Paige could be there after Susan Carmichael finally has that baby of hers and has to get up at all hours of the night just to feed the thing."

"Some women don't mind doing that," he informed her, although he remembered that Trana certainly had. More times than not, he was the one who slipped out of bed for those four o'clock feedings. "In fact, some women look forward to that quiet time alone with their new child."

"Damon, is there some reason you keep arguing with me?" The voice on the other end climbed to a higher level of annoyance. "Are you trying to back out on—" Blair's next words were covered by sudden static, then seconds later, the line went dead.

Relieved, not wanting to hear any more irate rantings from Blair, Damon pushed the off button, then the on button again to see if there was a dial tone. There wasn't. Smiling, though he couldn't imagine his battery going dead quite that quickly, he tossed the phone onto the bed. Finally, something went his way.

Feeling more troubled now than when he first called Blair, he lay down on the bed, too. While staring at the repetitious designs carved into the stark white ceiling high overhead, he understood what it felt like to be caught between the proverbial rock and a hard place. What was he to do?

"*Rinnnng.*"

Flopping onto his side, Damon glared at the odd shaped telephone sitting on his dresser. Evidently, Blair wasn't giving up her tirade just yet.

"Rinnnng."

At first, he considered not answering. But that would only enrage Blair more. He glanced at the corner of his desk where the bid for that resort job was tucked away inside a pristine white envelope, already addressed and ready to mail to John Bolin.

Groaning, he rolled off the bed and snatched the receiver from its arm before the third ring sounded. "Hello?"

"Something went wrong with your phone," Blair said, not bothering with a second round of greetings. "Did you forget to recharge the thing again? You know, I've told you and Jeri both about—" Again static smothered her voice then the Seascape Inn's telephone line went dead, too.

Thinking that odd, but pleased nonetheless, Damon wiggled the little brass arm several times to see if it returned a dial tone. It didn't. Smiling at how frustrated that had to make Blair, he decided fate had finally come around to his side. With neither phone working, he wouldn't have to listen to anymore of her rantings for awhile. But the contentment that brought him proved short lived. His black mood returned the moment he remembered the reason he'd called Blair to begin with. *Paige.*

He still had to deal with that problem.

Glancing again at the construction bid he had just spent two weeks preparing, his smile flattened, weighted by disgust. Blair was right about one thing. If he wanted Paige to give up the notion of living in Mt. Pine, one good way would be to find some way to come between her and Jeri again.

If he didn't do that, a lot of people would end up out of work, and his father's businesses would not make it through the end of the year. Without the businesses, he could no longer offer Jeri a very stable future; he would have a hard time even making his house payments. And he sure as heck wouldn't be able to afford the clothes Jeri would want now that she finally discovered her feminine side.

Dismally, Damon ran his palms over his face and sank back down on the bed. So what *was* the best way to go about wrecking Jeri and Paige's new friendship—and yet do it in the most painless way possible?

Standing at the window facing the pond where two brown ducks dipped and preened, Paige tried to figure out why Blair had sent her there if not to help Damon with Jeri. Was it because Blair was still so very angry with her for wanting to move? Was sending her there with such detrimental instructions a way of getting even for the hurt her decision to leave had to have caused her?

But if that was the reason, why would she chance hurting a twelve year old girl in the process?

Remembering how she'd deeply upset Jeri at first, Paige wanted to strangle Blair—or at the very least, give her a good, sharp piece of her mind. It was high time Blair was told to quit interfering in other people's lives.

With that thought, Paige picked up the telephone receiver and prepared to dial Blair's number, disappointed to find no dial tone. Thinking it an omen of some sort, she was just about to lay the receiver back in its cradle when suddenly she detected the tone she needed.

Dialing quickly, before the unreliable equipment went dead again, she tapped her foot impatiently, waiting for Blair to pick up. It being late Sunday afternoon, she fully expected Blair to be home.

"Hello?"

Anger prodding her, Paige wasted no time explaining why she had called, giving Blair no chance to speak until she'd finished. When she chanced to run out of breath, though not completely out of words yet, Blair grabbed the opportunity to defend herself.

"I didn't do it to hurt Jeri. That kid is tough as nails

anyway. And I didn't do it to try to make her into something she's not. It's not my responsibility how that child behaves. I did it for one reason only. Because I love you.''

Paige took a moment to try to find logic in that, but couldn't. ''How is sending me up here on such a wild goose chase in any way tied to love? Admit it. You intentionally set me up for eleven days of pure torture all because you were still angry over my decision to move and you wanted to find some way to get back at me.''

''You're right about one thing. I was and still am upset with you. But only because I know how very wrong it would be for you to move to Mt. Pine and spend all your savings on a small house and a dress shop that eventually you will not want. I tricked you into joining Damon and Jeri in Maine with the hope you'd get a little taste of what domestic life is really like. I thought maybe that would change your mind about moving.''

Paige threw up the hand not holding the phone, so frustrated she wanted to scream. ''I keep trying to tell you. This move is something I have wanted for a long, long time. It's not some short-lived fancy to be easily tossed aside. Unlike you, I don't enjoy living in New York City. For me, the lure of all that glitz and glamour wore off years ago.''

''But the important career you fought so hard to have is here. In New York. Not down in Texas. How can you just up and throw away a career that you've wanted and worked toward for as long as I can remember? When did you lose all your ambition?''

''I didn't lose my ambition. If anything, I was a bit too slow in finally finding it.''

''I don't understand.''

''That's because me having become the top designer for MissTeek Fashions was the result of your ambitions not mine. My ambition has always been to pursue a much simpler career, leaving me with enough freedom to settle down with the right man and start a family. That sort of life has always enticed me.''

"But look at all you have to lose," Blair argued, not yet giving up.

"I'm sorry, but all I can see is what I have to gain. Blair, I really am unhappy doing what I've been doing these past several years. The aggravation and stress that go with that job are just not worth it."

"Paige, please don't do this. Please don't toss aside a wonderful career. Don't ruin your life by marrying so young and tying yourself down with children. Please don't turn around and make the same mistakes Mother made. Don't let your life go by without ever fully realizing your talents. Don't throw away your dreams."

"You just don't get it, do you, Blair? Mother didn't throw away her dream of becoming a concert pianist. All she did was replace it with a *better* dream. She had fallen in love, so she married Dad, had us, and until the accident, lived a very full and happy life. She didn't need the concert stage to make her happy. All she needed was her own family."

"Do you honestly think she never regretted what she had to give up to have that family?"

"I never heard her complain. In fact, all I ever heard her say was how truly happy she was. I want that same degree of happiness. I realize there was a time I swore I'd never let myself fall in love again, never chance being as hurt as I was after Edward; but I've gotten over that. I'm now ready to risk it all." Too bad the one guy she would really love to risk it all with didn't feel the same way. His scars clearly ran much deeper than hers. "I refuse to end up like Damon. I refuse to go the rest of my life living out someone else's dream while my own dreams go overlooked. Somewhere out there is the right person for me, someone who can love me as much as I love him, and I hope to find him."

"But what about me?" Blair demanded. "I need you here. It was only through your association with MissTeek that I managed to snag some of the better paying modeling jobs. Until you started working there, Emilie had never considered me to represent any of her better fashions. And how am I going to bear living in this huge apartment all alone?''

Ah, so Blair's reasons to keep her in New York were not quite as selfless as they first seemed. For some reason, knowing that made Paige feel better. ''Sis, aren't you twisting that around a little? You are the one who introduced me to Emilie Teek during one of those shoots in Texas. And you can certainly find another roommate if you really want one. As for modeling jobs, you will always have far more offered than you can possibly handle. My job at MissTeek has absolutely nothing to do with how popular you've grown as a model. I'm sorry, but no more guilt trips for me. I love you dearly, but I'm through sacrificing my own happiness for yours. It's just not fair.''

''Obviously, you have no concept what love really is,'' Blair told her, lashing out in anger. ''Otherwise, you'd never have said any of that to me.''

Paige took a deep breath in an attempt to ease the weight pressing down on her heart, but it did little to help. ''I'm sorry you feel that way right now. Even so, it doesn't change the fact that I'll be moving to Mt. Pine the first part of next week.''

Having said that, Paige told her sister goodbye and hung up feeling a little sad, but at the same time oddly content. She'd just stood up against Blair's anger and survived.

The only thing that could make Paige feel any better about herself than she did at that moment would be if Damon Adams came bursting through her door, eager to announce his undying love.

If only that could happen.

With nothing to do during her last full afternoon at the Seascape Inn, Paige walked out onto the veranda a little after one o'clock and found Damon watching Richard and Jeri heading toward the ocean to go snorkeling.

''Can you believe it?'' he commented, pouting more

than frowning while he continued to watch the pair. "After those two already spent the entire morning together, they are now planning to spend most of the afternoon together."

"Are you jealous?" She studied his down turned mouth. How very much like a little boy he looked when sulking. It made her want to take him into her arms and comfort him.

But she didn't dare.

"Hell, yes, I'm jealous." He kicked at the planked floor to show just how so. "I finally finished that blasted bid I've been working on and got a copy of it off in the mail this morning. With that now out of the way, I had hoped Jeri and I could do something together. Just the two of us."

"But you have to remember, she's growing up," she explained, hoping to soothe his obviously hurt feelings. "You have to expect her to start finding other things to do with her time."

"I know." He pulled his gaze off his daughter's shrinking form to turn sad eyes to Paige. He looked like he'd aged years in the past several hours. "I've been dreading this day. I feel like I'm in the process of losing my best friend."

"You aren't losing her. She's just changing. It's all a natural part of her growing up."

"Well I don't like it."

Paige couldn't help but grin. "Nobody said you had to like it. But it would be a good idea to try to accept it."

He looked again at where Jeri and Richard were just about to disappear from sight, then let out a short breath. "I always thought I'd be prepared for this." He shoved his hands into his jeans pockets, twisted them around, then pulled them out again, clearly at a loss over what to do with them. "Richard picked her flowers, you know. It's hard to trust a guy who picks your daughter flowers."

"Oh, yes—definitely. Any guy who does that knows what he's doing. Flowers have always been very hard for a girl to say no to."

Damon's strangled reaction was immediate. "What do you mean by that?"

Grinning, Paige punched him lightly in the shoulder, aware if she hit him any harder than that as tense as he was, she could do serious damage to her knuckles. "Chill out, will you? Jeri's a sensible enough kid. She isn't about to do anything her own father wouldn't do."

"Oh, great." He moaned, then spun around, turning the backs of his sagging shoulders to the ocean. "Now I have that to worry about."

Feeling a little sorry for him, for he truly was upset, Paige tried to figure out some way to make the day pass more quickly for him. "What say I help you take your mind off your troubles for the next few hours? Let's go do something together." She tried to think of what. "I haven't been down the forest trails yet, nor have I ever made it out to Indian Point. I know we took the bicycles back," *thank God*, "but we could drive over in one of the cars."

At first, Damon looked as if he planned to accept that offer—with gratitude; but at the last minute he ran a splayed hand through his thick brown hair, then clutched it into a tight fist. "Sorry. I can't."

Looking even more solemn than before, he started toward the door. "I've got other things to do."

Not wanting him left alone with his misery, she tried again. "But just a second ago you told me you were free to spend the afternoon with Jeri. Did I say something to make you angry?"

"No," he answered, not looking at her. But the muscle pumping along the back of his finely chiseled jaw gave a far different answer. "I just want to be left alone, okay?"

"So you can brood about Jeri?"

His upper body rigid, he finally spun to face her. "You really should quit trying so damn hard to fit into our lives when the truth of it is, you never will."

After she gasped over that unexpected comment, Damon pressed his eyes shut, as if mentally counting to three, then walked quickly away, leaving Paige both speechless and devastated.

The pain was so intense, her only thought was to run as far away as possible.

❧ *Chapter 21* ❧

Damon locked himself inside his bedroom and refused to leave again for the rest of the afternoon, unable to gather the courage needed to go downstairs and face Paige. He'd hurt her with that last comment, exactly like he'd intended to. And he hated himself for it. Even more than he hated Blair.

Even when Jeri tried to get him to come out and play another game of croquet with them late that afternoon, Damon didn't budge. Nor did he, when she returned to see if he wanted to come downstairs for ice cream. Instead, he retired early, hoping sleep would help ease some of the guilt that gnawed at him, at least temporarily. But it didn't. He lay tossing restlessly beneath the light covers.

With so many thoughts plaguing him, Damon wasn't even aware he had dozed until a strange male voice startled him back awake.

"Damon. Open your eyes. We need to talk."

Thinking the voice had been part of a dream he didn't quite remember, Damon sat up, punched his pillow several times, tugged at his old, worn pajama bottoms, then plopped his head back down. A quick glance at the illuminated clock let him know it was after three o'clock. In ten short hours, Paige would leave for New York still thinking all was right with her decision to move to Mt. Pine.

If he intended to do something to change her mind before she left, and make Blair happy again, he would have to do it soon.

"But are you sure that's what's best?"

Damon sat bolt upright. The voice from his dream had followed him into wakefulness. He stared off in the direction he thought the voice had come from, but saw only the same familiar shapes and shadows as before. But for some odd reason, he thought he smelled gasoline. "Who said that?"

"Me. Umm, your conscience. I would like a word with you."

Oh, great, Damon thought, *on top of everything else, I'm going nuts.* He plopped his head back down to consider what could be done about that. Maybe Dr. Westworth knew somebody he could talk to. Someone who could straighten out his thinking again.

"There's nothing wrong with your thinking. It's just that I think we need to talk."

"About what?" Damon asked, though he wasn't all that comfortable with the idea of talking to himself aloud like that. Especially when he didn't seem to have a bit of control over one side of the conversation. This was a whole new experience for him.

"About what's going on with you."

"You mean about what's going on with *us*," Damon corrected, sitting up again.

"Whatever." There followed a noise that sounded like an annoyed huff.

"You know," he muttered more to himself than to the other voice, having already decided he was still dreaming so why bother? "It feels really odd for me to be sitting here in the dark, talking to something I can't even see."

"Would it make you feel better if you had something visual to talk to? Would it help you to quit asking so many questions about me if you thought you could see me?"

Damon didn't answer. What was the point? Eventually

he'd wake up for real and all this would go away, whether it appeared to him now or not.

"Okay, then, I'll do it, but only if I have your word there won't be anymore questions. Do I have that?"

With no intention of arguing with a figment from his own dream, Damon nodded as he glanced again toward the sound. Not expecting to see anything, Damon nearly jumped out of his skin when he saw the large, dark shape that suddenly formed at the foot of his bed. "Oh, Jesus!"

"Not hardly," the apparition commented then drifted to one side. *"He's way too busy these days to spend very much of His time doing one on ones like this. You'd really have to have one serious problem to get Him here."*

"Then who are you?" Damon asked, squinting to try to see the form better. With the only light slanting in through the turret windows directly behind it, he couldn't tell much. From what little he could make out, the specter had taken the shape of a broad-shouldered young man wearing what appeared to be an old style Army uniform. Although Damon couldn't quite make out a face due to the direction of the shadows, there was something weirdly familiar about him. "Or should I ask what are you?"

"Nope." It held up a hand, palm out, and drifted closer. *"You can't ask questions. Remember? I said I'd give you something to look at while we talk as long as you promised not to ask anymore questions. I'd also prefer you didn't talk about tonight with anyone else."*

Damon scowled, not so much because he'd just been outsmarted as because he had no idea what it was he'd been outsmarted by. What had he dreamed up for himself?

"That's good. Think of yourself as still asleep. It'll make it easier for you to cope with having talked to me come tomorrow."

Obviously, he couldn't wake up even if he wanted. "So what is it you want to talk about?"

"Technically, that was a question, but I'm willing to let that one slide. What I want to talk about is this contract Blair has you jumping through hoops for. I'm curious to

know why it is so important to you. I think I've got it all figured out but that.''

''Because, with construction work being as slow as it is right now down in northeast Texas, if I don't win that contract, my father's businesses will go down the drain.''

''That's something I don't understand. Why do you keep referring to the businesses as your father's when your father is dead, and has been for quite some time now?''

Damon started to ask how it knew that, then remembered he was the one directing the dream. Or at least trying to. Of course the apparition knew about his parents' deaths. ''I do that because my father is the one who started the businesses. And he's the one who kept them going through some pretty hard times. That doesn't change simply because he's gone now. Those businesses were started as a result of his dreams.''

''So then, by running that lumber yard, and that construction company, you are supporting your father's dreams, even in place of your own.''

Damon shrugged. ''That's basically it.''

''That's what I thought.'' The apparition drifted in a different direction, almost as if pacing. *''Why are you so dogged-determined to do that? Do you think your father would want you to continue carrying out his dreams like you are when deep down inside they aren't your dreams, too?''*

''That's a tough question to answer.'' Damon raked both hands through his hair. He'd never thought about it in terms of what his father might want had he ever realized that his son had other things he'd rather do with his life. ''I'm not sure what he'd want if he knew that. But then that's a moot point since it's not something I ever told him. I was too afraid it would hurt him to know I had other things that interested me.''

''You never bothered to tell him anything at all about these other desires you have? He never knew that what you really want is to be a coach? Why?''

Damon scooted back against his pillows to think about

that. He had no idea if he was still dreaming, or awake and imagining things—and frankly he no longer cared. He was finally getting some important matters straight in his head. "I'm not sure why I never told him. Would things be any different if I had?"

There was a pause. *"Okay, I'll turn that question back to you. Do you think things would be different if you'd told your father about your strong desire to be a teacher and a coach? Would your father have completely disregarded your needs and continued to urge you to follow in his footsteps? Or would he have seen everything a little differently and pointed you toward your own dreams?"*

Damon crossed his arms over his bare chest, considering all that. "I think had Dad known, he might have told me to do what I wanted with my life." Suddenly, his heart felt lighter. "He wouldn't have wanted to hurt me anymore than I wanted to hurt him. He would probably have found someone else to take over the businesses so I didn't have to."

The apparition stopped moving about and turned to face him. *"I think you're right. And I think he'd be very upset to know what else you're about to give up in a foolish attempt to save some dream that was never really yours."*

"You mean Paige?" Of course he did. "You're right, I should not be risking any happiness I might be able to find with her. Not for anything." With that realization now a very real part of him, Damon's mind raced on. "Or anyone."

Why hadn't he seen any of this before? In the past ten days Paige had become very important to him. More important than he'd ever thought a woman could be to him again. Important enough to risk it all—and that easily included his heart. And Paige had become important to Jeri, too. He might not be all that happy with the thought of losing his tomboy daughter, but Paige was right. It was a natural part of life. It was also a tumultuous part of life. A time when Jeri would need someone like Paige.

He had to consider what was truly best for his daughter, too. What was best for both of them.

One day, Jeri would leave home to find her own happiness. Of that much he was certain. And if he didn't act now, he could very well end up all alone then. Alone and miserable. Hating himself for what he'd lost.

Damon couldn't believe how easily everything was falling into place in his mind. There had been nothing to prevent him from pursuing his old dreams, and at the same time keep his father's two companies going by hiring someone else to do the job he now did. As for the bid he'd worked up, it was a good one. Why not let it stand on its own merit? And if he did get the contract, he could let Pete supervise the job. There was nothing to stop him from making any of those changes. More important, there was nothing to prevent him from trying to make Paige be a part of them.

He should not give up his one chance at true happiness, not even to cinch that lucrative job Blair offered. As for all those workers he'd worried about, even if he didn't get the contract, someone else in the area would. The work would be there for them whether he was the boss or not.

"Better get moving. Paige is a treasure you don't want to lose."

Damon saw no need to argue. Rolling off the bed, he snatched up the telephone receiver and put it to his ear, relieved to find it working again. Turning on a lamp so he could see the old-fashioned dial, he quickly spun Blair's number.

"Blair, it's me," Damon started, not giving her time to question his reason for calling at such a late hour. He rarely phoned her after midnight. When he glanced back to find the apparition nodding its approval, for the first time Damon saw its face. Again, the thing struck him as being familiar.

"Blair, listen closely, I have something important I want to say to you. I've decided I can't keep my end of the bargain, therefore I no longer expect you to keep yours.

I've finally realized the things in life that are the most important to me, and it just so happens that Paige and my daughter are at the very top of the list.''

"Paige?" she asked, clearly confused. "Since when is Paige so important to you?"

"Since I fell in love with her."

"You? In love with Paige?" To say Blair sounded upset was putting it mildly. "How could you do this to me?"

"I'm not trying to do anything to you, Blair. It's just that I've finally decided to do something *for* me. Or at least I hope so." He closed his heart against the fear that Paige might not feel the same way about him. He'd worry about that later. For now, he needed to get a few things straight with Blair. He stood facing the mirror, rubbing his stubbled jaw with his palm. "I mailed the bid to John this morning, and he can accept it or not. I'm sure not going to lose anymore sleep talking with myself about it. Not when I now realize the world won't come to some sad end if I don't get that contract."

"But your father's businesses might."

"True, but that's a risk I have to take. Which leaves me no longer at your beck and call."

"But you have to be. I still need your help convincing Paige to stay with me. I have to talk her into returning to her job at MissTeek. If I do that, Emilie has promised to name me the new MissTeek spokesmodel. Do you realize what that could mean to my career?"

Damon couldn't believe how self-centered she sounded. "Sorry, that's not my concern. You're my friend, and you've helped me through some hard times, but I can't let you continue to ruin Paige's life just to suit your own selfish needs." Much less ruin his own life. "Consider yourself on your own now."

Hanging up, Damon spun around to ask the apparition what he should do next. But the apparition was gone.

"Oh, great. Now what do I do?" He glanced back at his reflection and ran his hand over his face again.

First a shave.

Then a proposal.

He hurried to grab a pair of jeans, a shirt, and his travel kit. Now that he'd made up his mind, he was eager to know how she felt.

With his blood pumping faster and harder than he thought humanly possible, he managed to shave, brush his hair and teeth, and change into a pair of jeans and a light weight pullover shirt in fewer than five minutes. He barely took time to return his pajama bottoms and travel kit to his room before heading to her door. Leaning a fist against the door frame, he took a deep breath to calm the turmoil raging inside him, then knocked loudly three times. When she didn't immediately answer, he knocked three more.

"Paige?" he called to her in a voice loud enough to be detected inside, but not necessarily down the hall, where his daughter lay sleeping. "Paige, it's me, let me in."

No response.

Was she still mad at him for what he'd said earlier?

No doubt.

He knocked again, a little louder. "Paige, please. I've come to apologize." And a lot more. "Let me in." Still no response. He tried the handle and wasn't surprised to find it locked.

Growing impatient to spill his heart, he knocked a third time loud as he could. If Jeri woke up, so be it. He had to get Paige to open that door. "Come on, I know you are in there. Please, just let me in."

Nothing. Already, Damon tried to think of an alternative way into that room, but short of breaking down the door, he could think of nothing. Even a key wouldn't work if Paige didn't want it to. Dejected, he turned away. He really couldn't blame Paige for not answering his knock. Not after the way he'd hurt her.

"Dad? What's wrong?"

Damon hadn't heard Jeri open her door, and felt guilty to have waken his daughter at such an hour. "Nothing. Go back to sleep, slugger." He'd wait until morning to tell Paige all he had to tell her.

Jeri rubbed her eyes with the heels of her palms and glanced questioningly at him, then at Paige's still closed door. "Why are you dressed?"

"No reason. Go on back to sleep. It's late. We should both be in bed."

"Then why did you just knock on Paige's door?"

Did nothing ever get by this child? "I'd hoped to talk to her. I have something important to say to her."

"What?" Blinking groggily, she scratched her shoulder through her red night shirt. "That you love her?"

Damon didn't know how to answer that. He didn't want Jeri interfering in something this important. Still, he couldn't lie about it. "Yes."

For some reason, that didn't upset her like he'd expected. Being friendly to Paige was one thing, but being in love with her was quite another. Was Jeri really willing to accept that?

"But she won't let you inside to tell her?" Jeri looked surprised by that. "Why not?"

"We had a little falling out because of something I said to her earlier."

"Oh, so that's it," she replied, as if that had explained everything. "And now you want to apologize but she won't open the door and let you in."

"Exactly."

"So why don't you go in through one of her windows? Those screens come off real easy, you know."

The windows. Of course. He slapped his forehead for not thinking of that himself.

"If you want, Dad, I can stay out here in the hall and block her doorway should she decide to take off in this direction."

"You'd do that?"

"If it'll get you two back together, you bet." She frowned and shook her head as she curled her bare toes and shifted her weight to one leg. "Dad, you aren't getting any younger you know. If you don't find yourself somebody soon, you're soon going to be flat out of luck. And Paige is just about perfect for you."

Damon couldn't have been more floored. Maybe he was still asleep and this was all part of one long, weird dream. "You wouldn't mind if I started dating Paige?"

She shrugged. "Not anymore than you should mind if I started dating Richard. We do have to let other people into our lives, you know."

Damon refused to let those last comments get to him. Now was *not* the time to worry about Jeri dating.

"Go on back to bed, I'll handle this." He didn't wait to see if she obeyed.

Hurrying outside, he studied the two trees nearest her room, then chose the one that looked easiest to climb. Shimmying up Jeri style then jumping over to the roof, he headed for Paige's window. With those screens so easy to remove, he should be able to get inside to talk to her even if she didn't want him to.

As he crept closer, he was confident there would be no stopping him now—until he discovered all the windows closed. As warm as it had been all day, he would have thought she'd want them open.

"Paige?" Having already removed the screen, he tapped lightly on the pane. When no light came on within, he cupped his hands against the glass to see past his own moonlit reflection. His heart froze at what he found inside. Or rather what he *didn't* find. What he didn't find was Paige.

The room was vacant. The bed where she should be asleep was still made, the closet doors across the room stood folded back and except for a small stack of towels, it was empty. What looked like a note lay atop one of several colorful throw pillows.

His insides collapsed. *Paige was gone.*

Panicked, he flattened his hands on the glass and pushed up on the window. It opened. He hurried inside to read the note, hoping for some clue as to where she'd gone. The note was to Jeri, telling her Paige was headed back to New York to stay.

"Don't worry about the money you owe me for those clothes you ruined while you were still angry with me," it read. "Since I won't be moving to Mt. Pine where you can work off your debt like we agreed, I won't hold you to paying it back. I'm sorry things didn't work out for me. I think I would have enjoyed having you live nearby and be my good friend."

Damon grabbed hold of a bedside table to steady himself. Suddenly, he felt impaled with a hundred sharp spikes, each one intended to pierce his heart. With a fear so all-encompassing he never would have believed a person could experience it and still go on living, he ran out into the hall. He shoved the note into Jeri's hands as a way of explaining, then hurried to Miss Hattie's room to wake her. He had to know why Paige left. He had to know when.

"What time? She left about mid-afternoon," Miss Hattie told him, looking as if she thought he knew. She clutched her kelly green robe to her bosom with a wrinkled hand. "It wasn't too long after you two had talked for awhile out on the veranda that she went off for a very long walk. When she came back she looked so sad. She said something to me about being in everyone's way here, and how her sister was probably the only person who really wanted her around anyway. Not more than an hour later, she came back downstairs to tell me she was checking out. I pointed out that it was already nearly bedtime so she might as well stay until morning, but that didn't matter to her. She left anyway."

Heartsick, Damon gripped a fist to his stomach. *He* was the one who'd put those painful thoughts in Paige's head. In a foolish attempt to accomplish what Blair wanted, he had deliberately told Paige she could never fit into their lives, when the truth was, she'd already fit into both his and Jeri's.

How could he have done that?

Watching him closely, Miss Hattie pushed at her sleep

tangled white hair, now free from its usual bun, then explained further, "Paige wasn't making too much sense when she left here, and as you know, it's not really my place to ask questions."

Since when? Damon thought bitterly. Of all the times for Miss Hattie to decide to keep to herself, she picked this one. "So you just let her leave?"

Miss Hattie nodded. "Aye. Nothing else I could do." She looked apologetic. "I thought surely you knew. I thought surely she would have told you goodbye. She was gone even before I came up for bed."

Feeling his whole world crashing down over him, Damon apologized for waking her then turned to trudge slowly back to his room, his heart bursting with regrets. He passed Jeri heading back into her room while on his way, but all he could do was shrug helplessly to her imploring expression. Paige was gone. He'd run her off with his own careless words.

Would she ever forgive him?

Could she ever forgive him?

"You'll never know until you ask."

Damon spun around just as the door closed behind him. It was that same voice as before. But this time there was no image.

"Go into the village. She didn't get far."

Damon had no idea if it was madness that sent him flying across the room to grab his rental keys—or his own personal guardian angel—but fly he did. He scarcely touched the floor as he snatched up the keys and the wallet beside them, then barely hit every third step as he hurried down the stairs.

Tearing past the front desk where Miss Hattie kept a small lamp burning all night, he paused to wrestle with a front door that had become suddenly contrary. It was several seconds before he jerked bolt upright and turned to stare slack-jawed behind him. He gaped in disbelief at the glass-protected photograph Miss Hattie always kept at an angle to one side of the registration book.

His apparition.

Caught completely off guard by that realization, he took several steps toward the treasured portrait of Miss Hattie's late fiance all decked out in his officer's uniform. Having been commissioned so young, and bearing such a mischievous smile, the guy looked more like an overgrown boy playing dress up than the important decorated war hero he'd been.

So *that's* why the image had seemed so familiar to him. Damon picked up the old worn frame and stared dumbfounded at the image. The guy upstairs was Tony Freeport. Dear heavens. Beaulah Favish was right. There *were* ghosts at the Seascape Inn. Or at least there was one.

He swallowed hard, unable to believe who his guardian angel had turned out to be. But then maybe he'd just dreamed the whole incident, and having seen this photograph so many times through the years had caused him to include this man's image in the dream.

"Correction. I'm not now and never have been a guardian angel."

Damon jumped a foot, almost dropping the picture when he spun around to face the voice. No one was there. Not that that surprised him.

"I guess I'm more like a guardian ghost," the voice continued. *"Though I'm not your guardian ghost. But you and Beaulah are both right, this place does indeed have ghosts who come and go as they please. Three as a matter of fact. Me and both my folks. Sis never was much interested in sticking around earth."*

Damon stared again at the photo still in his hands. The more he heard, the less he was sure he was even awake.

"Swell looking fellow, aren't I?"

Swell looking? This was too much.

"But you'd better put that back where you found it and get on your way again. You have your future to rescue, remember?"

Damon hesitated.

"You aren't dreaming any of this, pal. Paige really has

left, and with the intention of never stepping foot in M
Pine again. Thanks to you, she's all mixed up about what
important to her now. If you don't get to the village befor
Horace wakes up, you'll miss what may be your onl
chance to turn that back around. Here, let me help ope
that contrary door. It likes to stick sometimes. And hurry
It'll be daylight soon and she'll have the gasoline sh
needs to be on her way again.''

At that moment the door clattered then opened presum
ably all on its own. When the screen door did the same
Damon took his cue. In seconds, he was outside, resumin
his wild dash out to the rental car he hadn't touched sinc
their arrival. Headed for Sea Haven Village as fast as th
car could safely travel, his heart felt like it might burst int
flame while he prayed fervently the voice proved right
That he would indeed find Paige and turn this whole sit
uation back around.

He nearly broke into tears when he rounded that las
curve and spotted her rental pulled off to the right side o
the street, nearly in front of the post office. Through th
dark windows, he could just make out the shape of he
head tilted against the headrest.

Prepared to drop to his knees and beg if he needed to
Damon tore out of his car and, with trembling hands and
a thundering pulse, rapped sharply on the window. As ex
pected, Paige came awake with a start.

"Damon?" she mouthed. "What are you doing here?'
She glanced out at the sky, as if gauging the hour of night
then leaned over to roll down the window.

When her face moved into the moonlight, he saw she'
been crying. A lot. Had his words about not fitting in to
their lives hurt her that much?

As painful as that thought was, it gave him hope.

"I'm so glad I found you," he told her, bending so they
could see each other more easily. "Paige, we need to talk
I have so much I need to tell you." About his feelings
About his mistakes. About what it had very nearly cos
him to be in league with her sister.

"Now?" She reached for the door unlock switch and the door handle at the same time.

Damon thought she was letting him inside, but instead she was letting herself out. With a fearful expression that cut right through his soul, she stood a few feet away, arms at her side, stiff as rails. "What is it you want to talk about?"

Damon ran a fidgety hand through his hair. He didn't know where to begin. "I've done some serious thinking in the past few hours and have changed my mind about a lot of things; and I wanted you to know about it."

"Thinking?" She dampened her lips. "About what?"

Damon's gaze locked with hers. He couldn't tell if those expressive brown eyes glimmered with renewed hope or yet more fear. "About us."

He moved closer, but was afraid to touch her. Afraid she'd pull away. "I know now how very important you are to me. Important enough I don't want to live through even one more tomorrow without you being some part of it."

"And I'm supposed to believe that after what you said to me yesterday?" She took a step away from him, as if afraid to accept his sudden change of heart. "What could possibly have happened to cause such a dramatic difference in your way of thinking?"

"I couldn't even begin to explain." At least not in a way that made sense. "Just believe me when I tell you that I've done a lot of soul searching these past several hours, and as a result everything is now very clear to me. I do not want to lose you."

Paige darted the tip of her tongue between her teeth, as if still hesitant to believe this unexpected change. "But what about those barriers of yours? The ones that have refused to let your heart get involved with anyone. What . happened to them?"

He blinked. Until now he hadn't noticed them gone. "I'm not sure."

"Well, what about all those times you were hurt back

in high school, and how they always left you feeling so injured? Isn't that what made you build those barriers in the first place? Have you put those aside forever? Just like that?"

"Yes." He was glad she brought that up. "I've given it a lot of thought, too. What you said about me having always associated with the wrong kind of girls struck me. I've since decided you might be onto something important there. When thinking back to those tender years, I realize now how very often I let Blair choose who we ran with and who we didn't."

Paige's expression relaxed a degree. It was the first indication he still had a chance.

"Yes, and we both know what type person that attracted Blair back then—the purely superficial type." She arched her eyebrows as if having just insulted him, then added, "Present company excluded of course."

"Present company not entirely excluded in this case," he admitted woefully. "I can see now that I was pretty superficial back then, too. Which helps explain at least part of the reason why I was never able to hold the interest of any of those girls. Looking back now, I realize no one could have done that. Those girls were constantly on the prowl. Constantly trying to prove to themselves and each other who they could conquer and how quickly."

Finally, Paige smiled with obvious understanding—that smile reaching Damon in places no one had touched before. She lifted her hand as if about to touch his cheek, then pulled it away, an act that left him aching. She still wasn't sure of him. "Sort of like Blair does even now."

"That's why I've concluded that maybe the biggest part of the problem wasn't with me to begin with. The biggest part of the problem was with them."

Finally, she cupped his cheek with warm, gentle fingers. "I'm glad you realize that. It's sort of what I already thought."

Overwhelmed by that tender touch, Damon fought an incredible desire to close his eyes and simply enjoy the compelling warmth. "I now know I judged the whole thing wrong."

Her smile widened, clearly what she'd wanted to hear. "And with that knowledge, you lost the need for those barriers around your heart."

"Completely." He couldn't resist the urge to pull her into his arms, and was relieved when she allowed him that pleasure. For a long moment, he held her close. "To tell you the truth, even before you had me considering any that, those long-held barriers of mine had already started to crumble down."

She pulled back so she could see his face. "Oh?"

"The fact of it is, I've been slowly falling in love with you since the first moment I saw you again. At first, I thought it was just desire I felt, but I have since discovered exactly how wrong that was."

"You have?"

He searched her upturned brown eyes, hoping to find even the slightest evidence that she felt the same way about him, but he just couldn't tell what thoughts ran through her head at the moment. "Look, I'm smart enough to know I've hurt you in a bad way, and that you certainly don't return any of these same wonderful feelings, at least not yet; but I'm hoping for a chance to change all that. Please, Paige. Give me that chance."

Paige studied Damon's worried expression for a long moment, far too astonished by what he'd said to respond right away. Just moments ago, she had been ready to crawl into some New York City manhole and wither away, her misery too overwhelming. She had truly believed, because of the demons from his past, Damon could never return her or anyone else's love. Because of that, were she to move to Mt. Pine, she would have spent every day of the rest of her life longing for something that could never be.

But now everything had changed. Suddenly, everything she had ever wanted lay at her feet. Damon's barriers had miraculously tumbled down, allowing him to love again. What was even more incredible was the fact that she was the one he'd chosen to love. And even *more* incredible was that she had Blair to thank for it.

Putting it together in her mind, Paige wanted to laugh out loud and cry all at the same time. Laugh at what Blair's reaction would be, and cry because her heart was filled with such amazing joy. "And who is it that says I don't love you?"

"Do you?"

He didn't as much as breathe while waiting for that answer. Part of her longed to make him suffer awhile, especially after all she'd just been through. But a larger part of her couldn't wait for him to know her true feelings. "Of course, I do."

His eyes widened with hope. "Since the moment we first saw each other again?"

Paige couldn't help it. She chuckled out loud at how very much he had underestimated her love. Reaching up to dab away a happy tear quivering at the corner of her eye, she admitted the truth. "Oh, no, since way before then. If you really want to know, I've loved you with every bit of my heart since I was Jeri's age."

Damon's joyous expression plummeted with sudden alarm. He took a tentative step back. "A twelve-year-old girl can love that deeply?"

"I'm afraid so," she warned him, aware of the thought that just struck him. "It could very well be that in about fifteen years, Paige and Richard will have this very same type conversation."

His eyes narrowed as if afraid to hope. "Fifteen years from now?"

She nodded, deciding he had enough to worry about for now.

His expression relaxed. "Since we should have other children by then to help fill the void, I suppose I could live with that."

"Other children?" Oh, she certainly liked the sound of that. She'd have more than just Jeri and Damon to treasure in the tomorrows to come. "How many?"

"How ever many we think we can handle." The playful glimmer had returned to his pale blue eyes. He moved close again. "I'm more than willing to do my part to see that they come promptly into existence."

"Oh, sure, you help create them, then dump them all off on me to raise," she complained, knowing very well that would not be the case. Damon had already proved what a devoted father he was.

"Wellll—" he stroked his handsome chin thoughtfully. "Since you are going to be busy with that dress shop of yours at times, and since I'll be busy going back to college to get that teaching degree, I suppose we'll have to make a team effort out of it."

"A team effort? Spoken like a true coach," she murmured, then leaned forward. She wanted to kiss the man who'd just opened her heart to the many wonderful treasures her tomorrows now offered.

*Turn the page
for a special preview of*

THE ENDLESS SKY

*An unforgettable romance
for Shirl Henke and
St. Martin's Paperbacks . . .*

The Bighorn Mountains,
Wyoming Territory, 1875

Stephanie watched Chase ride in on Thunderbolt, sliding from the magnificent stallion's back with the effortless ease of the high plains horse Indians. He was practically naked, clad only in breechclout and moccasins. If the proper ladies of Boston had swooned when he appeared dressed in immaculate white shirts and custom tailored wool suits, imagine how they'd react if he walked into one of their drawing rooms now!

He made his way to her after conferring briefly with Elk Bull. She refused to give him the satisfaction of waiting obediently like his horse until he deigned to speak to her. Instead she walked over to where several of the young women were unloading cook pots and other utensils and began helping with the task.

"You look too white," he said peremptorily, as he approached her.

Stephanie turned to him and sputtered, "And just what am I supposed to look like — a Celestial or an African?"

"You will use some walnut stain to darken your skin."

"Dye my skin!" she exclaimed aghast. He smiled sardonically. "What's the matter? Does the Boston matron shrink at the thought of dark skin?"

Her face reddened as she remembered loving the contrast between her paleness and his coppery darkness when they were in Boston. "I can't be what I'm not," she replied stubbornly.

"I'm not trying to remake you into a Cheyenne woman — as if I could. I only want to keep you from attracting any unwanted attention. If any white hunters or miners stumble on us, I'd hate to have to kill them just to silence them."

She looked at his implacable expression. "You'd actually do it, wouldn't you?"

"Go to Red Bead and have her disguise you. She'll know what to do," was all he replied before stalking off.

Stephanie seethed, resuming her tasks. If she made a loud clatter with the iron cook pots, no one commented on it. "I'm getting so sunburned I'll soon be dark enough to pass as an Indian anyway," she muttered to herself as she worked. She did not see Chase again until after the evening meal when she and several of the young women were on their way back from bathing in the river.

Stepping out from behind a copse of aspen, he barred her way. The other women quickly left them, knowing there was trouble between the White Wolf and his captive. Even her friend Kit Fox lowered her eyes in resignation and walked away. Stephanie looked up at him, waiting to see what he would do. He held a small vial in one hand. With the other he reached out and took hold of her wrist, heading back toward the river.

"I have already bathed," she said as anger and panic took hold of her in equal measure.

"But you have not done as I told you."

"No, I have not," she dared him, trying to yank her arm from the steely grip.

He refused to relinquish it. When she continued to balk, he slipped the small vial into his waistband and quickly picked her up, tossing her over his shoulder before she could do more than let out an outraged gasp. Approaching the riverbank, he slung her down and released her. They stood facing each other, eyes glowing in the dim light of evening. Slowly he withdrew the vial and uncorked it. A pungent not unpleasant smell assailed her nostrils. She wrinkled her nose as he offered it to her.

"Smear it on your face, neck, arms and hands."

"It stinks." She refused to take it.

"It's only walnut oil. As soon as the stain dries you can bathe away the odor."

"No whites will see me here. There's no reason for this."

He looked at the damp skin of her throat where a small pulse raced. She had left the tunic unlaced at the neckling. A small smile curled about his mouth as he fingered the lacings. "Well, at least you've finally taken my advice about loosening up."

She backed warily away. "I'll scream, Chase."

He smiled broadly now but it was not a nice smile. "Go ahead. Do you think any of my people will interfere between me and my captive?" He poured a bit of the dark oil into his palm and then slid it along the pale column of her neck, pulling her to him. She could feel the calluses on his hand, the slickness of the oil, the warmth of his breath as he drew her closer. His fingers dropped lower across her collarbone and she gasped, looking down to see the dark stain spread across her light skin. By now he had clasped her wrist in his other hand along with the small vial, all the while continuing the soft massaging motion along her shoulder, sliding the loosened tunic dangerously low. When he grazed the swell of her breast, she reached up and clasped his hand with her free one.

"Please . . . don't do this," she whispered hoarsely.

"I don't know. The thought of massaging all that lovely white skin does hold a certain allure," he murmured, noticing she did not pull away, only pressed her hand against his to stop him from reaching inside her tunic to caress her breast. He ached to do just that. Suddenly she seized the vial from him and slid from his grasp, standing still, her breasts rising and falling swiftly, her lips slightly parted, breathless. He could see the dark imprint of his touch across her throat, a stark contrast to the pallor of her face.

"I . . . I'll use the stain. Just leave me."

Silently as a wraith, he turned and did so. Stephanie watched him go, still feeling the tingling ache where he had touched her . . . and where he had not. With a ragged breath, she began to rub the pungent oil over her face and arms as the sun slipped beyond the western horizon and night fell.

When she returned to the camp, Red Bead looked up at her darkened skin and grunted in approval, then scuttled through the packs to give her a length of soft blue cloth, no doubt trade goods obtained from a raid. "Cover your hair with it when we travel," she said, dishing up a bowl filled with fresh berries and handing it to Stephanie. She used a small knife to cut off a hunk of the roasting venison haunch still spitted on the campfire and began to chew, then offered the blade to Stephanie to do likewise.

The meat smelled wonderful although she was still not used to the lack of salt. Her stomach gave a small growl. She used the knife to help herself.

The Red Bead said, "It was a good thing you did yesterday. Granite Arm told me how you saved her daughter." She paused but before Stephanie could make a reply she said, "Kit Fox wishes to wed the White Wolf."

"I know. She told me." Stephanie refused to venture more, wondering if Red Bead believed she was jealous.

"You are not like other whites I have known," the old woman said, then turned her attention to the food, staring silently into the flames as she ate.

They broke camp at dawn, continuing the trek north. Stephanie muttered to herself but wrapped the blue cloth about her head after plaiting her hair. She was ambivalent about running across any white travelers, devoutly wishing for rescue yet not wanting to bring harm to these people, many of whom had been most kind to her. Nor did she wish to see Chase carry out his treat and kill any witnesses in order to keep her.

Chase rode point through the day. She watched him on the ridge riding his magnificent stallion, Thunderbolt. The only time he rode the stallion was when he was with the band. What a splendid barbarian he was, riding bareback with long muscular legs gripping the sleek horse's sides and the wind whipping his long feathered braid. The sun gleamed on his sweat slicked skin, delineating the muscles of his shoulders, arms and chest. He did not wear a breast-plate today so the scars of his Sun Dance showed through the thick pelt of dark hair on his chest.

"You look at him with longing in your heart," Red Bead said, startling Stephanie. The old woman had approached silently, catching the white woman unawares.

A denial sprang to her lips but she looked into Red Bead's shrewd sympathetic eyes and nodded instead. "Once long ago, we were in love. But he left me. There is nothing that can change that."

Red Bead merely shrugged. "We do not always know what the Powers have in store."

Before Stephanie could reply to the enigmatic remark, Chase came streaking down the hill toward them, reining in next to Stands Tall and Bull Elk who rode at the head of the column of Cheyenne. They conferred briefly, then he approached the travois of Red Bead where Stephanie walked. Sliding from Thunderbolt's back he said, "Cover your hair completely," reaching out to pull the cloth shawl into a drooping hood that fell across her forehead, obscuring her face.

"Why? What is —" Before she could pull it back and look up at him, he reached out and seized her hand in an iron grip.

"Do as I say! A group of white men are just over that rise — miners looking to strike it rich in the Black Hills."

An expression of tortured ambivalence betrayed her before she could school her features to neutrality. Chase saw it and cursed. "Don't be a fool, Stevie. We outnumber them. I would have to kill them to protect my people."

"I won't reveal myself," she replied in a choked voice, knowing he would keep his word. She walked beside Red Bead under his watchful eye as he paced the restless stallion beside them.

She saw the miners when they crested the hill just as Chase had said, a rough looking company of about a dozen men. The leader was a gaunt looking fellow with a turkey feather in the greasy felt hat that shaded a face to which life had not been kind. Watery pale eyes narrowed as he studied the band of Indians whose path had crossed his, noting that they were not painted for war and had all their women and children with them.

"Howdy! Any of you speak American?" he asked, spitting a wad of tobacco on the ground and patting the repeating rifle he held in his hands. His men were well armed. He did not realize that the Cheyenne warriors were equally so. Chase had instructed that most of the men hide their Henrys and Winchesters in the baggage laden travois and carry only their bows and lances.

"I speak, yes," Stands Tall said in far more broken English than Stephanie had ever heard him use before. "We peaceful — good Indians."

So Chase came by his duplicity naturally, Stephanie thought with grim humor as she listened to the exchange. One of the men caught sight of a travois piled with beaver pelts and offered to buy them for a paltry sum, which Stands Tall refused. They haggled as the leaders around Elk Bull became increasingly restive. Then a rumble of horses' hooves sounded and more voices in English echoed across the open plain. From behind the next rise a column of cavalry out of Fort Fetterman came riding smartly toward them. Stephanie recognized the insignia and had even met the young captain who was leading the column. Every nerve in her body screamed at her to rip the covering off her hair and run to Gus Ansil.

Chase was not certain what she would do. Yesterday they had sighted the miners but only an hour ago had he run across the column of cavalry apparently sent to head off the men whe were illegally bound for the gold strikes in the Black Hills to the east. There was nothing they could do but pray the soldiers would let them pass peacefully. Stands Tall was now assuring the captain that they headed north to receive rations at Fort Stanbaugh and settle peacefully for the winter there.

The issue of rounding up all Indians on the northern plains had not yet been settled by Washington, although many commanders in the field frequently attacked villages under the pretext of hostile provocation by the Indians, charges unfounded more often than not. During the fall of 1875 matters were particularly delicate since the government was negotiating with various tribal leaders, chiefly the Sioux, in an attempt to get them to cede mineral rights to the sacred hills. Chase knew neither his Lakato allies nor the Cheyenne would ever give away their hunting grounds, but until the dust of endless talks settled, he prayed these troops would stand down during this encounter.

The warriors might be able to successfully engage both groups of whites in a fight, but in a pitched battle it would be an appalling disaster if they were encumbered with women, children and old people.

The Stephanie of old would never knowingly endanger children or old people, even to save herself. But that was the woman he remembered from another life, he reminded himself. He could not trust her now. If anything happened to cause a fight, he would be completely to blame. As the arrogant looking captain sought to end the haggling between Stands Tall and the miners, Chase reached down from Thunderbolt's back and swept Stephanie into his arms. She started to cry out but before she could do more than gasp, his mouth came down hard on hers. Stands Tall and several of the other Cheyenne leaders, who he had talked to before they encountered the enemy, all began to laugh.

"What's that buck doin?" one miner asked.

"Him just married. Now breechclout all time fall down. Then he fall on squaw," Stands Tall replied in the guttural dialect he had affected. Now even some of the other miners and soldiers joined in the laughter.

Chase heard the captain make some lewd remark as he carried Stephanie to the back of their caravan. With one hand he held the scarf tightly around her head while he pressed her against him with the other. His superbly trained horse responded to knee commands, stopping near the end of the long line of horsedrawn travois. He knew that Stands Tall had convinced the soldiers of the reason for his dramatic gesture. Now all he had to do was make Stephanie behave like an enamored bride. The thought gave him a sudden pang. *If only she could be my bride!* Her lips were startled and soft beneath his, tasting warm and sweet as he savaged them. Her body stiffened in surprise as she kicked and flailed, trying to push him away but he was far too strong. He deepened the kiss, taking advantage of her breathlessness by plunging his tongue inside her mouth and losing himself in the soulful hunger that had so long tormented him.

From among the cluster of women, Kit Fox watched the White Wolf carry her friend toward a big travois piled high with pelts for the cold winter camp in the mountains. He tossed her onto the pile of furs and covered her with his body as she thrashed, then grew suddenly quiescent. His whole body moved over her in a dance as ancient as time. In spite of the roughness of the initial encounter, Stephanie responded. Hesitant and inhibited as it was, the subtle relaxing, then retensing of her body gave her away. Her hands fell loose, no longer pushing against his body's invasion, and her legs ceased their thrashing. Instead her fingers curled against his shoulders and one leg instinctively raised and rubbed against his thigh. As Kit Fox watched, the movements spoke volumes to her.

They are destined to be lovers, even against their wills. Her heart ached, yet she faced the truth. The White Wolf had taken no other woman to his blankets since coming to live among the People. This was the reason. *Good-bye, White Wolf, Chase the Wind. I will grieve a while . . . then I will live once more.*

Stephanie felt the heat and hardness of his body as he slammed it into hers, driving the air from her lungs when he flung her onto the travois and followed her down into the soft furs. At least, that's why she told herself she did not cry out or fight him further. She would not respond to the harsh caresses he bestowed upon her as he forced her to lie silently beneath him, hidden from the soldiers. She *would* not. She tried lying limply beneath him at first, letting him play out the charade for the soldiers and miners. Their coarse, ugly laughter still faintly echoed but Stephanie could no longer hear it. The world receded until all her universe encompassed was the man holding her in his arms, pressing her into the soft furs. His every movement was a brazen caress, from the hot intimate invasion of his tongue in her mouth to the way his hips rocked suggestively against hers.

Her senses blazed to life, remembering how it had been between them every time they had touched before. With a small moan her hands reached up to his shoulders and her body opened to his, weeping with a want she could not comprehend, had never been able to comprehend from that first day in the snowbound country house in Massachusetts.

Then before she could utterly disgrace herself, she heard a loud command for the troops to move out, followed by the thundering vibrations of their horses' hooves. Disgruntled, the miners followed. Chase suddenly rolled off her and sprang from the travois. She lay breathless and stunned, staring at him as he stood towering over her. His breath came in gasps as if he'd run a great distance and his fists clenched and unclenched at his sides. The expression on his face was angry and at the same time agonized, as if he were in great pain.

Or had she imagined it? "It was not necessary to shame me. I would not have betrayed these people," she whispered hoarsely.

He just stared down at her for a moment. "I'm sorry. I could not risk my people's lives," he said in a low intense voice, still out of breath. He willed his rebellious body to obey him but just looking at her made it ache. The scarf covering her hair had pulled away now, revealing its bronzed splendor. Huge golden eyes glistened with tears in her small dark face. Thank heaven he had forced her to use the walnut oil. *That was not all you forced her to do*, his conscience tormented.

"You will never trust me," she said simply, too emotionally and physically wrung out to conceal her pain.

"I cannot even trust myself, Stevie," he replied. Then he spun on his heel and leaped on Thunderbolt's back, galloping away, leaving the caravan far behind.

Stephanie felt as if everyone around her were staring, but the Cheyenne were too polite for such a thing. They had surely seen the way she fell in with Chase's ruse — but not love. Never would she dare to call it love. Red faced beneath the stain darkening her skin, she climbed from the travois with trembling legs. That was when she met Kit Fox's eyes. And looked away quickly.

THE ENDLESS SKY

*by Shirl Henke—look for it
in January from
St. Martin's Paperbacks!*